EYE OF THE WHALE

ALSO BY DOUGLAS CARLTON ABRAMS

The Lost Diary of Don Juan

DOUGLAS CARLTON ABRAMS

EYE OF THE WHALE

A NOVEL

ATRIA BOOKS
New York London Toronto Sydney

ATRIA B O O K S

A Division of Simon & Schuster, Inc.
1230 Avenue of the Americas
New York, NY 10020

First Atria Books hardcover edition August 2009

ATRIA B O O K S and colophon are trademarks of Simon & Schuster, Inc.

For information about special discounts for bulk purchases,
please contact Simon & Schuster Special Sales at 1-866-506-1949
or business@simonandschuster.com.

The Simon & Schuster Speakers Bureau can bring authors to your
live event. For more information or to book an event, contact the
Simon & Schuster Speakers Bureau at 1-866-248-3049 or visit our
website at www.simonspeakers.com.

Designed by Davina Mock-Maniscalco

Manufactured in the United States of America

10   9   8   7   6   5   4   3   2   1

ISBN 978-1-4165-3254-5
ISBN 978-1-4391-6554-6 (ebook)

For the young and all who are working to protect them—
and especially for my children, Jesse, Kayla, and Eliana

Leviathan. . . .
On earth he has no equal. . . .
Will he speak soft words unto Thee?
—Job 41

NOTE TO READERS

WHILE THIS is a work of fiction, it was inspired by humpback whales that swam up the Sacramento River in California in 1985 and in 2007. The descriptions of whale behavior and intelligence are informed by the latest research into what we can and cannot know about these giants of the deep. The discoveries about endocrine disruption and the environment revealed in the story are also based on thousands of well-documented studies. I could never have written this novel without the expertise and guidance of dozens of scientists, physicians, scholars, and journalists who have worked tirelessly to uncover the truth about what is happening to marine and terrestrial life on our planet. I have tried in some small way to thank them in my acknowledgments. You can learn about their research and the facts on which the story is based at www.DouglasCarltonAbrams.com. Our understanding of this research and the story it tells about the future of life on our planet could not be more important.

EYE OF THE WHALE

PROLOGUE:
SIREN SONG

11:14 P.M.
Thursday, February 15
Near Socorro Island, Pacific coast of Mexico
18°48'N, 110°59'W
Clear night, wind SW 5 knots

APOLLO HOVERED SILENTLY *as a school of hundreds of hammer-heads encircled him in the rich upwelling—*

His massive forty-foot body hung just below the surface, cradled by the swell of the sea—

Moonlight filtered through the shrouded water of night—

Every inch of his skin straining to hear—

Waiting—

Silence—

Only the slow throb of his giant heart—the pulse pounding in his skull—

Slowly his tail floated up until he hung upside down—his twelve-foot pectoral fins splayed outward from his sides like a cross—

Rotating almost imperceptibly—he began to sing again—

Creaks and moans—cries and whistles—animated the water with the pulsing power of song—

The echoes cascaded back to him off the ocean floor as the sounds revealed the texture of the deep—

Then again silence—

At last—he heard two other males singing—amplifying the sound—

Then others—males and females—young and old—swam closer and closer—

THE *PACIFIC SQUALL* bobbed on top of the cresting waves, the steel hull of the research vessel vibrating from the whale song. The otherworldly music spilled out from the speakers strapped to the walls as whale biologist John Maddings accompanied on the cello. His weathered fingers, graying hairs surrounding each knuckle, pressed the strings against the neck as if taking its rhythmic pulse. The other hand lovingly rocked the delicate bow across the strings in a hypnotic melody.

With his eyes closed and his head tilted to the side in concentration, Maddings effortlessly played along with this year's song. He had begun to accompany whale song out of musical curiosity, but it had proved a powerful research method that let him enter and understand the structure in a way that his most technologically advanced spectrographic software could not. Now, six weeks into the breeding season, he knew this year's slowly evolving song practically by heart.

Although he had studied many kinds of whales, there was nothing quite like the song of the humpback. Its rhythm was scored to the rolling ocean; its haunting sounds gave voice to the abyss.

Maddings suddenly stopped playing. Quickly he put the cello in its case and jumped to the computer console. His trembling fingers flicked on a desk lamp. Its bulb cast a spotlight revealing the computer, a black synthesizer, and a photograph of a gray-haired woman in her fifties whose radiant smile made her beautiful.

Anxiously, Maddings adjusted the black knobs of the recording equipment, unable to believe the sounds coming from the directional hydrophone. Built in to the hull of the boat, this underwater microphone picked up the sounds echoing through the sea. Maddings made sure he was recording and then grasped the black joystick. He rotated the hydrophone 360 degrees. In every direction the song was the same—in every direction the song was new.

"Switch to the sonobuoys, old man. Switch to the sonobuoys." Maddings barked directions to himself in what was left of his British accent after years of living abroad. The other members of the crew were all asleep or up on deck.

Maddings squeezed his eyes closed to focus his mind completely on the sounds coming in from the sonobuoys. Used by the U.S. Navy to listen for enemy submarines, declassified sonobuoys now allowed marine biologists to listen for whales in vast expanses of the ocean. There was no doubt—the song was definitely diverging, shifting dramatically.

A wave of excitement flooded Maddings's body as his hands grew hot and his breath short. A voice in his head warned, *You're too old to get excited about what might just be your imagination or faulty equipment or both.* But he didn't believe this lying voice of caution.

Maddings wiped a trickle of sweat from his forehead. He hadn't felt like this in forty years, not since the day he and a colleague had discovered that the sounds made by the humpback whale were actually songs with recognizable structures. Four decades of study had documented repeatedly that the songs, sung exclusively by the males, evolved gradually over a season, even over years. New musical phrases were introduced by individual singers and gradually adopted by all males, but whole songs were not completely replaced in a night. What Maddings was hearing over the speakers was contradicting forty years of careful research.

He checked the recording levels again. The sound was getting louder as he picked up more singers. He turned the volume down to avoid distortion; the lights flickered green and stopped erupting red. Maddings needed confirmation. He grabbed the watertight case and pulled out the sat phone. From memory he dialed the number of his closest collaborator at the Woods Hole Oceanographic Institute.

"Mike, Maddings here. Sorry to wake you. Something . . . something unprecedented is happening."

"Maddings, good to hear from you. For you to use the word 'unprecedented' must mean you're talking about a goddamn miracle."

Maddings knew that neither of them believed in miracles, but he had woken Mike in the middle of the night only once before, and that call had made both of their careers. Perhaps that was why Mike was so uncharacteristically courteous even at this hour. "What is it?"

"I'm still in Socorro, recording song. There's rapid transformation. Mike, the song sung yesterday is gone. Overnight the humpback population is singing a completely new song."

"That's impossible."

"I know it is. I'm calling to find out whether you've heard about anything like this happening. I want to know if anyone else is observing it."

"Actually, there was some controversy about this a few days ago on WhaleNet. I invoked your research to dismiss her."

"Dismiss who?"

"That old graduate student of yours down in Bequia."

"*Elizabeth* . . ." Maddings said under his breath. A smile warmed his face as he began to shake his head in amazement and satisfaction. *Of course it would be Elizabeth,* he thought. *Brilliant Elizabeth.*

Elizabeth's face leaped to mind. Her unusual genetic heritage—half Jewish, half Native American—made her beautiful face look almost Asiatic. How she ever got a good Irish name like McKay, he never knew, but the Irish did seem to get around. Elizabeth was not only arguably the most gifted graduate student he'd ever taught, she was also a marvelous violin player and had been a vital member of his research quartet. That was until she had to follow her doctor husband across the country for his residency. It had been a great loss to the department and to him. He did become very fond of his students, which was a real liability, since they invariably left him to pursue their careers.

"Professor Maddings! Come quick!" The voice echoed down through the metal corridor from up on deck.

"I'll call you back, Mike."

Maddings felt the sharp pain in his not-so-young knees as he bounded up the stairs and practically stumbled to the gunnels, looking beyond. If it had not been for the ache in his joints, he would have sworn that he was dreaming. To see one whale breaching was always extraordinary, but to see so many was unfathomable.

As THE SONG ENDED Apollo thrashed his massive tail back and forth—propelling his forty-ton body straight out of the water

His black shimmering skin glittered in the moonlight as white foam spilled off like a waterfall—

His winglike fins rose slowly away from his body as he began to twist—

Pivoting on his fifteen-foot fluke—his back arching—the spray bristling from his body—

A moment of suspended time—weightless in the moonlight—

His earthbound bulk—refusing to linger in the sky any longer—fell back into the sea—

The resounding crack—the white lava waves—his flipper reached toward the sky as the dark waters enveloped his body at last—

All around him the others began following his lead—countless whales launching themselves skyward under the full moon—

They tore their bodies from the water in an endless cycle of flight and fall—erupting out of the molten water—

At last the moon reached its zenith—

Apollo and two other males began to swim quickly away from the rest of the group—

The others would follow north in the days and weeks ahead—

Yet Apollo's destination would be different from that of all the others—

ONE

12:00 P.M.
Five days earlier
Saturday, February 10
Shark Bay, Bequia, Caribbean Sea
13°01'N, 61°12'W

"THERE, LIZA!" Milton pointed toward the bay.

Elizabeth McKay saw the blow before it vanished in the wind. The aching tiredness in her legs from five hours of standing and scanning the horizon disappeared as the excitement of the chase began.

She looked through her large waterproof binoculars. The afternoon light reflected off the water like shards of glass, making her blue eyes burn, but she forced her eyelids open wider to take in more information. She squeezed the hard rubber eagerly when she saw the back of the whale floating in the water where it had surfaced.

"Head into the wind," she said as she braced her leg against the bench.

Milton had already anticipated her command and was steering upwind of the whale. It was hard to believe that eight years had passed since they started working together, when she first came to study North Atlantic humpback whales in their most southerly breeding grounds. Finding Milton had been like discovering a treasure of devotion: He had tirelessly helped her to navigate the dangers that she and her research subjects faced in these waters.

The old Evinrude 35 whined quietly as Milton drove his beloved lime-green boat into the trade winds that endlessly lashed these eastern Caribbean waters.

Elizabeth looked back at the viridescent mountains that thrust sharply from the water to a ridge stretching the length of the island like the spine of an emaciated animal. Bequia—or "bekway," as the natives called it—meant "Island of the Clouds" in Carib, but today there was not a cloud in the sky. The land was densely forested, mostly with the knotted and wind-curved trunks of white cedar, which the boatmen handpicked to fashion the ribs of their double-ender sailboats. From where she stood, Elizabeth could also see towering palms and prickly cactus, along with brightly colored houses that hugged the steep slopes and flat harbors. Their roofs were topped with corrugated metal, which the islanders used to capture rainwater.

Milton cut the engine, and they silently drifted back toward where they had seen the blow. "The whale he not far now," Milton said in the warm accent of the islander—a cross between a Scottish brogue and a Jamaican drawl. When Elizabeth heard Bequians speaking to one another, she sometimes had trouble understanding them, but when they spoke to outsiders, they often tried to speak "proper," as they called it. "There the whale!" Milton shouted.

Elizabeth looked where he was pointing and saw the glistening black back and dorsal fin just as the whale began to dive. Grabbing the camera from her yellow Pelican case, she anxiously pulled off the lens cap. *Will I get the image? Will I recognize it?* She pressed the shutter-release button halfway. As the image focused, the whale fluked up, and she saw the pattern on the tail. She stopped breathing as she shot several photos, but she could hardly restrain her enthusiasm. The tail sliced through the surface, and she shouted back, "It's Echo, Milton! It's Echo!"

She magnified the digital image on the camera's small screen to prove it to herself, but the three lines on his left fluke were unmistakable. With a little imagination, they looked like the ever widening circles of a radar display. These distinctive markings had inspired Elizabeth to name him Echo during her first season of fieldwork with Professor Maddings. Entering his unique tailprint into the fluke catalog had sealed her fate as a scientist intoxicated by the thrill of discovery and the patterns of nature.

Elizabeth scanned the water through her black binoculars with the precision of a radar-tracking device, searching for the wispy white plumes that would hang in the air for only a moment. Echo could stay down for as much as twenty minutes and surface anywhere within a radius of miles. Her stomach dropped at the thought of losing a chance to swim with Echo on her last day on the island.

Every minute that Elizabeth waited for Echo felt like an hour, but she did not dare get into the water too early and risk losing track of him. Handing the binoculars to Milton, Elizabeth pulled on her yellow fins. Her weight belt pressed down against her hips. She spat into her mask and positioned it on her forehead, ready to slip silently into the sea at any moment. Her long black hair was already braided, but she swept a few untamable strands out of her face and behind her ears.

With her mask and snorkel, she was limited to the border world of the surface, but scuba diving, with its clouds of bubbles, would disturb the whales and interfere with her recording. She had become quite expert at free diving and could hold her breath longer each year. Every movement was done precisely and quietly. Sound travels great distances in the water, as light cannot, making hearing as important to whales as sight is to humans. She didn't want to scare Echo away. Not all were benevolent in these waters.

As on many other small and remote Caribbean islands, almost everyone on Bequia depended on the sea for their livelihood. While some were master boat builders whose craftsmanship was prized far

and wide, most were simple fishermen. Yet a handful of men continued the hundred-year-old tradition that their ancestors had learned
aboard the Yankee whalers. They hunted in small sailboats, using
old-fashioned harpoons, and they were allowed to take four whales a
year by the International Whaling Commission. This was a small
number in comparison to that of the Japanese and Norwegians, who
each killed hundreds of whales annually.

In the distance Elizabeth saw the Japanese factory fishing boat
that had been trawling these waters all season. Her jaw tightened.
She knew they were offering development money on the island to
gain access to the fisheries and who knew what else. They had even
paid for the whaling station.

When she first came to the tight-knit community on Bequia
eight years ago, she quickly discovered that if she was going to have
any hope of doing her research, she would have to make friends with
the whalers—the local heroes who fought the giants.

As she got to know the whalermen, a mutual respect had devel-
oped between them. Milton had warned her against getting too
friendly with his half brother, Teo, who was the whaleboat captain
and a heartbreaker. Elizabeth knew she could handle herself, and to
her surprise, Captain Teo had a great deal of knowledge about the
whales. It was the Bequia whalers, after all, who had correctly guessed
that the males were whistling—the word they used for singing—
down in the depths.

Elizabeth continued to scan the horizon through her binoculars.
She had given Captain Teo an identical pair when it looked like he
might give up the hunt and start a whale-watching business. Elizabeth had explained that individual whales could be identified by the
pattern on their flukes, like a fingerprint, and he had told her how
devoted whale mothers were to their young. As they shared their
knowledge, they became friends and eventually lovers. It was still
hard for her to believe that she could have fallen for a whaler. She

could have escaped his handsome face and bewitching eyes—one green, one blue. She could have resisted the warmth and confidence of his island smile, but ultimately, she was caught by his love for the sea and his eagerness to share it with her.

For two months her desire and her doubt had wrestled like predator and prey. Elizabeth had ended their relationship over the phone the day after she met Frank for the first time, back in Boston. She knew that in the shelter of Frank's embrace, she could create a life and have a family. Despite what Frank said, she *did* want a family. Six years was not that long to be married, and Elizabeth argued that there was still plenty of time to have children after she finished her dissertation.

The blow finally came, *and it was only fifteen meters away.* Elizabeth threw down her waterproof notepad. She hoisted herself overboard and, biceps straining, lowered herself slowly into the water.

"Mind the sharks," Milton said softly as he handed her the video recorder. "Is plenty in these waters."

"Don't remind me." Elizabeth took the bulky gray waterproof housing that protected her video camera. She wished Milton wouldn't mention the sharks every time she got in the water. Many of the fishermen could not even swim, and Milton was even more afraid of sharks than she was.

Elizabeth pulled her mask down with one hand and then placed the snorkel in her mouth. She could hear her anxious breath rattling through the blue plastic tube and tried to slow it down. Ever since she had seen the movie *Jaws* as a girl, she had been afraid of sharks, which was very inconvenient for a marine biologist. She controlled her fear by never looking behind her in the water. If she was going to be eaten, she did not want to know in advance.

Elizabeth reminded herself of the facts that helped to keep her fears at bay. Unprovoked attacks by sharks were extremely rare. In these parts there were mostly reef sharks, which were rarely aggres-

sive. Even tiger sharks—while second only to white sharks in reported attacks on humans—were generally safe if one understood
their behavior.

She knew that those who thought the wild was ferocious and
endlessly dangerous were wrong. There was a homeostasis in nature
where predator and prey existed in close proximity. Only occasion-
ally at feeding time was the calm disrupted in a convulsion of violence as one animal died and another was able to continue living.
Survival was unkind, but it was not cruel.

Elizabeth kicked her fins slowly and smoothly, trying to make
as little disturbance as possible. Only forty or fifty feet below her,
she could see the marbled light dancing on the gray-brown coral
and a blue parrotfish darting around. The crackling of the reef's
snapping shrimp filled her ears, although most of the coral looked
bleached and dead. She felt a wave of sadness as she recalled how
colorful the reefs had looked when she first came to the island. She
thought of her colleagues who were trying to understand why the
reefs here and around the world were dying faster than anyone had
predicted. Was it warmer waters? Pollution? Disease? No one knew
for sure.

She turned her gaze to the gray housing of the video recorder she
held in front of her, putting her finger on the trigger, preparing to record Echo's every sound and movement. Elizabeth was one of the
few researchers who had started to record vocalizations while simul-
taneously observing and recording whale behavior. Whales spent the
vast majority of their lives in an alien and distant world, so the work
of studying them was long and difficult. Nonetheless, at moments
like this, it was thrilling.

Elizabeth kicked more quickly. Her hands floated ghostly white in
front of her. She stared at her naked ring finger. Tomorrow she would
be going home to California. While she hated to leave the whales, she
needed to return to Frank. Elizabeth remembered the fight they'd had

the day she left for the island, and her stomach tightened as she thought about Frank's ultimatum.

Echo appeared out of the shadows, interrupting any other thought, leaving only this moment of awe. She saw his huge head, from the rostrum on top down to the jaw, ending just before his enormous flippers. It was truly impossible to comprehend the vastness of his body. Behind the jawline, a third of the way along his length, she saw his eye looking at her serenely. With increasing size came ever greater calm in the order of nature. What had amazed Elizabeth most about these titans of the deep was not their power but their gentleness. In her imagination, whales were the very eye of the storm around which the whole world hurried and worried. She knew that Echo's massive heart was beating only once every three seconds as hers continued to flutter like that of a hummingbird. Humans were small and nervous creatures.

Echo's tail floated up until his body was pointing down at a forty-five-degree angle in the singing posture. As he sang, Elizabeth's rib cage began to vibrate. She recorded every discrete sound, every phrase, and tried to remember each of the recurring themes from her earlier recordings of this year's song. She drifted closer, the song growing louder.

High-pitched whistles and ethereal, ghostly moans surrounded her, vibrating through her. The deeper grunts and groans felt like a pressure wave, similar to the bass of a giant speaker pinning her to a wall. Her whole body shook, and her teeth started to rattle. The song began to overwhelm her senses as it spilled into her middle ear, disorienting her balance, invading her. She had never been this close before. She tried to steady herself but didn't know if she could withstand the intensity of the vibrations.

She was panting through her snorkel and starting to sweat under her mask. She needed to back up, but she did not want to leave, to miss anything. It was her last day of the season with the whales, and she would have to wait a whole year for another opportunity like this. She focused her mind on the sound, closing her eyes, becoming a part of the song.

When Elizabeth opened her eyes, she saw another whale swimming toward Echo. Her heart beat even more wildly. Interaction between whales was always the most dramatic and potentially important part of her work. It was where her research on communication came alive, and she said a scientist's prayer to the whales to give her something good, something she could write up and use to convince her department to give her another extension on her dissertation.

As she watched the languid aquatic dance of the two gentle giants, Elizabeth forgot about her deadlines. She knew that the function of the songs was one of the great mysteries of the ocean, with courtship and competition as the two predominant theories. What she was about to witness might reveal a piece of the puzzle.

Elizabeth released some of the air in her lungs and sank below the surface. If she was to understand the interaction, she had to know the sex of the new whale. Almost immediately, she could see the hemispherical lobe on its belly, revealing that this was a female. Elizabeth let out more air and sank down farther, holding the video camera out in front of her with rigid arms and pointing it where she was looking. The whale swam right next to her. Although four thousand times more powerful than Elizabeth, the female did not knock her out of the way. Instead, she gracefully raised her fourteen-foot flipper up over Elizabeth's head. And that was when Elizabeth saw it.

"Oh my God," she sputtered into her snorkel. She looked closer to see if she was imagining it. No researcher had ever seen what she was about to record on film.

TWO

THE FEMALE was in the process of giving birth. A tail, its tips curled over, was beginning to emerge from the whale's genital slit.

Elizabeth could not believe that she would be fortunate enough to witness a birth, let alone film it. In her shock, she had forgotten about breathing until her deflated chest began to ache. At times like this, she wished she could use scuba tanks.

Kicking gently to the surface, she blew water out of her snorkel and gasped for air. The whole time she continued looking down and pointing the camera at the female—she was not going to miss this for the world. Elizabeth double-checked the red indicator on the screen to make sure the camera was recording, and stayed as close as she could without scaring the mother. From what she could tell, the female did not seem agitated by her presence. Emboldened, Elizabeth let out more air from her lungs and silently descended again.

Another gasp of bubbles escaped as she recognized the notch missing from the female's tail. *It was Sliver.* She had seen Sliver several times over the course of her research, and now she felt like a midwife invited into the intimacy of the whale's birth.

Elizabeth was running out of air, but she refused to risk missing the birth.

Sliver was contracting her abdomen, trying to squeeze out the baby, just like any other mammalian mother. At last the rest of the ten-foot black body was born in a cloud of tissue and pink-tinged fluid. The calf had large fetal folds—creases caused by the cramped confines of the womb—which made the newborn look like it was made out of origami paper.

A six-foot placenta followed soon after. Reddish brown from blood and pink from exposed tissue, it drifted in the bright blue water like a giant jellyfish. Elizabeth shivered as she remembered the man-of-war she had accidentally brushed up against the year before. She recalled the sharp pain of its stinging cells, the flush of the hives that had covered her body like a burn, and the difficulty she'd had breathing as her tongue and throat swelled. Frank, a physician, now insisted that she carry epinephrine with her at all times just in case she got stung again.

Elizabeth was getting dizzy from lack of oxygen. She surfaced, blowing out the water in her snorkel and gasping, both for air and from the excitement of what she had just witnessed. Her hands were numb from the adrenaline pumping through her system, but she kept the camera pointed down.

As she descended slowly once again, she saw that Echo was supporting the calf. This surprised her. Most helper whales were females, "aunties," and there was no evidence of pair bonding in humpbacks. The male that impregnated Sliver eleven and a half months ago could be anywhere. Elizabeth could not understand why Echo, who most likely had no genetic relationship to the calf, was helping it to the surface.

Then she realized—something was wrong. She had not noticed it until now. She looked closely at the calf's body, her eyes straining to see through the streaks of sunlight spilling into the water. The baby rolled off Echo's rostrum and began to sink, listing to the side, not moving its flippers or tail flukes. Elizabeth knew from her time working with dolphins and belugas at the aquarium that cetacean babies usually swim at once. But this whale's body was limp and looked like a corpse slowly sinking in the water.

Elizabeth heard the mother's contact call: *w-OP.* And again a few moments later: *w-OP.* But there was no answer from the calf. She heard the sound again. Still no answer.

Sliver swam to the baby and nudged it with her head. The baby responded to its mother with a weak nod. It was not dead. But without the movement of its fins to keep it buoyant, the baby continued to descend. Sliver responded more urgently. She swam under her sinking baby, supported it across her head, and carried it to the surface forcefully. Her massive body created a current of water that pushed Elizabeth away.

Elizabeth's eyes were wide as she held her head above the water, waiting. She saw the two adult blows, but no breath from the baby draped across its mother's back. *What's wrong?* she wondered. *Why is this baby in distress? Had it been born prematurely? Had it been a prolonged labor?* She swam toward the calf, wanting to help it live. *But how?*

As they all bobbed above the surface, the calf's small blowhole caught her eye. It was slack. Elizabeth had an idea. It was crazy, but if it worked, it could save the calf's life.

Elizabeth flipped onto her back and began to propel herself with her fins back to Milton's wooden boat. She held the video camera against her chest and rocked back and forth, trying to make her body as streamlined as possible.

"Open the first aid kit!" she shouted as she reached the boat and hoisted her video camera onto the bench.

"You hurt?"

"No, just give me the case!" There was no time to explain.

"Blood in the water," Milton said as he handed her the first aid kit. Elizabeth pried open the hard plastic tabs and grabbed the pack of prefilled hypodermic needles. There were four Twinject pens, each calibrated for two doses—not enough for the calf's body weight. But dosing of epinephrine was not an exact science, and she had no alternative. The calf's muscles, including its heart, were not responding to life. The baby's whole body was shutting down. The cardiac stimulant in her hand was the only hope.

"Listen for the horn," Milton said, holding the air horn in his hand. It was their signal to alert her if he saw sharks.

Elizabeth's flippers propelled her forward quickly, and she twisted her body rhythmically to increase her speed. As she approached the whales, she tried to stay focused, but her eyes were drawn to the edges of her mask, scanning for sharks. Maybe she did want to know if she was going to be eaten.

"Bruuuuuuuuuuffff!"

Elizabeth froze. Sliver's protective underwater blow was unmistakable, as was the screen of bubbles. Elizabeth knew not to challenge a thirty-five-ton female driven by the strongest of instincts: protection of her young.

Elizabeth looked into Sliver's eye. The sclera was bulging, and it showed an anxious ring of white. *Of course she's stressed,* Elizabeth thought, and tried to calm her breath as she swam forward slowly. The baby could die at any moment from lack of oxygen. Elizabeth approached cautiously, looking for any further sign of agitation or aggression. One swipe of Sliver's tail or flipper could kill her instantly.

Instinctively, Elizabeth held up her hands, although she had no hope that this universal human gesture of peace would mean anything to a whale. *Was it possible for a whale to read emotion or intent?* Elizabeth gently moved her flippers back and forth as she held herself upright in the water.

Then she heard the jarring blast of the air horn, only slightly muffled through the water. She scanned around her and saw what was no doubt adding to Sliver's agitation—a Caribbean reef shark was biting into the placenta, its white mouth shaking back and forth as it tore off a piece. Its gullet convulsed and gills pulsated as it swallowed the sizable prize.

Another gray reef shark appeared, swimming around the placenta. Fear flooded Elizabeth's veins, paralyzing her limbs, even though she knew that reef sharks were relatively harmless to humans. Fighting to retain control, she took a deep breath. Finally, her muscles responded to her command, and she turned to face Sliver, who was watching her closely. The mother was still supporting her baby on her back, helping the calf to breathe.

Elizabeth kicked her fins slowly, approaching. Sliver's body was still, unthreatening. Her eye, although stressed, seemed to communicate something—*was it understanding?* Elizabeth had no time to waste, so she continued forward, realizing the danger she was in if she had misread Sliver.

A moment later, she reached out and touched the soft skin of the baby whale. She placed her finger in one of the smooth nostrils of the blowhole, but it did not close reflexively. She could hear the strained rumbling of its breath—the calf was trying to live. *Could Sliver hear her baby's weak heart beating against her back?*

Elizabeth moved down the body of the young whale toward the tail that was draped over its mother. The calf's smooth skin felt like a shelled hard-boiled egg. Elizabeth noticed several lesions, which surprised her—how could the calf have gotten lesions in its mother's womb?

There was no way to get to the underside of the tail, where the veins were visible. *This is not like working with dolphins at the aquarium,* Elizabeth thought. *How the hell am I going to do this on a humpback out here in the open sea?* She felt for the large veins of the tail fluke, which trainers and veterinarians used to administer injections in captive cetaceans.

She had never heard of anyone giving an injection to a humpback whale, but the physiology would no doubt be similar. She felt the little indentation where one of the veins curved along the shape of the tail. As she pushed on the black skin, she could feel the spongy wall of the vein, softer than the rubbery connective tissue on either side. The vein might be too deep for the short needle, but there was no time for an alternative. The baby's life was draining away.

The air horn sounded again.

She looked over and saw quite a few dorsal fins and tails slapping on the surface. A pack of sharks was fighting over the coveted spoils, but she could see from the delicately curving shape of their dorsals that they were all reef sharks. She sighed with relief.

Elizabeth quickly removed the plastic cap of one Twinject and wrapped her fist around the pen, jabbing it into the vein all the way up to the hub. The spring-loaded needle shot into the whale's body.

No response.

She clutched another pen and punched it into the vein.

Still no response.

Elizabeth's limp snorkel hung next to her face as she kicked with her feet to stay next to the whale's drifting body. Despite its size, the calf seemed so fragile.

Sliver began to sink so that only a small part of the calf's back floated above the surface. Elizabeth would need to make the next injection underwater. She bit down on the hard plastic mouthpiece of her snorkel and felt for the veins as she ducked her head beneath the surface.

She injected a third pen. Still nothing.

The calf's circulatory system was large, but she had expected to see some reaction by now. As she waited, she saw the frenzy of sharks still feasting on the delicacy of the placenta. They lashed at the red-brown mass and at one another.

Then she saw what she had feared most—a tiger shark moved in, scattering the reef sharks. The vertical bars along its twelve-foot length were unmistakable, and its dorsal was sturdier and more menacing than those of the reef sharks. She stared at its wide mouth of scalpel-sharp teeth and then saw it look at her through its large black eye.

It's just swimming, she told herself as she scanned its body for possible threat displays: pectoral fins pointing down, mouth gaping open, stiff movements. It was displaying none of these. Perhaps it was the whales that kept the tiger shark at a distance, or the placental feast. She kept telling herself that she was not in immediate danger, but she could not stop her heart from racing or the dizzy sensation caused by the cascade of fight-or-flight hormones in her body.

Sliver buoyed the calf back up, and Elizabeth took another giant breath once she reached the surface with them. It was as if Sliver were asking her to try again, although she knew the whale could not possibly have understood what she was doing. But somehow she must have known that Elizabeth was trying to help, or she surely would have protected her calf.

Elizabeth looked at the final pen in her fist and then felt for the vein with the fingertips of her other hand. She pounded against the whale's sloughing skin. The pen fired, and the epinephrine shot into the vein. *Breathe, dammit. Breathe.*

The calf's desperate gasp was fast and sharp as the blowhole opened wide. The baby's entire body seemed to convulse with the desire to live as it arched its back, lifted its flukes, and started throwing its head and tail to the side spasmodically. Elizabeth kicked backward quickly to avoid being hit by fifteen hundred pounds of newborn awkwardness. She heard a sputtering sound and then saw a tiny blow. The baby, still stimulated from the injection, rolled off its mother and started to beat its tail up and down eagerly. Elizabeth laughed with relief, and her chest swelled with joy as she saw the two fifteen-foot blows followed by the six-foot blow from the calf. Its burst of vapor was an explosion of hope and survival.

The three whales dove, the baby following the lead of its mother and escort. Elizabeth scanned the pattern on its tail, trying to memorize it. She noticed four very faint parallel lines on the left side and remembered the four injections. She'd call him Fourth Chance.

Elizabeth was alone on the surface. She looked around and realized that she had drifted twenty meters farther away from the boat, out into the open ocean. Milton knew not to approach too close while she was working with the whales, but now she heard the groan of the motor as it sped toward her. She was eager to climb in, knowing what was still lurking near the placenta. Some shark species preferred live prey, and she did not want to find out if tigers were one of them.

The bump came like a shoulder in her side. It was no doubt the infamous bump-and-bite behavior, and the shark was circling back for the second half of the equation. Elizabeth began to swim frantically, arm over arm, to the boat that was speeding toward her. In her panic, she literally tried to run from the shark, her legs kicking, her muscles steeled by the adrenaline, her chest jutting halfway out of the water.

"Shark! Liza! Shark!" Milton shouted from the boat—he must have seen the dorsal fin approaching her. Despite the frenzy and flurry of water, she felt as if time were slowing down, every second distended and terrifyingly long. A video she had seen flashed to mind. It was of a shark slowly biting off a woman's leg; it had been shockingly gradual and deliberate.

She could not help looking back at the dorsal that was only a dozen feet away. Though there was no way she would reach the boat in time, her body continued kicking desperately.

Suddenly, an enormous pressure wave of water rushed against her skin. She closed her eyes, anticipating the bite. The foaming water erupted like an underwater volcano.

Elizabeth was thrown forward.

A stream of moist air exploded above her as Echo surfaced. His exhalation was like a gunshot fired in her defense.

Elizabeth looked around her for the dorsal fin but saw nothing above the surface. She ducked her mask underwater, still searching for the shark. She was no longer breathing through her snorkel, and the salt water tasted like metallic blood. Stuffing the bite-piece into her mouth, she looked in every direction, trying to see beyond the dissipating bubbles.

In front of her, not more than a few feet away, was Echo's eye. The gaze was unnerving. She felt an intense familiarity, after all these years, and some sense of recognition beyond actual knowing.

She heard the scream of the motor and Milton's voice shouting her name, but it sounded far away. There was just this moment of presence.

Then Milton grabbed her wetsuit as Echo effortlessly sank away. Elizabeth looked up at Milton, still unable to speak. His strong fisherman's arms hauled her into the boat, and she fell against the wooden seat like deadweight, water pouring off her arms and legs.

"You all right?"

Elizabeth pulled off her mask as the adrenaline drained from her limbs. She looked up at Milton blankly, still in another world.

"That whale done save you, Liza."

Milton's words registered in her mind, along with the impossibility of their meaning. "Whales breach, Milton, that's what they do," Elizabeth said, trying to convince him—and herself—that her "rescue" was just ordinary whale behavior.

"This one done breach for save you, Liza."

"I wouldn't go that far, Milton." For a scientist, the idea that whales would care about humans was difficult to accept, not to mention impossible to prove.

"Dolphin save people—dog, too. Why shouldn't a whale save you so?" Milton was smiling, confident in his interpretation.

Elizabeth did not answer. Human-animal encounters like the one she had just experienced were always anecdotal and impossible to study. Her father's superstitious beliefs aside, animal intent was not provable. Elizabeth unclipped her weight belt and slowly peeled off her fins, feeling increasingly human.

Milton stopped smiling as the boat began to vibrate again with the sound of the whale song.

"Cut the engine," Elizabeth said. The boat went silent with a sputter. Elizabeth grabbed the waterproof case, the clear cover revealing the digital audio recorder inside. She dropped the hydrophone overboard and put on her headset.

"What's wrong?" Milton asked, perhaps noticing the expression on her face.

She pushed one earpiece closer to her ear, not believing what she was hearing. In her spiral flip pad, she quickly recorded the time and started making notes.

"What's wrong?" Milton asked again.

"The song is different—completely different."

"Maybe he just done tired of the old song."

"They don't just start singing new songs." She knew that the change in the song was as extraordinary as what she had witnessed in the water, perhaps more so.

With both hands, Elizabeth pressed the earphones against her ears, trying to hear the higher frequencies better. Her eyes grew wide and her mouth opened in mute recognition. The rapid transformation was unprecedented enough, but the sounds were totally impossible in a song.

"Are we recording?" Elizabeth asked anxiously, pointing to the pelican case on the bench next to him.

Milton looked down. "Yes, Liza, we getting every last word."

THREE

Moments later
Aboard the Masuyo Maru
1 mile off the coast of Bequia

TOKUJIRO KAZUMI peered through the enormous deck-mounted military binoculars from aboard the factory fishing ship. Through the eyepieces he saw the American researcher in her tiny hired boat. While he could see her long black braided hair, he could not see her beautiful face. He had been following her work since long before the recent *National Geographic* article. What he could not see in the sixty times magnification, he remembered from the full-page photograph in the magazine. Her face was wide, her high cheekbones like cliffs, her eyebrows arching over eyes that were so blue and so deep he could stare at them in the photo for hours. Her mixed race made the eyes linger, as the mind tried to understand what ancestry could have caused such a fusion of features and such consummate beauty. The magazine journalist must have wondered enough to ask and revealed the answer: a Jewish mother and a Native American father. The crossbreeds, like Elizabeth McKay and like him, were the hardiest and most vigorous, always taking the best qualities from each genetic strain. It was as true for humans as it was for dogs. He thought of his pet, Kioko, a mix breed, who had lived for eighteen years. It was not long enough. Kazumi still could not bring himself to imagine getting another.

The boat bobbed on the surface like a floating green buoy. *Sweet Madonna* was painted casually in red along the sideboard. He could barely make out the headphones pressed against her ears. *Listening to the whales,* Kazumi thought. He groaned, remembering her papers, which he had read online. Even the Scientific Committee of the International Whaling Commission had decided to discuss whale communication at the next meeting, largely because of her work. The day that humans could understand whale communication would spell the end of whaling forever. People did not want to eat food that was intelligent enough to talk.

Oil from whale blubber had become obsolete as a result of the discovery of petroleum. The only remaining market was for whale meat, and even there, demand had fallen over the past decade. Still, the whaling industry was actively working to expand the market by opening whale meat restaurants and getting whale meat into schools. As the executive director of the Japanese Department of Fisheries Development, Kazumi had been instrumental in getting thirty-five hundred schools to start serving fish sticks and burgers made out of whale meat. And, of course, there was China, an enormous untapped market for whale meat.

Kazumi looked up from the binoculars and saw the steep slopes of the island near the small boat. The lack of rainfall and arable land had made it one of the last islands to be colonized, and the fierceness of the Carib Indians had helped ensure their independence and that of the runaway slaves who came to join them. But eventually, all people could be bowed by force, as the British had proved so successfully all around the world.

Kazumi kept his receding gray hair perfectly tamed and wore a fashionably tailored blue suit despite the Caribbean heat. The British had never let the adversity of colonial life weaken their sense of propriety. At the elite boarding school that Kazumi had attended in England, the war had never ended, and he was seen as the enemy, despite the fact that his mother was British. Yet he never lost his love for England and felt that the British and the Japanese had many things in common, including their sense of propriety.

Kazumi gazed into the binoculars once again. The American was heading back to shore. Kazumi would hate to harm such beauty, but he was prepared to do whatever needed to be done—or, more accurately, to have Nilsen do whatever needed to be done.

IN THE NARROW CABIN, Halvard Nilsen's eyes were still blurry from a night of drinking on the island. He should have known better than to guzzle the strong rum—it contained twice as much alcohol as vodka—and his throbbing head reminded him of that fact. In the mirror across from his bunk, he looked at his disheveled hair, the rough stubble on his red cheeks, and the bags under his eyes. Nilsen pulled out a pack of cigarettes and lit one, a puff of smoke momentarily eclipsing his face.

He heard the high-pitched whine that he had been too liquored up to notice during the night. He scratched the bumps along the back of his neck. His eyes darted around the room, looking for any sign of movement. He saw the black speck bump along the wall of the small cabin, drunk on his blood. It hovered, heavy and sated, near the fluorescent light. Nilsen got up slowly, stalking one step at a time, raising his hands with the slow, deliberate patience of the hunter.

KAZUMI TURNED AWAY from watching the small boat when he heard Nilsen's heavy footsteps approach.

The Norwegian's ruddy face was lined and sun-damaged under his once white captain's hat. The stubble on his unshaved face rose into the beginnings of a mustache and goatee around his mouth. He wore a black T-shirt and jeans, disregarding the ship uniform, but technically, he did not work for the fishing fleet. Technically, he did not work for the government, as Kazumi did. His services were called "offshoring," and his salary was deposited into a numbered bank account in the Bahamas once a month.

Nilsen held up his right hand. On it was the crumpled remains of a large tropical mosquito, its legs and wings crushed, and a smear of blood across his palm. With his left hand, Nilsen pulled off each wing and each leg, dissecting his kill slowly. Once the mosquito had been utterly destroyed, Nilsen proceeded to suck the blood on his palm. "I got my blood back," he said, a smile spreading across his face.

Kazumi looked at him with disgust. "We have bigger problems than mosquitoes."

"That's why you woke me, *sir*?" There was always a sneer in Nilsen's voice. Kazumi knew that Nilsen did not respect him but had no choice other than to obey him. Few people ate whale meat these days, and as a former whaler, Nilsen needed work. Kazumi was willing to put up with the man's arrogance because he needed both his skills and his lack of moral qualms. Nilsen lit another cigarette and took a long drag.

"Take a look through the glass," Kazumi said. Their common language was English, although Kazumi emphasized his Oxford-educated accent to reinforce his superior position. Nilsen stepped up to look, and Kazumi winced at the smell of liquor, sweat, and old cigarette smoke that seemed to ooze from the whaler's every pore.

"What do you want me to do to him?" Nilsen said, referring to the local in the boat.

"Not him. Her."

"Her?" Nilsen's sneer had turned into a snicker.

"Elizabeth McKay is a marine biologist who thinks whales are smart—smart enough to use language."

"So can parrots."

Kazumi rolled his eyes. "We're not trying to convince the world to eat parrots, now, are we?"

"So what?"

"So we only have a few months before the vote. We can't afford to have a public relations disaster."

It had been over two decades since America and other cultural imperialists had forced the rest of the world to stop commercial whaling. Kazumi took great pride in the fact that a few nations like Japan, Norway, Iceland, and some island nations had managed to continue whaling through various means. They took several thousand a year, but that was a fraction of the whales being taken before the ban. Japanese scientists had shown that whale populations had recovered significantly. Kazumi was certain there were plenty of whales to support whaling in larger numbers, and he was leading an effort to overturn the out-of-date ban. Yet any vote at the International Whaling Commission was highly sensitive—people seemed to care more about whales than other seafood—and this American's research was politically explosive.

Established by whaling nations to regulate whaling, the IWC had become quite political and many member nations increasingly obstructionist. Fortunately, Kazumi and his allies had found a way to bring in new island nations that were supportive of his goals. At approximately 10,600,000 yen per whale, billions of yen were at stake. And then there was the matter of Kazumi's retirement, which was not too far off, and his "descent from heaven." He had been assured a lucrative board position by the whaling industry if everything went according to plan.

"What do you want me to do?" Nilsen asked with a smile. Kazumi knew Nilsen was always happiest when he had something to do.

Kazumi's face was impassive. "We're going to stop her from proving anything to anyone." He saw three blows from the whales that Elizabeth had been studying. The Japanese did not yet have permission to whale in these waters—but the local whalermen did. "Don't you think that Captain Teo would be interested to know about whales so close in?"

FOUR

ELIZABETH WAS STARTLED AWAKE by the cacophony of rain on the corrugated metal roof. The air in the one-room house she rented from Milton's family was thick and moist, and the blades of the wooden fan did little to cut through the heat. The blue walls were peeling, perspiring as everything did in the tropics. Only briefly, after a cold shower or the rare and welcome rain, did she ever get the layer of sweat off her skin.

She could smell the pungent smoke of the green mosquito coil that had long burned itself out. There was something about being stalked by a blood-sucking creature that robbed sleep of its rest. Fragments of dreams still flashed in her mind like scattered snapshots. She blinked, and recalled an image of a birthday cake floating on the water with burned-out candles.

She shook her father's voice from her head. Dreams were not messengers from the spirit world. They were simply the detritus of the brain's random firings during REM sleep. She was just feeling guilty about arriving back home the day before Frank's birthday. Maybe he was right. She was always trying to push the limits, get more time with the whales, and make the big discovery that would validate her research. But the new song she had recorded the day before could *be* that discovery; the extra day really might have made all the difference. She promised herself she would make it up to Frank.

Elizabeth sat up as her eyes focused on a mosquito that clung to the outside surface of the netting. It was still waiting, wanting, needing the blood protein in her veins that allowed it to lay its eggs. The numerous lenses of its compound eyes detected movement easily, so Elizabeth slowly placed one hand on either side of the fold where it rested. The mosquito did not move, perhaps exhausted by its all-night vigil, its maternal hunger for blood. The sting of her clapping hands was satisfying, but the mosquito was gone. She had missed and would have to leave the safety of the netting.

As a biologist, she was supposed to love all creatures great and small, but the truth was she disliked most insects. She thought of the disgusting cockroaches that would scurry over the countertops and on her bed in her aunt's apartment, when she was sent to live in New York at the age of seven. She shivered as she remembered the feeling of their wiggling antennae and their skittering flat bodies and hairy legs.

"You'll be better off with your aunt," her father had said the night they scattered her mother's ashes over the railing of the Golden Gate Bridge. It had been just the two of them. Elizabeth had tried to see below to where the racing current swept her mother's remains out to sea, but the lights of the bridge did not shine down to the water's surface. "The whales will watch over her now," her father had said. After that, whales had begun to appear in her dreams, always carrying her mother back to her, but inevitably, when she awoke, her mother was still dead, and she would feel her heart break all over again.

Elizabeth opened the slatted shutters, letting the cool trade winds blow in, and watched the downpour. She leaned out the window and gazed up at the dark clouds, feeling the drops splash on her face. Ever since she was a girl, she had loved rain. It reminded her of when she was young and still living in California, where water was scarce and always needed. It was easy to forget that for most of human history rain was the difference between life and death. Her father used to say that in rain was the secret of everything: Water runs down the rivers to the sea, then rises up to the clouds, and finally falls from the sky. All the things we do are the same. They come back to us just like rain. She watched the water sluice down Milton's green metal roof and into the pipe where it was captured and stored for drinking. And then the miserly squall stopped as quickly as it had started and the clouds were gone.

ELIZABETH'S LARGE BLUE DUFFEL BAG was packed. She was ready for the ferry to St. Vincent, then the flights to Barbados and Miami, and finally to San Francisco and home to Frank. Elizabeth remembered her wedding ring, hidden in a pocket of her bag. Her fingers were swollen from the humidity, and the ring resisted her efforts to put it back on. She sucked nervously on her finger, using her saliva as a lubricant, and wriggled the ring over her knuckle.

Relieved, she flipped open her cell phone and glanced at the photo of Frank. He smiled at her, handsome and confident. She touched the wide, open face and the laugh lines around his cheeks and eyes. Frank's forehead was broad and strong under short brown hair that was just beginning to recede. His cheeks and squared, dimpled chin had a day or two of a stubbly beard that made him look like he had just rolled out of bed—which was often the case, first as a medical student, then a resident, and now a fellow. His sparkling, mischievous, green-gray eyes stared at her.

It was these eyes that had first captivated her across the crowd at, of all places, a funeral. Professor Maddings's wife, Louisa, had died of ovarian cancer, and Elizabeth had left Bequia and the whale season early to go to the funeral. Death always demanded new life, and she was not the only woman who had met her future husband at the grave. Louisa had been one of Frank's patients during his medical school training. It was rare to meet a doctor, especially a student, who cared so much about his patients, but Elizabeth soon discovered that Frank's love was wild and fearless.

Right outside the church, he invited her for dinner. Later that night, when the owner of the Italian restaurant locked the door behind them, it was as if their hours together had been minutes. It may have been his eyes that she noticed first, but it was his questions that made her fall in love with him. He wanted to know everything about her, about the whales, about her world. He seemed to drink her up with the bottle of red wine, and she knew in an intoxicated cocktail of love and desire that this was the man she would marry. There was no careful consideration, no deliberating of variables—just one headlong plunge. From that first night, they spent every possible minute together. They shared a passion for the ocean, and three months later, on the ferry to Nantucket Island, Frank got down on one bended, trembling knee.

Elizabeth looked at the large diamond ring now. It was impressive but not very practical for field research. She and Frank had very little money: She was a graduate student at Woods Hole, and he was a medical student at Harvard. But they had not needed much. They spent most of their time in each other's arms and left his apartment only when absolutely necessary.

Elizabeth had tried to convince Frank to save money on an engagement ring and just get her one for the wedding, so they could take a longer honeymoon scuba diving in Belize. But on the advice of his father, Frank bought a two-carat princess-cut diamond. Frank's father was a nice man, but from a different generation, when big rings, big weddings, and big families were signs of having made it in America. There were times when Elizabeth wondered if Frank wanted a wife from a different generation.

Elizabeth plugged the audio cable of her DAT machine into the cheap boom box by her bed. The sound of Echo's song filled the room. The night before, she had listened to the song over and over again, trying to memorize the phrases and individual units. Now she kept rewinding and listening to one particular pair of upward sweeping sounds: "*w-OP-w-OP.*"

"What it mean?"

Elizabeth looked up through the open window and was startled to see Milton's dog, Catcher, his mouth open and pink tongue hanging out, panting. The mutt was part sheltie, with bright shining eyes and blond bushy ears that were cocked curiously at her. Elizabeth shook her head incredulously, knowing that the dog had not asked the question. Then, behind the shutter, Elizabeth saw Eldon, Milton's eight-year-old son, and she sighed, relieved that she was not losing her mind.

"It's a social sound—a contact call," Elizabeth explained. "The mother uses it to get her baby to come closer when it strays too far." Elizabeth and other researchers had known about these social sounds for many years, but she was one of the first to try to correlate the sounds with the social behavior. Whales had one of the most diverse sound repertoires of any species, but while song had been studied for decades, the social sounds were just beginning to be deciphered. It was like discovering an entire alien language and trying to understand it. Even SETI—the Search for Extraterrestrial Intelligence—had expressed interest in her research.

"Is a funny sound," the boy said.

"Whales make all sorts of sounds. Sometimes they sound like elephants trumpeting or dogs barking or birds chirping. Whales can sound like every animal you've ever heard." She knew she was exaggerating, but only slightly. The whales echoed the whole chorus of the natural world.

Elizabeth took out the tape, labeled it, and carefully packed it away with the others in her equipment bag. She put a fresh tape in the player and packed it in its yellow waterproof case. Like a professional photographer who always makes sure her camera is ready to shoot, Elizabeth always made sure she was ready to record. She felt a tinge of sadness. She wouldn't be making more recordings until next January, when she would return for the beginning of the whale season.

"Is a *mama* whale?" Milton's son said at last, after thinking about Elizabeth's explanation of a contact call.

"Generally, it is the mothers who use the call, but in this case, it's a male who's singing. Only the boys sing." It was strange to find these particular sounds, usually spoken between mother and child, in one of the songs, sung by a male.

The wooden slatted front door burst open.

"What is it?" Elizabeth asked as she stood up.

Milton had his hands on his knees and was trying to catch his breath. He was clearly in a panic. "Teo gone to get the whale family."

FIVE

ELIZABETH AND MILTON ran down the cracked concrete steps from the road, knowing that at any moment Teo could dig his killing lance into Echo, Sliver, or the baby. They looked down to make sure they didn't miss a step and then at each landing looked up and out at the horizon, scanning for the whaleboat. With one hand Elizabeth clutched her binoculars, and with the other she clasped her yellow case to her side to stop it from swinging and to protect the hydrophone inside. She had grabbed both instinctively when Milton had shouted to her, but now she regretted having the case, since it was slowing her down. Still, she managed to stay just a step behind Milton. Her feet knew the stairs, having descended them so many times in the predawn dark.

After stepping over a large rock in the path, Elizabeth was finally down at the beach. Half a dozen fishing boats, each painted a unique combination of bright colors, were hauled up on the sand. Milton and Elizabeth threw down the wooden skids, worn smooth and shiny by the hulls of countless boats. Each was the width of a forearm, and they laid them out like railroad ties.

Even without help, they could push the small green-and-yellow boat into the shallow water. Elizabeth hoisted herself into the boat, her lungs still burning. She tried to calm her breathing and scanned the horizon with her binoculars.

Milton released the pin and quickly lowered the Evinrude 35

into the water. He yanked on the starter cable. The engine sputtered but refused to turn over. Milton pulled on it again, but after the whine and complaint, nothing. Another six pulls, and Milton flipped back the engine cover. Elizabeth's stomach was twisting as she looked back at him.

"Is the damn wire." Milton jiggled a loose wire and lowered the cover. He kissed the tips of his fingers and then touched them to a sticker of the Virgin Mary that was stuck strategically to the engine cover. He again primed the hand pump on the tubing from the red gas tank and then gave the starter cable one last pull. The engine sputtered to life.

Milton gave the engine full throttle. Elizabeth's unbraided hair was blowing behind her. They were soon cutting through the waves and banging down into the troughs as they sped past Semple Cay. Elizabeth's heart was in her throat as she looked at the sterile white and gray whaling station. She shook from her mind the image of three carcasses—Echo, Sliver, and the baby—lying dead on the concrete ramp.

"Can't this boat go any faster? He's not going to remember Sliver," Elizabeth shouted back to Milton. She thought of the promise that Teo had made her many years ago. Echo was the first whale she had identified, and Sliver the first mother. She had made those two whales real for Teo as she pointed out the distinctive patterns on their tails. "Those are your whales, Liza," Teo had said. "We won't take them." But what if Teo didn't see the fluke pattern?

"Me pray Teo don't hurt the whale family," Milton said.

"It's *not* a family, Milton!" Elizabeth said, not meaning to speak so forcefully. She was trying hard to control her own feelings. Besides, the discovery that Echo was escorting Sliver was not proof of anything.

"Me know a proud papa when me see one," Milton shot back, unconvinced.

Elizabeth continued to scan the horizon without her binoculars, which were made useless by the rolling swell. Then she saw it. "There's the boat!" she shouted. Her heart sank as she saw that the mast had been unshipped. "Faster, Milton! Can't you make this goddamn boat go any faster?"

"We fighting the wind and the waves, Liza."

As they approached the twenty-seven-foot double-ender whaleboat, Elizabeth could see the hunt that was unfolding. Teo and his crew of five whalemen had harpooned the baby humpback. They had given it about twenty feet of line and were using it to lure the mother, an old trick learned from the Yankee whalers. A mother will never leave her calf.

Elizabeth knew the baby would be sending out its distress call as it strained against the rope. Elizabeth saw how small the blows were. It had to be confused and terrified.

Then she saw the dorsal fin of the mother breaking the surface as she circled around her baby and the whaleboat. Elizabeth steadied herself against the gunwale.

"Teo get an iron in the calf!" Milton shouted, now able to see the rope.

Elizabeth saw Teo in the bow of the boat, his leg snug in the knee chock as he readied the second iron, preparing to strike the mother as soon as she got close enough. His burnished copper face shone in the sunlight, and the cinnamon-wood harpoon was raised above his head. Jutting out of the shaft was an iron shank as long as his arm, and at its tip was a barbed blade.

"Stop!" Elizabeth cried, but her voice was swallowed by the whistling wind. She tried waving her arms, but all eyes were on the hunt. "Hurry, Milton, hurry," she said as they banged over the swell and cut through the wind.

If only Sliver would fluke up and Teo could recognize her. But she knew that Sliver wouldn't sound, wouldn't leave her baby. Then

Sliver did something that Elizabeth had never seen a mother do before.

Sliver's two enormous white pectoral fins towered out of the water on either side of the calf, curving toward each other. There was no way to describe this but to say that she was embracing her baby. Sliver must have come underneath so her belly could support her newborn. To help the tired baby breathe, Elizabeth thought at first. She had seen another mother whale take her "babe in arms" and strand it on her vast chest, perhaps to calm the calf. But no. That wasn't it.

Sliver wasn't willing to just help her baby die. As the mother whale began to roll away from the boat, Elizabeth realized she was trying to dislodge the harpoon. Sliver kept turning, the three-quarter-inch line wrapping around the mother and calf, yet the barb in the harpoon held fast. The mother was entangling herself, trapping herself as she tried to rescue her baby.

As they approached, Elizabeth waved her arms again and shouted Teo's name. But her voice was still lost in the wind. Then she covered her mouth in horror as Teo cocked his arm back.

Teo pitched the harpoon into Sliver's vulnerable left side just below her flipper. Elizabeth heard a cheer from the boat as the wound started to spray a four-foot jet of watery blood.

"Oh, God, no, oh, God."

The mother had left herself vulnerable to the whalers, and they had struck her near her lung. *"Teo!"* Elizabeth shouted again, and this time she was close enough to be heard.

Teo looked up at her.

"It's Sliver! Stop! It's Sliver!"

Teo's face fell as he realized what he had just done, but there was no time to answer.

Sliver continued rotating her giant body away from the whaleboat. The line was soon pulled taut, and the boat started to take on water.

"Loose the line, man, loose the line," Teo shouted, trying to save his boat and his crew. The men let the rope run out around the loggerhead.

"Cut it!" Elizabeth shouted, but the leading oarsman did not reach for the hatchet. Not unless Captain Teo gave the order.

Sliver continued rolling and quickly took up the slack. She and her baby were now tangled in eighty feet of rope. Elizabeth could see the baby pressed against Sliver's belly, the rough ropes starting to cut into its delicate skin.

"Get me closer," Elizabeth shouted, hoping to put herself and the boat between the whales and the whalers.

Milton gunned the engine, his eyes wide. He knew they were in danger, and he was nervous. The swell brought them within a few feet of the whale, and when he reversed the motor, it was too late.

Sliver thrust herself out of the water in a partial breach. The fifteen-ton head came crashing down toward Milton's boat.

"Jump, Milton," Elizabeth shouted moments before the jaw splintered the bow of his boat. Elizabeth and Milton were thrown out of the boat as the planks shattered.

Elizabeth surfaced and gasped for breath. She was floating in the water, surrounded by countless wooden pieces. Only five feet away, a thirty-five-ton animal was still entangled and trying with every ounce of its strength to get free.

"Milton," she shouted, "are you all right?" She knew that Milton, like many fishermen, could not swim.

"Me here at the whaleboat. Where you, Liza?" he yelled. He couldn't see her on the opposite side of the whale.

Elizabeth did not answer. She was no longer thinking of fleeing, as she saw Sliver's flipper floating just under the water next to her, still straining against the line that encircled mother and calf. Elizabeth reached her hand down to touch the knobby leading edge of the fin, which seemed to stop resisting for a moment.

"Liza, get away from the whale," Teo called out with the first traces of fear she had ever heard in his voice.

The water was unnaturally warm and smelled sickeningly sweet. It was dyed red with blood. Man-of-war birds, like vultures, were circling above.

A rifle shot startled Elizabeth. "Liza, get to the boat." It was Teo again.

Elizabeth saw her yellow Pelican case floating nearby. She took a few overarm strokes to grab it and then swam around Sliver's massive head. She looked for the whale's eye, hoping to be able to judge how far gone Sliver was, but it was underwater. When Elizabeth came alongside the boat, she handed up her case. For the second time in as many days, she felt hands grab for her arms and pull her into the boat.

"Cut her loose," Elizabeth demanded, panting and barely able to control her temper.

"She struck deep. If I cut her loose, she still die."

Elizabeth looked around at the faces of the whalers. She didn't know what she was looking for. She certainly wouldn't find support. This was their moment of glory.

Uree, the midship oarsman and the youngest man in the crew, looked up at her from where he was bent over listening to the center-board box. "The whale making noise," he said.

Elizabeth unclipped her case. She dropped the hydrophone into the water and put on the headphones, as if the sound could help her save Sliver and her calf. Elizabeth closed her eyes and tried to decode it. *Eeee-eeee-eeee.* It was a distress call, plaintive and haunting.

The moan of maternal anguish cracked open any pretense of

objectivity shielding Elizabeth's heart, and she had to choke back tears. Just the day before, she had witnessed the miracle of this mother giving birth and helped the baby to live. And now it was all for nothing—the calf and its mother were being murdered together. Elizabeth breathed deeply and squeezed her eyes shut, trying to will away the sight in front of her.

She knew this was the islanders' celebration and communion, but for her the butchery remained an annual penance. The whalers were holding on to the two ropes, the mother's wrapped around the loggerhead twice, as they pulled on the lines hand over hand, drawing the boat ever closer to the whale.

Teo picked up the eight-foot killing lance, its steel tip looming above him.

Elizabeth sprang to her feet before she had even considered her actions. She grabbed the thin brown metal shaft, smooth and worn from years of use. "Let her go."

"The harpoon done hit the lung. Is too late for this one."

"You promised me you wouldn't hurt her. You lied to me."

"I ain't know it was Sliver," Teo replied almost pleadingly. "I promise you."

They both stopped dead, the killing lance between them. Everyone heard the sound coming from the far side of the boat.

It was like a trumpet. Teo knew it well from when he had been foolish enough to try to strike a bull. Elizabeth let go of the metal shaft.

"Echo come to save his queen," Milton said, but there was fear, not joy, in his voice. The crew was looking down nervously, trying to see something, anything, in the dark blue of the deep water.

Nap, the lead oarsman, looked up and cried out, "Watch out—the whale!"

The tail towered above the boat like the hammer of God. It came crashing down on the water. Everyone fell onto the floorboards as the wake rocked the boat violently. All steadied themselves by grabbing onto the gunwales. Elizabeth braced herself against a bulk-head and wedged her leg underneath a seat. Echo continued lob-tailing, smacking his enormous flukes against the water next to the boat.

"If the whale come any closer, he shatter the boat," Teo said as he dropped the lance and grabbed the bomb gun. Elizabeth stood up and tried to steady herself as the boat continued to rock.

"Get out the way, Liza."

"Just cut the line!" Elizabeth said, the headphone shaken from one ear.

"Cap, shoot him, shoot him with the gun," Rafee, the boat-steerer, cried from the stern.

Teo took aim with the gun, waiting to see the chest or head.

"Wait!" Elizabeth shouted to Teo. "The sound—it's different." She had heard Sliver's call several times, but in the commotion she had not realized that it had changed.

Echo's tail sliced down into the water like a guillotine and disap-peared. "The bull done flee!" shouted Meekel, the tubsman.

Echo had sounded.

The crew returned to their seats. Some smiled in relief; others still looked haunted by fear.

Teo and Elizabeth turned back to the mother and calf. The calf hadn't surfaced for a long time, tangled as it was against its mother. Sliver had stopped trying to roll away from the boat. Then she lifted her great head out of the water, and in the eye of the whale, Elizabeth could see what had happened.

The baby was dead. The unmoving tip of the calf's fin just above the surface confirmed her intuition. Tied to her baby, chest to chest, the mother must have felt its heart stop beating. Was that why she had stopped resisting? Was that why she had changed her call to Echo? It wouldn't be long now for Sliver.

Stepping from seat to seat, Teo, with the killing lance in his hand, jumped onto the whale's back. Usually, it took several stabs to get at the heart or lungs, but Teo had a clear strike, and he raised the lance above his head like a sacrificial knife. He dug the killing lance deep into the heart as a bright red geyser of blood sprayed fifteen feet high and covered Teo and the boat. The men cheered as the thick blood came pouring down like rain.

Elizabeth covered her eyes with her hand as the blood streaked down her neck and face. She shot a glance at Teo, and he looked back at her, shaking his head ever so slightly. She felt sick and hopeless. With the whales both dead, a deep animal loneliness spread through her chest. It always took days after a whale hunt for that feeling of loss to pass, for her silent, tearless grieving to end. But this wasn't just any whale hunt, she thought, as she looked down at the lifeless bodies of Sliver and her baby. She longed for Frank. He always seemed to know how to handle the vicious and indifferent severing of death.

SIX

"GET ME DR. LOMBARDI. *Get me Dr. Lombardi now!*" A mask muffled the obstetrician's voice, but his order was clear. His hands, gloved and ghostly white, were shaking.

"Dr. Lombardi just got off. Dr. Wachowski is the neonatologist on duty."

"Dorothy, I need Frank for this one. Find him for me, *please*."

DR. FRANK LOMBARDI pressed down the plastic handle on the large stainless steel coffee thermos. Empty. Frank's eyes were closing, and he needed caffeine fast. He had assisted five deliveries, admitted three babies to the neonatal intensive care unit, and slept all of forty-five minutes in the last forty-eight hours. And he would still need to drive to the airport to meet Elizabeth. On the counter he spotted an abandoned three-quarters-full cup of coffee and opened the microwave to heat it up. Caffeine was caffeine.

"Dr. Lombardi to labor and delivery. Dr. Lombardi, please report to labor and delivery *immediately*."

Adrenaline rushed through his body. He looked at the coffee cup in his hand and lifted it to his lips. The bitter taste of cold, unsweetened coffee spilled over his tongue and down his throat. He threw the cup in the trash and ran down the hall to the operating room.

Frank rounded the corner of the scrub room, peering anxiously through the windows to the brightly lit OR at the limp infant being lifted onto the crash cart. He washed with lightning speed and backed into the room, snatching a towel from the scrub nurse and pulling on gloves. The exhausted mother lay on the bed, surrounded by nurses in purple scrubs and puffy blue caps. Frank spoke in an urgent yet reassuring tone that would encourage but not panic the mother. "Talk to your baby, Mrs. . . ."

"Bradley," one of the nurses filled in.

"Let her hear your voice, Mrs. Bradley."

A mother's voice often had a magical effect on her newborn. Through bleary eyes, Frank looked down at the sprawl of tiny blue limbs lying on the warming bed in front of him. He reached out his right hand to rock the tiny rounded back, trying to rouse the baby, while with his left hand, he held a miniature plastic oxygen mask over the baby's purple face. His hands worked swiftly and mechanically with long-practiced skill. He was not relying on magic, but he refused to rule out any help he could get.

Pulling off her own oxygen mask, the mother called out, "Cynthia, baby, wake up. Wake up, baby."

The unresponsive infant lay on the white blanket, her eyes nearly shut from swelling. The warmer above the baby glowed red. A scissor-shaped metal clamp was attached to the small remaining piece of umbilical cord. The father, who had been hiding in a corner, terrified, walked over and stared at his child.

"Mrs. Bradley, please keep talking to your baby," Frank said.

"Cynthia, wake up, baby, *please, wake up.*"

Frank was hovering with the endotracheal tube, a moment away from inserting it into the baby's mouth and down the throat. With his other hand, he continued trying to rouse the baby. The baby gasped, took her first breath, and began to wail, an anxious, reedy cry filled with terror.

After the frenzy of trying to get the baby to breathe, it was only now that Frank was able to look closely at her right arm. Where the hand should have been, there was just an undeveloped stump of a forearm. *Hadn't they spotted this on the ultrasound?* Something was wrong with this baby beyond a difficult birth. Frank wondered if she might also have a heart defect, which often accompanied physical deformities.

Tom Neumann, the obstetrician, was standing next to Frank, clearly shaken.

"Doctor, she's hemorrhaging," the nurse whispered, and Dr. Neumann shifted his attention back to the new mother, firmly massaging the uterus and quietly ordering the nurse to start IV medications.

"I have to take the baby to intensive care," Frank said to the nervous parents.

"What can I do?" the father asked.

"Help your wife rest."

Frank and the nurse wheeled the metal and wood crash cart down the hall. The Bradley baby, her blue skin turning ever more pink, lay crying in the clear plastic examining crib. The newborn screech-squawk had evolved over millennia to be so disturbing that it was impossible for mothers—or doctors—to ignore. Frank's shoulders and stomach were tense as he reached the NICU and began to give orders, trying to get this child the help she needed, although what that was, Frank did not yet know.

The nurses helped attach the Bradley baby to monitors that would sound alarms if her temperature, breathing, heart rate, or the oxygen in her blood fell below the normal range. As the baby's vital signs stabilized, Frank turned to the new nurse to ask her about the other infants. Kim was young and still learning but passionate, and he found her enthusiasm appealing. *Elizabeth has been away too long,* he thought with a pang of guilt. They spoke once a week on Sundays, but you could not hold a phone call in your arms. E-mails were worse. There was no life in an e-mail, and Elizabeth got to the cyber café on the other side of the island only once or twice during the weeks she was gone.

It was not just the month and a half they had been apart that had caused the loneliness in his marriage. Even when she was there, her mind and heart were always somewhere else. Had he made a mistake? Maybe they wanted different things. He had tried repeatedly to talk to her about children, but she always said they needed to wait until after she finished her dissertation. It had been six and a half years since they were married. How much longer would they have to wait?

The coffee had done nothing, and as the adrenaline from the birth dissipated, a wave of exhaustion crashed over him. He walked across the room to check the chart of the Alvarez baby. The NICU had several babies in clear plastic cocoons, with monitors that beeped periodically to show that the babies' vital signs were normal. Frank tried to warm up the metal chest piece of the stethoscope before placing it on the baby's tiny torso, already crowded with white and blue monitor pads.

"Are you going to talk to the parents about corrective surgery? It sure looks funny having the hole on his little thing in the wrong place," Kim said, referring to the baby's case of hypospadias.

"That's a little guy's privates you're talking about," Frank said.

"Sorry."

"How's the Chen preemie?"

"Stable."

"What is this—the Love Canal?" Dorothy, the overweight head nurse, walked into the room after reviewing charts.

Frank grimaced. "A certain percentage of abnormalities is normal."

"Well, we seem to have more than our share these days." Dorothy was noticing, as was he, a small upward trend in birth defects. Fortunately, Tom had been awarded a big grant for the Epidemiological Research Unit, or ERU, as it was called at the hospital.

The grant was to study birth defects in the whole Sacramento area. To Frank's surprise, the grant was not from the government or the university but from an organization called the Environmental Stewardship Consortium. Maybe it was one of those private-public partnerships the administration was always touting as the solution to cuts in government health-care dollars. Frank had seen the commercials for the Environmental Stewardship Consortium but knew nothing about them aside from the fact that they were clearly interested in helping hospital research.

"Have you seen the draft report from the ERU?" he asked.

"No sign of it," Dorothy said as they walked out of the room and over to the nursing station. Tom was hurrying down the hall on his way home.

"Hey, Tom. I was just wondering about the ERU report. I want to see if I'm—"

Tom glanced to the side, but he didn't slow down to talk. "Sorry—I'm behind on it." Seemed a little rude, but perhaps he was feeling guilty about missing the deadline, or perhaps he was still shaken from the difficult birth. Or maybe he was just tired, like Frank.

"Hey, Tom," Frank called after him. "My card key to the ERU isn't working."

"I think I heard security was doing something to upgrade the system. I'll have them get you a new card."

Frank flicked the plastic edge of the card key in the pocket of his white coat and watched Tom walk down the hall. He seemed to have a charmed life—his wife adored him and doted on him endlessly, he had great kids, a large house, important research, and now even a beautiful vacation home in Hawaii. *How the hell did he afford that on an obstetrician's salary?* Frank looked down, embarrassed for envying his friend.

"You look like shit," Dorothy said as she walked up to Frank, only her large girth and XXXL purple scrubs between them. "Elizabeth's coming home today, right? Don't you think you should get some rest and clean yourself up a little? Look presentable?"

"Are you trying to be nice, Dorothy?"

"The wards are empty, and Dr. Wachowski's here. Go home. We'll call you if something exciting happens."

Dorothy was right. He'd rest up, buy some flowers, and go meet Elizabeth's plane in San Francisco. Frank twisted his gold wedding band nervously and headed home.

SEVEN

THE ISLAND WAS CRAWLING with people. Unlike the old whaling station on Petit Nevis, which had room to spread out, Semple Cay was tiny, and people were packed together like ants on an anthill, coming and going, waiting to buy their share of the whale meat. One whale would bring a thousand pounds of meat and as much as fifteen hundred gallons of oil. In the past, everything was given, but now that the whales were scarce, people had to buy their meat and oil.

The cookout happened only when a whale was taken, and boats ferried celebrating crowds from all over Bequia. Small fires already burned around the island. Men drank Hairoun beer or St. Vincent's strong rum, cutting it with a swig of cold water between sips. Teo stood over on the bluff, watching the colorfully dressed crowd. He rested a shotgun on his shoulder, just to make sure everything was done in an orderly way and no one started thieving.

The tails of the cow and her calf lay on the concrete sloped slipway where they had been hauled up with the help of the winch. The once blue-gray water had turned crimson red. Whales were butchered in the water to cool the meat and keep it from spoiling. Waves slopped around the whales, surging against their limp bodies and brewing up a pink froth. A colossal pile of intestines, like a fleet of balloons come to grief, floated away on the receding tide.

The barefoot butcher, Noble, was hard at work in the belly of the cow, leaning against the backbone and using the sharp cutting spade to carve out two-foot-by-two-foot slabs of meat. The crew then used long flensing hooks to haul these blocks onto the concrete, where they were cut up and sold to the eagerly waiting families. Women were hard at work preserving the meat. Some *corned* it with salt and laid it on the rocks to dry, others cooked over the wood fires, *doving* it with onion, garlic, thyme, pepper, and oil.

The building had gray doors, above which were lattice screens, their square black holes looking out like hundreds of eyes. The roof of the whaling station was flat and surrounded by a white wooden fence. Children hung over the rooftop railing, trying to get a better view. They looked on with fascination like all who, still new to the world, wonder how one leaves it. Teo had been such a boy, watching his father bring in the whale, and he knew that the children's stomachs were groaning with hunger as they waited for the feast that would soon be theirs.

Several young boys were swimming in the bloodstained water around the carcass, eager to get as close as they could to the enormous monster. Numerous yachts carrying wealthy Americans, Canadians, and Europeans looked for anchorages in the rough shallows. Their countries had abandoned the hunt for the leviathan and now condemned it, but these foreign families could not hide their fascination.

The crew was working hard, and much of the blubber had already been flensed into three-foot-long white strips. These were being boiled down in cast-iron coppers, and the air was thick with the sticky smoke of cooking fat. Teo felt it on his skin and in his nose and lungs.

He glanced at the official from the Japanese government, standing on the bloodied slab in his suit and smiling as if he owned the place. He gave Teo a thumbs-up. Behind the man, Teo could see the enormous Japanese factory fishing boat in the distance. Some said it had received permission to fish these waters in exchange for development money. Teo's lip curled as he swallowed his distaste for the islanders' newest "investors." The old whaling station was good enough. They hadn't needed this new one or the devil's bargain that had been made to get it.

KAZUMI LOOKED AT the carcasses of the whales with pride, knowing the role he had played in the success of the hunt. The cultural celebration reminded him of the traditions he had witnessed during the dolphin hunt in Taiji, and as he looked into the faces of the young children, he knew they were dreaming of someday being on the whale crew. Traditions were important to hold on to; they were so quickly slipping away all around the world.

He had brought joy to the island and would soon bring prosperity. The large budget of the Japanese Fisheries Development Department allowed him to be a benefactor for many. He took special pride in knowing that these children would be studying at the new school he was instrumental in helping to fund. The department also supported individuals and institutions that were essential to its goals—including Elizabeth McKay's university.

RAFEE HELD OUT a part of the calf they had cut off, smiling wide. "Here your trophy, Cap."

Before Teo could respond, Uree shouted, "Cap, Noble say come quick." There was worry in his voice.

Teo hurried over to Noble, followed by Uree and Rafee.

"Cap, somethin wrong with the calf."

Teo looked at where the butcher had split open the calf and was shocked to find oozing sores and lumps like nothing he'd ever seen.

He winced at the strange odor coming from the whale's carcass. "Dump the calf. Take the motorboat and dump it."

"Whole whale?" Rafee asked.

"We eat the cow," Teo said.

"Cap, is a whale we wasting."

"I say dump it. *That final.*" His tone did not invite further comment.

Teo walked away from the crowd buzzing around the carcasses. Rafee was still looking after him, holding the whale part, incomprehension on his face. The whalermen were talking about how they were going to drag the calf back into the sea, but no one's heart was in it.

KAZUMI SAW THE WHALE PART that Rafee held, its pink flesh draped over his hands like a sacred offering.

"I'd be interested in buying that from you, sir. Name a price," Kazumi said.

"Sorry, this not for sale. This the captain's trophy. He'll be wanting it when he back in his right mind."

Kazumi noticed something strange about it, something that confirmed his worst fears about the whales. "Five hundred dollars, U.S."

"Happy to take your money, but is not mine to sell."

TEO LOOKED OUT from the cay into Friendship Bay. The bright blue, gray, and red roofs spread across the lush slope of the island. He had handed the shotgun to Rafee and told him to keep watch. Teo had had enough. The pleasure had gone out of it after he learned they were Liza's whales. And now he knew something was wrong, really wrong, with the calf.

The whaleboat would need to wait on the cay until the men were ready to sail it home. He looked down with pride at the planks of hand-hewn spruce and the ribs of white cedar. His father had made the boat, using only the horizon as a level. The boat had withstood much, even being dragged down to the depths by a bull whale. Teo's foot had gotten caught in the rope, and if it hadn't been for his filleting knife, he surely would have drowned.

Teo saw something shiny sticking out from under one of the wooden boards and reached for it. It was Liza's tape recorder. She had jumped into one of the motorboats and rushed to the ferry. It wasn't like Liza to forget her equipment, but she didn't seem herself after the hunt.

He rewound the tape and heard the sounds of the cow just before her end. On the slab, all that remained of her carcass was the spine and rib bones, stripped of meat and blubber. Next to his foot, a chunk of blubber had fallen out of one of the wooden tubs being carried to the coppers. The white cube was almost completely covered with tiny black ants trying to make sense of their prize.

EIGHT

ANTS HAD DISCOVERED the half bag of sugar. Elizabeth pulled it out with two fingers and threw it in the garbage with a shudder. The baking shelf was empty except for a box of birthday candles and an unopened bag of flour, both of which she set on the counter.

Elizabeth's eyes were so tired she had a hard time keeping them open. Her attempt to save Sliver and her calf had caused her to miss the early ferry. The later ferry had gotten her to St. Vincent in time to talk her way onto another flight to Barbados and then from Barbados to Miami, but there were no more flights from Miami that night. She had to spend the five overnight hours in the airport, waiting for the first departure. A screaming baby had prevented her from sleeping on the plane and turned her exhaustion into near delirium.

Frank had not received her message. His old cell phone had probably run out of charge, as it often did. He was not wearing his pager, and when Elizabeth finally spoke to Dorothy, she told Elizabeth that Frank had gone to the airport to get her.

Elizabeth looked at the beautiful bouquet of red roses on the round butcher-block table. She felt a wave of guilt, imagining him waiting at the airport. Red roses were the choice of the unrequited or the uncertain. Ordinarily, Frank bought her simple field flowers, her favorite. There was a note scribbled in his nearly indecipherable doctor scrawl. *Sorry I missed you at the airport. Looking forward to seeing you tonight.* Was she imagining resignation and hopelessness in the note?

She wanted to be awake for tonight. A nap would have been a good idea, but there was Frank's birthday cake to make, and she needed to check the WhaleNet discussion board. She had to know if anyone else had heard the song changes, and she wanted to post her audio files as soon as possible. What she had discovered would shock her colleagues, but if others could corroborate her findings, she would be part of one of the most significant discoveries in marine biology of the last decade or more.

Elizabeth found the recipe box that her mother-in-law had given her as an engagement present. Inside were all the recipes that Frank's mother had cooked for him as he was growing up, arranged alphabetically. The name of each dish was written in proud Italian capitals. Her mother-in-law rightly assumed that without an ounce of Sicilian blood, Elizabeth would know nothing about CANNOLI CON RICOTTA or PASTA CON LA SARDA or SPEDINI. She flipped through the stiff white cards, feeling another, even greater wave of guilt. Frank's parents owned an Italian restaurant in Waterbury, Connecticut, and she knew that for his family, love and food were synonymous. After her dissertation was finished, she again promised herself, she'd learn how to cook.

While cooking was an art that escaped Elizabeth, baking was a science that she at least understood. She kept flipping through the box looking for the recipe. At last she found the one card she had used before. The title for Italian cream cake was written in English, and the ingredients and directions were written out in red ink. Red meant that this was one of Frank's favorite recipes, and the three exclamation marks in the upper-right-hand corner indicated that it was his favorite food of all. Frank's mother had made this cake on every birthday since he was born. Baby Frank had probably gone directly from breast milk to Italian cream cake.

Elizabeth pulled the card and then knelt at her yellow Pelican case, which was lying by the front door. Holding the recipe card in her teeth, she used both hands to open the clasps. As she opened the cover, her heart started racing.

Where's the DAT recorder? In a flash of dread, she realized she must have left it on Teo's boat. She had been in such a hurry that she had grabbed her Pelican case and hadn't double-checked to make sure all her equipment was in place. She had not been in her right mind, but she was annoyed at her carelessness. She picked up the tape from the whale rescue that she had carefully removed and labeled that morning. Thank God, she still had the recordings from just before and after the song had changed. But now she would need to go into the office to turn the recordings into digital files and post them to WhaleNet.

There was still plenty of time before the guests—really just Tom and Jenny—arrived. Frank was coming home early to start cooking. He loved to cook, having learned it at his mother's side, although she thought it was somehow a character flaw that her son should enjoy it so much. Elizabeth wrote out a note to Frank and tucked the recipe into the Pelican case to take to the store.

FRANK PUT DOWN the two full bags of groceries and looked at the note that Elizabeth had written on the flip side of his note to her. The straight letters were efficient and well formed: *Don't let the party begin without me! Off to the office. Home around 1600.* He tossed the card on the table, disappointed that she had gone to the office before he even had a chance to see her. *What can't wait until tomorrow?*

He decided to change his mood with some music. There was no cooking without music, loud music, so he hit his "Italian cooking" playlist. He had not had time to cook a proper meal since medical school, and he looked at the kitchen like a long-absent lover. He took out a bottle of Riserva Barolo to let it breathe—and to taste it. He held the cool glass and ran his finger across the label. How long had it been since he had drunk a good bottle of wine and celebrated with friends? He recalled the life of joy and laughter he had known in Boston before residency and fellowship, before a blanket of numbness and exhaustion had enveloped him. The deep red wine stung his mouth, its blend of oak, black cherry, and plum awakening his tongue.

Flavor, his mother would always say, could not be added; it must be the foundation for everything, and so all Italian cooking began with soffritto. Frank chopped the onions and the parsley, then stirred the translucent heap as it cooked in the extra-virgin olive oil. Many made the mistake of cooking the garlic first, but if the garlic cooked too long, it would turn bitter. In Frank's opinion, one could never have enough garlic—he crushed a dozen cloves with the flat of his knife. Once the skin was removed, he chopped them finely to bring out their full flavor. Billy Joel's "Scenes from an Italian Restaurant" began to play. Holding down the tip of the blade with his left hand, Frank sliced the plump cloves along with the increasing tempo of the song.

He used the back of the knife to scrape the garlic into the pan. The oil welcomed the garlic as it sizzled and began to glow like edible gold. The aroma made him smile as he was transported back into his mother's kitchen, the heat of the stove against his skin, the steam of the boiling water in his nostrils, the smells that would embrace you with a love of life.

From the bag he pulled the package of black squid ink pasta. His stomach growled. *Pasta con frutti di mare con salsa fra diavolo.* He could practically taste the shellfish and the spicy garlic and tomato sauce. Frank opened the refrigerator. He stared at the barren cavern. In his mother's groaning refrigerator, you had to spend five minutes rearranging food to find space to fit an olive.

• • •

No one had posted anything about the whale song changing on the discussion board. A chill crawled up Elizabeth's spine in her sparsely furnished office. There were no personal effects on her laminate desk, no pictures of family, just piles of paper. Elizabeth drummed her fingers on one stack. *What if I'm wrong?* She could not imagine any errors she might have made in her recording or her deciphering, but she had been warned not to be a maverick, and challenging decades of research findings certainly would qualify her as one.

Dr. Skilling, her dissertation adviser, had often told her that academia was a shark tank. She thought about the whale birth and how she had escaped the tiger shark. *I am willing to take my chances,* she decided, and posted her audio recordings. After packing up quickly to go home, she reached for the door handle. It started to turn.

"Elizabeth!" It was Dr. Skilling. She was surprised to see him wearing a brown tweed coat with a maroon turtleneck and wire-framed reading glasses. He was usually dressed for fieldwork, but whether wearing jeans and a T-shirt or his academic uniform, he always looked effortlessly handsome. His light brown hair, strong jaw, and emerald-green eyes made him the object of endless gossip among both the students and the faculty. His celebrity status stoked the flames of fascination.

Dr. Skilling was the chair of the evolutionary biology department and head of the small Institute for Toxicology and Environmental Health. He was one of the world's leading experts on pelagic species and was conducting a major research study on apex predators— white sharks and killer whales—at the Farallon Islands. But most people knew him as "Dr. Shark," the host of numerous television documentaries.

"I was worried you wouldn't get back in time," he said.

"In time for what?" Elizabeth asked.

"To fill out the forms. Didn't you get my e-mail?"

"No, I'm afraid I didn't . . . What forms?"

"More bureaucratic bullshit," he said, handing the papers to her. "The department secretary needs them in her box by 9:00 A.M. to-morrow morning." His smile was reassuring, but somehow she didn't feel reassured. She missed Professor Maddings—he could find a way out of any dilemma. Yet Elizabeth remained grateful for Dr. Skilling's support in a hostile department. He was highly respected, which made him a powerful mentor.

She looked down at the papers he had given her. "Why do they need them?" Elizabeth asked.

"I explained in the e-mail that you're not going to be able to file your dissertation at the end of the semester if you don't get these forms in to the dean's office by the deadline."

"File my dissertation? But I'm still collecting my data."

Dr. Skilling sighed. "You have plenty of data, Elizabeth. Now what you need to do is finish your dissertation."

"I've discovered something new, which I think puts me really close to—"

"You don't *need* more data. You've been working on your disser-tation longer than anyone in the department's history. We're getting a lot of pressure from the dean's office."

"But I have another year of funding for my fieldwork."

"Elizabeth, the e-mail explained that, too . . . The department has voted to cut off your funding."

Elizabeth's knees went weak. She started to feel dizzy. The first thing she thought about was Milton's boat. "They can't cut my fund-ing. I have a grant."

"I'm afraid we don't have a choice, Elizabeth," he said, looking down. "Several people in the department . . . well, let's just say they don't believe that your research is serious science. The dean even got a call from the chancellor."

"Why does the chancellor care about my dissertation research?"

"It has come under criticism from outside the university."

"By whom?"

"Some . . . donors, I think. Look, I did everything I could. The department just wants you to finish your dissertation. If you do, maybe you can demonstrate to everyone the value of your work."

"It *is* valuable. I can prove it."

"Good, because you've got until March fifth to give the committee something we can sign off on."

"Or they're going to kick me out?"

"This shouldn't be news to you, Elizabeth—you were served notice last semester multiple times."

"But last fall you said—"

"Just get me the dissertation, please."

Elizabeth broke out in a cold sweat. Dr. Skilling was staring at her like the animal behaviorist that he was. She steeled herself and tried not to react.

"You know that's impossible," she said. "That's less than a month away."

"I'm afraid we have no choice, Elizabeth." Dr. Skilling turned to leave. "I know you can do it."

Elizabeth looked at her watch. It was 4:15 P.M. A sigh of exhaustion spread through her body. Her eyes burned, and it took all her effort to keep them open. She looked at the pages of forms. They would take her hours to fill out. Elizabeth sat back down at her desk and picked up the phone.

"Hello, Konditorei Bakery, can I help you?"

"Do you have Italian cream cake?"

"*Italian* cream cake?" the man on the other end said through a thick accent. "We got *Austrian* cake, no *Italian* cake."

She looked down at the recipe card. The red writing was shouting at her. "I'd like to order your best vanilla cream cake for four people. I'll pick it up at 6:30. Please write 'Happy Birthday, Frank' on it."

FRANK WENT UPSTAIRS and picked up his dirty clothes off the floor and threw them in the closet. Wrinkling his nose from the odor of his own sweat, he opened the window and turned on the fan above the bed. Downstairs, he took out a package of small white tea candles and placed them strategically around the living room. "Con te Partiro," sung by Andrea Bocelli, was now flooding through the house with all its operatic emotion.

ELIZABETH'S BODY felt heavy with exhaustion. The six weeks of fieldwork and sleep deprivation were catching up with her. She never slept very well when she was away from Frank. She looked down at the last page of the forms. There was still time to get home to the party—if she didn't crash. *I better put my head down for a minute, and then I'll be safe to drive, and awake for Frank.*

NINE

FRANK SAT at the round wooden table, which was cluttered with the remains of dinner. Three of the wineglasses were still half filled with red wine; the other was empty. The picked-at pasta lay next to the scattered remains of salad and broccoli rabe. No one had had much of an appetite. The roses in the center of the table seemed to be wilting already.

Frank stared at the one empty plate on the table. Elizabeth's voicemail had said that she would be back by seven at the latest—she had discovered papers that she needed to fill out at her office. At first he had worried that maybe something had happened, but this wasn't the first time she had lost track of time or fallen asleep at her desk. He had thought of calling her but kept telling himself she would walk in at any moment. Tom and his wife, Jenny, had encouraged him to call, but Frank kept saying, "She'll be here." It became a test for him, some kind of final exam of her love—and she had failed.

What had he done wrong? What hadn't he done to make Elizabeth love him or want to be with him as much as she wanted to be with her whales? He had known that she would never be like his mother; he had purposefully married her because she was strong and independent. His mother had never taken care of herself or her health, giving everything to her husband and children. He knew he didn't want a wife who was committing such slow suicide under the guise of love. He wanted a woman who would challenge him and be a true equal, but something had gone wrong. Their careers, certainly his as well as hers, had dragged them out of each other's arms, and now they could not find their way back. But maybe he had to face the truth—perhaps Elizabeth did not want a family or a marriage like he did. Maybe her science and her whales really were more important to her.

He looked at the box of brightly colored birthday candles languishing on the table. Pulling out a red one, he took up the lighter that had been waiting expectantly on the table. The wick ignited and glowed gold, the red wax starting to drip onto his finger. The burn cut through his numbness and his grief. After another few moments and a few more drops of sharp hot wax, he threw the snub candle into his wineglass. It hissed as it drowned, and gray smoke spiraled out of the glass.

He lit a green candle, watched it burn and drip onto his fingers, and then flicked it into the wineglass. The smoke snaked up, folding over itself until it was gone.

He lit another and drowned it, too. And another. And another.

Frank pushed his chair back and walked to the phone in the kitchen. He started to dial the number for Elizabeth's office. Then he hung up. He really did not want to know what the excuse was this time. Instead, he called the back line of the neonatal intensive care unit.

"NICU." Dorothy's voice made him smile, even in its brusqueness and impatience. There was always work to be done for Dorothy—and for him. There was no time to waste when babies were sick.

"How's the Bradley baby?" Frank asked. He was relieved to remember that there was so much greater suffering in the world than his—suffering he knew how to treat.

TEN

THE MOON HUNG like a searchlight in the sky, its glare rippling a path across the water. The fishing boat kept its engines quiet and slow. The factory ship could not get close enough to the cay, so Kazumi had dispatched one of the small catcher boats.

The rocks were treacherous and the currents around the island unpredictable. Kazumi had chosen a captain he could trust not only to steer clear of the shore but also to leave the expedition out of the ship's log.

There were still four hours of darkness in which to operate before the first fishermen would start to go out. They needed to accomplish their goal before they were seen. This would not be easy. Semple Cay was close to the island, and there might be curious eyes stumbling back from one of the rum shops. They would need to work without the benefit of floodlights. But nothing could be done about the full moon.

Pirates had once hidden among these islands and their innumerable cays because they were hard to patrol. Kazumi knew that the whole country had only two or three Coast Guard boats, and these would be docked back in St. Vincent at this hour. He had heard that drug dealers sometimes dropped shipments into the water at night near here, but what he needed to retrieve was more valuable to them than any cocaine shipment.

As they approached the cay, they saw the shine of an oily slick on the surface. Even at night, birds were feeding and fighting for pieces of the decomposing carcass. Small scraps of blubber and flesh were floating to the surface, dislodged by the fish that had come to feast. He could hear the birds squawking and flapping their wings at one another. The noise would hide the sound of the winch.

Kazumi raised his hand, and two divers jumped into the water, their faces hidden by their hoods, masks, and regulators. One was Nilsen and the other was a Japanese fisherman.

Tipped off by the birds, the divers found the carcass quickly. Its body was impossible to miss even in the dark water. The fish scattered as the divers approached, and then returned repeatedly, unwilling to give up the banquet.

Once the lift bags were in place, the divers used their regulators to fill them with air. Used for salvaging shipwrecks, these lift bags easily floated the calf. The divers then fastened a chain to the tail, and slowly, the winch pulled the body to the boat. Kazumi wanted to have the whale tested to know exactly what he was dealing with. He needed to know the truth, but it was equally important to ensure that others never did. As soon as samples were taken, the carcass would be destroyed.

ELEVEN

"**W**ELCOME HOME."

Elizabeth awoke with a start. "Connie?" she said.

A warm smile spread across Connie Kato's face. Her best friend had black bangs that she used unsuccessfully to obscure her pretty face. Connie's industrial-chic jacket and black-and-white–striped tights only seemed to accentuate the attractive body that was constantly getting her into trouble. Elizabeth and Connie had been best friends ever since Connie joined the evolutionary biology program two years ago, and they had been there for each other through all the inevitable dramas of love and life. Although they had very different politics—Connie's bordered on the radical—they found common cause as the only two female graduate students in the department. "What time is it?" Elizabeth asked, her eyes still trying to adjust to being awake.

"Almost eight o'clock."

"P.M.?"

"A.M."

"Oh, my God, I fell asleep. *I missed Frank's birthday party!*" As she spoke the words, she felt her throat constrict with dread. Elizabeth looked down at the papers. "These have to be at the department secretary's by nine."

"I can take them for you," Connie said, quickly scooping up the papers as Elizabeth grabbed her coat and bag.

"Thank you," Elizabeth said. "I know we need to sort out all the men in your life, but I've got to get home to mine—if he'll still have me."

Connie followed Elizabeth out to her car. "Elizabeth, I know you just got back, but have you thought about the invitation?"

"Connie, I'm a scientist, not an activist."

"If the whaling ban is reversed, there won't be any whales for *scientists* to study."

"I'll think about it," Elizabeth said, although she doubted anyone at the International Whaling Commission meeting in Seattle would listen to her. "Oh, I almost forgot." She pulled out a box lying on the passenger seat. "These are for you."

Connie looked at the box of Mama's Island fudge. "You remembered me . . . and my obsession."

They hugged each other, and then Elizabeth opened the door of her station wagon.

"Think about the IWC," Connie said.

"Who's going to care what I have to say? I'm not even a Ph.D.— and the way things are going, I may never become one." Elizabeth got into her station wagon.

"What are you talking about?"

"The department has cut off my funding."

"I told you your work is threatening."

"No, Connie, it's not threatening. It's just late. And now I've got three weeks to finish my dissertation."

"You'll show them all."

"No, I won't."

"Why not?"

"It's taken me five years to write the first half."

TWELVE

THE 1989 Ford Country Squire required several turns of the ignition before the engine turned over. The car had belonged to Frank's parents, and its wood-paneled exterior screamed "family car." All that was missing was the family. *Why isn't a marriage enough? Why does a couple only become a family when children are born?* Elizabeth wanted a family, but she wanted to finish her Ph.D. first. *I just need a little more time.* She pulled the gearshift into reverse and hit the accelerator. The heavy car lurched backward.

Elizabeth raced home through yellow lights and slowed only partly at stop signs. Davis was in the middle of the Central Valley's agricultural region, although its current crop was no longer corn and tomatoes but suburban children. As she passed a strip mall containing a coffee shop and a hair salon, she saw a ramshackle barn and an overgrown field across the street. The farms on the periphery of town always shocked her, like ghosts that still haunted the town, revealing the rich earth buried under the neatly paved streets and manicured lawns.

Pulling into the parking lot, she saw Frank carrying a worn cardboard box against his chest. T-shirts and a computer keyboard peeked out between the open flaps. She quickly rolled down the stiff window and shouted, "Frank—*I'm so, so sorry.*"

Frank stopped, looked at her, and then glanced back down at the box, which he dropped into the trunk of their other car, a beige Toyota Corolla. He turned away without saying a word. He was shaking his head. Elizabeth turned off the car and ran after him.

"Frank, please forgive me," Elizabeth said as she followed him through the gate to the small courtyard. They walked past the over-grown lavender and into their small town house. "I fell asleep at my desk. I wanted to be rested for your party, for our reunion."

Still no answer. He did not even turn around to talk to her.

"Dr. Skilling said I had to file some paperwork or I was going to lose my candidacy. Now he says I need to file my dissertation in three weeks or they're going to kick me out of the program."

Frank had picked up another box. This one also was not closed. She could see some of Frank's medical books inside.

Frank turned to face her, his brow furrowed in a scowl. "I can't do this anymore."

"Do what?"

Frank dropped the box on the ground. It landed with a thud. "Do this!" he said, his temper eclipsing his words with a cutting gesture.

Only then did the meaning of the boxes become clear. "You're leaving?" she asked.

Frank looked around the living room in exasperation for the words that had escaped him.

"I wanted to make you the cream cake. I got the re—"

"I don't need a cream cake. I need you. I need a family."

"You have me."

Frank stepped in close, wrapping his large hand around the nape of her neck, and pulled her face toward him. Elizabeth's eyes went wide as his lips sealed against hers. Surprised, she inhaled the sweet and familiar scent of Frank, and leaned into his embrace.

Grabbing both her shoulders, Frank wrenched her away from him and glared into her eyes. "Remember that? If you're not here, it dies."

"It's not dead. And we *will* have a family. I just need—"

"—more time," Frank finished. He'd heard it all before. He picked up an old plaid suitcase and a pile of gear he had not had a chance to box up. It was his old well-loved wetsuit, diving mask, snorkel, and fins. They stuck out at every angle, threatening to fall to the ground. "That's what you've been saying for five years!"

"Just until I finish."

"If it made a difference, I'd wait another five years, but it won't."

"What do you mean?"

"You're no closer to finishing than you were last year or the year before. Let's face it, Elizabeth. We want different lives."

"I want to have a family, Frank, I just don't want to sacrifice—"

"Families make sacrifices for each other." The plastic strap broke off the mask, and it dropped to the floor. They both looked at it.

"Maybe you shouldn't have sacrificed what *you* loved," Elizabeth said.

Frank did not answer as he walked out to the car. Elizabeth followed him. He threw everything into the trunk with the force of his anger. "Sometimes we sacrifice the things we love for the *people* we love." The driver's side door squeaked as he opened it and got in.

"Where are you going?" The words were out before she had thought them. The question seemed strange, but the answer made all the difference. Was he going to someone?

"I'm going to stay with Tom and his family."

She sighed with relief. At least this was about them and not someone else.

Frank turned the ignition. Elizabeth wished his car did not start so dependably. "I've made sacrifices," she said. He closed the door, but he rolled down the window. He was still willing to talk. "I moved to California for your residency—away from Professor Maddings and from my research subjects."

Frank shifted into reverse. "They're not your research subjects, Elizabeth. They're your family."

THIRTEEN

Three days later
Friday, February 16
Two hundred nautical miles off the Pacific coast of Mexico

APOLLO SWAM NORTHWEST *toward the summer feeding grounds—*
his long flippers not far from those of his two companions—

The three whales moved their flukes rhythmically and forcefully—
their grace belying the extraordinary thrust of the broad tails propelling
them onward—

Apollo could feel his companions by the lift and fall of water and the
low sounds of the contact calls that groaned from within their great
bodies—

These long utterances also revealed the seamounts and canyons on the
ocean floor far below—

Their course took them far west—past the continental shelf—the
waters descending deeply to the abyssal depths where the sperm whales
dove—

As Apollo and his companions surfaced—they let out great gusts of
air—emptying their lungs and filling them with the breath of life—

A strange sound—like nothing Apollo had ever heard—pulsed
through him—

He approached one of his companions—now held fast—unable to
move—caught by some strange tentacle—

Apollo saw his bulging eye—

And then a shattering eruption—so close it was deafening—the force throwing Apollo to the side—the air knocked from his mouth—his body heavier now—beginning to descend.

Only then did he taste the astringent tinge of red—and feel the heat of his companion's lifeblood—his companion's body limp—dead so fast—

The killer's tentacle began dragging his companion away—

Apollo saw the other whale fleeing—but the sound again was in the water—and the tentacle—and the eruption—

Blood closed in on both sides—like a red tide—

Apollo rotated his body to his second companion—touched him as he swam underneath—feeling for life—but there was none—

The great shadow of a ship hovered above, and his heart pounded in his chest—

Dive—

Dive—

Apollo stopped several lengths away—rolled his head to the side— and then saw the enormous gray ship looming out of the water to the sky—countless round eyes all along its body and its underbelly dark red like the blood that it drank.

KOJI ITO STOOD on the high bow of *Catcher Boat #1,* knowing what he needed to do, but unsure whether he could. Ito had the phone number and the test results—he just needed to make the call. But if he did, he would risk his job and possibly much more.

The gun smoke clung in a gray cloud around the harpooner, who wore a yellow plastic hard hat and an orange life vest like the other workers. The whales were pulled in, one on either side of the boat.

Ito knew they were somewhere off the coast of Mexico, a country that, unlike his own, seemed to think that whaling was wrong. The *Ryukyu Maru* whaling ship and its catcher boats needed to stay at least two hundred nautical miles off the coast, outside Mexico's exclusive economic zone, and in the open seas that were owned by no one.

Catcher Boat #1 had been rewarded by the sight of three adult humpbacks swimming north by northwest at an extraordinary eighteen kilometers per hour. The catcher ship fired two exploding grenade harpoons in quick succession, using both of its lines to catch two of the three whales.

Ito and several other workers tied large cables around each whale's tail to secure it as the boat raced back to the mother ship. The drag of the whales' forty-ton bodies caused the water to foam. On the side of the *Ryukyu Maru,* Ito read the English word RESEARCH in large capital letters, each many times larger than the height of an ordinary man. But today there were no foreign media or environmental groups nearby.

The factory ship hauled the lifeless whales effortlessly up the ramp and onto the processing deck. Ito and several other members of the testing crew took some standard morphometrics, measuring the total length, the width across the flukes, and flipper size. They cut out the gonads to determine the whales' reproductive state, their earplugs to tell their age, and their stomachs to see what they were eating. The scientist from the Japanese Cetology Research Center was looking for information that would demonstrate the health and abundance of humpback populations around the world. The whalers hoped to prove that the population had increased sufficiently and that they could begin commercial whaling once again.

Ito was simply a lab technician, not an official researcher, and he looked around nervously to see whether anyone was watching him. He stole a glance at the members of the flensing team, each in a green hard hat and a bright blue uniform. They were busy cutting away the whale blubber and meat and were joking about something he could not hear. According to the IWC treaty, the "by-products" of whales killed for research must not be wasted. The meat would be shipped to market in Tokyo.

Ito's official responsibilities were limited. He was taking tissue samples from various internal organs, and his hands now worked with practiced skill on the slippery stomach. His mind was free to think about what he was going to do. He had tried to speak to his supervisor but had been told to mind his own business. Ito knew whom he needed to call, but would the executive director of the Fisheries Development Department speak to *him*, an ordinary worker?

FOURTEEN

TEO WALKED UP the final cement step that led from the beach, his body bone-weary from a day like any other, out looking for whales. They still had another two whales in their quota for the season, but his heart was not in it. Every time he looked out at the horizon, he saw Elizabeth's face. He had stayed after the other men left to refinish the boat where it had been damaged by the tail of the bull, but he had also wanted to be alone.

"When the whaling captain gon choose heself a wife?" Eve, Maggie, and Cynthelia were sitting on a wooden stoop. It was Eve who had spoken. She had been widowed young, and Maggie's man had run off. Cynthelia was not yet married. They were all attractive women and dressed in shorts and T-shirts, like women who were still fishing for a man. "You just tell us which one you choose, and any of us gon make you a happy man!" Eve winked and Cynthelia giggled.

"I'm sure you know that a sailor he married to the sea. It wrong he break a lady's heart." Teo flashed them one of his famous smiles and then bowed his head and kept walking.

"Break me heart! Please break me heart," he heard Maggie call out after him. He chuckled at the proposal but knew that he could not do to hers what had been done to his.

A cheer rose up from the rum shop across the street, where his crew was playing a heated game of dominoes on the porch. The incessant beat of the soca music was punctuated every few moments by a sound like a pistol as one of the men slammed a domino down on the wooden table. The men considered the pieces they held like leaves in their knotted mahogany hands, and adjusted their strategy.

On the wall behind the men hung a turtle shell and the remains of a poster that had once said SAVE THE WHALES. The only word left was WHALES, and above it, someone had etched into the blue paint the word EAT.

All around the posters, like wallpaper, were magazine and newspaper articles: "The Man Who Battles the Giants," "Caribbean Whaler a Legend on Island," "The Last Great Whaler?" Teo remembered the words from one. It said he had the "rough way of the buccaneers but the charm of the captains that left many women gazing out to sea awaiting their return." Though he liked that description, it wasn't true, at least the part about many women. There had been only one woman, and she had left *him* gazing out to sea, thousands of miles away to America.

"Come have a drink, Cap." Rafee was waving him over.

He smiled as they all stared at him expectantly, but he had no time for drink. It muddied the mind, and a hunter always needed to have his wits about him. "Not tonight," Teo said.

"Nother time," Rafee replied, and the men returned to their game.

Teo walked under the arching rib bones of a humpback whale that marked the entry to his property. They were ghostly gray in the twilight. He touched the rough surface, paying his respects to the whale that he had killed as a boy at his father's side. He could still hear the cheering of the whalermen.

Some who had been in his father's crew remained in his. They were his men and he was their captain, and together they hunted the whale that fed the whole island when they were lucky enough to catch one.

The bare two-room house clearly belonged to a man who did not have a woman. All Teo owned of value was the boat, a few pieces of furniture, and a handful of pots and pans. He pulled the levered handle of the old fridge and opened the small door of the freezer compartment. In it was the whale part that Rafee had given him, wrapped carefully in white butcher paper. There had been something strange and wrong with it. He took out a chocolate-flavored Popsicle and, from the fridge, what was left of an open can of tuna.

Out on the deck, Teo looked down into a square plastic container, where half a dozen sea turtle hatchlings bumped into one another. He crumbled the tuna into the water as they swam around, nibbling at the meal. Their brownish-green shells were only three inches long. It would be several years until they were large enough to release back into the sea without getting eaten right from the start.

Teo sat down in a rickety wooden chair, its slatted seat and back rough and dried out by the salt air. Below him, a few stilts propped up the porch precariously. The house clung to the cliff as if desperately trying to avoid the hungry seas below.

It was threatening rain, and the whole sky looked gray and gloomy. Teo thought about his grandfather, his mother's father, who said it was the devil's work to kill the leviathan. He could hear his voice like a ghost: "When me a young man out fishing, before the Norwegians set up their whaling station at Glover Island, me never afraid of nothing and never felt lonely, neither. Me talk to the whale, and he answer me with his gentle blow—a great sigh—like he understand me and all the trouble of the world. But after a time—only take them two years to fish them out—me sit in me boat with nothing living to be seen anywhere. Me get this lonely feeling in me belly, like the whole world empty. Me miss them whales."

Something off of Mustique caught Teo's eye. It was near where Sliver and the calf had been killed. A whale was breaching. It was no doubt Echo, although from this distance, he couldn't be sure. All he could see in the gathering dusk was the whale tearing itself from the water again and again.

"Father be proud of you. You caught the whale at last and is the big man." Milton was standing on the porch. He hadn't bothered to knock. Family rarely does.

Teo decided not to take offense at Milton's reference to having gone three years without catching a whale. "Liza get off all right?"

"No thanks to you."

"I didn't know the whale was Liza's," Teo said. "I gon make it right." He held up Elizabeth's tape recorder.

"What you got that for?"

"She leave it in the whaleboat."

"She gon need it," Milton said nervously. They both knew that his boat now depended on it.

"I'm gonna get it to her. You have her address in California?"

Milton looked at him suspiciously. "You thinkin she have you just because her husband gon and left her."

"Did he now?" Teo said, his eyebrows blown high on his forehead by the news. "How you know?"

"I call her bout my boat. Didn't sound like sheself."

Teo was already thinking of what tack to take. "Well, maybe is time for tell Liza the truth about what the whale saying."

"What you know about the whale?"

"I'm a whaler, and *our* father was a whaler and his father before him."

Milton scowled at this reference to their father's giving Teo the whaleboat. Teo was an "inside" child and Milton an "outside" child—conceived on one of their father's fishing trips.

"So what that have to do with Liza? I thought you tell her everything you know."

"Not everything," Teo said.

"She better off without you." Milton no doubt knew that Teo's desire to see Liza was hardly just an interest in her research.

"Don't worry about your boat, Milton. Family watch out for its own. Is always a seat on the whaleboat for you."

"I rather starve."

"And your children?" Teo got up and went inside to the fridge. Milton followed him and watched as Teo took out a coffee can and removed the cover. There were rolls of ready cash in it, both colorful Eastern Caribbean dollars and green U.S. "You gonna need somethin til Liza can replace your boat." He handed Milton a roll of Eastern Caribbean bills and put the U.S. in his pocket.

Milton looked down. "We ain't need a handout," he said, choking on his pride but taking the money.

"Is not a handout. Is payment for keeping an eye on things while I gone."

FIFTEEN

KAZUMI TOOK THE CALL from the lab technician in a private room where he would not be overheard. The test results confirmed exactly what they had found in the diseased calf.

"You have copies of all the lab work?"

"Yes, sir, everything."

"Who else have you told?" Kazumi spoke calmly and smiled so that his voice would sound warm and encouraging. He knew that a great deal was at stake. Over 1.4 billion people relied on the oceans for their primary source of protein. Within fifty years, the edible fish in the sea would be largely gone due to overfishing and pollution, and this large percentage of the world's population would not be able to just start eating more chicken or beef. Baleen whales, which feed mostly on microscopic krill, would survive at least for a while, and the market for whale meat would be enormous, but only if people believed that it was a safe source of animal protein.

"I tried to tell the researcher from the center," Ito said.

After the calf's autopsy, Kazumi had sent a memo to the researchers at the center, telling them that all testing beyond basic morphology should be suspended. Managing public perception was essential. Other food industries had been ruined by health concerns, and the whaling industry was struggling to get started again. All seafood had some level of toxicity, and Kazumi was confident that they could show the public there were safe levels of whale consumption, like the tuna industry had already done. But if whales were showing up diseased and deformed, then it was only a small leap of the imagination for people to worry about what might happen to those who ate them.

"You did the right thing trying to tell him, and you did the right thing calling me," Kazumi said. "I will make sure the proper authorities are alerted. Fax the tests to me and then shred the copies you have. This is very sensitive information, as you no doubt know, and I will need to handle it personally."

"Yes, sir, I will do exactly as you say."

The call was over, but Kazumi could not resist the temptation now that he knew who the lab technician was. "How is your son, Mr. Ito?"

"My son, sir?"

"He works for an anti-whaling group, does he not? We keep a close watch on all of our opponents."

"We have not spoken in—"

"A son's actions bring shame on the whole family, don't they?"

"Yes, sir."

"Maybe you should speak to him . . . more often."

"Yes, sir."

"I will wait by the fax machine for your transmission."

SIXTEEN

5:00 P.M.
Next day
Saturday
Davis

Eᴌɪᴢᴀʙᴇᴛʜ sᴀᴛ on the brown couch, flipping through a box of photos. Her long hair was tangled and messy and pulled to one side, bound by a black hair band. The television was on with the sound off. She had just over two weeks to complete the final half of her dissertation, though it was no longer her greatest concern. She still wanted answers, but her most pressing questions had nothing to do with the whales. In the box of photos, she searched for reasons, for clues, for mistakes that might be corrected.

Elizabeth had gone to see Frank to apologize again. She had driven up in front of Tom's enormous plantation-style home in her run-down station wagon when she saw that young, perky nurse, Kim. Maybe Frank was leaving her for someone else after all; someone who would cook all of his mother's recipes, fill his fridge, and have his children. Elizabeth's foot instinctively hit the accelerator, and the car lurched forward quickly. She didn't stop driving until she was home. Only then, in her driveway, did she let her head collapse against the steering wheel. But even as sorrow and regret surged through her body, no tears would come.

It had been four days since he had left, but it seemed as long as the entire six weeks that she was away. Elizabeth continued flipping through the photos that were jumbled together in the box. She promised herself yet again that she would put these into orderly albums as soon as she had finished her degree. Elizabeth looked at a picture of herself on her fourth birthday, all pigtails and smiles. She was in her mother's arms, and her father was by their side. Her mother had light brown curly hair and blue eyes and was smiling at the camera. Her father, with his long black ponytail, was stone-faced, as if he knew what was to come. Three years later her mother would be dead from metastatic breast cancer.

After her mother died, her father was never the same. Her parents had loved each other the way people from different worlds can, with an almost desperate love, like two lifeboats lashed together in a storm of disapproval. Back then her father was fishing up in Alaska much of the year, out at sea for months at a time. It was the only fishing he could get with the fish stocks the way they were. She begged him to take her with him, but he said a fishing boat was no place for a seven-year-old girl. There were no other pictures of her childhood.

The rest of the photos in the box were of her and Frank. She stopped and pulled one out. She had found it—evidence of their happiness.

Frank was dressed like a Roman soldier, and in his strong arms he was carrying Elizabeth, wearing a mermaid costume. Her curled black hair flowed around her low-cut top, and her body was wrapped in sequined green fabric that ended in a wide blue tail. It was the Halloween before their marriage—her arms were wrapped around his neck and their eyes were lost in each other's. Perhaps it was the bright light of the flash, but their faces seemed to shine with love. She had never met anyone who loved being alive more than Frank.

Elizabeth continued flipping through the photos until she found one more piece of evidence. She swallowed, her throat dry, her mouth bitter with regret. The photo was from the last hospital

Christmas party. She wore a black dress with spaghetti straps, and Frank was wearing a blue suit, but it was the looks on their faces that interested her. They were proof positive of their estrangement. She held up the two photos. Like time-lapse photography, they revealed the death of a marriage. Both of their gazes looked vacant, distracted, and lonely. Frank had big bags under his eyes from exhaustion, and Elizabeth was staring away from the camera, clearly wanting to be somewhere else. There was space between their bodies, and his arm was behind her back not out of intimacy but out of formality.

The phone rang cheerfully. Elizabeth looked over as it continued to ring. The number "6" blinked red on her answering machine. She needed to call Professor Maddings back, but she could not bring herself to tell him that she was about to be kicked out of her program and that Frank had left her. Professor Maddings had been at their wedding.

Finally, the answering machine picked up. After a moment's pause, she could hear the message through the tinny speaker: "Elizabeth, it's Maddings again, calling you from Chile, where I've found the aggregation grounds of the blue whales. They are gathering by the dozens. I'm ringing you on a sat phone—must be costing the university a fortune . . ."

Her hand ached to pick up the phone.

"Elizabeth, you were right about the song change. It's been recorded in half a dozen other locations around the globe. I mobilized a team of graduate students, and they've time-mapped its diffusion . . . the radiation dynamics are classic—it's beautiful—like ripples of water in a pond. Elizabeth, what I'm trying to say, in my long-winded way, is that it all began with you in Bequia—"

Elizabeth lunged for the phone. Her heart was pounding. She got the handset to her mouth, her fingers trembling. "Professor Maddings."

"Elizabeth." Maddings uttered her name with such warmth that

it was as if he were greeting his own daughter. Her whole body re-laxed. "I knew that if I prattled on long enough, you might just pick up the phone and talk to me." Elizabeth smiled. He always could see right through her. "We also witnessed bizarre gatherings and breach-ing behavior at the breeding grounds off Socorro. And I've heard from three colleagues that these kinds of behaviors are being ob-served in other populations around the world— Elizabeth, I can tell something's wrong. You haven't given up on your music, have you?"

"Wrong? Why do you think something is wrong?" Professor Maddings was always after her about her music.

"I haven't heard you gasp with excitement once or interrupt me with your own even more brilliant ideas. So all I can think is that you have been neglecting your violin." Professor Maddings had often told her that music would get her through the low points that ac-company any career dependent on the vagaries of discovery.

"It wasn't just my violin I was neglecting," Elizabeth said, look-ing down at the photo.

"If I have to tell you again, I will—don't give up on your music. It will lead you into the heart of whale song. Now tell me what is wrong."

"Frank left."

"Left? You? Good Lord, what has gotten into him? You are the best student I've ever had. Doesn't he understand the first-class mind he's dealing with?"

"I guess he wanted a wife with more than a mind."

"What on earth does that deranged husband of yours—I know he's a good man and only temporarily certifiable for leaving you— but what does he want?"

"A family."

"Oh . . ." Professor Maddings said, realizing the evolutionary depth of the problem. "Well . . . we are no different than the rest of the animals in that desire. That's a hard one, but don't give up on the whales. They need you. We need you . . . Oh dear, my battery's running low, but I'll be watching you and that wonderful wayward husband of yours. Just show him that you want him—that's all we men, weak as we are, need to know—and then you can do what you please. Louisa always did. I'll be calling back to hear the happy—"

Elizabeth listened for a few moments to the dead line, not wanting to hang up. After putting the phone down, she walked over to the closet. She hesitated before opening it and again as she stared at the black case. At last she pulled out the delicate violin with its dark brown belly and long black neck. She cradled it in her arms as she adjusted the tension on the bow and placed it under her chin. She drew the bow across and then stopped to tune each of the four strings.

The feeling of the instrument came back to her as she began to play Professor Maddings's favorite piece, "Adagio for Strings" by Samuel Barber. He had said it intensified all emotion—joy or sadness, grief or exultation. Often she and three other graduate students had played it with Professor Maddings in the middle of a particularly thorny bit of analysis. He would tell them to rest the left hemisphere of their brain and relax into their right, to go beyond reason, beyond thought and into feeling and understanding. These were rehearsals of what he called his "research quartet."

As she played, tears began to fall down her cheeks. She recalled a story Professor Maddings had told her about a pilot whale who had grieved the death of a dolphin that was his companion for many years. The whale had fought the trainers when they tried to take the body away. Elizabeth was not willing to give up yet, either.

SEVENTEEN

2:00 P.M.
Eight days later
Sunday, February 25
La Pompe, Bequia

TOKUJIRO KAZUMI approached the small blue house with Nilsen. He had told the Norwegian just to smile and leave the conversation to him. Nilsen could sometimes be a bit trigger-happy. Kazumi knew there would be no need for guns or threats.

He pushed back his receding gray hair and then wiped the perspiration from his forehead with a handkerchief. His full eyebrows were still black, not gray, and peaked like an owl's. Kazumi thought about what he needed to do and felt a pang of shame. As a boy at boarding school he had dreamed of becoming so much more, of showing his English schoolmates that he was their equal. But it hadn't quite worked out. He had encountered prejudice throughout the Japanese government bureaucracy toward a "haafu"—a half-Japanese. He had taken the job in the Resource Management Department without conviction, but now he saw the righteousness of their cause, fighting against the cultural imperialists. Did they tell Americans not to eat hamburgers?

As he walked down the dirt path, he looked over to the small structure that the American researcher had rented from this family. He had always known that she was going to be a problem. Fortunately, their man at the university had been responsive to his concerns. But now they had an even bigger problem.

At the house, Kazumi waved away the cigarette smoke that hung around Nilsen like a perpetual gray cloud. A dog barked, and the door opened almost before he knocked. Standing in it was Milton Mulraine, a local fisherman and Elizabeth's research assistant.

The brown-haired dog wagged its tail and jumped on Kazumi's leg, licking his hand. Tears sprang to Kazumi's eyes as he remembered Kioko, who had died just the year before. He choked back his feelings and tried to smile. "You must be . . . Mr. Mulraine?" he said.

"Who want to know?"

"My name is Tokujiro Kazumi, and I am the executive director of the Japanese Fisheries Development Department. We are also the main sponsor of your new school." He gestured to the construction site across the street and the sign that proudly announced its donor country with a bright red circle. "I believe your own children are some of the top pupils. Am I correct?"

"You got that right," Milton said, standing taller.

"This is my colleague Halvard Nilsen." Nilsen, who as always looked like he needed a shave, nodded inscrutably. "May we come in?"

"Yes, please do. What can I get for your thirst?"

"Nothing, thank you," Kazumi said, stepping inside the small house. "I'm afraid we are in quite a hurry, but I hear that you might be able to help us in another way."

"Name it."

"We have been conducting some scientific research, and we've discovered that a piece of the newborn whale that was caught last week has gone missing."

"Oh, it ain't missing," Milton said.

"Do you know who has it? Did . . . Elizabeth take it?" Kazumi tried to pretend familiarity with the American he had never met.

"No, she know nothing about it, but Teo—"

"The whaler?"

"One and the same. He take it to her. Thought she might want to see it. Had something wrong with it," Milton said.

"I see." Kazumi tried not to react.

"You sure you ain't want something to drink? My wife make—"

"No, thank you," Kazumi said. "I heard Elizabeth was having problems with her funding." Milton's eyes fell. "Do you know whether she has the money to analyze the sample from the calf? Because I'm sure our department could help her out."

"She buying me a new boat, but I ain't know how much she got. You need her number?"

"No, that won't be necessary. We know how to get in touch with her. I'll make sure someone in our department pays her a visit."

"Tell her Milton send you."

"We'll be sure to do that." Kazumi looked at Nilsen, who was smiling broadly.

EIGHTEEN

4:45 P.M.
Five days later
Friday, March 2
Coast of Alabama

TEO JUMPED OFF THE YACHT onto the long wooden dock. He waved goodbye to his friend, who was piloting a sailboat up to the States. As the boat came about, the towering main sail and jib flapped like an enormous swan beating its wings.

The sun was low in the sky, and a dull light reflected off the gray water that surrounded the dock and lapped up against the barrier island. The strap of the cooler dug into Teo's shoulder. He walked down the dock and stepped onto the sandy shore. His legs were unsteady after a dozen days being rocked by the sea.

"Where you from?" The voice belonged to a large man who was wearing an I LOVE ALABAMA T-shirt. The bottoms of the letters were lost in the folds of his belly. The fisherman was tipped back in a metal beach chair, and a tall surfcasting rod was in the sand next to him. The dock had hidden him, but now Teo could see his burned face, covered in stubble, and the wide neck like a pelican's gullet swallowing a fish.

"From down the way. I just visiting a friend," Teo said.

The man looked suspicious, no doubt hearing his accent. "You one of them boat people?"

Teo put down the small duffel bag slung over his shoulder and reached into the cooler. "No, I am one of the rum people." He handed a bottle to the man, the golden brown liquid sparkling in the sun. Teo reminded himself to speak "American" to avoid suspicion. He could polish up his speech when necessary, although he didn't think there was anything wrong with the way Bequians spoke.

"Well, all right, then, you have a good time with your friend. And welcome to the land of opportunity."

TEO NEEDED TO FIND a way across the country. In town he saw a gas station, which also looked strangely like a church. There was an old-fashioned pump in front. On it was painted: DRIVING ON EMPTY? FILL UP WITH THE HOLY SPIRIT.

Teo stepped into the cool entryway. His eyes adjusted to the dim light, and he saw that it was indeed an old, run-down church with a dozen benches on either side.

"Can I help you?" A black woman stood behind a half door that led to an office.

"I'm looking for the bus station."

"Well, you've come to the right place. My name is Reverend Cissy, and I'm also the ticketing agent and gas station cashier." She added with a wink, "We call ourselves a full-service service station."

"I can see," Teo said with a wide smile. "I need to get to California. Davis, California."

"California? That's clear on the other side of the country. You are going to need a bus up to Mobile, and from there you can get a Greyhound to California."

Reverend Cissy sold him a ticket, which Teo paid for with U.S. dollars, and then made a nice donation to the collection box.

"The Lord thanks you," Reverend Cissy said, and then pointed him toward the kitchen so he could help himself to some ice.

• • •

WHEN TEO CAME BACK, he saw a police officer talking to the reverend.

"Cissy, I got a call about an illegal. Came on a boat. Have you seen him?"

"What does he look like?" Reverend Cissy asked.

"Light-brown-colored, not dark like you . . . more suntan. Toasted, not burnt, if you know what I mean."

The police officer's humor was lost on the reverend. "He got a ride," she said. "East toward Atlanta. Maybe you can catch him there."

The police officer left, and Teo came back in. "I think you have beautiful skin."

Reverend Cissy smiled. "We all came on a boat, whether we wanted to or not."

NINETEEN

7:00 A.M.
Next day
Saturday
Farallon Islands, California

"My name is Dr. Richard Skilling, and we are on 'sharkwatch' at the lighthouse on the Farallon Islands. We are surrounded by one of the most densely populated marine mammal sanctuaries in the world, and where there is prey, there are always predators. Each year some of the largest white sharks in the world come to these rugged and forbidding islands just twenty-seven miles from San Francisco, to eat seals and sea lions as part of their natural predation—"

"Cut. Can we pick it up from 'just twenty-seven miles' and avoid the word 'predation'? Maybe try something like 'gorging themselves' . . . 'feasting' . . . you know." John Fenster was directing his first IMAX movie, and he had promised Skilling that despite his long list of horror movie credits, he would be true to the science.

Jesus, Skilling thought, *I said "eat." Doesn't he think people can make the leap from eating to predation?* "You told me you weren't going to make another 'sharks as bloodthirsty killers' movie. People eat chickens and cows. Sharks eat seals and sea lions. I want viewers to know that they don't generally target people."

"Fine, Dr. Skilling, fine. You're the expert. Not to worry, there will be plenty of opportunities in the film to set the record straight. Tell us whatever you want, just keep the audience's spines tingling."

"Don't worry. My students are always on the edge of their seats."

Skilling had made numerous documentaries, but this was a big-budget movie, and he was the star. He had been recruited not only because he was one of the world's leading white shark experts, but also because he was that rarest of species: a Hollywood-handsome scientist.

They were filming at the skeletal gray lighthouse that crowned the granite peak of the largest island of the Farallon archipelago. Behind Skilling on the cement deck were two high-powered spotting scopes mounted on tripods. From this height all that was visible of the houses where the researchers lived were a pair of black gabled roofs.

Ordinarily, the almost constant wind that howled across Light-house Hill would make any interview impossible, but they were enjoying surprisingly clear and calm weather. The rocky islands looked almost inviting, which was about as deceptive as a shark's smile.

Skilling decided to approach from a different angle. Give them what they wanted, and then he could get the information in.

"Take two," Fenster said.

"Sharks live in our nightmares. They represent our greatest fears. They are humanity's ultimate predator. But as large as they loom in our imagination, we have until recently known very little about them. The truth is even more fascinating than our wildest fantasies."

Skilling picked up the jaws of an eighteen-foot shark and held them in front of him. The top rows of triangular-shaped teeth hovered just above his head, and the bottom rows hung just below his crotch. The jaws, which looked like they could have belonged to a Tyrannosaurus rex, were twice the width of his torso. He could see the film crew's eyes widen. He had them, as he always had his students whenever he displayed the jaws on the first day of class. Fear has a powerful way of focusing the mind.

"Great white sharks—or white sharks, as scientists call them—can grow upward of twenty-one feet long and can weigh just under five thousand pounds." Even Skilling's muscular arms were starting to shake from the weight of the massive jaws. He carefully put them down and, out of his pocket, pulled a two-inch tooth for a camera close-up. "White sharks have ragged, serrated teeth." He grabbed a mutilated surfboard from where it was leaning against the cement wall. "As you can see on the bottom, their pointed teeth pin their prey and prevent them from escaping. The crescent here on the top side of the board allows us to see the shape of their upper teeth, which they use to cut through large chunks of meat by shaking their head from side to side. They also thrash their tail back and forth to assist them in their sawing motion. It takes them a few seconds to sever the head off an elephant seal—that would take me ten minutes to remove, cutting through the muscle and bone with a hacksaw and cleaver.

"In recent years, researchers have discovered that many of our assumptions about white sharks were wrong. Once thought to be mindless killers, sharks are, in fact, cautious and stealthy hunters who stalk their prey from below and execute an attack that is well timed and well planned. Long thought to have poor vision, these ambush predators actually have keen eyesight and can tell not only where you are facing but even where your eyes are looking."

Skilling could not hide a sly smile. He took great satisfaction in the shark's hunting skills. "Yet their killing skills are far surpassed by our own. Last year sharks killed approximately seven people; most of these attacks were probably cases of mistaken identity. On the other hand, humans last year killed over a hundred million sharks, bringing some species to the brink of extinction. In the cruel practice of finning, just their fins are cut off for shark fin soup, and the rest of the body is thrown back into the water to slowly die. Who do you think is truly the most dangerous predator?"

As if by way of answer, a frothy white boil down in Fisherman's Bay revealed the presence of an unexpected but welcome visitor.

"Shark!" Skilling shouted. The others were all looking where Skilling had pointed, but by now he was on the radio, contacting his graduate students down below. "We've got a shark attack off Tower Point. Big blood slick. Meet me at the boat in two minutes."

SKILLING GUNNED THE MOTOR of the Boston Whaler, squinting, trying not to lose sight of the point of kill. Fenster and the cameraman talked excitedly up in the bow. Ben Lopez, a curly-haired graduate student, sat next to Skilling. "Ben, no matter what happens, keep this running and time coding," Skilling said quietly, handing him a pole that was attached to an underwater video camera. "Film crews come and go, but the research remains. It must always come first. Understood?" Ben nodded.

Skilling caught sight of the tail fin whipping back and forth, and then the dorsal, which was well over three feet. Skilling recognized over a hundred individual white sharks by sight, each one identified with a name he or his students had given it. But he had never seen one with a dorsal that big. It was hunting in "sisterhood territory," an area owned by some of the largest females.

When the boat arrived at the kill, the water was still stained with blood. A tornado of western gulls pecked at the remains of a blondish-brown pelt with one flipper dangling. The flayed underside revealed pink meat, red blood clots, and white muscle.

Skilling could tell from the large floating remains that this was a "super weaner." These baby elephant seals were not content to stop nursing after being weaned, and would steal the teat of another mother, displacing her pup. Instead of weighing the ordinary fifty to one hundred pounds, these overstuffed sausages grew to weigh up to three hundred pounds as they continued their rapacious diet. Skilling knew that weaning pups in general had only a 50 percent chance of surviving their first year. Finding food, avoiding being crushed by the bulk of two-ton elephant seal bulls, and escaping the jaws of white sharks was too much for many of them, including this one.

Skilling smiled. There was enough meat left to bring the shark back to finish off its meal. He would have a chance to tag her. They just needed to be patient.

The *Sailfish* pulled up next to them, and they lashed the Boston Whaler to the dive boat. Skilling looked at the metal cage, which no one had anticipated they would need today, since most of the sharks had already left on their migration. On Fenster's command, the crew quickly lowered the cage into the water.

Once he had awkwardly made it aboard the *Sailfish,* Fenster turned to face Skilling. "Dr. Skilling, I wonder if we could film you putting a satellite tag on this shark."

"Sure, if it surfaces again," Skilling said. He didn't like to over-promise. He was already assembling his aluminum tagging pole, which looked like a miniature, delicate harpoon. On the metal point of the pole, Skilling placed a barbed titanium tip. A leader line of monofilament connected this razor-sharp spearhead to the cylindrical satellite transmitter tag, which was about the size of a small microphone. Skilling wanted to be prepared—he might get only one chance to lodge the barbed point of the arrowhead into the dorsal muscle of the shark.

"Dr. Skilling . . ." Fenster began nervously. "I was actually wondering if you might be willing to tag the shark . . . in the water."

It was unusual but not unheard of for film crews to want him to tag the shark from the cage underwater; it was more dramatic. Skilling, however, wanted to make sure he didn't lose his chance to tag this possibly record-breaking shark, and working topside would allow him the greatest mobility. Still, he knew the Faustian bargain he had made. Despite his Ph.D., he was no different from any wildlife personality. TV Land was TV Land, and he knew what maintaining his reputation as Dr. Shark required. It was true that the underwater footage would be much more impressive. "All right," he said, "if that's what the film needs."

Tony, the cameraman, was getting into his wetsuit and preparing the "pig," the massive IMAX camera, which was all the bigger inside its yellow waterproof housing. Skilling pulled on his dry suit.

Fenster smiled weakly. He still did not look satisfied. "Do you ever tag the sharks from outside the cage?"

"Boil," Skilling shouted as he saw the turbulence in the water that preceded the shark's appearance. It was not far from the floating carcass. He raised the hatch on top of the floating cage. "Get in, Tony. Fast."

TWENTY

SKILLING'S HEART was pounding. The feel of the frigid water through his dry suit was like a dull ache, but he tried to focus his mind on what he had to do. He held the aluminum tagging pole, his hands covered by thin neoprene gloves to give him as much dexterity as possible. He didn't want to lose the two-thousand-dollar satellite tag and, more importantly, the opportunity.

As his eyes scanned the gray-green water, Skilling started to rehearse what he would say about the satellite tags—how they had allowed his colleagues to discover that white sharks migrate thousands of miles but that they were extremely territorial and returned to these same feeding grounds. It would be a long wait before he would get another chance to tag this shark if he missed it this year.

Skilling felt awkward in his dry suit and thirty-pound weight belt, like an astronaut in an alien environment. There was nothing about humans that was evolved to move in the watery world. The strong currents rocked the cage, and he had to hold on with his free hand to stay in place. The bright yellow housing for the IMAX camera was like a miniature submarine and made the small cage feel even smaller. Tony was on hookah, breathing air pumped in from the boat, but Skilling was on a rebreather. By recirculating his exhalations, the rebreather eliminated the bubbles that might attract the shark and interfere with the filming. The rebreather was expensive, but Fenster had included it in the movie budget, and now Skilling knew why.

Skilling looked around in all directions, orienting himself by the location of the carcass. It floated above him like a dark cloud, the flipper puffing out to one side. Light was streaming down all around it. The visibility was incredible, seventy-five feet at least, and he could see rock formations that were usually lost in the plankton-clotted water.

He shook his head as he remembered Fenster's question about leaving the cage—just what you might expect from a movie director if he was using some elasmo-model from the special effects department. But this was not "Bruce," the animatronic shark from *Jaws*. This was a real shark, and a big one.

Then he heard his father's voice in his head. *You really showed 'em what a Skilling is made of.* It was what his father always said when he threw a touchdown pass in a football game in high school. For a Skilling there was no such thing as defeat; there was only win or escalate. His father would be impressed if he left the cage. Maybe he'd never again have to hear him say to one of his fishing buddies back in Iowa, "Who in their right mind spends his life studying fish? Good for catching. Good for eating. But who the hell wants to know what they're thinking?" That always got a big laugh.

Suddenly, Skilling stopped thinking and stopped breathing, too. He spotted the large shape of the shark. "Holy Mother of God" were the garbled words that sputtered out of his Catholic childhood. Fear often has its own logic. Skilling couldn't imagine such a pious name making its way into the scientific literature. Simply "Mother" would have to do, and this shark could well be the matriarch. The absence of paired claspers—the equivalent of the shark's penis—told him that it was indeed a female.

Any desire to leave the cage had vanished. It was as big as he had imagined. By his estimate, the shark was twenty-one or maybe even twenty-two feet long, certainly a contender for the record. Its size also told him something else. This was a shark that could polish off a two-thousand-pound elephant seal bull. A super weaner pup would have just been a snack. There was no doubt in Skilling's mind that this shark was still hungry.

Mother was no longer rushing from the bottom for a killing blow. She didn't have to. Her victim could not fight back. Ambush had served its purpose. The shark looked almost docile as she swept her massive scythe-shaped tail and headed for the seal, or what was left of it. From her eye back to her gills, the shark had many deep gashes and severe bite marks that cut right down to the muscle. One of the gills was ripped and had a piece missing. There was no way to become a female of this size and age without enduring a fair share of scars from fighting or mating; the male shark would bite the female as they went into a mating spiral. Mating between whites was not all roses and candles, Skilling would tell his students, who would giggle as he told them about the hooks and spurs on the male's claspers.

Tony was filming as the shark tore into the carcass. She probably could have eaten the rest in one bite, but instead she chose to saw off a chunk, as if she were having appetizers. Her tail slashed from side to side, helping her tear through the meat. In the past, it was thought that there was only one shark at any given carcass, but researchers had since found that there were often several. Skilling hoped Mother would be dining alone.

The shark was too far from the cage, but if he moved out of the cage door a little, he might be able to reach its dorsal muscle with the titanium tip of the satellite tag. As the shark was busy tearing off a bite, shaking its head from side to side, Skilling realized this was his chance.

Skilling tried to get his resistant limbs to move. Every cell screamed at him to stay inside the cage as he unlatched the door and forced himself through it. Holding on to the bars with his free hand, he was so close—a foot or two away. He had to let go of the cage to reach the shark. He would never forgive himself if he missed this chance. With his blue diving fins, he pushed off from the cage.

Mother whipped her head to the side. Skilling froze as she stared at him with one black eye. The wash from the shark pushed him away from the cage. Practically hyperventilating, he sucked in oxygen, terror pumping through his limbs.

He reached behind him but could not feel the metal bars. The shark's slightly open mouth was a gash of black. A chaos of triangular white teeth stuck out of pink gums. Her black-tipped pectoral fins were splayed like wings, and her caudal fin hovered like a samurai's sword, ready to slice forward in attack.

Skilling started to back away quickly, kicking his feet as he reached behind him for the cage. *Don't turn your back. Don't turn your back.* He knew all predators preferred to attack from behind, as every attack exposed them to the risk of injury.

The shark started to rock her caudal fin back and forth as she approached slowly, perhaps intimidated by the size and unfamiliarity of the cage. Mother's snout had two holes for nostrils, and her extremely sensitive olfactory sacs were no doubt trying to decipher his scent. The dark pattern of spots making Mother look like she had a five o'clock shadow were sensory cells that could pick up electrical activity, such as his wildly beating heart and the muscles of his legs as he kicked. He was no longer thinking. His body was just reacting, a series of primordial moves that were far older than any rational thought.

Mother hovered for a second. Her hesitation gave him courage. The cage and boat must have looked like a large sea creature to the shark, but he'd seen them bite cages and boats and even rudders before.

He pointed his small aluminum spear at the shark. It was hardly a weapon. The dark unblinking eyes stared at him. Unlike fish, whose widely set eyes must scan for predators, sharks, like humans, could look straight at their prey.

As Skilling stared directly into the ancient unknown of the shark's eyes, all human arrogance was stripped away. The shark's massive back was gunmetal gray and its belly a ghostlike white. Its gill slits feathered like ripped paper as the giant continued to move slowly forward.

Skilling finally found the cage and fumbled behind him with blind hands. The door had swung closed, and the latch wasn't opening. He stole a nervous glance behind him. Tony was still filming but from as far back in the cage as he could get. *Doesn't he see me? Why isn't he opening the door?*

Skilling shook his hand to try to get Tony's attention, then quickly looked back at the shark. He didn't have another second to consider the cameraman. Mother rolled her pupils back, and her eyes turned white. Skilling dropped his tagging pole in a panic, knowing what would come next. He grabbed the icy bars and used all of his strength to heave himself through the water and around the side of the cage. The cage shuddered and the metal groaned as hundreds of teeth, each sharp as a scalpel, collided with the side of the cage, inches from his hand and body. Mother's white-and-gray torpedo snout was distended, her lower jaw gaping open in a silent roar. The skin above her upper jaw was creased by her massive bite. Her teeth and gums jutted out from the top of her jaw, like a rabid beast baring its fangs.

Unable to move backward, the shark kept thrusting forward as she shook her head, trying to free herself. She had discovered that the cage was not prey, and was hunting what was. Skilling was looking down the cavernous gullet and saw the cartilaginous gill arches expanding to devour him. Several teeth had broken off and were falling like white triangular leaves through the water.

As Mother finally freed herself, Skilling managed to squeeze through the gap between the boat's propeller and the back wall of the cage, where Tony was still filming. Her eyes rolled back in her head, Mother was trying to bite whatever was alive. As she sensed the electrical current of the motor, her jaws clamped down on the boat's propeller. She let go with an angry shiver of her head, thrust her caudal fin three or four times, and was gone into the deep. Skilling knew that if these stealthy hunters did not succeed on the first strike, they would often circle around and approach from a new angle. He had to get into the cage, and fast.

Skilling moved as quickly as he could to the front, scanning the water for the shark. This time Tony had the presence of mind to help unlatch the door. Skilling slipped inside quickly as the gate banged open against the cage. He was safe.

Out of the depths, Mother launched herself at them, the bars of the doorway distending around her snout, her jaws reaching for the elusive prey. Skilling grabbed the yellow camera from Tony and used it as a shield against the shark, who had thrust her head halfway into the cage. Tony was frozen, his body pressed against the back bars. Skilling waved his hand in front of Tony's mask and pointed his thumb up. Tony didn't have to be told twice as he pulled himself through the hatch at the surface. He didn't look back for the camera, which Skilling was using to fend off the shark. Mother opened her mouth wider and bit into the housing of the camera, yanking it out of Skilling's hands. The shark whipped its tail from side to side, each thrust the force of a car crash. As Mother wrenched her head free, the camera was torn from Skilling's hands.

Skilling watched Mother retreat into the jagged streaks of sunlight as the crushed yellow housing of the IMAX camera fell out of sight. He climbed through the hatch and back onto the deck of the *Sailfish*.

"Are you all right?" Fenster said anxiously, and then noticed that Skilling had not passed the pig up. "Where's the camera?"

Skilling stared down at the deck, his whole body shaking from shock. He clenched his fists to stop his numb hands from trembling, but he could not stop the nausea and dizziness.

"Where's the camera!"

"The shark decided it didn't want to have its picture taken after all," Skilling said, his voice chillingly calm and lacking any humor.

Fenster opened his mouth to speak and then closed it.

Skilling wasn't looking at him anymore. He was scanning the water for the shark. It hadn't come back for the small piece of sealskin that was left. All Skilling could see on the surface were the distant dorsal fins of several transient killer whales. They cut through the water like tall black filleting knives. On another day, this would have been a source of interest, but now he longed only to see Mother again. Despite the fact that she had just tried to devour him, he felt heartsick. His respect for her was as close to worshipful awe as he had ever experienced.

TWENTY-ONE

APOLLO LISTENED—*he could hear the clicking and sonar blasts of a pod of killer whales hunting nearby—six or seven perhaps—from their sounds—*

A dangerous number if they were hungry—and killers were always hungry—

His eyes strained to see black and white skin in the shadowy gray water—

He began to swim away—trying to get as far from the sounds as possible—then all at once he stopped—hearing the cause of the killers' excitement—

The distress call was clearly from a calf—not his kind—but certainly a whale—migrating with its mother back to the northern feeding grounds—like Apollo's own young would be doing shortly—

The piercing screech of a newborn's terror is understandable by all—

Apollo tilted the white expanse of his large pectoral fins—gracefully—like the changing wind—

He pivoted the forty tons of his body and began to swim toward the menacing sounds—

He drew closer and could see that the large male killers were deliberately colliding with the mother whale—separating her from her calf—

The female killers and their young were drowning the newborn—holding its head and blowhole underwater—

Suddenly they noticed Apollo and shifted their attack to the intruder—

Several of the largest killer males left the mother that they were corralling—one sank its sharp teeth into Apollo's tail—

He tried to shake it off as others bit into his flippers—dragging him down—

More seemed to join the pack—now there were twice as many—

Several buzzed him with their sonar—the pulsed shots rattling his sensitive hearing—

The water was filled with their barking and trumpeting—

He let out a bellowing roar in defense—then whipped his flukes from side to side—

One of the big males sped toward him in a bluff charge—another was not bluffing and slammed the hard top of its rostrum into the sensitive portion of Apollo's side where his lungs were—

Another tried to bite his back where it narrowed behind his dorsal—

The calf and mother had fled—his sacrifice would save the life of the calf and possibly that of the mother as well—

He surfaced to breathe as a killer launched its body onto his head, cutting off his breath by covering his blowhole with its bulk—others piled on and pushed him underwater—

One tore into his back with its teeth—he flinched from the pain—air escaping from his mouth—

His tongue—the part they prized most—raked against his baleen combs—

He knew they often devoured the tongue and left the rest uneaten—

Apollo made one final attempt to flee—

TWENTY-TWO

8:05 A.M.
Davis

ON THE WALL hung a whale calendar. March's picture was of a humpback breaching, as if it were escaping the water and flying through the air. The first few days of the month had a red line struck through them, and the fifth of March was boxed in overlapping red squares that framed the word DUE. Elizabeth had been working on her dissertation for almost two weeks but only had two days left to finish.

She sat at the round kitchen table next to a half-empty pot of coffee. The soundless television was playing in the background, keeping her company. Somehow, having other people in the house, even if they were only on the television screen, made her less lonely. The screen flashed an image of a beautiful stand of redwood trees. It soothed her. Over the trees appeared the green logo for the Environmental Stewardship Consortium and the words OUR RESOURCES, OUR FUTURE. It was a welcome relief from the car and detergent advertisements.

She turned back to her computer and continued typing on her silver laptop in a white heat, trying feverishly to meet the deadline. Professor Maddings's call had sparked her into action. Nothing was going to stop her from finishing her dissertation and getting her Ph.D. It was no longer just her career that was at stake, it was also her marriage—she would prove to Frank that she could finish and that they could start a family together. Next to her was a printout of what was already done: her introduction, literature review, methods, and results chapters. The cover sheet presented the unassuming but potentially explosive title: "Social Sounds in Whale Song: Evidence That Whale Communication Is Language?"

To argue that whales communicated with a few discrete calls was one thing, but to say that they actually had a language, as humans did, was extremely controversial. Languages had *words* with symbolic meaning and syntax, allowing humans to form sentences and communicate extremely complex ideas. If whales had language, it meant that their social sounds were not just vocalizations, like a mother calling to her baby, but had independent, symbolic meaning and could communicate far more information. A whale could refer to a baby that was not actually even there. Perhaps most controversial, if whale communication was a language, then there was the possibility of translation—of communicating between our two species.

Elizabeth knew she would need to address all of this in the chapter she was about to write: her discussion and conclusions. She glanced nervously at the calendar. And then there was the small problem of not knowing what her conclusions were. She did not know if the data justified going so far as to claim that whales might have language, not to mention that such a conclusion would almost certainly jeopardize her career. But she did not honestly know how to account for what she had observed. The rapid song change suggested that the song itself had meaning, and the refrain of social sounds that appeared in the song led her to believe that they were being used in some kind of symbolic semantic way.

To distract herself from writing something that might bury her career, Elizabeth tried to call her husband for the fifth time. The image of him and Kim came to mind, and she hung up before the call connected. The minute she hung up, the handset rang.

"Frank?" she said, thinking for a moment that the call had gone through after all or that he had called her back.

"No, Liza, is me."

"*Teo?* How did you get my number?"

"Milton gave it to me. He tell me about your husband, too."

"That's not your concern."

"Maybe it is, maybe it isn't . . . I got a present for you."

"My DAT recorder?"

"I got that, too."

"I'm happy to pay for the postage."

"That won't be necessary."

Elizabeth was distracted by a news report that flashed across her TV screen. In amazement, she read the words in the headline: HUMP-BACK WHALE SPOTTED IN SAN FRANCISCO BAY.

"Teo, I'll have to call you back."

Elizabeth hung up and knelt in front of the television, turning up the volume.

"This morning a humpback whale showed up off of San Francisco's Fisherman's Wharf. It was quite a crowd pleaser. We're going to go live to Jenny Cho, who's got a whale of a story for us."

"This whale-watching tour didn't have to go very far today to see a whale. All they had to do was escort this humpback whale as it swam through the bay. It seems to be heading inland toward the estuary. You may remember other humpback whales taking a similar course—our old friend Humphrey in 1985, and then a mother-and-calf pair named Delta and Dawn in 2007. But what's unusual about this whale is it seems to be singing. Thanks to the hydrophone built into this boat, we are able to hear the whale's song."

Elizabeth's spine started to tingle—it was identical to the song sung by Echo thousands of miles away, in an entirely different ocean. It was obviously not Echo. There was no way he had swum around the tip of South America in three weeks, but sound could travel much faster than any whale. The song could be propagated across the entire distance over a matter of days. Maddings had said the song was spreading around the world and migrating from ocean to ocean. And here was the proof.

"Oh my God," Elizabeth whispered to herself. "It's really true."

"What makes the whale sing?" the television reporter asked. "Is it love? Or is it joy?"

The hairs on the back of Elizabeth's neck were standing on end. Right in the middle of the song, she heard them: the social sounds she had recorded in Bequia.

She grabbed her digital SLR and her video camera in its gray housing. Without her DAT recorder, it was all she had. The door slammed behind her as she ran to find the wayward whale. Something deep in the pit of her stomach told her that this was not a song of love or joy.

TWENTY-THREE

8:30 A.M.
Downtown San Francisco

Reginald Gates stepped into one of the two elevators that reached the forty-sixth floor of the Transamerica building. He took a deep breath, trying to calm himself, and straightened his yellow tie in the reflective metal doors. Looking the part was important, and his tie complemented his gray suit nicely. Gates blinked his tired eyes and tried to suppress a yawn. He had been up most of the night staring at the spreadsheet, trying to will the quarterly numbers to change, but no matter what he did, they were still not coming out as he needed.

The doors of the elevator opened, and he walked over to his longtime secretary. Wilma—or Willie, as she was called—was like a surrogate mother and had moved with him up the corporate ladder. She was even willing to work on a Saturday, like today, when it was required.

"Mr. Heizer is waiting for you," she said, rolling her eyes nervously in the direction of the CEO's office. "Your jelly donut and double pick-you-up are on your desk. There's also some fresh fruit, which it wouldn't kill you to eat every now and then."

"Thanks, tell him I'll be right there . . . Oh, and will you copy these papers from the ESC for the *file*." Willie looked up at him, transformed into his accomplice. "I want to take it home with me tonight for safekeeping," he added.

Through the large windows, he could see the entire Bay Area and arching Bay Bridge. Despite its grandeur, he had already become indifferent to the view. Most of his time was spent with his back to the window, poring over spreadsheets and other financial documents. Growing up in North Richmond, California, Gates had seen the famous four-sided pyramid for as long as he could remember, and a view like this would have made his jaw drop in wide-eyed amazement. Even as a poor African American kid from the ghetto, he had known that someday he would work in an office on the top floor.

Gates had spent the last ten years working his way up to chief financial officer at Heizer Chemical Industries International. He was looking forward to taking his wife and baby away for a much delayed vacation. Maybe this summer, as soon as all the remodeling was done on the new house.

Gates's cell phone rang, and a picture on the screen showed his beautiful wife holding their six-month-old girl in her arms. He did not have time to answer it, so he hit "ignore." He'd call her back later.

The phone rang again.

"Baby, I can't talk now. I've got to meet with Jim."

"Reggie, something's wrong with Justine. She's not playing, and she won't eat. She doesn't seem like herself, and I'm worried."

"She's going to be fine. I'll call you back when I'm done giving the bad news."

"I'm going to take her in to see Dr. Lombardi."

"Can't this wait until Monday?"

"No, it can't."

"I'm sure there are good doctors near Blackhawk. You don't need to take her all the way back up there."

"I trust him."

"I'll call you later." Gates gathered up his spreadsheets and walked over to report the numbers to Heizer.

• • •

WHY THE HELL do CEOs always do this power-play crap and look out the window when they're unhappy? Gates felt like a schoolboy at the principal's office, but the problem had nothing to do with his performance. It had to do with that of the company.

"Reggie, I think you know that your bonus is pegged to making our numbers this quarter."

"Jim, I realize that, and I tried everything I could to make them different, but I can't invent numbers that don't exist."

Jim Heizer, the son of the company's founder, turned away from the window to face Gates. He looked overstuffed in his green suit, and when he spoke, his double chin jiggled like the pale throat of a toad. "I didn't say invent numbers. I just said to be creative with the numbers. I'm sure you'll do what needs to be done." Gates knew what he was being asked to do, and his body felt hot and uncomfortable. "I promoted you because I knew I could count on you, Reggie. Don't let me down."

Gates got up to leave.

"And don't forget the Chinese investors. They will be at the Rio Vista plant at four o'clock."

"We've got the executive committee meeting until three. Can't someone else take them around?"

"I don't trust anyone else with this one. We need their money, and we need it in this quarter. You know that plant better than anyone." Heizer smiled. "You can take my helicopter."

For a moment Gates forgot the pressures he was under. He walked over to the window where his boss was pointing and saw a shiny royal blue helicopter perched on a white rooftop helipad.

"I thought the neighbors had gotten the heliport closed."

"We were able to work with our friends in the city to overcome their concerns. Have a good ride."

• • •

GATES FELT the smooth, black leather of his seat. Beside him was a little tray with snacks, water, and orange juice. The soundproofed walls kept out most of the noise, so all Gates could hear was the light fluttering of the rotor outside.

When the helicopter took off, he felt his stomach drop and tried hard to stop himself from giggling. He felt like a dumb kid again, but the ride was more fun than anything he could remember. Out the window he saw the fan of gray streets and gray rooftops. Ahead he could see a patch of green around Coit Tower, the prison island of Alcatraz floating off in the bay, and behind it the brown-green hills that surrounded the Bay Area. Out to the left, he could even see the Golden Gate Bridge. When the helicopter pulled over the aquamarine water of the bay, he sighed and started to relax.

Before long the helicopter was flying over his old neighborhood of North Richmond, where the small urban houses and apartment buildings were packed tightly together. He remembered, as a kid, hearing the sounds of drive-bys and gang shoot-outs, and was grateful that his daughter would have a different life. He looked at his black titanium watch, its face smiling success at him. It was only 3:10; perhaps there was time for a quick flyover.

He opened the window to the cockpit. "How far out of our way is Blackhawk? I just bought a house there."

"No time at all. There's not much traffic up here," the pilot said, accustomed to accommodating any requests his executive passengers made. Gates gave the pilot his address to put into the GPS, and the helicopter started to bank to the right. Below, Gates could see where the blue-green water of the bay turned into the muddy brown water of the delta formed by the drainage of the Sacramento and other rivers.

As they headed southeast, they flew over large unpopulated tracts of land just outside the Bay Area. The brown hills looked almost like the back of a living animal. He wished he could show his wife and daughter how beautiful it was.

Then they were back over civilization, the cul-de-sac suburban developments of Martinez and Walnut Creek, where the houses seemed so crammed together. He was pleased that he could afford something better. They were approaching Blackhawk, and he could see the golf course surrounding the homes like a large interconnected lawn.

"There it is," the pilot said, pointing to one of numerous gray roofs.

Gates's heart sank. From up here, the homes looked no different from the countless other homes they had flown over. The roofs were a little larger and the address more exclusive, but in truth, they were houses packed together by a developer who was trying to make as much money as possible.

"Thanks," Gates said, sorry he had come. The pilot banked to the left and headed north to the chemical plant.

They flew back along the delta and up the Sacramento River. The farmland on the outskirts of Sacramento was a patchwork of green and brown fields.

He saw a crowd of people on a bridge below, and a flotilla of fishing boats. "What's going on?" he asked, opening the window to the cockpit again.

"Haven't you heard? A whale swam up the Sacramento."

"You're kidding. All the way up here?"

"Amazing, isn't it? Just like Humphrey and those other two whales. Must be something the whales like up here."

Gates looked for the whale in the muddy brown water. Today whales were simply curiosities, giants from another world, but at one time they had been a vital part of the global economy. Cities like San Francisco had grown up around whale fisheries and had relied on their oil to fuel industry. Gates thought of the historical plaque he passed every day on his way into the office; it announced that the hull of a whaling ship, the *Niantic,* was buried directly beneath the skyscraper. Gates loved history and knew that the future belonged to those who understood that some things, including the thirst for vital resources, never change.

The helicopter was arriving at the chemical plant. It was strange to see it for the first time from above. It looked like a maze of pipelines, whole building-sized towers made entirely out of tubes transporting chemicals to large circular holding tanks. Several smokestacks pumped out large gray clouds. As a child, he had called the stacks from the Richmond refinery "the cloud-makers."

After landing, Gates was introduced to the group of Chinese investors, who were all wearing yellow hard hats. He put one on his head and welcomed the group to the plant. After the translator had interpreted, they smiled and greeted one another awkwardly. All around them, workers were dressed in gray coveralls and wore the required yellow hard hats. Gates always thought the hard hats were a little silly, since there was really nothing to fall on your head. The place was not dangerous, like a construction site.

He led the group into one of the testing chambers and explained, "Here we are making a compound called Bisphenol A, a vital ingredient in polycarbonate plastic and epoxy resins." He tapped on a plastic water bottle that had been left there for tours. "It makes plastic clear and shatterproof, very useful. Global production is over two million metric tons a year, and our factories around the world make over 20 percent of the world supply. It can also be made into flame retardants and has been used as a fungicide." Next to him, one of the workers was checking gauges and writing numbers down on a clipboard. After the translator was finished, Gates encouraged her to lead the visitors on to the next stop.

"How's the baby, Reggie?"

Gates did a double take.

The worker raised her safety glasses. "It's Janice."

"Oh, Janice, how are you?" Gates said, out of politeness, but he felt embarrassed by her familiarity. He glanced toward where the Chinese investors were getting into what looked like an oversized golf cart.

"How's it going up there? You taking care of everyone?"

"You know I am. Good to see you, Janice."

At the next stop Gates continued the tour and showed the Chinese investors where they were making other chemicals, including very profitable flame retardants. He pulled on the sleeve of his suit coat to explain that these compounds stopped fabric and other materials from burning. "Here in California, all bedding and furniture must use flame retardants. We are the third-largest supplier in this annual market of 2.4 billion dollars."

His cell phone rang. It was his wife. *Oh, Christ, I forgot to call.*

"Are there any more questions?" Gates asked, hoping he could end the tour quickly and answer his wife's call. The investors all got very excited. "They only have one question," the translator said. "Where's the whale?"

TWENTY-FOUR

4:15 P.M.
Liberty Slough, California

APOLLO WAS SWIMMING QUICKLY—still unsure if he had really escaped—

He heard only the constant droning of boat engines—but he had long ago stopped hearing the sounds of the killers—

He was trailing blood from the bite on his back—chunks of his flippers and tail were missing—but that was all—

Was it the shallow waters that the killers were unwilling to enter or the harbor seals that had distracted them with an easier meal—

Apollo did not know at what point he would be safe and swam onward—as their clicking sounds became increasingly distant—

He finally slowed as the water was ever more murky—he tilted his massive forty-foot body downward—his tail floating up and his rostrum pointing down—

Apollo sang the song once again and then continued upstream—the currents of brackish water washing over his body—the thin water less buoyant—the noise of the boats assaulting from all sides—the brownish channel an echo chamber of sound—

But he swam on against the current—far from the ocean—

At last he squeezed through the narrow pilings—the waters ending in land—and he began to sing once again—

The waters had grown stale and bland as he left the living seas— now far from where all life had been born—

TWENTY-FIVE

5:00 P.M.

THE SUN WAS THREATENING to set as Elizabeth sped past rows and rows of cornfields and endless expanses of bright green grass that would be rolled up and sent to landscape lawns and golf courses around the country. She saw large factory farms of cows and lambs that were being fattened up for the slaughter. Silver-feathered vultures circled overhead.

Elizabeth glanced down at the map spread out on her steering wheel as she tried to navigate the back roads. The wood-paneled Country Squire was barreling too fast. She slammed on the brakes and just missed sliding into an irrigation ditch. The screech of her tires sent a clutch of red-winged blackbirds darting overhead, their red epaulets like bloody badges on otherwise jet-black wings. A snowy egret that had been hunting nearby sailed away to safer ground.

This was pristine and remote delta farmland. Although it was only two hours from downtown San Francisco and an hour from Sacramento, the area still looked wild and desolate. The only sign of modernity was the electrical cables, held up by what looked like long-legged steel giants that grasped the wires in their hands and marched in an endless row. In the distance, Elizabeth saw some factories belching smoke, but they were quite far away.

Unlike humpbacks that had entered the river in years past, this whale had not meandered but had sped up the Sacramento River in a day, entrapping himself in a muddy dead-end slough only a half hour from the university.

Elizabeth had called Connie on the cell phone, and Connie had been able to get her the location of the whale. Elizabeth had not bothered to ask whether Connie had gotten the information from the police radio, which she said she had listened to avidly since she was a child, or from Skilling, who apparently had been called in as a local expert. *He knows nothing about humpbacks,* Elizabeth thought, but if there were television cameras, she had a feeling Skilling would be there.

As Elizabeth turned on to the levee road, she saw a sign warning her that she was entering private property. Although surrounded by fallow brown fields, the slough itself was lined with green trees and grass, an oasis of water in the dry agricultural land. The oaks, cypress, and native grasses around the slough were all bent by the wind that blew constantly across the flat delta. The muddy brown water rippled and shimmered in the low afternoon sun. It was hard to imagine that a whale could be swimming in the small and no doubt shallow slough, which was no more than five hundred feet long and two hundred feet across. The whale would be lucky if it was fifty feet deep.

A black-and-white California Highway Patrol car blocked the road, and behind it she could see white news vans with tall transmitting antennas spiraling toward the orange sky. A helicopter circled above, trying to get close-up footage of the whale. The constant drumming of its rotors and its downdraft were probably frightening the whale and keeping it submerged.

Elizabeth pulled over and got out. The gray gravel crunched under her sneakers. Up ahead was a concrete bridge. How, she wondered, had the whale squeezed through the narrowly spaced pilings? Across the slough, the land opened up into a brown grassy expanse, like the Okavango Delta in southern Africa, which she had visited as a biology student in college to study lions and elephants. On the opposite bank, she also saw a burned-out, overturned car that had been stripped of its parts. As the helicopter took off, she saw the whale start to lobtail, beating its tail against the surface. She scrambled to get the lens cap off her digital camera and pointed it at the whale's flukes.

"Can I help you, ma'am?" said an officer, dressed in a beige uniform with a six-pointed star on his chest, like some old-fashioned sheriff in a lawless town.

"I'm a marine biologist at the University of California, Davis. I'm here for the whale."

"Let me call Incident Command and see if we can get you clearance. What is your name?"

Incident Command, what is that? Elizabeth wondered after having been allowed to pass. *Who authorized my entry? Was it Skilling?* she wondered as she saw him being interviewed by half a dozen television reporters.

"Why do you think the whale swam here?" she heard one of the reporters ask.

"There are three possibilities we're exploring," Skilling replied. "It could be confused. Whales swim against the northern currents, and it could have been confused by the outgoing tide from the bay. It also appears to have fresh wounds and could have been fleeing killer whales."

"But why would it swim so far upriver?" another reporter asked.

"The third and most likely possibility is that the whale is simply sick. My hunch is that it has some kind of parasitic infection of the inner ear or of the brain that has caused it to become confused and disoriented."

"Do you think you can save it?" another interviewer asked.

"Probably not." Skilling paused to let the full force of his conclusion sink in. "Our main concern is that it might run aground, and then we're going to have a big smelly carcass to deal with."

"It's not a carcass yet," Elizabeth said before she realized she had said it.

The large black television cameras turned to face her. One of the reporters pushed a microphone into Elizabeth's face, eager for controversy—and for more encouraging news.

"What do you think is wrong with the whale?"

"I don't know," Elizabeth said, "but it is making unusual sounds that have been recorded in several other locations around the world."

Before Elizabeth could explain, a female reporter assaulted her with more questions. "What kind of unusual sounds? What do you think the whale is trying to say? Is the whale giving us some kind of message?"

Every ounce of Elizabeth's scientific body recoiled at the conclusions that this reporter was drawing so quickly. "We really do not have any evidence to suggest that the whale is communicating with us. Like Professor Skilling—"

The television reporters, realizing that they were not going to get anything more controversial from Elizabeth, quickly turned away to wrap up their stories. She overheard the credulous reporter conclude by saying, "Is the whale lost, or here for a reason? Stay tuned as we discover what this whale might want us to know." Elizabeth rolled her eyes.

"That's one way to get the whole world—not just your colleagues—to think you are crazy," Skilling said from behind Elizabeth.

She turned around sheepishly. "I didn't mean it to be taken that way."

"Welcome to the media. Subtlety is not their business."

"Sorry about cutting in like that. I didn't mean—"

"It's okay. How are you doing?" There was genuine concern in Skilling's voice.

"I'm going to deliver the dissertation on Monday."

Professor Skilling's eyes went wide with surprise. "I'm glad to hear it, but I meant with your husband."

"I didn't know my personal life was world news."

"There are no secrets in our department—at least not personal ones."

"Okay, I guess . . ." Elizabeth was eager to change the subject. "Dr. Skilling, that whale is singing the same song as the whale I was recording in Bequia. The song seems to be migrating around the world, which I'm sure you know is highly unusual. I want to study this whale."

"You'll have to get a permit from NOAA," he said, referring to the National Oceanic and Atmospheric Administration, which had the jurisdiction to protect the whale.

"That could take weeks."

"Yes, it probably will."

"Dr. Skilling," one of the newscasters said, "could we do a retake? The light was not as good as we'd like."

"Sure," Skilling said, quite familiar with the media's needs. He turned to Elizabeth. "Let me know if I can do anything."

"You can accept my dissertation," she said as he started to walk away.

"Just make it acceptable," he said without turning around.

Elizabeth saw that Connie had arrived with a group of protesters who were holding up SAVE THE WHALES signs. Connie seemed to be involved in almost every issue that dealt with the health of the oceans, but she was particularly devoted to stopping the return of commercial whaling. Elizabeth wondered how the protesters had gotten through. Then she noticed that crowds were arriving to see the whale.

Connie and Elizabeth met on the bridge that crossed the slough. They both looked down at the whale's dorsal fin, which was all that was visible in the muddy water. A rigid-hulled Coast Guard boat was patrolling the waters nearby.

Elizabeth felt the bridge vibrating from the whale's song. "I've got to record this whale," she said, knowing that it would be impossible with the protection zone the Coast Guard had set up.

"How are you going to do that?" Connie asked.

"I'm going to come back after dark."

TWENTY-SIX

FRANK STARED DOWN at the menu in front of him. Tom had recommended the lobster and the restaurant and the whole idea of going out with Kim. The lights in the seafood restaurant were dim, and a candle flickered in a red globe between them. Nets and nautical gear hung from the ceiling and walls. The restaurant reminded Frank of Elizabeth and their time diving together. The restaurant was a mistake, as was the whole idea of going out on a date.

Tom seemed certain that Frank needed a wife like his. Jenny had been a nurse, and they seemed to have a perfect family, but Frank still wasn't sure what he needed.

"You're thinking of her, aren't you?" Kim smiled with understanding. Her short blond hair framed her attractive face. She wore a red dress that clung to her slender body quite differently than her scrubs.

"Yeah, how did you know?"

"I've been out with enough men to recognize the symptoms of 'I'm not over her yet' syndrome."

"Incurable?"

"I'm not sure. I'll need to conduct a history . . . and a physical." Kim was being playful, and Frank smiled at her use of medical terminology. He decided to play along.

"I'm ready for the examination."

"Why did you leave her?"

Frank played with his silverware. "I guess I felt alone in my marriage. When you've worked thirty-six hours straight, you want to come home to someone who's happy to see you. Elizabeth was never there."

"What do you want?"

"I know what I don't want. I don't want to choose between having children and the woman I love—"

"The woman you love?" Kim said, looking surprised and disappointed.

Frank heard his words echoed from Kim's lips. She put her gold napkin down on the table, pushed her chair back, and said, "I think we can skip the physical exam. I already have my prognosis."

Frank knew it, too. He shook his head with recognition. "Incurable."

"Good night, Dr. Lombardi."

Frank looked at his empty plate. Children or no children, he wanted Elizabeth.

"Do you know what you want?"

Frank looked up and saw the waitress. "Excuse me?"

"Do you know what you want?"

Frank smiled and said, "Yes . . . I think I finally do."

TWENTY-SEVEN

Midnight

ELIZABETH STOOD in her kitchen, dressed in her black wetsuit, with her video camera bag over her shoulder. She looked down at her wedding ring, shining brightly under the fluorescent light. Her hands were swelling for some bizarre reason, and the ring felt tight and uncomfortable. It would be safer for the whale and for her ring if she took it off. She moistened her finger in her mouth and tried to pull the ring over her plump knuckle. The metal dug into her skin but would not budge. *Olive oil,* she thought, and then smeared the cooking oil on her finger. This time it slipped right off, and she placed the ring in a small dish by the side of the sink.

ELIZABETH PARKED THE CAR far away from the levee, where the police car still blocked the way. The wind was blowing hard, rustling the grass and making the trees at the edge of the water sway like ghosts.

In one hand she had her mask, snorkel, and fins, and in the other she carried the heavy video hydrophone in its plastic housing. The night was moonless, and she knew she wouldn't see anything on her video camera, but Teo still had her DAT recorder. The video camera would record a digital audio signal that she could work with.

Elizabeth felt like a frogman as she sneaked along the irrigation ditch and over the levee that rose like an ancient American Indian burial mound. Even with her wetsuit on, she could feel that the air was cold, and she knew the water would be even colder. The fog was rolling in, and Elizabeth shivered as she carefully walked down the steep slope to the water. The crickets were so loud they sounded like an alarm.

Halfway down the hillside, the rocky ground gave way, and Elizabeth fell hard on her hip. She saved the video hydrophone by sacrificing her elbow and, dropping her fins and mask, caught herself with her other hand. She kept sliding—right into a blackberry bramble. The long, thorny vines scraped across her face and pierced her wetsuit, but it was her palm that stung the most from the sharp rocks and broken glass.

A police flashlight swept across the area. "Protesters?" she heard one of the officers say as she held her breath, both to stay silent and to try to endure the pain. "Or rats?"

The thought of rats made her cringe. She stayed perfectly still, looking for anything that might be moving.

After a few minutes, the police officers gave up their search. Carefully, she tried detaching herself from the thorns that only grudgingly let go.

Not willing to risk slipping again or being spotted, Elizabeth crawled to the water's edge. She listened for blows, but all she heard was the water lapping against the rocks.

Then all other sensations—the pain, the cold—disappeared as she heard the exhalation like a dragon's blast not far from the bank. By the starlight, she could see the high back of the humpback slipping under the water. The damp air fell against her face like a fisherman's kiss, filled with the salty smell of the sea. She and the whale were breathing the same air. This was not just a fact but an intimacy.

Elizabeth sucked the blood trickling from the palm of her right hand and pulled on her mask and flippers.

She slid into the water, which was even colder than she'd expected. Pulling the mask over her eyes, she stared into the black depths. A tremor of fear snaked up her spine as she swam out into the slough. *What the hell am I doing in this dark, deserted water with a forty-ton animal?*

Then the whale began to sing. In the narrow waterway, the sounds were amplified. They penetrated her body, deeply piercing her ears and skin. As with Echo in Bequia, she felt a pressure wave against her chest that made it difficult to breathe. She turned on the camera, knowing that its audio would capture each and every sound the whale produced. In the darkness, it felt as if the sounds had shape and form. There it was again—that social sound in the song that occurred together with the contact calls: *EEh-EEh-EEh.* Unlike the continuous tone of distress calls, this sound was shorter and more abrupt. It reverberated through her, making her body shake and tremble. It was the same sound Sliver had made after her baby had died, but what did it mean?

One of the law enforcement agencies turned on a floodlight. She took a gulp of air and dove below the surface. The whale stopped vocalizing and swam past her. In the light spilling in from the surface, she saw the whale's outstretched fin, as if he were extending it to her. She released a gasp of air and slowly stretched her hand back to him. She thought of the X-ray photos she had seen of a whale's flipper, revealing a bone structure that was startlingly similar to a human hand. Then they both surfaced to breathe.

Forty-five minutes of swimming and recording passed in what seemed like moments. When she checked her camera, she discovered that she was out of memory. The floodlight swept across the water, and she had to duck beneath the surface yet again. There was no more she could do tonight, so she swam toward the shore, landing as far from the authorities as she could.

Dragging herself onto the muddy bank, she pulled off her fins. She now had a deeper understanding of the sounds and fresh ideas for ways to test their meaning.

As Elizabeth turned around to climb back up the levee, the bright beam of a police flashlight blinded her.

"I'm going to have to arrest you for trespassing and for violation of the Marine Mammal Protection Act."

CONNIE KEPT A CLOSE WATCH on Elizabeth from the bridge where she and the other protesters were holding a candlelight vigil. Her organization, the Ocean Warriors, worked to spread the word that over a thousand whales were still being killed each year from whaling and from Navy sonar.

"Oh, no!" Connie said as she saw the police officer approaching Elizabeth. *Not good. Not good. Be strategic.* Connie looked around and saw a group of college guys whose main goal seemed to be to drink beer and heckle the protesters. She knew the activists were spoiling for a fight.

Connie slipped away from the others and walked behind the college students, who were watching the arrest taking place across the slough with keen interest. She picked up one of the beer bottles they had not broken on the rocks along the shore and launched it at the activists, careful to hit the concrete bridge rather than her friends. The reaction was immediate. First there was shouting, and then several of the protesters ran at the college students, who weren't quite sure what was going on.

Connie shouted from the bridge to a police officer, who hurried toward the brawl. Connie ran along the levee road, trying to watch her steps on the dark and uneven surface. She called down to where the police officer was trying to reach Elizabeth without slipping.

"Aren't you Professor—McKay—the world-famous—marine biologist?" Connie said, trying to catch her breath. "I hear they've put you—in charge—of the research—team."

The young police officer looked back and forth between Elizabeth below him and Connie above. In the floodlight, Connie could see his young, fresh face and short-cropped red hair. At that moment the police officer's shoulder microphone began to crackle. "I need Code Two backup."

The police officer glanced at Connie and Elizabeth another time and then spoke into the shoulder mike. "Ten-four. Sacramento Fifteen thirty-five en route."

"I know who the hell you are. Just get your ass over here," the other police officer shouted back through the shoulder mike.

The young police officer cringed. "I'm sorry, Professor," he said over his shoulder as he hurried up the hill. "I was told to arrest anyone who— I'm really sorry."

The police officer had clawed his way up the steep levee, and Connie gave him a hand up. "Don't worry about it," she said with a smile. "You were just doing your job, Officer Clark." She was shining her flashlight at his ID tag.

"Thanks," he said abashedly. He ran off to help his partner, who was trying to break up the fistfight that had broken out between the protesters and the college students.

"Let's get you out of here," Connie said to Elizabeth, helping her friend up over the edge of the levee.

"World famous?" Elizabeth said with a smile.

"Almost."

"Thanks."

"Don't mention it. Now let's get you home and dry."

"I can't. I've got to get to the office."

"Now?"

"I heard something in the recordings that I need to compare to the sound files I recorded in Bequia three weeks ago."

"What did you hear?"

"There's a distress call in the song. I need to find out why."

"Of course it's distressed," Connie said. "It's trapped."

"I don't think so . . ." Elizabeth said, remembering what she had heard on the television news broadcast. "The whale was making the distress call as it swam into the delta and all the way up the river."

TWENTY-EIGHT

12:30 A.M.
Sunday
Davis

Nilsen took a long draw on the unfiltered cigarette he was smoking, his only companion during the night. As the smoke filled his lungs and the nicotine reached his blood, his whole body started to relax, and for a moment he forgot where he was and the intense boredom of waiting.

Whaling required endless patience as one awaited some small disturbance on the surface of the water, hours upon endless hours of nothing, until finally, there was a frenzy of activity.

When was that damn island whaler going to arrive? It'd been two weeks since he'd left the island, and there was still no sign of him. Kazumi, the bastard, was hell-bent on recovering that worthless piece of whale. Easy for him. He didn't have to stand for hours in the dark, legs aching. Nilsen would finish this job and then go back home to the land and sea that he loved. He leaned against one of the pines in the small cluster of trees and looked up at the windows of the researcher's town house. Still dark.

TWENTY-NINE

2:00 A.M.

DESPITE THE OFFICE KEY in her hand, Elizabeth felt like she was breaking in. She had often worked late into the night and was not easily spooked by empty buildings. But something had changed in her relationship to the department. She did not quite know what. Was it their decision to cut off her funding? Was it the mysterious call from one of the university's donors? Or was it the pressure to finish her dissertation on an impossible schedule?

The hallway was dark, lit only by an ethereal blue glow from the circular tank in which white ghostlike jellies pulsed and undulated through the water. Elizabeth was grateful for their rhythmic motion, which reminded her of the sea and the sway of the tides even in this landlocked region. The fluorescent lights sputtered before coming to life. Although she had changed into dry clothes, her hair was still wet, and she was shivering.

At the wooden door to her department, Elizabeth paused. The glass window had been pasted over with flyers, and it was impossible to see who was inside. She swung it open quickly and then sighed. Maybe she was just spooked from her brush with the law. No, there was something else, something about her department. It felt hostile and unwelcoming.

Elizabeth downloaded the photos she had taken at the slough earlier and compared them to the fluke identification registry that had pictures of all known whales migrating along the West Coast.

There were fresh bite marks on one fluke, which supported Skilling's theory that the whale might have been chased into the bay by killer whales. She zoomed into the image and saw several white lines that crossed like a triangle or an abstract "A." They reminded her of a fluke ID she had seen several years ago, when she had worked on maintaining the registry. She found that image and compared it with the one she had taken. Aside from the killer whale teeth marks, the flukes were identical. The whale was a male in the Socorro Island population that migrated to several feeding grounds, often passing close to Vancouver. His name was Apollo.

"Well, Apollo, what are you and your friends saying?" Elizabeth whispered to herself.

She settled into the familiar work of analyzing the song and began to look for recurring patterns: subphrases, phrases, and themes. Whale song was generally between the length of a ballad and a movement in a symphony. And it was structured in many ways like human songs: similar rhythms, similar-length phrases, even rhyme. As Elizabeth listened to sounds that resembled a trumpet, she marveled at how the whales even balanced percussive sounds with pure tones in roughly the same proportions that people do.

Ordinarily, Elizabeth would have focused on the overall structure, but today she was more interested in the dozens of occurrences of what she and other researchers had long identified as "social sounds"—sounds used in everyday whale behavior and interactions. There were two such sounds, one of which was repeated, and they seemed to be inserted into the song almost like a chorus or a refrain.

It was just after dawn when Connie arrived. Apparently, she had been delayed by bailing out several of her fellow activists from jail.

"Listen to this sound from the slough," Elizabeth said, and played the sound that was always repeated in pairs in the whale's song. It was a low-pitched sound, but it was often very soft: *w-OP. w-OP.* "Now listen to this." She played an identical phrase. "I recorded this sound on several occasions when calves had strayed from their mothers. I think it's a contact call between mother and calf."

"Is the whale in the slough a female?"

"No, I got a good fluke ID, and it's a male. His name is Apollo."

"But why would this whale . . . I mean, there's no calf with it . . . and it's not even a mother."

"I know. It's strange, but this is the second male that I've heard use this sound in its song. What if the contact call from a mother to a baby actually meant 'baby'?"

"I'm not sure I follow. Are you saying they have a word for 'baby'?"

"Well, whales don't have words, but what if that vocalization meant 'baby'?"

"What does this have to do with distress? You said there was a distress call."

"There is—or at least I think there is." Elizabeth wished she had the tape from Teo in which Sliver's distress call had changed to the one she was hearing in the new song.

"So . . . you're saying that this whale's baby is in distress?"

Elizabeth shook her head and said, "I don't know. It doesn't make a lot of sense, does it?"

"Maybe the whale started making the distress sound when it entered the bay," Connie offered.

"That would make sense, except for the fact that whales all around the world are singing this same song—and there's a distress call in all of them." Elizabeth knew she could do no more. She needed to get home and finish her dissertation. Someday she would sleep again, but not today.

"Elizabeth . . ."

She had not seen Dr. Skilling come in. "Yes."

"Tomorrow is the deadline."

"I know, but I need more time. I'm still working on my conclusions."

"We're out of time, Elizabeth. I won't be able to reverse the decision of the committee."

THIRTY

ELIZABETH WALKED UP to her home with a feeling of dread. It was not just that she had under twenty-four hours to finish her dissertation, or her worry for Apollo, both of which were very much on her mind. It was also returning to an empty house and her increasing sense of hopelessness about saving her marriage.

She stepped inside her small walled courtyard and saw the unpruned rosebush. The fragrance reminded her of the bubble bath her mother used to buy. She leaned over, and her nose touched the soft pink petals. Her mother would sit in her piping-hot bath by candlelight, and when she was done, Elizabeth would slip in, the glowing light filling the room like a holy sanctuary. The warm bath was like her mother's arms enveloping her. When her mother got sick, Elizabeth would run the bath for her and wash her soft skin.

The front door was ajar.

"Frank?" *Has he come home?* "Frank?" She pushed the door open.

"No, is your Teo." He was sitting on her couch, grinning like the cat that ate the canary.

"Teo! What are you doing here?" Elizabeth tried to get over the shock of seeing Teo in her living room. "And what are you doing letting yourself into my house?"

"Now, is that island hospitality?"

"You're not on the island."

"I know. I just take a bus through every state between Alabama and California."

"How did you get in?"

Teo held up a fishing knife with a long, thin blade that tapered to a point. "Good for filleting fish and picking locks."

Elizabeth felt a shiver at the sight of the blade. "Why are you here?"

"You leave this in my boat. Don't you remember?" He held up the silver DAT machine, which was slightly larger than his hand.

"You could have mailed it to me."

"But then I have to wait a whole year to see you." Teo smiled a big island smile, and his eyes—one green and one blue—stared at her.

"I'm married, Teo."

"Then why aren't you wearing your ring?"

Covering her left hand protectively with her right, Elizabeth walked into the kitchen and let out a small gasp as she saw the empty dish. "It was right in here," she said, looking all around the kitchen counter.

"I heard Frank's gone and run off. Like I told you, some people understand the sea, and others, they don't." Teo followed her into the kitchen. His face must have registered his surprise at seeing her down on all fours.

"I can't find my ring."

"Maybe it's not the right one."

Elizabeth got up and shot him an annoyed glance. "Frank is coming back."

"But what if he don't?"

"I know you have come a long way, and I thank you, but you really need to go. My research is due tomorrow." Elizabeth moved closer to usher Teo to the door, but he held firm, bringing them within a foot of each other. "I'm afraid—" she started.

"I listen to that tape, Liza. You think the whale is saying something, don't you?"

"It's using a distress call," she said with a sigh. She was grateful for the change of subject but did not have time to explain.

"Yeah, I hear that sound on the tape."

"You did? You know the sound for distress?"

"I'm a whaler, Liza. I am the distress. But there's more than one kind of distress, you know."

"What are you talking about?"

"There some things I never get around to telling you."

"Why wouldn't you have told me?"

"Island people don't give away all their secrets to those . . . who just passing through."

"I told you it was a mistake."

Her words had stung. She could see it on his face, but he ignored them. "Can I play it for you? Then I'll go."

"Promise?"

"I promise," he said, his voice low.

They sat on the couch and listened to the recording. The sound was the one Elizabeth had heard before: *eeee-eeee-eeee*. "You hear that cry—is a long, steady moan. They only use that cry if they think there's a chance for them. You can hear the sadness in it, is almost pitiful. Now listen to it change." The second sound was the unfamiliar distress call that she had heard in Echo's and Apollo's new song. It was also the sound that Sliver made after the whalers had killed her calf: *EEh-EEh-EEh*. "This one sound desperate. You can hear the hurry in it. They only use that one when they held fast and all hope is lost."

Elizabeth's mind was spinning with possibilities. She realized that Teo might be useful in helping her to decipher the song, and she could tell he knew it, too.

"Well, I guess I should be going now," Teo said.

"Do you have a place to go?"

"I guess I'll just take the bus back."

"Have you eaten? At least let me feed you."

"That would be nice. I eat last in Utah. I think it was Utah."

Elizabeth laughed, imagining Teo in a truck stop or a convenience store. In the fridge she found a pizza, but there was mold growing on it. She dumped it in the trash. Prying open the cardboard box of leftover Chinese food produced a rancid odor that made her wince. It followed the pizza box. In the freezer, she found some fish sticks. "Now that's my kind of meal," he said when he saw that it was the only thing in the freezer. "That and some coffee, and I'm satisfied." He was tilting his head to the pot of coffee she had made the previous morning. They ate and laughed—it was good, being around someone who knew her so well. "Maybe I take a day or two to look around. Never been to California before."

Elizabeth hesitated. She knew she was being reeled in so slowly she could hardly feel the pull of the line. Her mind came up with four or five quick rationalizations that echoed the mix of gratitude and pity and curiosity that she was feeling.

"One night—on the couch," she said.

His smile was grateful. "It'll be a king's four-poster after my trip from the island."

"You sailed from Bequia?"

"I'd have sailed around the world if you were waiting."

"I'm not waiting, Teo, and you shouldn't be, either."

"You never gave me a real chance."

"I made my choice," Elizabeth said.

"And I made mine."

Elizabeth turned away from Teo. She prayed that Frank would come back to her, so she would never have to choose again.

• • •

ELIZABETH WORKED all afternoon at the dining room table as Teo went for a long walk. When he came back, he had a couple of burritos for dinner. Her stomach grumbled. She was surprised by her appetite, as she devoured her burrito.

Around midnight, Elizabeth wrote the concluding lines of her dissertation, which included all the maybes and possiblies that science required. Proving anything scientifically was difficult, especially something as elusive and intangible as the linguistic intelligence of whales. "The complex vocalizations of humpbacks and other baleen and toothed whales require further study and analysis. Although current research is inconclusive, it is possible that humpback social sounds may form the basis of a meaningful social language." This seemed reasonable and prudently cautious, and the fact of the matter was she did not have the evidence yet to argue for something stronger.

Elizabeth headed upstairs and locked the door to her bedroom. She remembered the words of an old song from the island she often heard sung by the children—"Mr. Dog, he came to town." She shook her head and whispered the final line: "But I've already got a wedding gown."

"Frank will come back," she said under her breath. "I know he will."

THIRTY-ONE

AFTER ELIZABETH headed upstairs for the night, Teo pulled the package out of the cooler, which he had hidden outside. The ice was almost gone, but the water was still cold, and the package remained solid. He stowed it in the empty freezer in the back on the bottom shelf. It seemed unlikely that Elizabeth would find it there. From what he could tell, she lived on cups of coffee and takeout, but he wanted to be extra careful. He didn't know how Elizabeth would respond to what was in the package. The memories were no doubt still fresh, and he had no desire to remind her of that day. He placed the half-empty box of fish sticks in front of the package to hide it.

Teo turned out the light and sank into the large couch. The cool dark of the night closed in around him like the sea. As his eyes adjusted, he saw a square of white light on the floor cast from a street lamp. He breathed in deep and exhaled. Usually he liked to be alone in the dark with his thoughts, but tonight they were troubling. *I shoulda give up the whale hunt for her, if she a had me. Damn that Norwegian whaler. I wish he never tell me about Liza's whale.* Teo figured there must have been a reason that Nilsen had told him, but why had the man wanted him to kill Liza's whales?

The phone rang next to Teo. It kept ringing, but Elizabeth didn't answer it. The machine picked up, and he could hear the message.

"Elizabeth. I want to talk. I know now what's most important to me. Call me. Please."

Teo turned his head slowly toward the now-silent answering

machine. The band of light from outside fell across its metal surface. The number "1" blinked red. His rough, long fingers, so used to the fearless taking of life, trembled as they moved slowly toward the machine. He stopped, glanced at the stairs to Elizabeth's room, and then pressed "erase." The number "1" changed to "0."

Teo was not proud of what he had done but knew he needed more time. He hadn't come all this way to be turned around and sent home without a chance. He stared out the window, past the streetlight, out into a clump of trees. Then he spotted something.

It was the orange glow of a cigarette being smoked. Someone was out there. Someone was spying on Elizabeth. Teo exhaled deeply. All hunters needed patience and restraint.

THIRTY-TWO

7:00 A.M.
Next day
Monday, March 5
Davis

Eᴌɪᴢᴀʙᴇᴛʜ ᴡᴀꜱ ʀɪᴅɪɴɢ on Apollo's back. The smooth motion was like flying, and she felt an indescribable sense of joy and freedom. But her father was standing on the bank of the slough, his hair parted into two braids, his copper face stern. He was pointing down. She didn't want to look; she wanted to keep riding the whale forever. Her father glared at her, his finger motioning toward the ground.

Now standing on the bank, she could see what he saw. A frog was struggling to walk in the mud. When she knelt and turned it over with her finger, she saw that it was missing its hind legs.

The clock radio blared as Elizabeth tried to shake herself from the dream. She lay back against her pillow and then looked over at the time: 7:03 A.M. She had to get the dissertation to the department and meet Connie at the slough.

Eᴌɪᴢᴀʙᴇᴛʜ ʜᴇᴀʀᴅ ᴛʜᴇ ʙʟᴏᴡ and looked quickly for Apollo, who had surfaced not far from the shore. Even from the levee she could see that his skin was beginning to slough off. "Apollo's skin is deteriorating," she said, turning to Connie.

A crop duster buzzed overhead. "Maybe he's sick from the spraying," Connie said.

"They're spreading it on food. How bad can it be?"

"I grew up in the Valley, remember? I've seen what it can do to people."

Elizabeth felt a wave of nausea but breathed through it and told herself she was just overtired. "More likely he's just sick because he's in fresh water."

As Apollo began to dive she could see the large cut on the whale's back. In the slough it was likely to get infected. She walked quickly, knowing that time was short. If he became septic, he could die in a matter of days.

THIS PLACE *is becoming a circus,* Coast Guard Lieutenant Isaac James thought as he looked out at the hundreds of people who were walking and standing along the levee road trying to catch a glimpse of the whale. They were missing work and school just to see the show. It was his job to shut the show down as quickly as possible.

He stood at the door of the white portable that had been delivered to serve as the mobile command unit. Lieutenant James wore a blue baseball cap with the words COAST GUARD written in gold across the front. His winter uniform, with its navy blue shirt and trousers, kept out the morning chill as his tie fluttered in the wind. He wore a blue name badge above his right breast pocket, and over his left hung several multicolored rows of ribbons for extraordinary service. Even on his large chest, they hardly fit. Everyone had told him that he was commander material, maybe even admiral. But for now he was just a lieutenant. Maybe they had thought his farm-boy face and dimpled chin would appeal in front of the camera, or that his relaxed attitude would work well with other agencies. He recalled the words of his boss: *This is your big break. Don't screw it up.*

Lieutenant James looked at his dive watch. He had five minutes until he was supposed to start the interagency briefing, but he had no idea where to begin. He had been sent over from Sector San Francisco to direct the rescue, but his commanding officer had neglected to tell them how exactly to help this whale. He smiled when he thought of the other order he had been given as he left home that morning. His twin six-year-old daughters had stood at the door in their dolphin pajamas, waving goodbye. "Go save the whale, Daddy!"

As if Lieutenant James was not under enough pressure, the lieutenant governor had made it his personal mission to make sure the whale rescue was successful. He had mobilized the ICS—Incident Command System—which was used in cases of natural disaster. They were treating the whale's entrapment like an oil spill. There were representatives from the Office of Emergency Services, Fish and Game, and Highway Patrol, but everyone would look to him, because the Coast Guard was supposed to be responsible for the water. *Boats, maybe, but not whales.*

Lieutenant James needed someone who knew something about whales. NOAA had a stranding network for marine mammals, but the closest coordinator was down in southern California. He had called the Marine Mammal Center, but their veterinarian was out of the country. He still did not have an animal person he could rely on.

People claiming to be experts were calling in with all sorts of crazy ideas, and it was hard to know whom to take seriously. A bigshot biologist from the university named Richard Skilling had shown up. At first Lieutenant James was happy to have a biologist, since everyone else was from enforcement, but there was something about this man that he did not trust. Maybe it was just horse sense—growing up on a farm had given him an instinct about animals and people. Or maybe it was the fact that Skilling came across as arrogant. Or maybe it was because the professor thought the whale was sick and likely to die, an outcome he was not willing to accept.

Lieutenant James grabbed the small metal handle of the flimsy door, ready to close it and begin the meeting. His black handheld crackled. "Lieutenant, there's a woman here says she's a marine biologist, specializes in humpback whale something. I told her you already had advisers from the university."

"It's okay. You can let her through."

From the doorway, he watched her walk toward him. *Could she be the help I need?* He looked down from the raised portable at her and introduced himself. "I'm Lieutenant James, incident commander. And you are?"

"Elizabeth McKay."

"And what do you know about whales?"

"I specialize in humpback whale communication."

"Communication, huh? You talk to whales?" His hopes for help were quickly disappearing.

"I study their songs and their social sounds."

"Really? Can you tell him to leave, Professor?"

"Afraid not, but I discovered something that might help your rescue operation."

"And what's that?" Lieutenant James said, expecting to hear yet another well-meaning but totally useless suggestion on how to get a forty-ton whale back out to the ocean.

"I've deciphered a distress call, one that I've recorded in other parts of the world. Perhaps if we understood why he's in distress, we could get him to leave."

Lieutenant James decided he liked this woman and her confidence, but most of all, she had said the magic word. The Coast Guard was all about responding to distress calls.

"Professor McKay, why don't you come inside?"

THIRTY-THREE

AT ONE END of the portable, representatives from what looked to Elizabeth like different law enforcement agencies crowded around a table. In the corner, black sunglasses pushed back on his head, was Skilling, whose slight scowl revealed that he was not particularly pleased to see her. "Shouldn't you be working on your dissertation?" he said.

"It's on your desk."

Skilling looked taken aback, as if he had not really expected Elizabeth to be able to finish. He nodded, and the corners of his mouth turned down like those of a grouper.

"So," Lieutenant James asked, "what are we going to do to get this whale out?"

Skilling was the first to speak. "Officers, this whale is sick and liable to die any day. After careful deliberation with my colleagues, we have come to the conclusion that most probably this whale has eaten sardines and anchovies with a high concentration of domoic acid. This happens from HABs—harmful algae blooms—and has most likely damaged its hippocampus. The navigational system in its brain is no longer functioning, and the condition is probably incurable. Once my team and I dissect the whale, we will be able to confirm this finding, but the only humane decision is to euthanize it."

Kill it? Elizabeth thought, shocked at the idea. How could Skilling be so sure about his diagnosis, not to mention his prognosis that the whale could not be saved? Other whales had been rescued from the Sacramento River before. This was not the first whale to have lost its way and become entrapped in the delta. What was behind Skilling's eagerness to kill Apollo? But before she could say anything, a large man in a khaki shirt and green pants spoke.

"Well, if it's sick, we should put it out of its misery. At Fish and Game we often have to shoot deer and even bears that are wounded."

"This is not a deer or a bear," Elizabeth said, unable to stop herself.

A highway patrolman was clearly entertained by the whole discussion. "You're going to kill this whale in front of that crowd? You want a riot on your hands?"

"Gentlemen, I don't think we are in a position to make that decision," Lieutenant James said. "The lieutenant governor is going to be here in a few hours, and he wants to know how we are going to save this whale, not kill it. Whale experts, what are our options?"

"In 1985," Elizabeth said, "Humphrey, another humpback, was lured out of a slough like this one by playing feeding calls."

"It's not clear whether it was the feeding calls that made any difference," Skilling said. "I'd recommend playing the sounds of killer whales. That might scare the whale, but I think you're wasting your time."

"Feeding calls and killer whale sounds?" Lieutenant James said. "Any objections? Good, I'll inform the lieutenant governor—" The sound of one of the television helicopters rattled overhead. "And then we need to brief the media. Can we begin the operation at 1300, Professors?" Skilling looked slightly surprised at Elizabeth's being addressed as a professor. Elizabeth was also embarrassed by this jump in rank, but she said nothing, knowing that this new status might give her the credibility she needed to help save Apollo. "1300?" Lieutenant James repeated eagerly.

Both Skilling and Elizabeth nodded, although neither of them knew how they were going to get the equipment and the sound files there in time.

THIRTY-FOUR

1:00 P.M.

ELIZABETH AND LIEUTENANT JAMES stood in the bow of the rigid-hulled inflatable boat. On the side of the bright orange buoyancy tube, U.S. COAST GUARD was written in large white letters. The low winter sun glinted off the steel cabin and the black machine gun mounted in the bow. The presence of the weapon made Elizabeth uncomfortable, but Lieutenant James acted like it was not even there. The late-winter wind was blowing cold across the delta, sneaking up the legs of her jeans and under her fleece jacket.

Skilling had returned to the office to read her dissertation and attend the department meeting, but he had e-mailed the killer whale sound files to her. Elizabeth broke out in a sweat, realizing that they were reading her work. She took comfort in the fact that it could be weeks before they voted on whether to approve it.

The cold breeze caught the sweat on her neck and made her shiver. She tried to focus on the equipment in front of her. Two strong Coast Guard seamen were lowering a heavy steel navy loudspeaker into the water. The skeletal frame, like a box with no sides, surrounded the speaker that hung suspended in the center. Once it was tied off and floating a few feet below the surface, everything was in place. Elizabeth held the DAT machine in her hand.

Apollo surfaced twenty feet from the boat, allowing Elizabeth to see the wound on his back more closely. The skin was ripped open, exposing white blubber and the pink muscle beneath. It was a deep cut, and the laceration looked serrated, perhaps from the teeth of a killer whale or a boat strike. Seeing the injury up close renewed her sense of urgency to help this whale get back to the ocean.

"Ready?" Lieutenant James asked.

"I guess so," Elizabeth said as she played the tape.

"Steer us toward the bridge," the lieutenant commanded the coxswain standing at the wheel in the cabin.

They could not see Apollo in the murky water and waited for him to surface. She put on her headphones and could hear through the hydrophone that the feeding call was pumping out into the water loudly. It sounded like the wailing siren from an emergency vehicle—*AHhh-ooOO*—first falling and then rising.

After several minutes, she raised the volume, but still nothing.

Ten very long minutes passed, and finally, Apollo surfaced at the other end of the slough. Elizabeth was disappointed but not surprised. When this rescue technique had been tried two decades earlier with Humphrey, he had come to the boat immediately. But the feeding sounds had had an opposite effect on a subsequent pair of whales, Dawn and Delta. Something in the pit of her stomach had told her that this time it was not going to work.

"Try the killer whale sounds," Lieutenant James commanded. "Bring the boat back behind the whale, and let's see if we can herd him down the slough."

"Lieutenant, I really would not recommend playing predatory sounds to a forty-ton whale in an enclosed space," Elizabeth said.

"Do we have another choice?"

Elizabeth paused. She wasn't sure whether to say what she was thinking.

"Do we have another choice, Professor?"

She winced. "Just call me Elizabeth."

"Okay, do we have a choice, Elizabeth?"

"Last night I recorded two social sounds in the song—"

"That was you last night?"

Elizabeth swallowed and continued, deciding not to address the various laws she had broken. "One sound for distress and the other a mother-calf contact call."

"I thought this was a bull."

"It is."

"Unless a lot has changed in the animal world since I left the farm, bulls don't have calves."

"They don't."

"Then what are you suggesting?"

"I'm not suggesting anything. I'm exploring the possibility that this whale is trying to communica—"

"With us?"

"No, not with us, with other whales. We just happen to be lucky enough to overhear it." The whale's song started to vibrate the steel hull of the inflatable.

"Why would it come here to communicate with other whales?" Lieutenant James spoke slowly, trying to follow what she was saying.

"Perhaps it *is* lost, or it could have been chased into the bay by killer whales. We don't really know."

"You really believe this whale is saying something?"

"I'm a scientist, Lieutenant. I don't believe anything. I formulate research questions, and then I test them."

"Such as?"

"Why are whales all around the world repeating this same song? Why are social sounds embedded in the song? What do these social sounds mean?"

"These are all very interesting scientific questions, Professor, but what does this have to do with rescuing this whale?"

"Apollo."

"Excuse me?"

"His name is Apollo. I found his tailprint in the fluke registry."

Lieutenant James looked taken aback to be on a first-name basis with the whale. "Well, then, how does this help us to rescue Apollo?"

"If this whale is making some kind of a distress call, maybe we can find some way to calm it and get it to leave."

Lieutenant James was shaking his head doubtfully.

Elizabeth urged, "Give me one week. Get me a letter of authorization so I don't have to do my research in the middle of the night, and I'll find you a way to get this whale out." Or at least she hoped she would.

Lieutenant James's cell phone rang. When he looked at the caller ID, he stood up straighter before answering. "Yes, sir . . . I understand perfectly, sir. We will have this resolved as quickly as possible. I will brief you within the hour." He hung up and turned to Elizabeth. "Play the killer whales."

Elizabeth shook her head and played the file. She listened through the hydrophone at the high-pitched screeches and gunshot-like popping sounds. She had heard that the concussion of these sounds was like being beaten with a club.

Apollo moved so quickly that the bow wave swamped the small orange boat and heaved it sideways. Elizabeth dropped the recorder and fell backward into the icy water.

She came to the surface and gasped for air as she saw Apollo slashing at the boat with his giant tail. It was crashing down like a mallet and sending white boiling spray in all directions. She could hear the killer whale sounds, felt them hit against her body. If only she'd had a chance to turn off the player!

Then the sounds stopped, and so did Apollo's attack against the boat. Lieutenant James must have hit the right button.

THIRTY-FIVE

*T*HE SOUNDS OF FEEDING *echoed through Apollo—his stomach rumbling with a season's starvation—his blubber stores as thin as they had ever been—*

Apollo remembered the feasting of the cold summer waters where the rustling of krill was calling with life—he and the others drawing bubbles around the shoal of tiny crustaceans—circling—circling—creating the net—closer and closer—and when all knew that the feast was ready—erupting upward as one—mouths wide open—an explosion of spray—filling—closing—straining—devouring—

But there were no krill in these narrows—their salty swarms were absent in this lifeless water—

The sounds changed—no longer of kin—they were now of killers! He could hear the sharp-edged pitch of their frenzied screams—the pulses like teeth once again striking his skin—

The wound was still fresh on his back—the raw edges of skin rubbing—

He charged toward the sound and began slashing his tail in defense—but there were no killers in the water—just the slow drone of a boat—

And then he saw it suspended in the water—struggling to reach the surface—he searched for an eye but could not find one—then drew the creature close with his flipper—tucking it against his body—then rolling to lift it onto his belly—

THIRTY-SIX

ELIZABETH FELT HER BODY pushed over and up. The slough was parting, and the brown water began to spill away from her. She couldn't believe it. She was on all fours, crouching on the belly of the whale.

Above her Elizabeth saw the towering pectoral fins. The massive four-hundred-pound flippers could easily crush her, but she was being held as gently as a calf cradled by its mother. After she had recovered from the shock and realized that she was not dreaming, she heard cheering. It was coming from the spectators lining the banks.

Elizabeth smiled a nervous half-smile, knowing that her colleagues and the Coast Guard might not be as impressed. While riding on whales was acceptable at marine parks, she knew it was considered interfering with a wild whale by researchers and, even more importantly, by law enforcement. She looked down at her hands, and what she saw made her heart sink.

The whale's skin was not only blistering and sloughing off, but there were raised white plaques, like mold on cheese, and these lumps were already starting to ooze. She also saw white lesions and more superficial pockmarks. She wondered whether all of this could have happened so quickly, just from the fresh water.

The cheering had not stopped. Elizabeth raised her hand modestly to acknowledge the crowd and let them know she was all right. They cheered all the louder. She quickly slipped into the water to swim back to the boat.

The whale swam toward her, and just above the surface she saw his gray-brown eye. It caused her to tremble even more than the freezing water.

Through the clouding lens she recognized a light she had seen in other whales she had studied. It was not just perceptiveness or intelligence. It was the familiarity of something long forgotten, which she could feel but had never been able to give voice to.

Several large, blue-suited Coast Guard seamen helped Elizabeth over the orange gunwale of the boat. Water poured off her soaked clothes. As they wrapped a rough wool blanket around her, she felt it scrape against her neck. She could feel her body's heat captured by the wool and was grateful for the warmth. Someone handed her a cup of coffee from a thermos. She smiled as she smelled its bitter aroma, and everything else seemed to disappear for a moment in a cloud of steam.

Lieutenant James came up to her. "They've agreed to make you a co-investigator on the permit for the Marine Mammal Center. You got your week."

"And then what?"

"Let's hope it doesn't come to that."

WHEN ELIZABETH reached shore, the television film crews attacked her.

"Can you really talk to the whale?"

"Are you like Dr. Dolittle?"

"What's wrong with it?"

"I don't know," she said, remembering her mistake the day before.

"Is the whale sick?" a reporter asked as the crop duster flew overhead.

"I'm not sure, but I think we need to institute a no-fly zone to avoid harming it any more."

"What did you see when you were on the whale?"

"His skin is blistering—he's not healthy."

"What do you think is making the whale sick?"

"I don't know," she said, remembering Connie's words, "but the crop dusting can't be good for him. I would strongly encourage the farmers in this area to stop spraying until the whale is safely back in the ocean."

"So how did it feel to be on the belly of a whale?"

Elizabeth smiled. "I guess it's better than being *in* the belly of a whale."

Everyone laughed as she excused herself. Elizabeth squeezed the water out of her braid. She was grateful to have her hair braided, or she would have looked even more like a wet rat on television. She wondered if Frank would see the program, and she hoped she had looked at least halfway decent.

"Excuse me, Ms. McKay . . ."

Elizabeth turned around. Bruce Wood, a reporter from the *Sacramento Times,* handed her his card with a wry smile. "I'd like to do a story about you and the whales you talk to."

"Why don't you write an article on the effects of crop dusting?"

"Crop dusting is not news in the Central Valley, but whales and the women who love them will be of interest to our readers."

"I'll keep it in mind," Elizabeth said as she met up with Connie, who had a tiny video camcorder in her hand. It looked like something an international spy might use.

"Home movies of the great Dr. Elizabeth Dolittle. You can't trust the news to get the story right." Connie handed Elizabeth a slip of paper. "I got you the name and number of someone who might be able to help stop the spraying. He's the head of the Valley Chamber of Commerce. He'll know who's responsible."

"Why me? You're the activist."

"He's much more likely to take a call from a celebrity."

"What are you talking about?" Elizabeth said testily, pulling the wool blanket more tightly around her. They crossed the police tape surrounding Incident Command and moved through the crowd of people still lining the shore of the levee.

Before Connie could answer, people began to recognize Elizabeth as the woman they had just seen on the whale. They moved apart to make way for her, staring silently. Elizabeth felt strange, as if she had returned from an alien world. Embarrassment flushed through her body like a red rash. She heard someone clap and then others joined in, and soon the whole crowd was applauding. It continued as Elizabeth walked down the levee. What she had done to deserve the applause, she wasn't sure. What she meant to these people, she didn't know. But she had given them something they longed for, and they were clearly deeply grateful.

THIRTY-SEVEN

4:00 P.M.
Davis

"**D**ON'T YOU KNOW smoking bad for your health?" Teo pressed his filleting knife to Nilsen's neck and pushed his chest firmly against the other man's back. It had been easy to recognize Nilsen from the island—he was, after all, the one who had told Teo about the whales. He had also been the one who had cut a member of Teo's crew in a bar fight. "Tell me why you spying on Liza before I slit your throat and watch the smoke come out."

Nilsen exhaled and said calmly, "You got this wrong."

"Have I now?"

"We've got twenty-five thousand dollars for that package you brought from the island."

"That a lot of money for a couple kilos of whale meat." Teo was having fun with the man, but he was also thinking fast about why they were willing to part with so much cash.

"The offer is for twenty-five thousand *U.S.* dollars," Nilsen said, still surprisingly relaxed for someone whose throat could be slit at any moment. Teo considered the offer. He could do a lot with that kind of money, but what kind of a bargain was he making with the devil? He knew Nilsen worked for the Japanese, who were trying to bring back commercial whaling. He did not object to it— they were fishermen, just like him—but they'd wipe out the whales in a few seasons. Then there'd be no more catching days, not for anyone.

Teo thought about the package in Elizabeth's freezer. He'd need to move it to keep it—and Elizabeth—safe.

"Well, I got an offer for you. Get the hell out of here and never come back. Then I won't slit your throat. That's *my* final offer."

THIRTY-EIGHT

5:00 P.M.
Liberty Slough

Elizabeth was feeling queasy again as she got into the car. Connie had decided to stay with the whale and coordinate the protesters, who still held signs demanding an end to Japanese "scientific" whaling and to sonar testing.

It was highly unlikely that the crop dusting could have caused her to feel ill so quickly, particularly as it was not affecting the rest of the crowd in the same way. Still, she thought it best to minimize the stress on the whale, whether from pesticides or the noise of the airplane. She would talk to Lieutenant James about the no-fly zone, but she decided to try the number Connie had given her.

Out of her bag she pulled her old silver cell phone and flipped it open. She dialed the number. As it rang, she drove out of the field where her car and now several hundred others were parked.

"Valley Chamber of Commerce. Can I help you?" The receptionist's warm voice allowed Elizabeth's shoulders to relax.

"George Conley, please."

"Who may I tell him is calling?"

"My name is Elizabeth McKay."

"Will he know what this is about?"

"I'm one of the researchers working with the whale trapped in the slough."

After a short delay, a man with a deep voice said, "This is George

Conley. And you must be the whale whisperer? I just saw you on top of the whale."

"You did?"

"I've been watching everything on the webcam—it's not every day we have a whale visiting the Valley."

"Well, that's why I'm calling. I'd like your help getting the farms near the slough to stop spraying until the whale leaves."

"Spraying crops is a highly time-sensitive operation."

"It might just be a week or two."

"I wish I could help you, Ms. McKay, but those fields around the slough are owned by G&G Foods, one of the largest agribusinesses in the world. If they don't spray now, they could lose hundreds of thousands of dollars to pests, and then the farmworkers won't have crops to pick. Do you want me to ask them to put people out of work? How would those workers feed their children?"

The guy sure had a way of making a request sound heartless and unreasonable.

"The whale might be sick and—"

"Businesses can't stop because a whale decided to pay us a visit."

"We think the water in the slough might—"

"Ms. McKay, our members are good businesses. That agribusiness grows food for families to eat. The oil refinery makes gasoline for families to drive their cars. The chemical factory makes plastics for products like baby bottles. These businesses give people what they need."

"I have no doubt, Mr. Conley. We're just concerned about controlling any chemical exposure that the whale might be experiencing."

"Ms. McKay, all of the companies in our area obey strict federal and state regulations. Scientific research has shown time and time again that the pesticides the agribusinesses use are safe—unless, of course, you're a pest. So please, if you know what's good for you and everyone else . . . don't start being a pest."

There was something strangely defensive and even threatening in his rant, but Elizabeth had to get off the phone as a wave of nausea rolled through her body. "Thank you for your time, Mr. Conley." At a stop sign, she took several deep breaths to prevent herself from vomiting. She jumped at the foghorn blast of an eighteen-wheeler waiting impatiently behind her, and looked up to see its big steel grille and shiny glass headlights in her rearview mirror. She accelerated quickly. Elizabeth was out in the middle of miles of agricultural land, and the winter sun had already fallen below the horizon. Perhaps the tone of the phone call had shaken her more than she realized.

He swallowed another antacid. More heartburn.

"ESC."

"It's George Conley. I need to speak with Ms. Hanson right away."

"One moment, please."

"George, so good to hear from you." Amanda Hanson spoke in a voice that was so smooth and calm that it always made him nervous. He imagined her holding the receiver with her perfectly manicured red nails. Perhaps it was just that he knew her reputation from the business and philanthropy circles in which they traveled, but she made him think of a black widow spider. From what he had heard, she wove her intrigues as if she had eight legs, and she was apparently not unwilling to eat her mates—or anyone else who got in her way.

"I'm very sorry to bother you, Ms. Hanson, but I thought you might want to know that Elizabeth McKay, that whale whisperer, just called me. She's poking around the slough and talking to the media. We could have a problem with that whale."

"Really? With the whale?" Her voice was cool and unflustered, as usual.

"That scientist is worried about crop dusting hurting the whale, but she could find out that there are greater dangers out there than a few fields of tomatoes."

"Thank you for calling, George. We will certainly look into the problem."

THIRTY-NINE

5:30 P.M.

As soon as Connie saw the caller ID on her cell phone, her heart started pounding. She needed privacy and hurried some distance away from the protesters.

"Tano's nervous." The Internet call from Japan was clipped, forcing Connie to press the phone closer to her ear. She looked at her watch—it was 10:30 A.M. Tokyo time. Jake and Tano were no doubt making final preparations.

"Of course he's nervous. It's dangerous," Connie whispered forcefully into the phone. "All actions are dangerous, especially one like this." She could tell there was something else behind Jake's call.

Tano was the nicest person Connie had ever met: sincere and earnest and polite. He was not like so many of the activists, who were angry at the world, wounded by people, and seeking refuge in their love of animals. Tano was the future of the anti-whaling movement in Japan. He had gone out on a whale watch with his biology class at university, fallen in love with the whales, and now wanted to save them. He also happened to have fallen in love with Connie. She knew it would never work and that love was only a distraction from the war they were fighting. It had already complicated her relationship with Jake.

"I am worried about Tano," Jake said.

"Do you think he can be trusted tonight?"

"I think so. He's committed, just nervous. We both are." Jake was fishing. "You should be here with us."

"I am there with you."

"I don't understand why you need a Ph.D. You already know everything you need to lead this organization."

"If we are ever going to make a real difference, I need to know the science." It was true, but she had also come back to help her parents, who had been farmers in the Valley and were now dying from respiratory illnesses.

"Whatever you say, *Dr.* Kato . . . Are you worried about us?"

"Of course I'm worried about you."

"Then it's not over."

Why the hell do I have to deal with my troops falling for me? "It's over, Jake."

"You've met someone?"

"No."

"It's not over until you sleep with someone else. Not until you've got the smell of someone else on your skin," Jake said. Connie regretted her recent night with Skilling. She remembered how she had showered for an hour in scalding-hot water to try to get his scent off her body. She knew Jake would go ballistic if he knew that another man had slept with his girlfriend—even his ex-girlfriend. She had wanted to tell Elizabeth but was embarrassed and hadn't yet worked up the courage.

"Stay focused, Jake. Where's Tano?"

"He just walked in."

"Let me speak to him."

"He can hear you."

"Do me proud, Tano. Do your father proud."

Tano's father, Koji Ito, worked for the whaling industry. They had not spoken since Tano abandoned his plans to work for the whaling fleet.

"You sure tonight is a good idea, Connie?"

"The timing is perfect—right before the vote on commercial whaling and with people worrying about Apollo. It has to be now."

"Yeah, you're right," Jake said, trying to encourage his comrade in arms. "Tell your friend Elizabeth that she's a big hero over here. She's really pissed off the Japanese Cetology Research Center."

"How do you know?"

"Remember the back door that Yoshi hacked into their intranet? Well, he's been reading their e-mail. Seems she's a real publicity nightmare for them."

"Their nightmare is just starting. You got the files I sent?"

"Yes."

"Be careful."

"Tell Tano and me you love us," Jake said with nervous laughter. "Give us something to live for."

"Love is not the only thing to live for," Connie snapped. Then she was sorry she'd said it. Why was it so much easier for her to hate than to love? "Be safe tonight," she added quickly.

FORTY

ELIZABETH PUSHED through the glass doors of Haring Hall. Her nausea had subsided. She wanted to hear—and at the same time did not want to hear—whether her committee had started reading, although she doubted it. Skilling often left early and would be long gone. The thought was a source of relief as she opened the wooden door to the department. She could focus on the recordings and hopefully come up with something that might help Lieutenant James save Apollo.

She turned on the lights and wondered if she had stepped into the wrong office. Her desktop computer and sound equipment were missing. The modular desk where she worked was empty—even her papers and coffee cup were gone.

"I'm glad you're here. I wanted to tell you myself."

She spun around and was facing Skilling. "What happened to my computer . . . and my data?"

"The committee reviewed your dissertation all morning and announced their decision at the department meeting this afternoon."

"Already? What was your decision?"

"I'm afraid the committee thought your conclusions were unsubstantiated, and they decided not to approve your dissertation."

"So you want me to revise it?"

"The department voted to terminate your candidacy, Elizabeth, effective immediately."

"You're kicking me out?"

"Not me. The department."

"Is this personal? Because I challenged you at the slough?"

"Elizabeth, this has nothing to do with me. I have always had your best interests at heart."

"I don't get it. Tell me what's wrong and I'll revise it. I just need a few more days."

"The committee felt that six years was more than enough time. It may take a few weeks for the dean's office to notify you of the decision, but I didn't want you to have to hear it from them."

"But, Dr. Skilling, you're the head of the committee. Didn't you support me?"

"I did the best I could, Elizabeth."

"You voted for me, didn't you?"

Skilling looked down.

Elizabeth felt as if the floor had dropped out from under her. "I thought you were on my side. You're my adviser."

"I told you not to throw away your career on worthless research. Neither you nor I nor anyone else is going to be able to understand what this whale or any other is saying, because whales aren't 'saying' anything."

Elizabeth was sweating but persisted. "But the social sounds in the song—"

"Prove nothing."

Elizabeth began to feel dizzy, and her mouth was dry. She tried to swallow. She looked away from Skilling's eyes, focusing instead on his pressed white shirt.

Skilling put his hand on Elizabeth's shoulder and stared at her.

"Animals just respond instinctively. Killing. Mating . . ." His hand rested a little too long on her shoulder as he tilted his head to the side and gazed into her eyes. "I know this has been a hard time for you, Elizabeth, but I'm here for you." A whiff of Skilling's musky cologne triggered her gag reflex. As she opened her mouth to speak, the bile rose up in her throat.

FORTY-ONE

8:00 P.M.

"**A**ND THEN I threw up all over him," Elizabeth said. She propped herself up in bed as Connie sat by her side, cackling a sinister, delighted laugh.

Elizabeth couldn't help chuckling, despite the fact that she felt sick and depressed. "Maybe Skilling's right. What if I *have* wasted my career?"

"How can you say that? You are about to make one of the biggest scientific breakthroughs of our generation."

"Thanks, Connie, for trying to cheer me up."

"Don't 'Thanks, Connie' me. I'm not trying to cheer you up. Don't you realize what your work means?"

Elizabeth looked down.

"You don't, do you? Well, let me tell you." Connie stood up, clearly moved by what she was about to say. "For thousands of years we've separated ourselves from all other animals and denied their intelligence—using and destroying them as we see fit. If you're right, it means that we were wrong. It means maybe, if we start listening to them, we can finally find our way back to living in harmony with the rest of life. That's what it means."

"You're a good friend, Connie."

"No, I'm not," Connie said, looking at her watch. She sat back down on the bed next to Elizabeth. "I've been a good enemy, but never really a good friend."

"What are you talking about? You're a great friend."

"Jake and Tano are risking their lives tonight. I should be with them. I should have—"

Before Connie could finish, there was a knock at the door, and Teo walked in carrying a tray of food. "Some fish broth. Make you healthy and strong."

"Thanks, Teo, and thanks for helping me last night," Elizabeth said.

Teo smiled and then turned quietly to go. At the door, he said, "Liza, if is all right with you, I might stay a few more days, just for keep an eye on things."

"I'll be fine, Teo."

"Elizabeth, you don't need to do it all by yourself," Connie said. "Until Frank comes back, it isn't a bad idea for Teo to stick around."

"If is all right with you, Liza," Teo repeated.

"Okay, Teo, maybe a few more days."

Teo left and Connie watched him go. *"Liza?"*

"That's what he used to call me."

"You never told me about him."

"It was a long time ago . . . before I met Frank."

"He came all the way from the Caribbean? You sure there's nothing boiling besides the soup?"

"I'm married."

Connie's raised eyebrows showed that she was surprised by the forcefulness of the response. "I didn't say you weren't."

"What if Frank doesn't come back?" Elizabeth asked Connie.

"He'll come back. He's just confused. Now eat something. It'll be good for you," Connie said, offering her the bowl.

Elizabeth smelled the fishy broth. "I can't." She got up to go to the bathroom.

"Well, if you don't want the fish soup, I might taste it myself. I think I might like island cooking."

"Help yourself," Elizabeth said as she walked into the bathroom. She smiled at the thought of the whale activist and the whaler.

TEO WALKED INTO the kitchen to wash the smell of fish off his hands. Something glittered on the floor under the refrigerator.

He stooped down and fished it out. It was a diamond ring—Elizabeth's. He picked it up carefully and was about to head upstairs. The ring would cheer Elizabeth up, he was sure of it, but then he thought again. Perhaps he might hold on to it a little longer, until it was clear that Frank really was coming back. Maybe there was still a chance for him.

THROUGH THE BATHROOM DOOR, Elizabeth called to Connie, "I've got to get back to Apollo. I only have six days left, and he might not last much longer." Elizabeth leaned on the sink. She looked at herself in the mirror . . . she was pale . . . her limbs felt heavy . . . and then everything went black.

FORTY-TWO

10:15 P.M.
Sacramento

WHEN ELIZABETH came around, she felt the rough white sheets under her hands and the plastic mattress beneath. Fluorescent lights filled the room with an unnatural white glow. She was tilted up in bed with an IV drip in her left arm. Hospital monitors flashed and beeped all around her, confirming the fact that she was alive. All she remembered was looking in the mirror and then being in Connie's car, battling waves of nausea each time she tried to sit up. *What is wrong with me?* she wondered. She turned her head to the side and saw Connie sitting next to her.

"What happened?" Her own voice seemed distant and hollow in her throat.

"You passed out in your bathroom. You woke up, but you've been pretty out of it ever since. They're doing some bloodwork."

"Where are we?" Elizabeth asked anxiously.

"At the hospital."

"Which hospital?"

"The Medical Center."

"Get me out of here," Elizabeth said, trying to get up.

"How are you feeling?" Frank stood by the curtain.

"I should go," Connie said.

"Are you okay?" Frank asked again.

"Yeah, I guess I'm just working a little too hard. You remember, that was the problem you thought was incurable."

Frank pretended to ignore her comment. "Did you get my call? You never—"

"What call?"

Frank touched Elizabeth's wrist gently and then took her pulse. "You took off your ring."

Before she could tell Frank that she had lost it in the house, David Chin, one of the ER doctors, and Tom Neumann walked into the room. Elizabeth knew both of them as colleagues and friends of Frank's, and she felt uncomfortable being their patient.

"How is everyone doing?" asked Dr. Chin. Frank and Elizabeth looked at him blankly without speaking. "Well, okay then," he said. "Let's get down to it. It doesn't seem like there is anything seriously wrong. Just dehydration."

Elizabeth's shoulders relaxed. Maybe she hadn't been poisoned at the slough.

"The bloodwork also showed something else," Tom said, unable to contain himself.

"Maybe we should leave you with the test results," Dr. Chin said, handing the chart to Frank. Dr. Chin and Tom left the room, both unable to suppress their smiles.

Frank quickly flipped open the chart. "Oh, my God."

"What's wrong?" Elizabeth asked.

Frank handed her the chart. She scanned the page and she saw the words: "Pregnancy test: positive."

"I'm pregnant?" Elizabeth said, not quite believing it. Thoughts flashed through her mind with staggering speed. *My marriage may be over. I've just been kicked out of graduate school. I have no way to support a child.*

"You're pregnant," Frank said again, perhaps trying to convince himself.

"What are we going to do?" Elizabeth said, biting her lip. Staring into Frank's face, she felt a vulnerability she had never before experienced.

Frank moved toward Elizabeth, put down the metal railing of the hospital bed, and sat beside her. His loving smile made her eyes water. "What do you want to do?" he said.

Tears spilled over from Elizabeth's eyes. She quickly tried to wipe them away. "I want this baby . . . but I want to have it with you."

Frank took Elizabeth's hand and squeezed it.

"Will you come home?" Elizabeth asked.

FORTY-THREE

Liberty Slough

THE TINTED WINDOW lowered silently into the rear door of the black town car, revealing a woman whom he had talked to only on the telephone. By the light inside the car, he could see that Amanda Hanson was older than he had imagined from her smooth, youthful voice. He could tell that her auburn hair was dyed to hide the gray, and even a face-lift or two could not hide fifty or more years of gravity.

"It's an honor," she said, looking up at him.

"Ms. Hanson, the honor is mine." His hands were buried in the pockets of his field coat to keep them warm, and his raised shoulders shielded his neck against the wind that encircled them.

"This whole thing," the woman said, waving to the slough where Apollo still lingered, "is getting very awkward. Having all this attention here is making my clients very uncomfortable."

"I have the situation under control. This will be over within a week or sooner."

"Ms. McKay," the woman continued, "has the entire world waiting for her to talk with that whale."

"You don't have to worry about her, and this whale will be put out of its misery very soon. My friends have arranged for the necessary equipment. It should be here within a few days."

"I'm glad to hear it. We've had our people inside speak to the lieutenant governor about the situation, and I think he understands our concerns."

"Good, this will all be over shortly."

"Don't disappoint us, and we won't disappoint you."

The window rose smoothly. Then the car drove off, and he was left in the empty field, dust devils spinning around him.

FORTY-FOUR

10:35 P.M.
Sacramento

"**W**HAT'S GOING ON?" Connie asked as she stepped back into the room.

"I'm pregnant," Elizabeth said. "And Frank's coming home."

"You're pregnant? You're pregnant!" Connie shouted.

Elizabeth was surprised by Connie's enthusiasm. She was the last person on the planet Elizabeth thought would get excited about a baby.

"How have you been feeling so far?" Tom asked, wheeling an ultrasound over.

"Just some nausea . . . and vomiting." Elizabeth smiled at Connie.

"I'm afraid that's normal. Any bleeding?"

"I guess a little, about a week ago. I don't have regular periods."

"I don't want to be overprotective," Frank cut in, "but don't you think it's probably not the best idea to swim with a forty-ton whale at the moment?"

"I want to keep you overnight, but I'm not overly worried," Tom said as Frank's eyes narrowed and his lips pursed. "Since the bleeding has stopped, it's probably fine. Besides, you have a whale to save."

Frank let out a sigh in exasperation.

Tom pretended to ignore him. "Now, let's have a look at little Frank or little Elizabeth."

On the 3-D ultrasound, the nine-week-old fetus looked like a whole person, only in miniature. She could see its rapidly beating heart. As they rubbed the sonogram wand through the gel on her belly to get a better look, the baby's face turned and seemed to gaze at them through the ghost eyes in its skull. Elizabeth was not prepared for the flood of affection she felt for this person she had not even known she was carrying. She stared at the screen, in awe of the new life floating inside her, this tiny and most precious of sea creatures.

FORTY-FIVE

Two hours later
Rush hour
Tokyo, Japan

THE HACHIKO CROSSING in the famously crowded Shibuya center had been chosen strategically. The NHK Broadcasting Center, Japan's public broadcaster, was not far away, and with a little luck, the action would be broadcast by satellite all over Japan and on Japanese-language television around the world.

The entire facade of the twenty-story building was covered with 1.5 million computer-controlled LED screens. As Jake and Tano pulled up, the screens were displaying a video advertisement of a blond model dressed in black, strutting down a fashion runway. This image dissolved into a pristine grove of blooming *sakura,* Japanese flowering cherry trees, which was then replaced by the logo of the Environmental Stewardship Consortium and the words in both Japanese and English: OUR RESOURCES, OUR FUTURE. Jake noticed that his breathing was shallow. He tried to deepen his breath to relax, to stay in the present moment.

The building also was not far from the Meiji Shrine in Yoyogi Park, where Jake had spent many days trying to meditate under a ginkgo tree. Jake loved Shinto shrines and had admired Japanese culture ever since he had studied aikido as a short and much-picked-on high school student. He had become fascinated with the figure of the samurai and the code of Bushido, which demanded that one face one's death with honor. Jake had tried to face the world without fear, as a samurai would. In college, he had majored in Japanese and had tried to condition his mind as rigorously as the Zen masters demanded. Yet he was never very successful at meditating. Eventually, he had discovered a shortcut to enlightenment that allowed him to face and conquer all of his fears. Tonight he hoped to revisit his enlightenment.

In their impossibly small car, Jake and Tano pulled into the garage. Disguised in white janitorial jumpsuits, they made their way from the parking garage to the very heart of this building-turned-billboard.

They knew where the screens' control room was located, thanks to the blueprint of the building they'd gotten from the archives of the city-planning department. Yoshi, the organization's computer genius, had interviewed for a job there and discovered that the room was unmanned after 6:00 P.M.

Yoshi had also hacked into the system, found a master list of the building's entrance codes, and written the program they would need to control the massive screen display. But Yoshi could not get the program past the firewall. Jake and Tano needed to get into the room itself to install the program.

Inside the room, Jake and Tano unzipped their white jumpsuits, revealing cold-weather jackets and pants. Tano was right—they looked more like mountain climbers than eco-activists. Jake opened a small laptop and connected the cable using the diagram Yoshi had prepared. He glanced at the door, where they had placed a bundle of thin red cylinders wrapped with black duct tape.

"Jake, you afraid?" Tano asked from over his shoulder.

Jake glanced up to see sweat running down Tano's face. He knew it was not from the heat. Tano's black glasses were fogging up. "I'm never afraid when I know I'm doing the right thing," Jake said, his fingers hovering over the keyboard. "We're ready. Are you?"

Tano nodded.

Jake pressed "enter."

On the monitors, they could see the advertisement go black as an image of humpback whales replaced it. A mother, her baby, and a male escort swam together underwater, a video clip that Connie had "borrowed" from her friend Elizabeth. The film switched to footage of the Japanese whaling fleet, exploding harpoons, and Japanese whale meat products. The film ended with footage of Elizabeth on Apollo's stomach and the words in Japanese and English: CAN WE SAVE THEM? CAN WE SAVE OURSELVES?

Tano placed the call to the television station. As the clip played again, they knew they should go. It would not be long now.

They locked the door and then squeezed epoxy glue into the keyhole. They fastened the red-and-black bundle to the door handle and then lit the fuses. Although they were harmless flares, the noise and light they gave off might scare away the guards for an additional thirty minutes. Plan A required them to get back to the car and leave before they were discovered. Down the hall, Jake saw a small group of guards racing toward them.

"In here," Jake said, trying to retrace their steps back down the stairs, but there were more police coming up the stairwell—these were officers from the *koban* police boxes. There was no choice but to head up: Plan B. This was the moment that Jake had hoped for and Tano had dreaded.

Jake pushed open the door to the roof, Tano not far behind, and the police not far behind him. Sweat made Jake's shirt stick to his back as he and Tano raced for the corner ledge. As they pulled themselves up onto the foot-wide barrier, Jake could see the neon lights of Shibuya center all around him, even above him, eerily reflecting off the low-hanging clouds.

The police stopped when they saw Jake and Tano balancing on the ledge. They were probably worried that the "terrorists" might be content to take their own lives.

Jake looked down and saw that an enormous crowd had gathered to watch the images of the whales and whaling. He smiled. The first part of their mission had succeeded.

The cold winter wind blew around them, but it was a welcome relief as it cooled Jake's head and neck. They ripped off their jackets as the police officers shouted at them to stand still. Each of them wore what looked like a backpack but was actually an ultra-low-profile BASE-jumping parachute connected to a body harness.

"Ready?" Jake shouted.

Tano didn't answer. His hands were trembling. On a building this low, it was go and throw, and there would be no margin for error.

"It's no different from what we practiced—just pull the cord! Three, two, one, JUMP!"

Jake watched Tano throw his small round pilot chute a moment before he did.

As Jake left the ledge, all fear dissipated, and each second expanded into a timeless moment of focused and deliberate action, like that of a samurai wielding his sword. Jake kept his head up, arching his stiff back, his knees and arms bent. He must have looked like a frog from below. And then his chute snapped open. The sound was like the crack of a giant towel. His feet kicked out as his body was jerked back from the downward pull of gravity. Above him, the chute opened into a large rectangular black flag with the words SAVE APOLLO! SAVE THE WHALES! spray-painted across it in white.

Oh Christ! His chute had opened backward. He knew instantly that he had a 180 as the spreading force of the lines turned him around to face the building. He was too close to turn. Terror flooded his body as he headed toward its glass face, blinded by the bright light of the LCD screens.

Jake grabbed both rear risers and pulled his knees up to his chest as he slammed against the building, the soles of his boots cushioning the blow. The chances of entanglement and a straight drop were enormous. His stomach muscles clenched tight as a fist. He was at the mercy of physics, but now every cell in Jake screamed to survive.

He hung on the rear risers as he swung backward, dropping fast. When he saw there were ten feet between him and the building, he let go of his left riser and hung on the right as his chute pivoted, turning him away from the building. He grabbed his yellow toggles to release the control lines.

The flight was only a few seconds. He was coming in fast. At last he pulled down on the toggles, flattening out his angle of descent. Landing hard, he rolled on the side of his leg, his black parachute trailing behind him. He stood quickly if unsteadily: he was not hurt. As he pulled on the cutaway handle to release his parachute, he looked around for Tano. Had he made it to the car? They would laugh over a Sapporo tonight about his brush with death.

Then Jake saw a crowd of onlookers surrounding Tano's body. He gasped in disbelief. "Tano!" he shouted, pushing through the crowd, and then crouched beside his friend. Tano's face stared up blankly, life gone from his eyes. What the hell had happened?

Jake knew a 180 was often caused by wind or body position and that he was lucky to be alive, but he couldn't begin to understand what had caused Tano's mishap. He scanned Tano's body for some explanation. Then his stomach lurched as he saw it—the one-inch piece of flat webbing that attached the bridle of the pilot chute to the harness had been threaded through Tano's leg strap by mistake. His parachute had not even opened.

Jake heard sirens. He looked up at the advancing police.

FORTY-SIX

10:45 A.M.
Next day
Tuesday
Ten miles from Liberty Slough

Eᴌɪᴢᴀʙᴇᴛʜ sᴀᴛ in the passenger seat of Connie's car, wishing her friend would pay more attention to the road and less to the radio. Perhaps it was the fact that she was pregnant, but she suddenly felt more cautious. Connie had been kind enough to pick her up from the hospital and take her to Apollo, so she did not want to complain.

"Can I help you?" Elizabeth finally said.

"No, I've got it." Connie was switching between the AM and FM news radio stations that she had programmed into her car stereo. There were no music stations. She seemed anxious and upset, as if she hadn't slept all night.

"Are you okay?" Elizabeth asked.

"I'm fine," Connie said, but she didn't sound it. Her tone was harsh. She was driving fast, and the flat country roads were narrow, with steep drainage ditches on either side.

Elizabeth heard the siren and saw the flashing lights in her side-view mirror.

"Damn," Connie said as she panicked and stepped on the gas.

"Connie, what are you doing? Pull over."

Connie came to her senses and pulled over. "Sorry, I'm not myself . . ."

The black Crown Victoria sedan must have been an undercover police car. The dash-mounted siren flashed blue lights like a law enforcement discotheque. The officer who walked toward them was dressed in a navy blue uniform and wore mirrored aviator sunglasses.

Connie lowered the window.

"Let's see some ID from both of you."

"Both of us?" Connie asked. "I was the one driving."

"I'm going to have to check for warrants." Perhaps Connie's little sprint from the long arm of the law had made him suspect that they were fugitives or criminals or had something else to hide.

Elizabeth handed over her driver's license. Connie was still looking in her bag, but she didn't seem in any particular hurry to find her license.

"Elizabeth McKay," the officer said with a smile, and she wondered if he, too, had seen her on Apollo's belly. Had anyone not seen her? "Ms. McKay, please step out of the car." That seemed strange to Elizabeth, but she did as she was told. The space was quite narrow between the car and where the road sloped down to the irrigation ditch. "Turn around. I'm going to need to check you for weapons."

"Are you with the sheriff's department?" Connie asked. She must have thought this seemed strange, too.

The officer held up his hand to shut Connie down. "I'll be with you in a minute, ma'am." Elizabeth wished Connie would be a little less confrontational.

Elizabeth turned around and faced the car. The officer tapped Elizabeth's legs to get her to spread them apart and then began to pat her down, starting with her shoulders and torso. As he touched her, he said, "I'm not sure you ladies realize what can happen to you out here." The officer patted the outside of her legs. "There are a lot of dangerous people around here. Meth heads, poachers, car thieves . . ." The officer touched Elizabeth on her inner thigh and lingered there.

Elizabeth's heart was pounding with fear. Something was wrong. Police officers didn't do this, and if they did, it was wrong. As she felt him grope her, she slapped his hand away.

Connie was out of the car now. "What the hell are you doing? What's your badge number, Officer? What's your name?"

The officer was already walking back to his car. "You ladies have a nice day, and remember what I said."

"That was harassment! *What is your badge number?*" Connie was shouting and pursuing the officer, who was getting in his car.

"Forget it," Elizabeth said as she grabbed Connie's arm. "Let's get the hell out of here."

The black sedan sped off ahead of them.

"Who was that?" Elizabeth asked.

Connie's face was twisted in rage as she stomped on the gas and headed toward the slough. "Some fake cop."

"Maybe a pervert?" Elizabeth guessed.

"More likely a messenger," Connie replied.

FORTY-SEVEN

11:10 A.M.
Liberty Slough

CONNIE DROVE into the field that had become the slough parking lot, still listening anxiously to the radio. It looked to Elizabeth as though Connie's hand was trembling. The incident with the fake officer had clearly affected Connie as much as it had her. Elizabeth was still feeling nervous and a little paranoid. As they drove toward a parking spot, Connie found the news she was looking for.

"In Tokyo, Japan, two eco-terrorists—"

"They're eco-*activists*!" Connie shouted at the radio.

"—broke into a building in downtown Tokyo and hijacked an electronic billboard to display footage of swimming humpback whales and Japanese whaling practices. When the police arrived, the two men BASE-jumped from the building. One of the parachutes had SAVE APOLLO! SAVE THE WHALES! written on it. The other parachute reportedly did not open. A Japanese national, identified as Tano Ito, died on impact—"

Connie slammed on the brakes. "Tano . . ." she whispered.

"The other eco-terrorist was arrested."

"Jake . . ."

"An organization called the Ocean Warriors has claimed responsibility."

"Your Jake and Tano?" Elizabeth said, horrified. "Did you know they—"

"Yes," Connie said, clenching the wheel and staring straight ahead.

"I'm sorry," Elizabeth said softly.

"People die," Connie said, her voice cracking. Tears streaked down her face as she stepped on the gas and pulled between two parked cars.

"I'm sorry," Elizabeth repeated. She wanted to say something more, but before she could, there was a rap on the window. She rolled it down as Connie looked away.

"Where have you been?" Lieutenant James asked. "Everyone is telling me to euthanize this whale—somehow even the lieutenant governor has decided it might be the most humane thing to do—and you just disappeared."

"I'm sorry. I was at the hospital."

"You okay?"

"Yeah."

"Good, because we're running out of time. They could take this out of my hands at any moment."

"I'll come up with something."

"I don't want something. I want a way to get this whale out alive. I'm risking my career, buying you time. Don't let me and everyone else down, Professor."

Lieutenant James walked off to talk to some man in a suit. Elizabeth recognized him as a representative from the Office of Emergency Services, which no doubt reported back to the lieutenant governor.

Connie was still crying silently.

"Can I do—"

"Go save that goddamn whale. That's what you can do. Tano died for the whales. You can make his death mean something."

"I'll try," Elizabeth said, but as she got out of the car and walked to the portable, she knew it was impossible. What had her mother's death meant? She understood the desire to see life and death as part of some grand drama, to give them some greater meaning, but it was a lie. Life was just life, and death was just death. She looked down at her belly and felt a tingling in her abdomen. She was surprised by a new desire to reconsider this biologist's creed.

FORTY-EIGHT

11:35 A.M.

THERE WERE no enforcement people in the portable. Elizabeth glanced around the three narrow rooms that served as Incident Command. On one end was the command room, which was filled with communication equipment, and on the other was the meeting room. In the middle was the cramped office space, with a few desks, a radio, and a phone. Elizabeth was grateful for the privacy as she sat at one of the desks and turned on her laptop. Thank God the department hadn't confiscated it, too. Dr. Skilling was right that the data technically belonged to the grant, but she had collected it. Skilling always had discouraged her from posting her data to the web, telling her to guard it jealously. Maddings, however, had believed that true intelligence was always distributed and collaborative. Fortunately, she had listened to Maddings.

Elizabeth went to the WhaleNet site. To her amazement, on the discussion board there were hundreds, perhaps thousands, of postings from people all over the world. These had links to websites that people had put up with pictures of Elizabeth and Apollo. She was flabbergasted. She had no idea that her work with Apollo had awakened such concern.

Elizabeth felt strengthened by this support and was all the more determined not to let people down. She went to the site's archives, much of which she and Maddings had contributed. She clicked on the sound files from both the slough and Bequia and listened as the spectrogram scrolled across the screen. Something still did not make sense to her, and she knew it was important. What was the meaning of the difference between the two distress calls? Why had the mother used the shorter and more urgent distress call after her baby had died? And why had Echo fled on hearing it?

Elizabeth remembered a video file Professor Maddings had posted a few years earlier that included a baby contact call and this shorter, more urgent distress call. She searched through the archive, found the video, and opened it. On her screen, a small window displayed a bull shark swimming toward a baby humpback that was with its mother and another female, perhaps a midwife whale. The hair on her neck stood on end and goose bumps covered her arms as she remembered her own encounter with the tiger shark in Bequia. She breathed in hard and exhaled slowly, trying to focus on the sounds.

Listen. Listen.

First she heard the sound for "baby." Then she heard the distress call—the short, urgent one. The sound fell abruptly at the end. The mother humpback was facing away from the shark, resting near the bottom, as tired mother whales often do. In the video, her body was like a gray cloud. The midwife whale seemed to see the shark first and must have tried warning the sleeping mother, who turned to face her baby immediately after hearing the call.

As Elizabeth replayed the video, she was able to see the sound visually portrayed on the spectrograph. First she saw the soft and fluid mother-baby call—*w-OP.* It looked like an Arabic word sweeping upward as it scrolled across the screen. Then she saw the dramatic, wider-frequency distress call, *EEh-EEh-EEh,* like three sharp downward slopes.

One of the overnight security officers had walked in for his coffee break. The man's slurping, sniffling, and shifting in his chair was distracting Elizabeth. She needed some music to help her focus, so she chose a piece that reminded her of Maddings and his encouragement.

Samuel Barber's "Adagio for Strings" filled the portable. *Don't give up on the music, Elizabeth.* It was Professor Maddings's voice in her head. She smiled. It was as if he were with her in the room. She remembered what he had always told her: *You can't understand the communication if you don't understand the emotion.*

It dawned on her that Professor Maddings was not just making some pop-psychology remark. He was proposing a grand theory of biology—making the claim that humans might understand the cries and chatter of other animals if they understood the emotion behind the utterance.

All animal communication was similar in many ways. Maddings delighted in showing his students how a mouse's squeak, when dropped three octaves, sounded like a lion's roar. The emotions were the same: fear, anger, concern, and—although no scientist would wager a career on attributing such a human emotion to an animal— perhaps even love.

To her, it seemed so patently obvious: It confirmed that every-thing humans do comes from the 2.5 billion years of animal life from which they evolved. But for many others, it was extremely controver-sial, if not impossible, because it contradicted cherished beliefs about human uniqueness and superiority. While living with her aunt in New York, she had attended Hebrew school and had been taught how Adam had been given dominion over the animals but was later banished from the Garden. A flaming sword now hovered above the gate to Eden, forever separating humans from their past and the ani-mals they had once known.

Having finished his coffee and donut, the officer got up to leave. In the reflection on her laptop screen, Elizabeth saw the man put his hand in her backpack and pull out her cell phone.

"Excuse me, that's my bag."

"Oh . . . ah . . . sorry," the officer said. "I thought this was Bob's. He asked me to get him his cell phone." Elizabeth noticed that this officer was dressed in the same uniform as the one who had stopped them on the road.

"Are you with one of the enforcement agencies?"

"Ah, no," the officer said, edging to the door. "Private security."

"Who do you work for?"

"We're contracted by the state." He hurried out of the portable, the door banging behind him.

Elizabeth pulled her backpack next to her and looked over her shoulder nervously, wondering where Lieutenant James was. She would feel safer if he was around, but she also knew that she'd better have some answers for him when she saw him next. Elizabeth opened the door of the portable and saw hundreds of people standing and sitting on the levee road. Some had even brought beach chairs. It was the middle of the day on a Tuesday, but people were putting the rest of their lives on hold for the opportunity to get a glimpse of Apollo.

The phone rang. Connie had arrived with Teo, and they had brought lunch. Elizabeth told security to let them through.

She returned to her laptop and clicked on the audio file from the whale hunt. The recording of the harpooned mother and calf filled the portable along with Barber's "Adagio," which continued playing. The anguish of the mother's calls wove together with the cello's slow and methodical crescendo. Elizabeth now listened to the emotion, and there it was—in the mother's calls, she could hear the baby tied against her chest, could hear the moment of the baby's death, and the mother's certain knowledge of her own. She heard the distress call change—felt the difference in her body. Her eyes grew wide with understanding.

FORTY-NINE

"IT's NOT A DISTRESS CALL—it's an alarm call! *A danger call!*" Elizabeth said, hardly able to control her excitement as Connie walked into the portable followed by Teo, a pizza box in his hand.

"What danger?" Teo asked.

"The whale sound—I know what it is."

"You do?"

"You showed me," said Elizabeth.

"Did I?" Teo stood up taller, like a proud rooster.

"You explained the two different distress calls the day you arrived. So tonight I went back to the tape I recorded as Sliver and her calf were dying."

Teo put down the pizza box and looked up uncomfortably. "Liza, afore you go on, I need for you to know I not mean to kill your whales."

"Kill Elizabeth's whales?" Connie cut in.

"Teo's a whaler on Bequia." Elizabeth had purposefully neglected to mention this fact to Connie.

"You're a *whaler*?"

"I pledged my life to it," Teo said. He turned back to Elizabeth. "But I not know they your whales. I never strike them if I know they yours."

"I can't believe you're a whaler—and I can't believe you let him stay in your house," Connie said.

"Teo's a friend, whaler or not. Look, we can deal with this

later," Elizabeth said firmly. "We have a whale to rescue, remember?"

"*Sorry,*" Connie spat out.

Elizabeth turned to Teo. "After you harpooned the baby—"

"*Harpooned the baby,*" Connie said, shaking her head.

Elizabeth was undaunted and continued, "The mother was vocalizing the sounds, *eeee—eeee—eeee.* A typical distress call, not unlike ones that have been recorded when whales are caught in other kinds of ropes. Do you remember you said you could hear the sadness? It's like someone marooned on an island calling, 'Heeeelp! Heeeelp!' Even if you didn't speak the language, you would know what that person was saying. But once the mother was also harpooned—I think once she knew her baby was dead and that she was dying—she changed the call to her escort. *EEh—EEh—EEh.* The call falls like *Watch out!* or *Run!* or *Go!* I don't think this is a distress call at all. I think it's a *danger* call."

Elizabeth could see from Teo's wide eyes that he understood immediately. "What's the difference?" Connie asked with annoyance.

"A distress call is what an animal uses to get help," Elizabeth said. "A danger call is what an animal uses to warn others."

Teo's discomfort with the idea was written in the wrinkled lines of his forehead. "You saying Sliver trying to save Echo?" Such concern, such feeling in an animal he thought of as food, obviously did not quite sit right. Elizabeth almost thought she saw empathy in his eyes.

"While there was hope, she was calling her escort to come save her and her calf. But when she knew there was no hope, she was telling him to save himself."

"That explain why he disappear so quick," Teo said, "not taking the boat down with him." Elizabeth remembered the terrifying moment when the whale's tail had battered the boat and Teo had grabbed the bomb gun.

"What does all this have to do with Apollo?" Connie asked, still spoiling for a fight.

"Apollo is repeating the danger call here in the slough. His vocalizations translate roughly as *Baby. Baby. Danger.*"

"But what exactly is the danger?" Connie asked. Elizabeth didn't know the answer to the question, but she did know that she'd need to find out soon if Apollo was going to live.

FIFTY

2:00 *P.M.*

ELIZABETH WAS SITTING OUTSIDE at an aluminum picnic table with Connie and Teo. The day had gotten warmer, and it felt good to be out of the stuffy portable. They were finishing their pizza and watching Apollo surface for a breath every four or five minutes. Elizabeth wondered if the frequency of Apollo's breaths might indicate that his health was deteriorating.

A Coast Guard seaman opened the door of the portable. "Professor McKay, our base dispatcher says he's got a whale inspector calling from a ship in the Pacific. His name is Ito? Says it's urgent."

Elizabeth and Connie looked at each other as they both stood up. They went into the portable and hit the speakerphone button.

"No one can know I call you . . ."

"Why *are* you calling me?"

"My son die to tell world about you, and you must tell world the truth."

"I'm not sure I understand."

"Kill my son." The man was speaking through tears. "They threaten me."

"Why?"

"I inspector for *Ryukyu Maru*. I test all whale tissue. Chromium—very, very high." Elizabeth was surprised. She knew that chromium was a chemical that had caused disease in a whole town when it was released into the groundwater by a California utility some years back. "Also PCBs and phthalates. Lesions and tumors, many, many whales."

Elizabeth thought of the calf that she'd seen in Bequia. "Have you told anyone about your findings?"

"I try. If anyone know I call . . ." The man's voice lowered.

"Don't worry," Elizabeth said. "Can you send me any of your test results?"

"They want me destroy, but I not do it. They destroy my life, kill my son." The man was weeping.

"I am so sorry. I will do what I can."

"You must tell the world the truth."

"Will you fax me the data?"

"Yes, I fax you." He was whispering now. Elizabeth told him the fax number. "I go now. I go now." His voice was soft and small, like a little boy's. He hung up the phone.

Connie was crying again. It was true; people died. But those who were left behind were never the same. Elizabeth opened her arms to Connie, who hesitated and then accepted her embrace.

"I'm fine," Connie said as she wept. "I'm fine."

A few minutes later, the fax machine in the portable rang. Connie dried her eyes as they watched it spit out paper.

Elizabeth knew she needed to learn more about what was happening to the whales, but she suspected this was not just about the whales. She put her hand on her abdomen and wondered about the meaning of the whale's song for the baby she was carrying.

"Connie, can you give me a ride?" Elizabeth said, taking the fax. "I need to research these chemicals and find out what the danger really is."

FIFTY-ONE

IN THE BIOLOGICAL and agricultural sciences section on the third floor of the library, Elizabeth hurried past the journals bound in blue, green, and black, with sober and dependably practical names like *Current Biology, Genes and Development, The Journal of Molecular Evolution,* and *American Naturalist.* These journals, however, were mostly historical. What she needed to know could be found only in the most current database.

Elizabeth saw a computer tucked privately in a corner and sat down. The department had already retracted her log-in privileges. It was surprisingly swift for a bureaucratic university. One would think that they had more important things to do than stop her from remotely accessing the library databases. Fortunately, at the library, she did not need a log-in ID. The whole electronic archives of the university were accessible through the black screen stirring to life in front of her.

Elizabeth was not sure what she was looking for, but she took out Ito's fax and typed in one of the chemicals on the list. The computer brought up numerous articles, including one entitled "Is Pollution the AIDS of the Ocean? Fire Retardants and Immunological Disorders in Marine Life."

She typed in the rest of the chemicals and read through dozens of articles, many of them about the effects on whales and other marine mammals. She knew about the plastic island out in the Pacific that was the size of the state of Texas, but what she discovered was that plastics were now in practically every drop of ocean water. She remembered, as a girl, seeing the barges in New York taking the trash out to dump in the ocean, and here she was seeing what this relationship to the marine world had brought. As she researched disease and birth defects in animals, she kept coming across other articles on the possible links to human birth defects. One study had found high levels of birth defects among mothers in the Faroe Islands who had eaten whale meat before getting pregnant. The article and several others explained that a baby inherits the "toxic load" of the mother. In other words, even before it is born, the baby is contaminated with the toxins its mother has been exposed to by her environment.

Elizabeth's cell phone rang.

"Are you home?" It was Frank.

"Almost."

"Have you been with the whale?" Frank said. He was trying to be supportive.

"I'm at the library researching birth defects."

"What in the world would possess you to do that?"

"I got a call today. Something is wrong with the whales and their offspring, and I think that human babies—"

"You should be resting."

"You know more about this than I do. Can you help me?"

There was silence on the other end of the line.

"Frank, I need you."

She listened anxiously for him to say something. "I'm just getting off. I'll be there in half an hour."

"Do you study here often?" She heard the warm, familiar voice behind her, and her body responded instinctively.

"Only when it's a matter of life and death," Elizabeth said, turning around and looking into Frank's chocolate-brown eyes.

"We have to hurr—"

Frank kissed her lips, gently, sweetly, lingering. "You look beautiful. Pregnancy really suits you."

"I bet you say that to all of your wives," Elizabeth replied, then moved quickly through the stacks, with Frank just a step behind.

"Where are we going? I thought you wanted me to help you research."

"This is research. We need to talk to someone." As they hustled down the stairs, Elizabeth handed him a printout from a professor's website. It announced a lecture by a professor named Gladys Ginsburg.

The sliding glass doors opened, and a burst of cold air accosted them. "But this is tonight—in Berkeley," Frank said.

"In forty minutes," Elizabeth replied, heading to the car.

"Berkeley is over an hour away," Frank protested.

"Not the way I drive."

FIFTY-TWO

ELIZABETH AND FRANK arrived at Room 22 in Warren Hall just as Professor Ginsburg was being introduced. They would have to wait to talk to her about Apollo and the whales, but Elizabeth was glad to have made it in time for the lecture. The sheer volume of evidence that Elizabeth had discovered in the library suggested that widespread chemicals were affecting animal and human health—especially babies. She hoped that Professor Ginsburg would explain how all of these individual studies might fit together.

The large hall in the Berkeley School of Public Health was filled to capacity, and the only seats were near the front. Elizabeth and Frank walked down the aisle as inconspicuously as possible.

As the dean finished his introduction, the excitement was palpable in the air. ". . . what I'm trying to say in these rather long introductory remarks is that no one since Rachel Carson has done more to educate us on the role of toxins in our environment and in our lives. It is my privilege to introduce Professor Gladys Ginsburg." There was a polite and respectful clapping from Professor Ginsburg's colleagues, whose professional decorum prevented them from expressing the depth of their admiration. Yet this was a public lecture, and throughout the audience, a number of people who did not have to worry about the opinions of their colleagues leaped to their feet and gave her a standing ovation.

"Thank you very much," Dr. Ginsburg said, smiling, clearly moved. Elizabeth imagined it must be some small validation for the hours she spent in airplanes and hotel rooms around the world, trying to sound the alarm about the dangers she and her colleagues had discovered.

Dr. Ginsburg stood only a foot taller than the wooden podium, with styled gray hair and a grandmother's warm smile, but her voice was strong and confident. "We all know that we are facing grave dangers in our *outer* world."

The first slide appeared on the screen behind her. Four pictures revealed the dangers of global warming: smokestacks spewing carbon emissions into a sky turned gray by pollution, the white spiraling cloud of a hurricane seen from space, the bones of a dead animal in a desert landscape, and a polar bear on a melting ice floe.

She clicked her remote, and the full, round belly of a pregnant woman appeared on the screen. The mother's hands cradled the top and bottom of her near-term womb. "But what about the *inner* world?" Dr. Ginsburg asked. "We face dangers here that are equally grave." The screen filled with a picture of the translucent pink body of a baby floating in a black sac, like an astronaut in space. Its tiny hands floated above its chest, its thumb practically touching its lips. "A recent study of umbilical cord blood found over 413 toxic industrial chemicals and on average more than 200 different chemicals per child. Since World War Two, approximately 80,000 chemicals have been invented, and thousands of these have been produced in quantities in excess of millions of pounds per year. Only a small percentage of these chemicals have ever been tested to discover their effects on animals and humans—"

"*Dr.* Ginsburg," interrupted a man in the back of the room, "the chemical companies follow strict state and federal regulations. How can you mislead this audience by suggesting that they are putting us and our children at risk?" The man was standing. He had short black hair and wore a double-breasted blue suit. His voice was smooth and deep.

"I am happy to answer all questions at the end," Dr. Ginsburg said wearily. "However, since you raise the issue of testing, I will address it now. The government only tests chemicals that are known to be health hazards, and very few chemicals are known in advance to cause problems. In other words, chemicals are innocent until proven guilty. In addition, when tests are conducted, they are done on one chemical at a time. We are exposed to great chemical cocktails that compound and exacerbate our reactions. Scientists are starting to discover interaction effects that can dramatically increase the danger."

The man sat down. Elizabeth could see a smug smile on his face. He seemed satisfied with having sown a little doubt in the audience's mind.

"Let's look at what these dangers are," Dr. Ginsburg said, returning to her presentation. "We are starting to discover that many of these synthetic chemicals play havoc with our physiology and that of other animals. They disrupt the endocrine or hormonal systems that regulate everything from our mood to our development to our fertility. What global warming is doing to the environment, endocrine disruption is doing to our bodies."

Dr. Ginsburg showed a collection of pictures of fish with enormous, bulbous tumors, frogs with too many legs, alligators with tiny penises, and seagulls with deformed beaks. She explained the exposures that may have caused each of these problems.

"*Dr.* Ginsburg," the man interrupted again, "so far, you are talking just about fish and birds. How do we know that the dangers are the same for humans?"

People were turning around and getting impatient with the intrusions, but Dr. Ginsburg seemed to know from experience that it was not possible to leave a heckler's objections unanswered. "For too long we have thought of the land and the sea as separate and ourselves as somehow different from the rest of life, but increasingly, we are seeing that all life is connected at a chemical level. We share 97 percent of our DNA with chimpanzees and 60 percent of our DNA with something as distant as a fruit fly. Common sense would tell us that what affects them will eventually affect us. But we don't just need to rely on common sense. Unfortunately, we have mounting evidence of the effects of these chemicals on humans. Let me give you one graphic example." The next slide was a neck-down photo of a naked baby.

There was an audible gasp in the room. The genitals were very hard to distinguish.

"This," Dr. Ginsburg explained gravely, "is an extreme case of hypospadias—where the urethral hole of the penis is not in the correct place. Here you can see the rather large hole is at the base of the scrotum, almost like a vagina. The sample of cord blood from this child contained 271 industrial chemicals that did not exist a hundred years ago."

"How many cases are we talking about here, *Dr.* Ginsburg?" said the man in the back.

"Hypospadias has tripled in the last thirty years to one in every hundred births; undescended testes have doubled; and testicular cancer is also rising. Just as worrisome as these individual conditions is the overall decline in the birth of boys. North of the Arctic Circle, where many of these chemicals end up, twice as many girls as boys are being born. Much closer to home, in the heavily polluted town of Sarnia, Canada, three girls are now born for every one boy. The town only discovered this startling fact because they had so many girls' softball teams and so few boys'. A recent study has found an unexpected drop in the number of boys throughout much of the Northern Hemisphere. The number of 'missing boys' in the U.S. and Japan alone is estimated at over 250,000."

"Why is this happening, Dr. Ginsburg?" a woman in the front asked, with obvious worry in her voice.

"I guess we might as well take questions as we go. I understand that what I am saying is difficult to hear and raises numerous questions and concerns. Many of these chemicals look a lot like estrogen—the female hormone. Our hormonal and other bodily processes are so sensitive that the presence of toxins in the parts per billion can have profound developmental consequences."

Another hand shot up in the air. "What kinds of exposures are we talking about?"

"Let me give you one example. Will you hold up the water bottle in front of you for the others to see?" Elizabeth recognized it as the hard plastic bottle favored by backpackers and athletes. Professor Ginsburg clicked past several slides to one of plastic baby bottles. "That water bottle and these on the screen are made out of a plastic that utilizes a chemical called Bisphenol A. It is also used in PVC pipe and to coat children's teeth so they don't get cavities. Seven billion pounds of this plastic chemical are produced and put into our environment every year, a little over a pound for each person on the planet. Exposing pregnant rats to tiny amounts of these plastic-making compounds resulted in their babies having precancerous lesions in their breasts when they reached puberty.

"This and other studies are showing that many adult diseases can be preprogrammed into our genes by exposure to toxins in the womb and during childhood. This is nothing less than a revolution in our scientific understanding of toxins and public health. We once believed that 'the solution to pollution was dilution.' In other words, if you kept your exposure under a supposedly safe level, there was no problem. We now see that this is not the case. Minute quantities can alter the expression of our genes and cause lasting health problems. Other possible dangers of Bisphenol A include impaired brain development, hyperactivity, Down syndrome, prostate cancer, low sperm count, long-term memory loss, dementia, and even obesity and diabetes. Bisphenol A is just one chemical of the thousands our bodies have to contend with. You probably have always looked at the ingredients that you couldn't pronounce in the products in your home, and something deep inside said that these were probably not good for you. The truth is, you were right. Many of them aren't."

"Dr. Ginsburg, you are only presenting part of the data." It was the man in the blue suit in the back of the room. "There have been numerous industry studies that have shown these chemicals are safe."

"There are many reasons that the design of certain studies hides the true dangers—which I don't have time to go into—but let me show you one slide that I think will present the problem of relying on companies who have billions of dollars at stake to conduct their own health research. There have been 180 animal studies of Bisphenol A at levels beneath FDA/EPA safety standards." Dr. Ginsburg clicked on the next slide. "In the studies funded by the government, 14 found no effect, and 153 found an effect." She switched to the next slide. "In the studies funded by industry, 13 found no effect, and 0 found an effect." There was an audible murmur in the room.

The man who had asked so many questions got up to leave, perhaps realizing that he had done what he could or that this audience was increasingly unsympathetic to his position.

"Sir, before you leave, would you share with the audience whether you work for an industry lobbying group or a product defense firm?" When the audience showed surprise at this last term, Dr. Ginsburg added, "Yes, even products now have lawyers."

The heckler looked over his shoulder but left without answering. Dr. Ginsburg turned her intense gaze back to the audience.

"We worry about chemical weapons in the hands of terrorists, but we are using chemical weapons against ourselves. Endocrine disruption is a time bomb that could lead to the extinction of our species and much other life on the planet. We have spread these chemicals so far and wide that there is no longer any hope that one person can avoid exposure through food and lifestyle choices. Eating organic and other precautions are important, but they are not enough. What is required is collective action. Our survival depends on it. But I must share with you my greatest fear. There may be fates worse than extinction. If we don't address the problem and we do survive, we may do so as such a disease-riddled, suffering species that we may someday wish we had been wiped out."

ELIZABETH SAT THERE stunned. It was difficult to accept the magnitude of the danger. Even as scientists, she and Frank had not yet known that the problem was so great. Clearly some people—no doubt many—were trying to obscure the data. After the applause died down, she and Frank walked up to speak with Professor Ginsburg as other audience members gathered around.

"Dr. Ginsburg, my name is Elizabeth McKay, and I am a marine biologist."

"Oh yes, I've seen you with that whale, Apollo."

"That's why I'm here. I'm trying to understand what might be happening to the whales. Could endocrine disruption and the kind of environmental toxicity you were describing lead to lesions and tumors in newborn whales?"

"Absolutely," said Professor Ginsburg. "We're starting to find these problems in marine as well as terrestrial life. To prove the relationship, of course, you need to do testing."

"What tests do you recommend?"

"You're at UC Davis, aren't you?"

Elizabeth decided not to explain that she had been kicked out. "Near there."

"Well, I work a lot with Pete Sanchez at UCD. He's a toxicologist with a state-of-the-art lab. If you can get tissue and water samples, he can do the testing."

Frank said, "Have you mapped the distribution of these chemicals? For example, in Northern California?"

"We're working on that now. Actually, most of our mapping gets done in Pete's lab. That's his specialty. Would you like me to let him know you'll be in touch?"

"Yes, thank you," Elizabeth said, knowing what she had to do next.

IN THE ROW where the heckler had been sitting, Amanda Hanson flipped open her thin silver cell phone.

"Elizabeth McKay is a bigger problem than I thought. I want to know everything she knows, the minute she knows it. Did you get her phone?"

"Our security officer was . . . unsuccessful."

Hanson inhaled deeply, trying to control her temper, remembering what her yoga teacher had said about deep breathing and relaxation. "What are you going to do *now*?"

"We've figured out how to do it remotely. With the transmission of one firmware patch, her cell phone will tell us everything we want to know and more."

FIFTY-THREE

9:00 P.M.

"GOD, THAT WAS DEPRESSING," Frank said. He and Elizabeth were outside the lecture hall, trying to process the disturbing information. But most of all, they were thinking about their child. The future of the species was no longer an abstract fear—part of that future was right in Elizabeth's womb. "She seems so cheerful, even though she's telling us that the world is ending."

"It's not over yet, Frank. There's still a chance to turn it around." Elizabeth's stomach growled with hunger. The fate of the whales and the world would have to wait until after she had eaten. Her child was hungry, and there was no way to feed a child on despair.

Elizabeth and Frank stepped into Saul's to grab a quick sandwich. The long deli display case was practically overflowing. All around them hung New York photos and memorabilia. Elizabeth remembered all the delicatessens she had eaten pickles in, studied in, and heard people argue in while growing up in New York.

While they waited, Elizabeth thought about the talk. She had a better idea what might have caused the health problems in the whale calf in Bequia. She kept thinking of the meaning of the sounds in the song. *Baby. Baby. Danger.*

"Professor Maddings said that the new song originated in Bequia," Elizabeth said, as much to herself as to Frank. "Echo began singing it after Sliver's calf was born sick."

"Do you think the song is about Sliver's sick baby?"

While Frank was clearly dubious, she appreciated that he was trying to help. "No. If that were the case, why would the song have spread around the world? Why would other whales have chosen to adopt it as well?"

Frank paid the cashier and took the bag of food. Inside were two sandwiches and two large kosher pickles as well as the potato knish, half a pound of macaroni salad, and bagel with cream cheese Elizabeth had also ordered. Feeling a little embarrassed by her appetite, she moved toward the door.

Elizabeth noticed a black-and-white picture on the wall. It was of an old synagogue. She ran her fingertips across a line of Hebrew carved into the synagogue's stone wall. She noticed two words repeated in a row. She did not recognize the words, but she recognized the letters from her Hebrew school classes. In some ancient languages, she had learned, repetition was an intensifier—or perhaps a multiplier.

Her heart started to race. "That's it," she mumbled to herself, her mouth full of bagel. "That's it."

"What?" Frank asked as he caught up to her.

"I think I know why the whale is repeating the sound for 'baby.'"

They pushed their way through the glass door. As she spoke, little puffs of moisture were visible in the cold night air. "They're not saying *Baby—danger*. They're saying *Babies—danger*. It's plural."

FIFTY-FOUR

9:00 A.M.
Next day
Wednesday
Sacramento

Elizabeth looked down at her ring finger. It felt all the more naked now that she and Frank were back together. Together but not actually together. On their way home from Berkeley, Frank had been paged to the hospital.

When she got home, Elizabeth realized that in the flurry of everything, she had forgotten to tell Frank about Teo. She called Frank's cell phone, but the voice mail box was full. She didn't want him coming home and finding Teo there. She'd swing by the hospital and tell him after her meeting with Bruce Wood, the reporter.

The reception area of the *Sacramento Times* spilled over into the offices of its reporters. The large open room was filled with the hum of people talking. Everyone walked quickly and she could feel the tension in the air. At a daily paper, every hour counted toward making deadline.

"He can see you now," said the secretary, who was smiling and starry-eyed at having met the "whale lady." Frank had convinced Elizabeth to try out her theory with one journalist before announcing it on live television at the press conference. She had seen how easily her words could be misunderstood or misconstrued.

The metro news area was a maze of cubicles, the dividers rising high enough so that people were hidden while seated but could stand up and shout above them. Fixed to columns in various places were televisions tuned to CNN. Bruce Wood was leaning far back in his chair, his fingers laced behind his head. As soon as she saw his wry expression, she regretted having come.

"Your message said that you wanted to talk about pollution. Does this have to do with crop dusting?"

"Not only. This is a much greater threat."

"Look, Elizabeth, I already told you that pollution is not news in the Central Valley. I was hoping you were coming in for a feature story on whale whispering."

"I realize that this might be beyond the interest of metro. That's why I called to see if the news reporter and the science reporter might be able to sit in on the interview."

"Based on what you said in the message—that the whales are worried about their babies—the editors weren't convinced that we were dealing with news—or, quite frankly, science."

"I realize this may be hard to accept, but I've identified two calls—one for 'danger' and one for 'baby,' which is repeated, possibly as a plural."

'Danger' and 'baby'?" The reporter spoke very slowly, as if he were speaking to an imbecile or a lunatic.

Elizabeth steeled herself and persevered. "I believe the whale is warning other whales that their offspring are in danger."

"I see. Well, for every . . . whale . . . that has a doomsday projection, there is probably another whale that is saying everything is coming up roses. Uh, not sure if whales know about roses . . . coming up seaweed?"

"I can see that you don't believe anything I'm saying."

"No, frankly, I don't."

"I realize that it's hard for us to imagine that whales are intelligent enough to communicate or care about one another."

"I once read that they were about as smart as dogs. I've met some smart dogs in my day, but they couldn't do much more than fetch and roll over."

Elizabeth remembered something Maddings had said about cynics being heartbroken optimists who never wanted to have their heart broken again. Wood, like so many others, would never be able to risk believing what she was telling him. Elizabeth got up, realizing there was no reason to continue the conversation.

The newspaper on Wood's desk reported another homicide down by the river. Elizabeth turned back to the reporter and jabbed her finger down on the front page. "Murder and war, your so-called news stories, are not really news at all. Those stories are as old as our species. The real news is what is happening for the first time in the history of our planet."

As Elizabeth walked away, Wood stood and called out to her over his cubicle wall. "Call me if you want to be profiled in the pets and people section."

FIFTY-FIVE

9:10 A.M.
Davis

Frank was exhausted and glad to be coming home, if only for a few hours of desperately needed sleep. He imagined Elizabeth's long black hair tickling his nose as he curled up against her that night. For now he was just grateful to lie down for a few hours in his own bed.

Frank tried to find the right key as he inserted several that all looked alike. The knob started turning by itself. Standing in the doorway was a swarthy, broad-shouldered man with two different-colored eyes.

"Who are you?"

"And you must be the long-lost husband. Frank, is it?"

"Yeah, and who the hell are you?"

"My name is Teo." He sized Frank up from head to toe. "So you the one Liza left me for?"

"Liza? You mean Elizabeth."

"Before she your Elizabeth, she my Liza. Come in. She be back anytime. We cooking up some breakfast."

"Elizabeth doesn't cook."

"Maybe she just like island cooking." Teo was baiting him. Frank saw the kitchen knife in his hand.

"What are you doing in my house?"

"Your house? I thought you left. I guess that means Liza can do as she please, and it please her to have me here." Teo started walking back into the kitchen.

"I don't believe this."

"Believe it, man," Teo called out. "Just ask her."

Frank's mind was reeling. Was she playing him? Had she cuckolded him? "Get out of my house!" He didn't care whether the man had a knife or not.

"Is Liza's house now. Remember? I leave if she tell me to."

Frank's blood was pumping into his fists. He turned and slammed the door behind him.

FIFTY-SIX

11:35 A.M.
Sacramento

FRANK HAD TRIED ELIZABETH on her cell without success. Maybe she had turned it off while she was in the meeting with the journalist. She often forgot to turn it back on. He paused before entering the exam room and shook his head, trying to get rid of the thoughts that kept circling in his mind like a dog chasing its tail. Whatever he was feeling about Elizabeth and Teo, he would need to leave it in the hall. He looked down at the chart for six-month-old Justine Gates.

Frank opened the door. Delores Gates, Justine's nervous mother, had stopped in on her way to the surgeon. She stared at him, desperate for help. Frank looked at the baby girl in her arms. Justine was dressed in a pressed pink sailor's outfit. Her brown eyes looked at him with wonder, and the fluorescent light reflected off her smooth cheeks and button nose. Frank hoped his child would be as adorable.

Justine's mother was smartly dressed in a pink pantsuit, and her long, straightened hair did not have a strand out of place. She wore black cat's-eye glasses, which somehow made her look both more beautiful and more intelligent. Her husband stepped back into the room from taking a cell phone call in the hall. "Sorry, it was the office." He was apologizing more to his wife than to Frank, and her raised eyebrow registered her displeasure at her husband's priorities. "There's an emergency at the Rio Vista chemical plant."

"You work at a chemical plant?" Frank asked, knowing that worker exposure was often a risk factor for children and wondering if he should factor it in to his differential diagnosis.

"I'm the chief financial officer for Heizer Chemical Industries International," Gates said as he tilted his head back and looked down his nose at Frank. He squared the shoulders of his green pin-striped Italian suit, which probably cost more than Frank made in a week, maybe even a month. Yet when they had first met, Frank had felt the strong grip of someone who had once worked with his hands. Gates's arrogant reaction hinted at the insecurity of a man who fears slipping back to where he began.

Frank tried to ignore the father's arrogance and gather the information he needed. "Do you spend much time at the plant itself?"

"Our company has thirty-five plants around the world, Dr. Lombardi. I work out of the headquarters in San Francisco."

"I am asking . . . for health reasons," Frank said, trying to recover from the awkwardness of the moment.

"Periodically, I need to go to one of the plants for an audit or other emergency. Why?"

"On-the-job exposure is one concern, but let's not jump to conclusions or a diagnosis. The tests should be back tomorrow, so we will know for sure. Now there is no sense worrying until we know what we are dealing with."

"Thank you, Doctor," Justine's mother said, pulling her child more tightly into her arms, as if she were trying to protect her from whatever news they might hear the next day.

"I'll see you tomorrow," Frank said, stepping out of the room.

Elizabeth was standing in the hall. "I missed you last night—" she said with a seductive smile.

Frank was not smiling. "Apparently, you had plenty of company."

"Are you talking about Teo?"

"Yeah, *Teo*." Frank's voice was hollow and cruel. "What is he doing here? I thought that was over before we were even together."

"It was over—it is over. I tried to leave a message on your cell phone to tell you he was in town and needed a place to stay. He's still a friend."

"Sounds like a *very* good friend."

Elizabeth did not know how to answer. "What are you saying?"

"It's not what I am saying. It's what he said." Frank's voice was raised.

"Dr. Lombardi, please report to the NICU."

"I've got to go."

"Frank, this is crazy. Call me so we can talk?"

"Talk to *Teo*. And get him out of our house."

ELIZABETH ALMOST KNOCKED the door down, and Teo jumped out of the kitchen with a knife.

"You better protect yourself," she said.

"Oh, is you, Liza," Teo said, returning to the kitchen.

"What did you say to Frank?"

"I just tell him the truth. That we together. Like we were."

"*Were*, Teo!"

"We were never over. You never give me a real chance."

"I knew what I wanted, and you were not it. Now get out of my house."

Teo stepped toward her and grabbed her arm. Moving in as if they were dancing, he kissed her hard on the lips.

Elizabeth struggled against him and reached behind her for something—anything—she could use to defend herself. Her fingers grazed a knife sitting on the counter, but Teo knocked it just out of reach before she could get her hand around it. Teo smiled at his victory and stepped back. As he did, Elizabeth slapped him across the face as hard as she could. "I'm married, Teo. I'm married—and I'm pregnant."

FIFTY-SEVEN

1:30 P.M.
Liberty Slough

APOLLO WAS BEING ATTACKED *from every direction—the pound-*
ing and clanging shook his entire body—piercing his skull like sharp
teeth—overwhelming his hearing—confusing all of his senses—

His eyes searched in the dark water for the danger—as the sound
closed in from all sides—

He stayed away from the shore—where the sound echoed toward
him—but there was no escaping the cacophony—

Boats were corralling him like a pod of killers—

He began to slap his tail against the water—but the noise would not
stop—

He had only one defense—to fight sound with sound—

He began to sing—

ELIZABETH WAS STILL ANGRY as she drove up to the slough, a long
line of cars in front of her. Signs indicating that this was private property
were posted all along the road. A black security car—not a police car—
was preventing the would-be whale watchers from driving or walking
onto the levee. Elizabeth pulled off into a field and got out of her car.
The sound of metal hammering against metal assaulted her ears.

She started to run to the slough, past the white television vans
that were also being kept out of the area. They recognized her and

rushed toward her, grabbing their cameras and assaulting her with questions.

"Why are they closing down the slough?"

"What's wrong with the whale?"

"Have you determined what the whale is saying?"

"I'm from CNN . . ."

Elizabeth kept walking quickly but could no longer run through the thick crowd of reporters and cameramen who surrounded her. She was surprised to see that the number of reporters had only grown larger. Judging by the languages on the microphones being thrust in her face, there were now television reporters from many other countries, including Japan. Elizabeth thought of Ito and her unsuccessful attempt to explain her findings to Bruce Wood. She was losing her nerve.

"I'm sorry," she responded. "You'll have to wait until the daily press briefing for any news."

Elizabeth hurried up the steep incline that led to the top of the levee. When she got to the yellow tape blocking off the road, a security guard moved toward her quickly.

"I'm afraid this is private property."

"The levee road is public access."

"This area is off-limits."

"I am part of the research team," Elizabeth said, looking at the small ring of boats trying to herd Apollo toward the bridge. They were hammering steel pipes that descended into the water. Apollo was clearly agitated, slapping his tail.

"Our orders—"

"I don't give a damn what your orders are. I have a permit to study this whale," she said as she continued walking.

"Ms. McKay, your permit has been revoked."

Elizabeth's heart stopped at having the security guard address her by name. Still she kept walking. *Who revoked my permit? And who told this security guard?* She needed to talk to Lieutenant James as quickly as possible. Something was definitely not right.

"Ms. McKay, I am going to have to ask you to *stop.*" The force of the man's voice was threatening, and Elizabeth turned to see him resting his hand on the grip of the gun in his holster.

"Are you going to shoot me on national—make that international—television?" she asked as she pointed to the television cameras filming the interaction and eagerly awaiting a story. A shooting would move up the segment in the nightly news. *Pregnant whale researcher shot trying to protect Apollo!*

Then Elizabeth's stomach dropped as she recognized the man in the aviator sunglasses. It was him: the fake police officer who had stopped her and Connie on the road. She couldn't move. He saw her reaction and was smiling. The security guard spoke into the black plastic mouthpiece fastened to the shoulder of his jacket. Elizabeth imagined that he was calling reinforcements or other security guards farther up the slough.

The renewed sound of clanging shook her free and gave her courage. She turned and kept walking up the slough, watching what was unfolding in the water.

Elizabeth knew what the Coast Guard boats were trying to do. *Oikomi* was a Japanese method of herding dolphins to slaughter, and it had been effective in the past for scaring whales out of waterways like this. She saw Skilling standing next to Lieutenant James on the orange rigid-hulled inflatable. It was no doubt Skilling's idea, and while it was not an entirely bad one, she had a feeling it was not going to work this time. Her intuition was confirmed by Apollo's refusal to move. Instead of swimming toward the bridge, he stayed in the center of the slough.

She saw the stalk of his tail rise just above the surface, his flukes tilting sharply down in the singing position.

• • •

LIEUTENANT JAMES had a throbbing headache, no doubt caused by the loud banging of metal poles that was shaking his skull and his boat.

"Well, Dr. Skilling, it looks like this whale is not willing to be corralled."

"If this were a healthy whale, I guarantee it would have worked. I can tell you with a hundred percent confidence: This whale is sick and needs to be euthanized."

"Professor McKay says that the whale is—"

"Elizabeth McKay is a failed graduate student whose fringe research was rejected by her thesis committee. The media is making her out to be the good guy and me to be the bad guy, but I'm not the bad guy. I want what is best for the whales. Dissecting this whale will help us to understand harmful algae blooms and their effect on marine mammals. It might even allow us to prevent this from happening in the future. I'm the good guy, not Elizabeth."

Lieutenant James was surprised by the professor's rant. "We're all trying to help the whale, Dr. Skilling." His head was pounding now. Through the loudspeaker mounted on top of the orange boat, he called off the small armada banging the pipes, and the slough fell blessedly silent. Dr. Skilling did not say another word as the boat made its way back to the bank, and as soon as they had landed, he stormed off.

FIFTY-EIGHT

2:10 P.M.

LIEUTENANT JAMES lifted the yellow cautionary tape that was stretched all around the portable and let Elizabeth through.

"It's okay, I need her," Lieutenant James said to the two armed security guards detaining her. They had apparently been warned of her presence by the phony police officer, who was nothing more than a gun for hire. But hired by whom?

"I hear my letter of authorization has been revoked."

"I got the call this morning," Lieutenant James said, not looking at her, obviously trying to control his temper.

Elizabeth followed his rapid march back to the white portable. "Who is doing this?" She knew that whoever had gotten her authorization canceled was also behind the barricading of the slough.

"The people who own the land."

"Who are they?"

"Some consortium . . . they sure have a lot of pull in Sacramento." Elizabeth thought of Connie's certainty that the whalers were behind everything. Was she right?

"Why are they doing this?"

"I don't know, but they are making my life—and yours—a lot harder."

"But why?"

"I don't know why. And frankly, all I want to know is how—how the hell I'm going to get this whale out of here." Lieutenant James, she thought, was not someone who swore regularly or let his irritation show.

"I think I know what the whale is trying to communicate."

Lieutenant James let out a deep sigh. "That's nice, Elizabeth, but it doesn't change the fact that if Apollo is not swimming back out to sea by the end of the week, my orders are to euthanize him."

"I suppose Skilling and his team are salivating to get their hands on the carcass."

"That's not my concern, Professor. Some of the scientists on the conference call this morning said we should drag it out by the tail. Please tell me something I can do instead."

"That would be a disaster."

"I know." Lieutenant James was shaking his head. "I need your help with something else."

"What?"

"Do the press conference with me? It's in fifteen . . ." Lieutenant James looked at his watch. "Ten minutes. The media's breathing down my neck—they've got television stations from Japan and England and Spain and France and Brazil and God knows where else. At least you've got some good news for them."

"Good news?" Elizabeth didn't think that what she had to say would be seen as good news.

"Help me out, Professor. Tell them what you've figured out. At least it's progress. Maybe it will keep them from making me kill this whale."

"Okay," Elizabeth said, "but I need you to help me out with something, too."

"Name it."

"Get one of the NOAA or Fish and Game guys to take a water sample."

"What do you want that for?"

"I'm still trying to figure out a why."

THE PRESS "ROOM" was simply a podium set up in a field where the wind was whipping around and howling into the microphones.

"Today at 1330 we attempted a Japanese dolphin herding technique that has worked to rescue whales in the past. Unfortunately, the whale did not respond favorably, and when it became clear that the sound was agitating the whale, the operation was terminated. The whale returned to singing its song shortly before the operation ended. I would now like to invite marine biologist Elizabeth McKay to discuss her findings on the possible significance of the whale's song."

Elizabeth was standing behind Lieutenant James and took a deep breath. She heard Ito's voice: *You must tell the world the truth.* She stepped up to the podium as if ascending the gallows. She heard the rapid-fire shutters of the photojournalists. The cameramen were jockeying for position; even though it was still day, they had their bright lights shining on her.

"I want to begin by saying that my findings remain preliminary at best. Nonetheless, I have found social sounds embedded in the whale's song, which in and of itself is unusual. These social sounds are functioning like a refrain in the song. One of these sounds is a danger call, and the other is a contact call used particularly for calves."

"What do these sounds mean?"

"They translate roughly as 'Babies in danger.'"

The reporters started shouting questions. This was not scientific jargon. This was about babies in danger. Finally, Elizabeth pointed to one reporter raising her hand in front.

"Why do you think Apollo is 'singing' about this?"

"I don't know, but it may have something to do with the fact that whale calves are being born sick."

"Why are they sick?"

"Again, we don't know for sure, but it seems that pollution and chemical contamination may be at least partly responsible."

"You really expect us to believe that whales talk to each other about pollution?" It was the *Sacramento Times* reporter Bruce Wood.

Before she could answer, a newscaster asked, "Are whales really that intelligent?"

Elizabeth thought about what Professor Maddings had once said: *The most accurate measure of intelligence is simply the ability to survive, and by this standard, human intelligence remains an unproven evolutionary experiment.*

"How intelligent whales are is not yet clear," Elizabeth finally said. "Given that humans are the ones creating the pollution, I guess some might also wonder how intelligent *we* are."

The reporters laughed.

"Thank you very much," Elizabeth said as she stepped back from the podium. Lieutenant James escorted her away from the press. Elizabeth looked out at the whale, who surfaced and exhaled with a mighty white cloud of mist. *Why won't you leave, Apollo?*

FIFTY-NINE

ELIZABETH NO LONGER felt safe at the slough. The police and other enforcement officers were increasingly scarce, replaced by private security personnel. She remembered how one had tried to steal her cell phone and knew she would be safer at home. Maybe Connie was right. Maybe the whalers did see Apollo as a public relations nightmare and were trying to shut her down.

"Elizabeth McKay, if I am not mistaken." Elizabeth turned around and was surprised to hear that the British accent belonged to a tall Japanese man with gray hair. "May I have a word with you?"

"I'm not doing any more press interviews today."

"I'm not with the press; I'm with the Japanese Fisheries Development Department. You may know we are one of the supporters of the Japanese Cetology Research Center." Elizabeth knew the name of this infamous "research" institution. It was responsible for overseeing what it called scientific whaling, but most people believed it was a pretext for the Japanese whaling industry to continue hunting despite the ban on commercial whaling. The whales that were killed for research were then carved up and sold on the Japanese market.

"Yes, I'm quite familiar with the JCRC's reputation."

"Don't believe everything you've heard. We are expanding the center to examine issues of whale intelligence and would like to offer you a position."

"You're kidding."

"The starting salary is two hundred thousand dollars a year, with an almost unlimited budget."

"Isn't that a somewhat unusual offer to a graduate student who doesn't even have a Ph.D.?"

"The entire resources of the whale fleet will be at your disposal."

"So I can record the distress sounds of dying whales?" Elizabeth said, turning to leave.

"Ms. McKay, whaling is inevitable in our emptying oceans. You can help us to make it more humane." Kazumi was following behind her.

"I'm not interested in being the doctor at the extermination camp."

"Ms. McKay, we may be able to help you with your candidacy."

"Can you? Were you responsible for getting me kicked out?"

"We have some influence at the university and may be able to reverse what was no doubt a hasty decision."

Elizabeth could not believe what she was hearing. Connie had been right. "Did you also get my research permit revoked?"

"I don't know what you are talking about."

She opened the door to the station wagon.

"All we are asking in return for our help is the package that Teo Juval brought you."

"I don't know what *you* are talking about."

KAZUMI WATCHED ELIZABETH drive away. She was even more beautiful in person than she had been in the magazine. He was sorry about what now would be necessary. Kazumi pressed the speed dial number on his cell phone. He had only one bar, but the call connected.

SIXTY

4:05 P.M.
Davis

Teo threw a shirt into his old duffel bag. He did not have much, and he did not need much. For so many years, he had thought he needed Elizabeth, but now he knew she was not for the having. He would go back to his whales and his people, and he would be content. Maybe he'd even settle down with one of the island women who would take him.

He wrote out a note telling Elizabeth that he had left a "present" for her in the freezer of the community room. He was no longer worried about reminding her of Sliver and her calf, but he knew the package—and Elizabeth—would be safer if it was not in her house.

He pulled the duffel over his shoulder and headed for the door.

Nilsen watched as an endless parade of schoolchildren marched in front of his car. An orange-vested crossing guard held up a big red stop sign. Nilsen could feel the weight of his gun where it hung in the shoulder holster. This time he would have the upper hand with that island whaler. He'd wanted to act sooner, but Kazumi had been strangely unwilling, wanting to take steps first himself. He didn't know what they were, but they had failed, and now he had permission to take care of the whaler and his girlfriend.

Children looked through the windshield at him. Once they were out of the crosswalk, he stepped on the gas and drove quickly. He'd get the package and settle the score. He rubbed his neck where the islander had pressed it with a knife.

TEO CLOSED THE DOOR behind him and headed down the path. He needed to get to the bus terminal, where he'd buy a ticket to Miami. From there he'd catch one of the cargo boats that went to the islands.

"Teo!"

Elizabeth was walking up the path from the parking lot.

"I was afraid you had already left."

"Leaving now."

"Teo, what's the package?"

Teo led Elizabeth past the mailboxes and the green lawn where the children were playing, past the pool, and finally to the community room. He was about to open the lock with his knife when Elizabeth pulled out her key. She dangled it in front of him.

After opening the freezer, Teo moved a box that contained the leftovers of someone's wedding cake.

"Is back here." He pulled out the package, carefully wrapped in white butcher paper. It was still frozen. "They offer me twenty-five thousand U.S. dollars, but I keep it for you. I wait for the right time. Then I see it put you in danger and I hide it."

Elizabeth tore open the paper, but she wasn't sure what she was looking at. It was a black tube.

"Is the calf privates."

"You brought me a whale *penis*?"

"I doubt the postman take it," Teo said defensively.

"You brought this all the way from Bequia and across the country on a Greyhound bus?"

"I keep it on ice so it don't spoil."

"But why?"

"Is something wrong with this whale, real wrong. Look at this."

SIXTY-ONE

National Institute of Ecotoxicology
Montreal, Canada

MADDINGS'S NOSE AND CHEEKS were still red and stung from the wind that had greeted him at the airport on landing in Montreal. Although now indoors, he was shivering in the cold dissection lab. He pulled his white cardigan more tightly around his neck and wondered if the shocking sight in front of him was partly to blame for his trembling.

It had been only that morning at his office in Cambridge that he'd received the call from Michel Roland at the Faculté de Médecine Vétérinaire of the University of Montreal. As soon as he had heard the request, he canceled all of his appointments and took the next plane from Logan.

Roland had asked him to come up to investigate a carcass. Maddings knew that Roland, the head of the National Institute of Ecotoxicology, had seen just about everything since dissecting his first beluga in 1982. Yet his voice sounded extremely agitated on the phone, which was why Maddings had flown up immediately. As one of the world's leading experts on whale anatomy, Maddings thought he had seen everything, too.

"I don't believe it. I need confirmation," Roland had said in his succinct Québécois French accent. The mystery hidden in the corpse of this whale would make it famous in the scientific world, and

Roland no doubt wanted an expert like Maddings to witness—and validate—his findings.

Maddings looked down at DL-406. DL was for *Delphinapterus leucas,* the beluga's Latin name. The beluga lay on the table, its pursed lips much flatter and more humanlike than a dolphin's. The skin of the corpse was gray. It would not have changed to the characteristic white for several more years—that is, if the whale had lived. Maddings marveled at how much the face of the beluga looked like a human embryo, with its large, bulbous head. A smile haunted its face even after death.

They could tell by the enamel rings of this whale's teeth—just as botanists can read the age of a tree by the rings of its trunk—that it was not even two years old and was still no doubt nursing. That was the problem.

Maddings had read about highly contaminated stillborn beluga whales found washed up on the shore. It was yet more evidence that the mother's toxins were passed through the placenta. After birth, this baby would have nursed on a diet of rich milk that came as it did in all mammals, from the mother's fat stores. But this whale had been receiving a steady diet of contaminants along with its mother's milk.

Pulling on his surgical gloves, Maddings realized this must be the reason that the beluga whale population had not recovered. Four decades ago, when the public had discovered the extent of the contamination, the government had cleaned up the waters of the estuary near Montreal, but these immortal contaminants were still living in the bodies of the whales and being passed on from generation to generation. *Would this not also be true for humans?*

Roland walked into the room, looking like he had aged quite a bit since Maddings had seen him last. Behind his large horn-rimmed glasses, there were purple bags under his eyes. Maddings also recognized the thick nose and strong chin of the French trappers who had settled this area two hundred years ago. Roland's hair, parted in the center, now had wisps of gray.

"So sorry. I was on the phone with the health minister. Thank you for coming."

"I'm just glad I was able to get here."

"This is my Book of the Dead," Roland said as he closed up his log and handed it to one of his assistants, a red-haired woman with a thin, birdlike face. During the earlier dissection, Roland had found and recorded an astonishing litany of diseases that he now began to identify, touching the flat side of the scalpel to each area.

"Here you can see lesions in the adrenal and thyroid glands; malignant tumors in the breasts and uterus; gum disease and missing teeth; ulcers in the mouth, throat, and stomach. And over here, you can see pneumonia and emphysema, as black and extensive as in a lifelong smoker. And down here, bladder cancer, which, perhaps not surprisingly, is quite similar to what many workers at a nearby aluminum factory suffer from. Throughout, there is also widespread bacterial infection, suggesting a highly compromised immune system."

Maddings shook his head at this litany of misery that would have rivaled Job's.

"All of these we have seen before, but this is why I asked you to fly up. This we have never seen in a female." Roland pointed down to the base of the abdominal cavity.

"*My Lord,*" Maddings said as he saw what Roland was pointing his scalpel at: two grape-sized testicles that were connected to the rest of a male reproductive tract, including the epididymis, the hothouse where sperm were grown, and the tubular vas deferens, through which they were discharged from the body.

Roland had found in this whale the extremely rare biological phenomenon of hermaphroditism. An animal having both male and female reproductive tracts was almost never seen in wildlife and had never been discovered in whales. Maddings knew that the sex of a baby, whether human or any other mammal, was set during the first few months of life. Exquisitely sensitive chemical signals determined whether a creature became male or female. Was this a true hermaphrodite—with both male and female parts? Or was this female really a male whose normal development had been arrested?

Maddings was wondering what could have caused this. As if Roland's research assistant had read his mind, he came running into the operating room breathlessly. He spoke in English when he recognized the famed Professor Maddings standing in their lab.

"Dr. Roland, the report on the tissue sample has just arrived from the Fisheries and Oceans lab. They found mercury, DDT, and PCBs." The assistant paused, knowing that what he was about to say next would be controversial. "The PCBs in the whale's body were over five hundred parts per million."

Maddings couldn't believe his ears, but it was Roland who answered, "That's impossible. That's ten times higher than the contamination level for hazardous waste." Roland looked at the report and shook his head. "By law, this whale would need a special permit to swim through Canadian waters."

Maddings was thinking about the data from the *Odyssey*, a five-year voyage that several of his colleagues had just completed, trying to establish baseline levels of contamination in the world's oceans. The level of toxic pollution in even the most remote locations and in sea life everywhere was staggering. Perhaps this whale was demonstrating the aberrant development and disease such contaminants were causing. Pollution was replacing the harpoon as the greatest threat to whales, but pollution, unlike the harpoon, was a danger not only to whales.

As he looked down at the silent whale, he thought of the high-pitched squeaks, squeals, and whistles that had earned the beluga its nickname, the "sea canary." Perhaps the corpse in front of him really was the canary in the coal mine.

Maddings went outside to escape the smell in the operating room. It was as if the whale had begun decaying even before its death. He breathed the cold air, which seemed so fresh and filled with life. Was this deformity of the genitals a unique case, or was it a growing phenomenon? Maddings feared he knew the answer.

SIXTY-TWO

Davis

ELIZABETH STARED into the open package at the nipple slits on either side of the black and shriveled skin of the penis.

"His boy thing got girl things," Teo said with all the scientific precision of a five-year-old. But Teo knew whales, and he knew what was wrong with this one.

"I can see that," Elizabeth said, unable to tear her eyes away.

"The whalers aint want anyone to know," Teo said.

Elizabeth thought of Pete Sanchez, the toxicologist Professor Ginsburg had told her about. "We've got to take a sample to get tested," she said to Teo. "And find out what caused this."

Elizabeth and Teo took the package back to the town house, away from the curious eyes of four older women who had come to play bridge. With the digital camera, Elizabeth took some photos of the whale penis and its unusual nipple slits.

"The whalers be back for it. They aint give up until they get it," Teo warned.

Elizabeth used Teo's sharp knife to cut off a sample of the defrosting whale skin, taking it from the already cut edge and careful to make sure she did not change its appearance. She did not know what the whalers had seen, but she wanted them to think that it was untouched. She wrapped the small piece of black skin in a paper napkin and then put it in the empty box of fish sticks that Teo handed her. She grabbed her jacket and headed for the door.

"Elizabeth," Teo said.

She looked back at Teo in surprise. He'd never called her Elizabeth before, always Liza. He said, "I hear what you say. That you want your man back. I hear you real good."

"Thank you, Teo."

"Maybe I see you next year."

"We'll see, Teo. But tell Milton I'll get him his boat one way or another."

"I know you will."

At the door, Elizabeth stopped. "Thank you, Teo . . . thank you for caring about the whales."

TEO WRAPPED the butcher paper back around the whale part and headed out the door to leave it in the community room. He would call the whalers and tell them where it was. It was the only way to ensure that they would leave Elizabeth alone.

Over the tall fence that surrounded the small courtyard, Teo could see Nilsen walking up the path, his right hand in the pocket of his black leather jacket.

Teo hurried back into the house. He threw his duffel in the back room and quickly placed the whale part in the freezer. He'd left the front door slightly open. When Nilsen opened it, Teo jumped off the couch in feigned surprise.

Nilsen pulled out a gun from his pocket and pointed it at Teo's chest. "Are you going to give me the package, or am I going to have to get it from your girlfriend?"

Teo couldn't help himself. "She aint me girlfriend no more."

"Where is it?" Nilsen spat out.

"Is in the freezer."

Nilsen urged Teo toward the kitchen with the gun.

Teo had no choice but to turn his back on Nilsen as he opened the freezer. He was about to reach for the package when he felt the nose of the gun against his back.

"You never should have put a knife to my throat."

"I aint mean anything by it."

"Well, I don't mean anything by this."

SIXTY-THREE

4:30 P.M.
Sacramento

FRANK WALKED INTO the doctors' lounge. Tom was watching a clinical video on the television, shaking his head and mumbling to himself.

"What's wrong?" Frank asked.

"Look at this," Tom said without taking his eyes off the screen. "I've never seen anything like it." Frank saw the sperm magnified over a thousand times. They looked like liquid pins, their tails lashing. But many were not moving at all. Then Frank saw what Tom was pointing at.

"Is this a joke?" Frank said.

Tom shook his head.

"What is it—some kind of cloning experiment gone wrong?"

"No," Tom said. "It's a video of a sperm sample from a man in Denmark. A colleague sent it to me for a second opinion. They've been seeing lots of cases like this." Frank knew Tom was an expert in "dysfunctional" sperm. He examined the image again closely. The sperm had two heads and were swimming erratically in a circle.

"What's the diagnosis?"

"No one knows, but this man is not alone. I just read a review study that said sperm counts are down fifty percent in the last sixty years."

"Fifty percent?"

"I guess it's good for my fertility clinic. I'm in a growth business."

"Never thought of it that way. But if it continues at this rate, our whole species could . . ."

"Ironic, isn't it? We could go from a population explosion to zero population."

Frank sat thinking about this possibility for a second before his thoughts were interrupted by the hospital loudspeaker. "Dr. Lombardi, please report to the reception desk."

"WHAT THE HELL do you want?" Frank demanded when he saw who it was.

Teo held up Elizabeth's wedding ring, the large square-cut diamond sparkling under the fluorescent light. "I found it on the kitchen floor under the fridge."

"You stole her ring?"

"I never going to keep it. I was thinking I could get her to love me, but now that I meet you and know that she pregnant, it just don't seem right."

Despite his dislike of Teo, Frank's shoulders started to relax. "Thanks," he said, taking the ring.

"I came here as a test, and Liza—your Elizabeth—pass. Or maybe I fail. Hold on to her. Strong ones always get away if you don't hold them fast." Teo turned to leave.

"What happened to your head?" Frank asked. Teo's hair was matted with blood. Nilsen had knocked him out, no doubt with the butt of his gun.

"Is nothing. Just a farewell present."

"Let me have a look. It might need stitches."

SIXTY-FOUR

5:00 P.M.
Davis

ELIZABETH WAS TIRED and glad to be home. She was also glad to have the whale sample in the hands of a toxicologist. Outside in her small courtyard, the wind made the rosebush sway. The pink of the flowers was washed out by the gathering night, but their fragrance filled her nose. She took a deep breath and willed her body to relax.

The rosebush was desperately in need of pruning, or any attention at all. One of the branches snagged her jacket. Why hadn't she asked her mother to show her how to garden? As a girl, she had always felt like there would be more time. She pulled off the branch, careful to avoid the thorns crowding up the stem. She looked at their shape, interested in them because her mother had been. The spikes reminded her of tiny shark's teeth. Always the biologist, Elizabeth marveled at the limited number of shapes in the natural world. The very laws of physics, she knew, dictated this fact.

Once inside the house, she noticed a pile of mail that Teo must have gathered from where it had fallen through the door slot. The bills could wait. First she needed a shower.

The hot water felt sublime, and she closed her eyes as she remembered the events of the last several weeks. Elizabeth heard a noise. Maybe it was her neighbors getting home. She peeked out of the translucent shower curtain, hearing the music from the movie *Psycho* in her head. How many showers had that movie ruined? She rolled her eyes at her imagination and picked up the shampoo. Then she remembered what Dr. Ginsburg had said about the toxic chemicals in ordinary household products. The ingredients list was an inch and a half long. Even with her chemistry classes, she couldn't pronounce half of the names and certainly didn't know what they were. The shampoo bottle thudded as it hit the plastic trash can next to the sink.

After the shower, Elizabeth put on a terry-cloth robe and wrapped her hair in a blue towel. Absentmindedly, she picked up the mail and began to flip through it. Bills, bills, junk. Then she saw something strange.

There was a letter with no stamp or return address. She pulled it out and looked at her name, handwritten on the envelope. The writing was precise, like that of an engineer or architect: ELIZABETH MCKAY. There was no address. It must have been dropped off.

She ripped it open.

The envelope's only contents was a folded piece of newspaper, which she opened. Her chest seized with terror, and her fingertips went numb as she dropped it on the counter.

It was her graduate school head shot that had been printed in one of the newspaper articles. Someone had burned out her eyes with a cigarette.

SIXTY-FIVE

5:30 P.M.
Sacramento

FRANK WALKED QUICKLY toward the exam room where the family was waiting. He took some deep breaths and tried to stay hopeful. He had not seen the test yet and was worried. This girl had found her way into his heart, had cracked open his shell of detachment. What had begun simply as professional concern about Justine's condition was now real and unavoidable human compassion.

During residency, they had tried to beat this out of him under the banner of scientific objectivity. Frank had sworn to himself that he would not get numb, would not stop caring, but that was before the endless hours, the countless patients. It had happened without his even knowing. The truth was that most of the doctors who cared about their patients eventually experienced emotional burnout. Distancing oneself was a necessary part of survival in a field with a staggering amount of unexplainable and incomprehensible suffering. It was one thing for an adult who had smoked all his life to be diagnosed with lung cancer, but for a kid to get cancer . . . It was the kind of thing that made you shake your fist at the sky and doubt the existence of God. Frank had done both.

As Frank hurried down the hall, he recalled Professor Ginsburg's lecture. Maybe the cases of childhood cancer had less to do with God and more to do with humanity. Frank glanced at the dark glass door of the Epidemiological Research Unit as he walked quickly down the hall. He noticed the words written in cheerful white letters: SPON-SORED BY THE ENVIRONMENTAL STEWARDSHIP CONSORTIUM.

When he arrived at the exam room, Frank felt flushed as he took the chart from the door and flipped through it. The results of the biopsy were not there.

"Kim," Frank said, then hesitated as he recalled their failed date. "Can you please call pathology and have them fax over the test results for the Gates baby, stat?"

"Yes, Doctor." Her tone was professional. Thank God she wasn't going to hold it against him. Frank turned back to the exam room and took a deep breath. It would be awkward to be in the room without the results, but Frank did not want to keep the family waiting any longer. He opened the door.

Justine, once again on her mother's lap, was smiling as she pointed at a picture in a board book. In quick diagnostic observation, Frank noticed the bags under Delores Gates's eye makeup as well as how her husband played nervously with his black watch.

"Not a lot of sleep last night?" Frank asked, knowing that much suffering could be relieved just by its acknowledgment.

"No, not much," she said.

Frank sat down on a rolling stool and approached slowly, not wanting to scare Justine. "Now, let's have a look at the surgeon's handiwork."

Frank gently pulled back the dressing tape and gauze bandage on the girl's neck. When she flinched, he stopped and waited. Then he finished removing the gauze so slowly the girl did not even seem to notice. He stared at the centimeter-long incision where the pediatric surgeon had removed a lymph node. A red line showed where she had been cut, and across it were the sutures of black nylon thread. They looked like fishing line knotted on one side, straight as the rungs on a ship's ladder. The incision was healing fine, and any redness was hidden by the girl's beautiful coffee-colored skin.

"The lab test should be here any minute," he said, looking back at the parents. The mother's hands were clenched, and the father was tapping one of his black leather shoes. Frank reminded himself to breathe. If he calmed himself, it helped his patients and their families stay calm as well.

"What would it mean," Gates asked, "if our baby has this disease?"

"Lymphoma," Frank said, "is a cancer of the lymph system, of the immune system."

"Will our baby die?" Ms. Gates asked.

"We'll know more once we get the tests back," Frank said. "Let's wait—"

"Doctor, if my baby's going to die, I want to know." Gates was speaking with executive authority. He was a man who clearly felt most comfortable with the hard truth of numbers, but there was no certainty on the profit and loss of life, only probabilities. Frank knew that many people took a prognosis as prophecy and died on the exact day predicted. He refused to give a death sentence to anyone, regardless of the "facts."

"I understand, Mr. Gates. We all want to know what might happen to Justine, but much depends on the kind of lymphoma, its severity, where it is in the body, and how far it has spread. And much depends on her."

"Last time I was here," Gates said, "you asked me about my job at the chemical company and how far we live from the plant. Does this have something to do with our baby being sick? Because we don't live near the plant—we live in *Blackhawk*." He said the name of the most exclusive town in the Bay Area with hard-earned pride. Frank noticed Gates glance at his wife, who was scowling but said nothing.

"It may not be the result of exposure, but that is one of the risk factors," Frank said.

"Dr. Lombardi, I spoke to a friend of mine," Ms. Gates said. "She has a toddler who was diagnosed with this same disease a year ago."

"A neighbor?" Frank asked.

"Used to be," Gates said.

There was a knock at the door. Kim handed him the lab results.

"Thank you." Frank was still trying to be hopeful. The blood test was often a false positive. The biopsy would tell them for sure. "Now let's see," he said, and then began to review the tissue diagnosis on the first page, outlining everything that the pathologist had found. Then he flipped to the conclusion on the second page. He felt his face fall. *Lymphoblastic lymphoma/acute lymphoblastic leukemia.*

"The test was positive," Frank said as he looked down, unable to face the parents.

"Positive—that's good, right?" Ms. Gates said, forcing a smile.

Frank looked into her worried brown eyes. "I'm afraid not. I'm very sorry."

Ms. Gates burst into tears, which caused Justine to start crying, too. She pulled her child against her, trying to comfort them both as she rocked back and forth. "My baby, oh, my baby, my baby . . ."

SIXTY-SIX

Lieutenant James poured himself a cup of coffee from the glass pot. The steam felt damp against his tired face. The kitchen was still dark except for the light from the streetlamp outside and the orange glowing light on the coffeemaker. His wife was still asleep, as were his twin daughters. He had gotten home late the night before, too late to read them a book or say good night, but they always wanted him to kiss them, even if they were asleep. He had walked into their bedroom, pulled up their covers, and kissed their warm cheeks. They smelled like baking loaves of bread.

The phone rang, and Lieutenant James jumped to the counter to answer it, hoping it wouldn't wake up his wife or his girls. *Who is calling at this hour?*

"Isaac, it's Commander Swift."

"Sir."

"The facts on the ground are changing. We've got to get that whale out of there by tomorrow, or we're going to have to euthanize it."

"Sir, I thought we had at least until the end of the week. As I'm sure you know, Humphrey was upriver for twenty days before he was rescued."

"This operation is costing the state much more than Humphrey ever did, and money is only one of the factors."

"Factors, sir?"

There was an awkward silence. "Isaac, your order is to get that whale out today or kill it tomorrow."

"I don't know how to get it out, Commander."

"Well, find out how, or we have no other choice. I want to hear back from you by 1400. Understood?"

"Yes, sir."

As Lieutenant James hung up, he heard little feet on the stairs. His brown-haired daughters came running at him with big smiles, and each hugged a leg as he turned around. His girls were getting so tall they now came up to his waist. Kayla was in her pajamas and held a book in her hand. Eliana was already dressed and held her blue sneakers against her chest.

"I can do it, Daddy. I can do it myself." Eliana had been trying to learn to tie her shoes for months. The fact that she was already six and her twin sister knew how to do it was a source of serious embarrassment. Lieutenant James squatted down as she slipped her sneakers on over her frilly white socks. She picked up the laces of her left sneaker and wrapped them around each other, her face in deep concentration. But she got lost in the twisting and threw her laces down in defeat, all the more frustrated because she had thought she could do it.

"Remember the rabbit ears," Lieutenant James said as he took the laces and looped each one. "Wind one ear around the other and come through the rabbit hole like this. Now you try with the other foot."

"No, I can't do it." Eliana was frowning, and her arms were crossed over her chest.

"You can do it, Elly," her sister said as she sat down to read.

Lieutenant James held up his pointer finger like the number one. "One more try? Just one more try?" He smiled, found her downcast eyes, and spoke in a playful voice. "Just one more little try."

Eliana snatched the laces of the other sneaker and slowly formed them into rabbit ears, then twisted one around the other and finally pushed it through the rabbit hole.

Lieutenant James pulled the laces tight. "You did it." She gave him a big hug, proud of her accomplishment.

Lieutenant James's wife, Janet, was watching from the doorway to the kitchen with a smile. Her long red hair hung down over her pink robe, and her freckled skin and light blue eyes looked pretty, as they always did in the morning, even without makeup.

"Sorry about the call," he said.

"Apollo?" she asked.

"Yeah, they want me to kill it if it's not gone by tomorrow. I don't understand what the rush is."

Kayla looked up from her book. "Daddy, don't kill the whale." Lieutenant James realized that he should have been more careful about what he said in front of his daughters. He pursed his lips as he pulled on his black coat and Coast Guard cap. He was at the door when Kayla came running over. It was still dark and cold outside. "Please, Daddy, promise me you won't kill the whale."

Lieutenant James bent over and put his hands on his daughter's shoulders. "I'm going to do everything I can to help this whale, but if it doesn't want to leave or if it is sick, then we might have to put it to sleep."

"No, Daddy, don't." Kayla was crying. She knew what putting it to sleep meant.

Eliana came to the door and held up her finger. "One more try, Daddy. Just one more little try."

SIXTY-SEVEN

9:00 A.M.
Davis

ELIZABETH DID NOT SUBSCRIBE to the *Sacramento Times,* but there it was on the doorstep. Someone had unfolded it and laid it out for her to see. She felt dizzy and sick to her stomach as she read the front-page headline: A WHALE OF A TALE: FAILED GRADUATE STUDENT NO WHALE WHISPERER.

Elizabeth's hands were shaking as she picked up the paper. She dreaded reading what the article said, but she could not stop herself. It would be worse not knowing what her neighbors and friends were being told about her.

"Since the whale's arrival in the San Francisco Bay and its journey up the Sacramento River, former graduate student Elizabeth McKay has been telling the media that the entrapped whale has a story to tell." The article went on to say that Lieutenant Isaac James had given Elizabeth "unprecedented access to the entrapped whale" and that he had disregarded the recommendations of many more senior scientists who were advising him that the whale was sick and should be euthanized "out of compassion." It explained that she had recently been kicked out of her graduate program. Skilling was quoted as saying, "I spoke with Ms. McKay many times about the fanciful nature of her research, that it was based on unsubstantiated findings." The article even suggested that she was possibly mentally unstable.

• • •

Elizabeth drove across the causeway toward the medical center, the steering wheel of the old station wagon vibrating. She squeezed her hands around the hard plastic, hoping it might stop the wheel—and her—from shaking. The beauty of the floodplain and wildlife sanctuary spread out on either side of the causeway, soothing Elizabeth's anxious mind. In comparison to the picture and the newspaper article, the argument with Frank about Teo seemed trivial. She had tried to call, but his cell phone kept going to voice mail. It would be better to see him, to tell him in person, to hold him. God, she needed his arms to comfort her.

As she drove, she could not stop thinking about the photo with its burned-out eyes. How far would the whalers go? When she'd seen the picture, she had immediately checked the freezer to see if the whale package was still there. It was not. In its place was a brief note Teo had scribbled: "Package to the whalers. Hoping it helps you and the whales."

Snowy egrets and a great blue heron stood elegantly in the distance, and a red-tailed hawk flew over the car. The smell of brine and fish made her wince. Had she forgotten to wash her wetsuit? Elizabeth looked in her rearview mirror and saw the messy backseat of the station wagon. Her wetsuit and fins were stacked on top of equipment, files, books, clothes, and other chaos that she'd never had a chance to clear out. She was a bit of a packrat; Frank had always complained about her unwillingness to let go of anything that might someday be useful. As she rolled down her window, the wind felt good on her face and helped with the smell.

Elizabeth's cell phone rang. She looked at the caller ID. *Restricted.* She flipped open the phone and held it to her ear as she continued driving with her other hand.

"Hello, Elizabeth, I see you've been making headlines." The voice was a woman's, and it sounded menacingly sweet.

"Who is this?"

"One of your secret admirers."

"Very funny."

"We can ruin your career—or at least what's left of it."

"What do you want from me?"

"We want you to stop being the self-appointed spokesperson for the whale."

"Why?"

"It doesn't matter why. We just want you to stop talking about things that you don't know anything about and scaring people unnecessarily."

"How did you get my number?"

"We know a lot about you, Elizabeth."

"You can't stop me from telling people the truth."

"Oh, yes, we can." The calmness of the voice sent chills up Elizabeth's spine. "Let's just say we have legal and *extra*legal means to keep you quiet. If you know what is good for you and your baby, you'll do as I say."

"How do you know about my baby?"

"You're not listening, Elizabeth. I told you that we know a lot about you."

"How dare you!"

"If you don't believe what I say, Elizabeth, just look behind you . . ."

Elizabeth's eyes flared up toward the rearview mirror. There was no car behind her.

"In the backseat," the voice added.

Elizabeth's heart was pounding against her rib cage. Was there someone in the car? She saw nothing but the pile of her debris.

As if reading her thoughts again, the woman's voice whispered, "Under the wetsuit."

Elizabeth glanced at the red brake lights of the truck in front of her and then quickly reached into the backseat, knocking her wetsuit to the floor. Underneath she saw a baby's car seat. In it was a blue baby's outfit. As she looked closer, she saw something sticking out of the collar. It was the silver head and vacant black eye of a large dead fish. She screamed and stepped on the gas instinctively. Her eyes shot back to the road, but it was too late. She was going to crash into the truck in front of her.

Elizabeth yanked the wheel to the right to avoid the truck and cut across the access lane, hurtling toward the railing of the causeway and the floodplain below.

SIXTY-EIGHT

THE STATION WAGON hurtled toward the concrete guardrail. The front wheel well hit first, and the car screeched along the barrier, shooting sparks in every direction. Within seconds, the full weight of the heavy car collided broadside. The car tipped up on its side as it rode on two wheels, preparing to fall over the low guardrail.

Elizabeth looked down at the water in the floodplain below her, seeing the car's reflection. She yanked the wheel to the left, but the momentum carried her fifty meters down the guardrail, sparks still flying, metal grinding, as the car finally bucked and stopped with a groan.

The old car had no air bags, and there was nothing cushioning her body as it absorbed the shock of the crash. From what she could tell, she had not hit her head and was not badly injured. Shaking and numb, she got out of the car to look for damage. The side of the car was bashed in, and the right front wheel well was punched into a permanent scream. But the tire was intact and still looked drivable.

A car stopped behind her, and a man got out. "Are you all right?"

"Yeah, thanks."

"You sure?"

"Yeah, I'm fine. I'm fine. Thank you."

The man looked at her suspiciously, perhaps wondering if she was in shock. He wasn't the only one who was wondering if she was in her right mind. Risking her and her baby's life *was* crazy.

It began to drizzle as Elizabeth got back into the station wagon. *Maybe I am in shock,* she thought as she stared blankly, watching the drops tapping against her windshield. She shifted the car into drive and headed back to the slough to see Apollo. To say goodbye.

"How COULD YOU run a public relations hatchet job like that?" Bruce Wood asked, although it was more of an accusation than a question. He was standing in the doorway of his editor's office, his black eyes narrowed in anger. For all he knew, the whale researcher *was* crazy, but this was unprofessional and exactly the kind of garbage that was ruining journalism.

The piles of paper on the desk almost hid the editor's rosacea-reddened face. His unkempt gray hair was brushed across his balding head. "When my best investigative journalist decides to cover garden parties and school bonds, I have to turn to the wires."

"The wires? The public relations wire, maybe."

"Subscriptions are down. Advertising revenue is dropping. The staff is shrinking. I need to print something, don't I?"

Wood remembered Elizabeth's comments about pollution. Maybe there was a story here after all. Someone was clearly trying to discredit her. "I'm going to find out who's behind that wire story and why they have it in for that graduate student. Then maybe I'll have some real news for you."

SIXTY-NINE

Sacramento

Frank closed his cell phone. He couldn't reach Elizabeth on hers but had left her a message, which she was either not hearing or unwilling to return.

Tom walked up to the nurses' station, distracting Frank from his worry about Elizabeth. "Frank, sorry about security. I told them to hurry up." Tom glanced to the side.

"Thanks," Frank said, but he wasn't buying it. How could it take a month to reset some access codes? The Epidemiological Research Unit was finding something that they didn't want others to know. Frank knew from playing poker with Tom that he was a terrible bluffer. His eyes always looked to the side when he was lying.

Tom turned to fill out a prescription. His card key was in the pocket of his white coat. Frank clasped his hand on Tom's shoulder affectionately. "I want to thank you for your and Jenny's help during this trying time for me and Elizabeth."

"It's nothing," Tom said, seeming a little uncomfortable with the physical intimacy.

"No, really, Tom, it's meant a lot to me." As he looked into Tom's eyes and held his shoulder, Frank used his other hand to pluck Tom's card key from his pocket.

"Anytime," Tom said.

Frank started down the hall. "Hey, wait a minute," he heard Tom say. Frank froze and then slowly turned around. "You forgot your coffee."

Frank sighed and smiled. "You can have it."

Tom tipped the Styrofoam cup to his lips and drank it in one gulp like a shot, then lifted it in the air as if toasting Frank. "The coffee hasn't gotten any better."

"Some things never do," Frank said, hurrying down the hall.

He looked both ways to see if anyone was coming. The hall was empty. He slid Tom's card key into the reader and heard the door unlock. Frank slipped inside quickly and closed the door.

On Tom's desk was a picture of his family in front of their large vacation home in Hawaii. Tom, Jenny, and their two boys beamed with almost unnatural wholesomeness and all-American good looks. Obstetricians weren't buying big vacation homes in Hawaii—plastic surgeons or dermatologists, maybe, but not obstetricians. Tom must have either come from money or been moonlighting.

There was another photo on the desk of Tom's softball team. Tom and Jenny had been nothing but kind to him, and Frank felt guilty about suspecting his friend. But something was suspicious. When he had asked security about his key, they said he had not been authorized to get a new one.

Frank pressed the power button on the computer, and the monitor flashed to life. An external hard drive resting on the desk hummed as its light turned red and then green. Frank swiped Tom's card key on another reader next to the computer, but then it asked for his password.

Frank sat back in his chair. *How am I ever going to figure out his password?* He was not particularly good at code cracking—that was always Elizabeth's skill. Her mind was always good at puzzles. His was not. *Come on, think. Children? Everyone uses their children's names.* Frank typed in the names of Tom's two boys, but neither worked. He slumped in the chair, defeated. He stared at the picture of Tom's soft-

ball team. He knew Tom was a passionate—his wife said obsessive—
softball player. Some doctors lived for golf. Tom lived for softball.
What's the name of his team? The Hawks? No, no . . . the Eagles!

Six little black circles appeared in the dialogue box as Frank
typed "Eagles."

He was in.

Frank looked up the birth defects statistics that the research unit
was collecting for the regional health registry. The summary page
listed two stats.

"Prematurity as a percentage of all births: 12.3%."

"Birth defects as a percentage of births: 3.5%."

Frank sighed with a combination of relief and frustration. He
knew these numbers were consistent with the national averages, and
he was relieved that there was no great epidemic of prematurity or
birth defects. But his gut told him these statistics were wrong. He
had witnessed more than his share of abnormal births.

He clicked on the icon for the database of birth defects and
began to navigate through the records. Under the child's name each
electronic record had the diagnosis and a picture of the condition.
There was everything from a slightly cleft palate to spina bifida, and
this was just in the first two letters of the alphabet. He started in on
the C's. Frank stopped. *Where's the Bradley baby?* He recalled the
missing hand and the heart defect of the baby he had delivered a
month before. *Did I skip over it?*

He looked back through "B," but there was no Bradley. *Could
they be almost a month behind in entering data?* The record in front of
him was of a tiny preemie born the week before. Many of the other
records were more recent. He started to check for other patients of
his and discovered that some of them had not been entered into the
epidemiological database, either.

Frank looked around nervously. Someone was clearly falsifying the
data to make it look like there was a normal incidence of prematurity

and birth defects. He looked back at the main database of all births and checked the coding for the Bradley baby. It said: "Birth outcome undetermined." *That's crazy,* Frank thought. *The diagnosis is right there in the record.* Quickly, he checked several other babies who had been born with birth defects and found that they, too, were labeled "Birth outcome undetermined."

Frank saved the databases to the external hard drive and then unplugged it from the main computer. He looked around for something to hide the hard drive in. Sticking out of the garbage was a small pizza box.

Frank left the office and closed the door behind him.

"Are you stealing my pizza?"

Frank turned around and saw Tom standing there.

Before Frank could respond, they were paged overhead: *"Dr. Neumann and Dr. Lombardi, please report to the birthing center."*

SEVENTY

Liberty Slough

*A*POLLO'S EYES *were clouding over—and he was seeing through an increasingly white film—*

He could hear the splashing of flippers and feel the ripples of the creatures approaching—

He continued singing—the waters vibrating—

Still he did not move—

Then he felt the net around his flukes—like those that had caused so many whales to drown—

His heart began to beat faster—and he began to thrash his tail—

Suddenly he heard the roaring of a boat and was being dragged backward—

He continued thrashing and resisted with all of his strength—

His backward slide stopped—the roaring increased—the whining sharp in his ears and the net straining where it circled his flukes—

ELIZABETH STOOD ON the concrete bridge, watching the disaster unfold in front of her. Apollo was thrusting his mighty tail, straining against the tether of the industrial-gauge rope being used to drag him out. The divers had fastened a padded rubber harness around the caudal peduncle, the part of the stalk just before the tail. Elizabeth looked behind her at the muscular forty-seven-foot motor lifeboat on the other side of the bridge from Apollo. It had been brought in for the operation and was pulling at full throttle. But it was not moving forward. The rope was taut and lurching back and forth, straining to the point of breaking.

Elizabeth felt helpless. She had no better ideas, and even if she had, there was little chance that anyone would have acted on them. The television reporters had shown little interest in her when she had arrived at the slough. A Dr. Dolittle was one thing; an insane graduate student was another. Even Lieutenant James had told her that he'd been ordered to take her off the whale rescue team. She was here simply as a private citizen, an ordinary spectator. Fortunately, after a court order, the owner of the land was once again allowing people to use the levee road, which was public property.

She looked out at the levee wall on one side and the line of trees hugging the shore on the other. While the landowners were not preventing the public from entering, they were not making it easy. Black security cars blocked off the road, and people had to walk quite a distance. Even with this barrier and the discouraging news broadcasts, there were still two or three hundred people standing or sitting along the levee. A troop of young Cub Scouts wearing blue uniforms and bright orange neckerchiefs held up a banner that said: SAVE APOLLO. They hadn't lost hope. The white television vans were still there, and a helicopter circled like a buzzard, waiting for the whale to die.

Elizabeth was startled by a sound like a shotgun. The rope had snapped, and the eighty-ton shock load had turned it into a deadly coil. Ducking quickly behind the concrete barrier, she heard it come flying toward where she stood on the bridge. The rope lashed in fury and continued toward the boat, rearing up like a serpent and tearing off the antennas mounted on top of the wheelhouse before finally shattering the glass of the back windows into countless pieces. Several of the Coast Guard seamen had dropped to the deck. All, including Lieutenant James, were still moving and did not seem to be seriously hurt. Even at this distance, she could hear James's voice saying, "Dammit. Damn that stubborn whale."

In the brown water below the bridge, Elizabeth saw her faceless reflection. The rescue efforts had failed. She had failed. It was just a matter of time before they euthanized the whale. Someone wanted this whale out now—whether alive or dead. When she had arrived at the slough, she'd discovered that her laptop was missing—stolen. Whoever had put the dead fish in her car had taken her laptop out. Maybe Connie was right. Maybe it was the whalers. Well, they had won, and she and Apollo had lost.

"Aren't you supposed to be saving this whale?"

Elizabeth looked over and saw Teo walking up the bridge.

SEVENTY-ONE

"I THOUGHT YOU had left," Elizabeth said, even as she herself was turning to leave.

"I decide to stay around and keep an eye on you til Frank come home. Connie say I could stay a few days at her place."

"What makes you so sure he'll come back?"

"He see it right, don't you worry."

Elizabeth kept walking toward the bank.

"Where you going?"

"Home."

"Giving up?"

"There's nothing more I can do for Apollo."

"You can find out what wrong with that calf. Is no whaling if the whale all covered in diseases."

Elizabeth hadn't heard from Pete Sanchez, but she wasn't sure how those test results would make any difference to Apollo. "I have to think about my own baby now."

Teo followed Elizabeth back across the bridge. "If is true what you say about the whale warning, you think your baby'll be safe?"

"They threatened my child, Teo." She stopped at the bank where the bridge started, trying not to look at him. "I'm afraid."

"Of course you afraid. Courage don't mean you not afraid. I been scared plenty. Courage mean doing what you must though you never been more afraid in your whole life."

Elizabeth heard Teo's words, but she had made up her mind. She was giving up being a scientist, giving up on her quest to understand the whales. She had sacrificed so much already, and she was not going to sacrifice her child, too. Stepping off the cement bridge and onto the gravel path, she turned to say goodbye to Teo, knowing she was also saying goodbye to the whales and to eight years of her life.

Elizabeth saw the sun glittering on the water. She felt a dull, gnawing ache in her stomach and bit her lip to stop herself from crying. She looked into Teo's face and then looked down, ashamed of her failure.

In the mud next to his dirty white sneakers, she saw something. It was a dead frog. She stooped down and turned it over with her finger. It had a double pair of back legs, the extra set growing out of its stomach. Its mouth hung agape. She looked closer. Something in its mouth was shiny, reflecting the low sun. With her forefinger, she opened its mouth. On the frog's tongue, an eye stared back at her.

SEVENTY-TWO

FRANK AND TOM stood along the wall of the birthing room wearing blue surgical gowns, white latex gloves, and pink paper masks over their faces. Frank listened to the moans of the young woman struggling to bring her first baby into the world. The mother gripped the hand of the labor nurse as if her reassuring grasp could help her baby come into the world sooner.

The baby was premature, and the heart tracing had been irregular. Frank glanced around the room for family. There was no father in the room, no grandparents, no sister, not even a friend. The young unwed mother was not over sixteen and clearly terrified. Frank thought of the statues of the Virgin Mary in his childhood church.

He glanced over at Tom, who was scrupulously avoiding his eyes. "I can't believe you would do it!" Frank whispered forcefully, careful to keep the nurse at the bedside from hearing them.

"Do what?" Tom said, glancing at Frank for only a brief moment.

Frank could see that he was sweating under his mask, and it was not just because the birthing room was heated. "What you did to the database."

"What are you talking about?" Tom asked, looking to the side again.

"You miscoded the birth defects." Frank was getting angry at his friend's denial. The woman's cries intensified.

"So mistakes were made in the data entry."

"You knew exactly what you were doing. You were falsifying the data to make it look like there were a normal number of birth defects."

"It's just a research study."

"This is not just a research study. These are our patients. We use that information to diagnose and treat them."

"I had no choice."

Frank sighed. At least Tom was admitting that he had done it. "What do you mean?"

"They have me."

"Who?"

Tom stared at Frank. His eyes looked nervous but also strangely relieved, as if he had been desperate to tell someone the truth. "I just wanted to do research. The hospital said there was no way without a funding source. That's when they called."

The laboring woman's primal groans filled the room with each contraction. Tom glanced down at where the labor nurse was checking the young woman. Almost ready but not yet.

Frank asked again, "Who's 'they'? The Environmental Steward-ship Consortium?"

"Yeah. They offered to support my research if I made a few cosmetic changes to my design, and I didn't think much about it. I figured that's how you get ahead in the field. You do research. You get funded. You publish articles. I was willing to play ball, but I didn't realize the game they were playing."

"What did they want?"

"They started to redline my articles and to change my conclusions. When I told them I wouldn't do it, they started to threaten me. They know what I've already done. Now I can't get out." Tom's eyes looked fearful above the mask. "What are you going to do, Frank, now that you know?"

"What are *you* going to do?"

"This could ruin my career."

"Yeah, it could."

"Jenny doesn't work. I've got kids to feed."

"What about *these* kids?" Frank said, tilting his head toward the child about to be born.

Tom pushed his gloved palms together in front of his scrubs, as if he were praying. Frank could see that Tom was trying to stop their shaking; he wasn't succeeding.

Leaning over Tom's shoulder, Frank asked, "Who is the Environmental Stewardship Consortium? Who are they, really?"

Tom did not have a chance to answer. He had to move swiftly into action as the baby began crowning. He gently started to stretch the membranes around the head. *"No empuje, señorita, no empuje."*

The new mother uttered one long, last groan, and the baby's head pushed through the birth canal, followed quickly by the shoulders, torso, and four limbs, whole and complete. The little boy had a full head of black hair and a reddish-brown face. He was screaming with life and health.

Dorothy came huffing into the room, her rubber-soled shoes squeaking on the linoleum floor. "Mr. Gates is in your office, Dr. Lombardi. He says he needs to talk with you immediately. Says it's urgent."

Is something wrong with Justine? Frank wondered, and glanced back at the newborn.

"The baby's fine," Tom said. "I'll take care of him. Go."

SEVENTY-THREE

GATES WAS HOLDING a photo of Frank and Elizabeth that he had picked up from the desk.

"Is something wrong, Mr. Gates? Is it Justine?"

Gates looked up and then carefully placed the picture frame back on the desk. "There is something wrong. But it's not just Justine."

"I don't understand."

"Dr. Lombardi, we're not making anything in our factories that the other large chemical companies around the world aren't making—hell, we're a lot better than some about following environmental regulations. The problem is, we're creating things that have never existed before, so no one really knows what the long-term effects will be. Much of the time, companies are left in a gray area."

"I'm not following you, Mr. Gates."

"We didn't always live in Blackhawk, Dr. Lombardi. I worked my way up through the company. I started out at the West Sacramento plant, got my MBA at night. I wanted to show my boss that I could play the game, maximize profits. I decided to build employee houses on land owned by the chemical plant. It was cheaper. I made the decision to build the house where my baby got sick."

Frank wondered why Gates was telling him all of this. Had he come for absolution? Many people treated doctors like priests and confessed their sins. "Mr. Gates, no one man caused this problem," Frank said, trying to console him.

"I know this is not just about one man, or one chemical company, or one oil company, or one agribusiness—it's about all of them. It's about the cost of doing business. I know, because twelve years ago, I helped set up a group called the Environmental Stewardship Consortium to try to protect our interests. We saw what was happening to the tobacco companies. We knew if the truth got out and there was litigation, it could cost us billions."

"What truth?"

Gates set his black leather briefcase on the desk, took out a file, and handed it to Frank. "These were all supposed to have been shredded, but I kept them just in case the good old boys on our board ever decided they didn't like having an outspoken black man around. You might say it was my unemployment insurance. I know what you were asking about the day my wife and I were in your office, before our whole world collapsed."

"What do you want me to do with this?"

"I'm sure you will figure out something."

Gates was at the door. "I think we learned the wrong lesson from tobacco, Dr. Lombardi. I pray God will forgive me. I know my wife never will."

SEVENTY-FOUR

"THE SAMPLES are very hot," Pete Sanchez said as he came back in. The fluorescent lights on the ceiling of the wet lab were unrelentingly bright. Elizabeth could not help feeling like one of the specimens in the fish tanks around her. "We'll get the full tests back in a week. I'm still waiting on the whale tissue, too. But I did some preliminary tests that can give you a sense of what's to come.

"The sample from Liberty Slough is some of the most polluted water I've seen. It has pesticides, probably agricultural runoff from the fields—phthalates and Bisphenol A, likely from the plastics factory—and benzene and phenols, no doubt from the oil refinery."

"It must be some kind of toxic waste dump," Elizabeth said.

"I wish it were that simple."

"What do you mean?"

"All of the samples were hot, even the whale tissue. It had many of the same pollutants as the frog and the water—PCBs, pesticides, you name it."

"But the whale sample is from a completely different ocean."

"Water doesn't obey our maps," Pete said dryly. "There really is only one ocean. One of my colleagues just found the highest levels of heavy metal and persistent organic pollutants in free-ranging wildlife near the Gilbert Islands. Do you know where the Gilbert Islands are?"

"No, I don't."

"Neither did I. They're out in the middle of the Pacific Ocean. They're about as remote as you can get, and researchers found chromium levels that were off the charts."

There it was again—the same metal that the whale inspector had said he was finding in the whales. "What are these pollutants doing?" she asked.

"We're discovering all sorts of mysteries surrounding the way that chemicals and life interact," Pete said. "I'll show you."

Elizabeth knew that this was about much more than saving Apollo. With a growing sense of dread filling her body, she followed Pete over to a collection of cages. Suddenly, she wasn't sure she wanted to hear what Pete was about to tell her; yet she knew that if she had any hope of helping her own baby, or anyone else's, she had to know the truth.

"You've heard of arsenic, right? Probably as a poison that's been used in countless murder mysteries—that's at a high dose. Well, at a lower level, it undermines how your body fights tumors." Pete pointed at one of the cages. Elizabeth winced at the sight of the swollen white rats in the cage, which looked like they were covered in lumps. "But even lower levels of contaminants can compromise your health. Look at the rats in these two cages."

Elizabeth saw two other rats, their red eyes looking up at her nervously. One was extremely thin, and the other was grossly obese, four times the size of the other.

"These rats have consumed the same number of calories and have had identical activity levels, but this rat"—Pete pointed to the obese one—"was given one part per billion of a chemical called BPA right after birth."

"One part per billion?"

"That's like one drop in an Olympic-sized swimming pool.

Sounds like such a tiny amount. I know it's hard to imagine it could be harmful."

"So why do some people get sick and others don't?"

"Our inherited genes play a role. No two animals—including humans—will respond in exactly the same way. And there are other factors, such as stress."

"Stress?" Elizabeth said dubiously. "Stress can't change the realities of chemistry."

"See for yourself. Look at these tadpoles," he said. Elizabeth bent down and looked into a fish tank filled with them. "They are swimming in water contaminated with a pesticide. They seem largely unaffected, but look what happens when they are stressed." He pointed to another tank where a small wire cage hung over the edge. Inside of the cage was a California newt with a black back and an orange belly. "When tadpoles in the contaminated water smell a newt—their traditional predator—they are fifty times more likely to die than tadpoles swimming in uncontaminated water."

Elizabeth saw many of the tadpoles in the second aquarium floating belly-up. She was trying to accept the magnitude of the dangers that faced her and her child. For some reason, seeing the tadpoles floating on the surface made these dangers real. "Is there any hope for us, Pete?"

"I'll show you something that gives me hope." Pete brought her over to a series of large plastic tubs. In the first was a patch of desolate black soil. "Many of us were asked to recommend solutions to an oil spill that took place up in Washington recently. I decided to test a theory about mushrooms being the earth's mechanism for regenerating itself, so I sprinkled mushroom spores, and this is what happened after four weeks." Inside the second plastic container, brown mushrooms were crowded together so densely that it was hard to see the soil. "Do you want to see what happened after ten weeks?"

Elizabeth nodded.

Pete took her outside to the courtyard. The soil-filled square tub was covered with flowers and bugs, and even a robin perched on the rim.

"Life is simply the balance of destruction and restoration. I have no doubt life will survive. The question is whether we and other so-called intelligent species will."

The cell phone in Elizabeth's hand started to vibrate. It was Frank.

SEVENTY-FIVE

"THIS IS Lieutenant Governor Farthing. Is this Lieutenant Isaac James?"

"Yes, sir."

"Commander Swift tells me that he is planning to remove you from your post. He says you are not following orders." The lieutenant governor's voice had the calm cadence of power.

Lieutenant James swallowed hard. "I'm trying to do my duty, sir. I know how much you have been a supporter of saving this whale, and I understood my orders to be its rescue." He swallowed again and looked up at the light blue piece of construction paper on the wall—his daughter's picture of Apollo.

"We've done all we can for the whale, son. My scientific advisers have convinced me that the whale is sick and suffering. The humane thing to do is to euthanize it."

Lieutenant James wondered which group had gotten to the lieutenant governor and how large their campaign contribution was. Despite Skilling's belief that the whale was at death's door, several other scientific advisers believed the whale had more time, including Elizabeth. "Sir, honestly, I don't want to risk my men getting close to the whale again. This whale has a lot of fight in it. I have talked to the zoo people about their elephant darting gun, but the Fish and Game people tell me etorphine is too dangerous to introduce into a marine environment." Lieutenant James hoped this might delay what was becoming increasingly inevitable.

"I am aware of these concerns. One of the scientists has arranged for the delivery of an exploding harpoon."

"A harpoon, sir?"

"An on-site veterinarian will be tasked with firing it."

"What about the Marine Mammal Protection Act, sir?"

"This has been cleared with the National Marine Fisheries Service. Sunrise will be 6:00 A.M.—that's in thirteen hours and thirty minutes. I want you to make sure this is handled before then."

Lieutenant James was surprised by this request.

"Is that understood?"

"Yes, sir."

"We've roped off the area, but the media is very persistent."

"*We've* roped it off, sir? I thought that was done by private security officers."

"The Office of Emergency Services consented. We don't want this turning into a circus. I trust you understand."

"Yes, sir."

"Any questions?"

"Just one, sir. I would like to have your orders in writing." Lieutenant James was stalling.

"I'm beginning to understand Commander Swift's frustration. The orders will be faxed over later today. If they are not carried out by tomorrow at sunrise, Lieutenant, I'd look for a new career, if I were you. Is that clear?"

"Very clear, sir."

SEVENTY-SIX

5:00 P.M.
Davis

ELIZABETH EXCUSED HERSELF and hurried away to answer the call.

"Elizabeth, I just saw the article. Are you okay?"

"Yeah."

"I have something to show you that might explain who's behind it. Where are you?"

"I'm at the toxicology lab at the vet school."

"I'm on my way. I can smell the vet school from here."

Elizabeth smiled for the first time since she had seen the article. Having her spouse on her side made all the difference. She could stand against the rest of the world if necessary.

FRANK WALKED INTO the toxicology lab. He had on a pink shirt and a frog-patterned green and yellow necktie. The shirt and tie did not exactly match, but now even Frank's lack of color coordination seemed endearing to Elizabeth.

"I should have trusted you. I'm sorry for getting angry," he said.

"Teo told me what he said. I can understand why you were jealous."

"It's the Italian in me."

"Maybe it's the human in you." She took his hand and pulled him close. "Frank, you're the man I want . . . the only man."

Frank smiled like a schoolboy at his first dance. *Maddings was right*, Elizabeth thought. *That really was all Frank needed to hear. Why did it take me so long to say it?*

"Look," Frank said. "Finish your Ph.D., and we'll go wherever we can both get jobs. Maybe I can take a teaching position with shorter hours. We can be together and have our family. We've been waiting long enough."

"I am thinking of giving up. You and Dr. Skilling were right. I have been at it too long."

"Giving up? You can't do that."

"But—"

"If you give it up, you'll never be happy."

Now it was Elizabeth who was smiling from ear to ear. "Really, you mean it?"

"Of course I do. I was an idiot for suggesting that you should."

"Maybe I can talk to Dr. Skilling and change my dissertation topic."

"No," Frank said, shaking his head. "You can find another program, maybe go back to Woods Hole. You're not going to change anything—and certainly not for *Skilling*." Frank's face showed a scowl of disgust as he said the name. "I found out a lot about Tricky Dick Skilling. You need to see this." Frank looked around to make sure they were alone, then took a file out of his bag and placed it on the gray countertop. "The memos and reports in this file show that many of the chemical companies, oil companies, and agribusinesses are well aware of the dangers of their products but have decided to cover them up."

"The companies in the Valley are doing this?"

"These are not just companies in the Valley. These are international conglomerates—some of the biggest companies in the world." As he flipped through the file, Elizabeth saw that all the internal memos were marked confidential. "It was more important to them to protect their profits and to avoid government regulation. So they buried their findings and fought anyone who was trying to reveal the health dangers to the public."

"How could they get away with this?"

"The companies have tried awfully hard to cover up their tracks and confuse the issues." Frank pointed to one memo that discussed the creation of the Environmental Stewardship Consortium. "These companies set up this product defense group to try to obscure the data and buy off scientists—"

"Dr. Richard Skilling," Elizabeth read under a column of "sympathetic" scientists. Next to them were earmarked payments for testifying in Congress and for signing their names to pro-industry research articles.

"Yeah, good old Dick Skilling. He's made a fortune from industry. They even gave him royalties on a patent to hide the money they were paying him."

Elizabeth was amazed. Skilling had betrayed her and even tried to seduce her, but she'd never imagined that he could be so corrupt. She was feeling tired and defeated—and hungry. "So what?" she finally said. "Everyone knows that there's a cost of doing business. How do we prove that any of this matters?"

Out of his leather doctor's bag, Frank pulled what looked like an external hard drive, no bigger than a paperback book. The drive's gray metal reflected the lights overhead. Frank was smiling like the Cheshire cat. "The cases in this database show the real cost of doing business *like this*." He turned to Pete, who had just come back into the room. "Dr. Ginsburg said you're mapping toxins. I assume you're working with GIS?"

Pete's eyes widened with excitement. "We've got one of the best systems. It's my pride and joy." Geographic Information Systems allowed scientists to map data, often using satellite images.

"Ever work with health data like birth defects?" Frank asked.

"With whatever we can get. Privacy laws make it hard."

"What if I said that on this hard drive I had the birth defects and childhood cancer records for the entire Sacramento Valley region?"

"With home addresses?"

"Everything."

"I'd say that you had brought me the GIS Holy Grail. We've been trying to get that data for years."

"Well, here it is. Can you map it?" Frank asked.

Pete was turning on his computer eagerly. "I'm sure I can make you a pretty picture."

Pete had a map of Northern California up on his screen. It looked like a weather map, with concentric irregular shapes of color superimposed on satellite images. "While we wait for my software to read your data set, let me show you what we're finding."

"What are we seeing here?" Frank asked, pointing to the red area.

"The red zones are the hottest. That's where the highest levels of toxic contamination are found." Pete zoomed out to a satellite map of the whole planet. The red zones were much smaller, pockmarking the globe. "As you can see, there are hot zones in the arctic and other places of relatively low population, simply because of the way these persistent organic pollutants travel with the wind and ocean currents."

"Are these all the chemicals we've mapped?"

"Oh no, that's just one well-studied contaminant. But if you study one contaminant, you don't see the bigger patterns. Let me show you the top fifty." As Pete did so, the red began blending together increasingly and was harder to differentiate. "And here are the top two hundred that have been found in some measure in nearly everyone who's been tested." The world was awash in the color red. The whole globe was a hot zone.

"The data set has been geocoded," Pete said. "Let's see what we have." He zoomed back in toward the surface of the planet as if falling back to earth. Elizabeth noticed the distinct peninsular shape of the Bay Area, like two pincers separated by the thin expanse of the Golden Gate Bridge. To the west she could see the small dots of the Farallon Islands. The image moved east and zoomed in toward the area of the slough.

"These are the hot zones close to the local assets of the companies in the consortium," Frank said, pointing to the screen; the factories, refineries, and fields of the companies could be seen from the aerial view. "They have a similar photo in one of the reports in the file." The zones of contamination seemed to bleed out from the industrial sites, but what was surprising was that the slough was shaded red from three different directions.

"Now let me overlay your data," Pete said. With a few keystrokes, a sparse collection of small diamonds appeared randomly on the map.

Frank's shoulders dropped. It was not revealing what he'd thought it might. "Hey, wait a second," he said, remembering the miscoding. "In the birth outcome column, try changing 'undetermined' to 'defect.'" Pete did a find-and-replace in the data file and then hit "enter."

Frank gasped audibly as he ran his finger over the screen. "Ever wish you weren't right?" he said. On the screen were densely clustered blinking diamonds on the housing developments on the outskirts of Liberty Slough. The slough and Apollo were at the center of it all. No wonder the Environmental Stewardship Consortium wanted to get that whale out of there—before anyone started testing the water.

ELIZABETH AND FRANK thanked Pete and then headed out of the lab, taking the file and the hard drive with them. Elizabeth's cell phone vibrated again. She flipped it open and said hello.

"It's Bruce Wood from the *Sacramento Times*."

"You have some nerve, calling me after what you wrote."

"You didn't happen to notice that there was no byline, did you?" Wood said, not a hint of guilt or remorse in his voice. "I didn't write the article. Comes over the wire practically ready to print—from a PR agency. That kind of crap is ruining my profession."

"So why are you calling me?"

"I did some investigating about who was behind the article, and I'm thinking maybe there's a story here after all. I thought you might have some leads for me."

Elizabeth was walking toward the car. *Can I trust him?* she wondered, glancing over at Frank. He was always telling her to trust her instincts. Something deep in the pit of her stomach told her she could. "I think I might have a file full of them."

SEVENTY-SEVEN

7:05 P.M.

"**D**OCUMENTS WERE TAKEN from the council." Amanda Hanson's usually calm voice sounded worried. "They were given to the husband of that marine biologist," she continued. "They've both seen its contents, and she's going to give it to a reporter." The firmware patch downloaded into Elizabeth's cell had turned it into a bug that was transmitting Elizabeth's conversations even when she was not on the phone.

"What are you doing about it?"

"I'm calling you," Hanson replied.

"Why me?"

"Your name is all over that file."

"There must be someone who usually deals with this."

"We're not the mob. I've taken care of the one who gave them the documents, but you need to get the documents back and make sure they don't tell anyone what they've seen—ever."

REGGIE GATES STOOD across the street, watching silently as his three-car garage burned. The bright orange and yellow flames had consumed most of his sprawling gray neocolonial house, and the garage was the last to burn. The fire had spread fast, unnaturally fast. He heard something explode inside as firemen rushed around him, trying desperately to keep the fire from igniting the trees and the neighboring houses.

Gates didn't notice his wife walk up to him until she was standing right beside him, Justine in her arms. The fire fascinated the girl, and her delicate mouth hung open.

Gates took Justine into his arms and hugged her as his wife rested her head on his broad shoulder.

Frank held Elizabeth tight as they stood outside the lab. Neither one wanted to separate. Amid all the shocking events of the day, Elizabeth felt a deep sense of relief and calm in his arms.

Frank's beeper squawked at his waist.

"Oh, Christ, it's the ER," Frank said as he looked at the number. His voice was weary and disappointed. "I'm supposed to be off, but I'm at the top of the 'go-to' list, and Bill is home throwing up."

Elizabeth's shoulders dropped in familiar resignation.

"Let me walk you to your car," Frank said.

"You don't have to," Elizabeth said, not wanting to have to explain her accident. Frank would just worry.

"I want to," Frank insisted, and put his arm around her shoulder protectively. The sky was overcast. The forecast had said a storm was coming, but so far, there had only been on-and-off light rain.

Elizabeth's stomach clenched as they walked under the bright fluorescent streetlights. Parking lots always seemed to be menacing at night with no one around. She was glad that Frank was there after all.

"Oh my God, what happened?" he exclaimed.

"Just a little fender bender."

"Fender bender? There's no longer a fender to bend. Were you hurt?"

"It was nothing, really. A little scare." Elizabeth opened the door, which squeaked even more than before. As she stuffed the file into her already overstuffed bag, the newspaper picture fell out and into an oily puddle.

Frank crouched to take a closer look. "Who did this?"

Elizabeth shivered as she looked down at the burned-out eyes floating in the water. "I don't know," she said.

"I'm going to call the hospital and tell them I can't come."

"Don't be silly. They're just trying to scare us."

"They succeeded."

"I'll be fine until you come back."

"I'm not leaving you."

"Frank, who's the hospital going to call? Who's going to take care of those mothers and their babies?"

"What about this mother and her baby?"

"We'll be fine until you come home."

"I don't want you going home," Frank said. "Go to Connie's."

"Frank, I just—"

"Elizabeth, I love you. I need to know that you're safe."

"But—"

"Did you hear me?"

"Yes."

"Tell me what I said. I need to know that you heard me."

"You love me. You need me to be safe."

"That's right."

"I love you, too, Frank." She curled in close, and Frank held her tight.

"I almost forgot," Frank said, pulling a ring box out of his pocket. "I found your ring."

"Where did you find it?"

"Uh . . . around," Frank said. "Look, I traded it in."

Elizabeth opened the ring box. Her jaw dropped. Inside the box was a white gold ring with small diamonds set into the band. It was beautiful, practical, and unostentatious.

He said, "My father was wrong. A man doesn't show his love to a woman by—"

Elizabeth's lips were pressed against Frank's. He clenched her hard to his chest, and they kissed passionately. It had been a long time since they had shared a kiss like this, a kiss that could cut away their loneliness, like a scalpel wielded with exquisite skill.

SEVENTY-EIGHT

7:30 P.M.
Davis

"Lieutenant James has been ordered to kill Apollo."

Elizabeth started to panic and almost dropped her cell phone. Her heart was pounding so hard she could feel it in her throat. "Connie, where are you?"

"I'm at the slough with Teo. Lieutenant James says he's out of time. They're going to harpoon Apollo by 6:00 A.M. tomorrow."

"This is Skilling. He's convinced them that the whale is dying."

"We're doing everything we can to slow them down, but we need to convince Apollo we've heard his message and he can go."

"Connie, I told you. It's not like that. Apollo is not trying to communicate with us, he's— Wait a second. He may not be communicating with us, but he *is* communicating." *Hadn't Frank just needed to know that I heard him?* Maybe whales were no different. There was no whale to respond to Apollo, but she could. Elizabeth made a loud, tire-scraping U-turn. "I have to get something at my house, but I'll be right there."

Elizabeth pulled into her reserved space in the parking lot closest to her house. The other seven spaces were empty. The wind was blowing hard, swirling leaves into spirals that seemed to take shape as if they were scarecrows coming to life. Their town house was on a greenbelt, away from the rest of the development. She had always appreciated this seclusion, but tonight the lot felt dark and frightening. *We have legal and extralegal means to keep you quiet.* The anonymous woman's voice echoed in her head.

The door of the station wagon creaked again as she opened it. After the accident, the car really was about ready to die. *Who will hear me if I scream?* Certainly not the crazy woman who lived in the one-bedroom next door and never left her house. Elizabeth had not met her or even heard her in all the time they had lived next to each other.

She walked quickly down the narrow path to her unit. The fluorescent lampposts glared down at her like glowing white eyes, but there were no lights in any of the windows she passed.

Elizabeth started to get the creeps, as if she were being watched, as if she were being stalked. She put the key in the lock and looked over her shoulder, then tucked the thick file under her arm, needing both hands to open the door. The hair on her neck was standing on end. She looked into the dark house and flipped on the light. *Just get in, get the audio disk, and get out.*

She put the file down on the round butcher-block table and ran into the back room, where she rummaged through a box full of her backup field data. There it was. She grabbed it and took a deep breath as she opened the door.

A bolt of electricity flooded through her body, knocking her backward into the house. She felt like she had been struck by lightning. Severe pain shot down her spine and through her limbs as she collapsed to the ground, convulsing and shaking. She was being electrocuted. All the neurotransmitters in her muscles were being disrupted, and she lost any ability to move. Bursts of white light like fireworks exploded in front of her eyes. She knew she must be dying. Her limbs were stiff, and she flopped on the floor like a caught fish. All she could manage to utter were the stifled words "Oh my God . . . Oh my God . . ."

As quickly as it had started, it stopped. Her eyes began to focus. She saw two barbed electrodes, like those from a Taser, still attached to her shirt. A sharp pain pierced her arm. Dr. Skilling was kneeling over her, injecting her with a large syringe.

She tried to resist, but Skilling held her down. A wave of terror filled her body as completely as the charge had. *What is he injecting me with? Please don't let him kill my baby!* She struggled, but it only made the needle stick hurt more. Through the fog in her head, she groped for a plan. *Go for the eyes, go for the eyes . . .*

Skilling grabbed her wrists and held them away from his face. His eyes looked black and disklike, predatory and empty. Elizabeth felt as if her brain and her body were separating, going in different directions, snapped apart by the grip of the drug. Her arms were useless, pinned above her head by his hands. She looked down and saw her legs flailing, lashing out instinctively, like those of a wild animal trying to fight him off.

Her knee hit its target, right between his legs. Skilling let go of her arms as he clutched himself. She rolled away and began scrambling toward the door on her hands and knees, feeling a sudden burst of hope. She was getting there. *Keep going. Don't look back.* The door began to retreat, to move away from her. Desperately, she lunged for the door handle and felt its cold metal in her hand. She turned it. It opened. *I'm free. I'm safe.*

The whole door began to turn. Like Alice in the rabbit hole, she fell down and down through the door.

. . .

ELIZABETH'S CHEEK hit the ground hard. Skilling turned her over. Her eyes were wide open, vibrating slightly, saliva dripping from her mouth, her breathing noisy but regular. She was completely immobilized. He could do what was, unfortunately, now necessary.

SEVENTY-NINE

Frank tried calling Connie's house again, but there was no answer. Connie wasn't picking up her cell phone, either. *Maybe they are at the slough. Maybe there's no cell reception.* Frank knew that all of Elizabeth's best intentions to rest might not allow her to stay put. She was a force of nature. Such forces were not always easy to live with, but they were a privilege to experience up close. Why did he almost have to lose her before he realized what she meant to him?

"This is Connie Kato. If you want to overthrow the status quo, leave a message. Otherwise, don't call back." *Beep.*

"Connie, this is Frank. I'm worried about Elizabeth. She was supposed to go to your house. She's not picking up her cell, and there's no answer at home. I hope you are together somewhere. Please call me on my cell. Thanks."

"Dorothy," Frank said as he walked toward the door, "I've got to go find Elizabeth. I've got my pager if you need anything."

"Glad you two are back together. It's about time you came to your senses."

EIGHTY

T HE NIGHT was velvet black, and the layer of marine fog enveloped what little light was shed by the headlights of Skilling's BMW Z3 Roadster. The car's fabric top did not keep out the winter chill, but it did conceal the unconscious body in the passenger seat next to him.

He had chosen the car because its long wheelbase and fluted side vents reminded him unmistakably of his streamlined sharks. But tonight, with the top up, the Roadster felt cramped, like the cabin of a small boat. He had bought it—thanks to the money from the consortium—as a sports car, not as a hearse. The sooner he got rid of Elizabeth's body, the better.

As he continued to drive, he lit a cigarette. He needed to calm his nerves. He had tried to quit for years, had pretty much succeeded, but when he got nervous, he craved nicotine. The pack of cigarettes he kept in his car had come in handy in preparing the newspaper photo for Elizabeth. If only she had listened to his warning, none of this would have been necessary.

Skilling inhaled, breathing in the scent of cigarette smoke mixed with that of the car's leather interior, then exhaled in a long, slow breath. Everything was going to work out. Animals killed other animals. It was the law of nature. Some were predators and some were prey. He felt a cascade of endorphins pumping through his blood. Not since he was in the water trying to tag Mother had he felt so alive.

Skilling pulled into the dock where his boat was moored. As the clouds parted he saw the moon, just past full. The dock was empty, as he knew it would be. The active fishermen would be home asleep for another few hours. Many of the boats were all but abandoned, their owners unable to turn a profit from the dwindling fish stocks. The owner of the boat next to him had neglected to take down its ragged flag. Red and white stripes and a blue sea of stars flapped angrily in the wind. There was a "For Sale" sign in the window.

Just to be certain, Skilling wrapped Elizabeth in a blanket and carried her over his shoulder like a long carpet. A seagull flew onto the dock and cocked its head to eye him closely. Seagulls always knew. They could smell death long before it happened. They were the vultures of the sea and would appear at a shark attack almost before the shark.

He set Elizabeth down in the open cabin. His twenty-five-foot sport fishing boat had yellow-and-black trim and was perfectly designed for his work studying big marine animals. The walk-through transom at the stern made access in and out of the water easy and allowed him to pull seal carcasses onboard to dissect. He fastened the microphone-shaped satellite tag to a heavy wooden tagging pole, which he would have to use until he could get another aluminum one. Tagging Mother was all he could think about, what he dreamed about every night. He would not miss the chance again, should his little excursion present the opportunity.

Skilling cast off the lines. Sitting in the cushioned white captain's seat, he turned on the twin Honda 150s. They jumped to life eagerly, like racehorses. These brand-new four-stroke engines had been paid for by his research stipend from the Japanese whalers for his services on the IWC Scientific Committee. There were so many funding sources, if researchers were willing to open their eyes. The engines hummed as he quietly backed out of the slip. He passed the pleasure yachts, their unrigged masts looking like lonely crosses.

He clutched the rubberized steering wheel, in the middle of which was glued a gold doubloon. One of his colleagues had given it to him: a not totally flattering allusion to Moby Dick's peg-legged whaler. A curious sea otter poked its head above the water, and the red light blinked on the piling that marked the end of the harbor.

He headed into the blanket of gray. The radar was set to a four-mile radius, but even in the bay, the waters were rough, and there was a lot of interference. This scatter was hard to distinguish from the actual targets, the rocks and boats he was trying hard to avoid.

Skilling set his waypoints for a course to the Emperor's Bathtub, on the windward side of Southeast Farallon Island. The Bathtub, a narrow but deep eddy in Maintop Bay, had the perfect geography to make it a feeding trough for white sharks. The drain of the Bathtub was just wide enough for the graceful turns of the sharks, so they could strike unseen and exit quickly. It was practically like a fast-food drive-through.

The actual coordinates he entered were not just of the cove but were even better. They came from the three radio acoustic position-ing sonobuoys that he had installed a few months back with the help of the sea urchin fisherman—the only person who was brave enough or fool enough to dive with the Farallon whites. The RAPS data al-lowed him to track individual sharks with pinpoint accuracy to study their small-scale movements. The most recent transmission had indi-cated that a shark named Scar Eye was out there in Maintop Bay. He hoped Mother might be as well.

When he'd gotten the call from the consortium about Elizabeth, he'd known immediately where he would take her. It had not been a rational thought, but it had struck him as having a certain amusing poetic justice—the whale researcher eaten by a shark.

• • •

Elizabeth started to groan, and he glanced down into the cabin. The drug was wearing off. Ketamine had been a convenient and effective drug for his purposes. The anesthetic had shut down Elizabeth's cerebral cortex and all conscious thought while allowing her to continue breathing. White sharks much preferred live prey.

"Jesus," Skilling said as he saw the walls of Alcatraz towering in front of him. He slammed the throttle astern just in time to avoid running aground on the rocks of the island prison. As he swung the boat around, he heard one of the propellers grind on an underwater rock. *Christ, Richie, can't you drive a goddamn boat?*

Skilling started on his course again, a little shaken and more careful to keep his eye on the radar. He changed the screen to a wider view as the foghorn from Alcatraz wailed behind him—a little late. *They really got the best of you, didn't they, Richie?* It was that same voice. He wasn't going crazy. Everyone heard voices. Sane people, like him, just realized they were the workings of their own mind.

The voice did what it always did. It got him thinking about how he was getting a raw deal. How his colleagues were keeping him down, preventing him from becoming the chair of the department, stopping him from serving on important scientific committees. They were just jealous that he was the famous Dr. Shark.

Why did he always have to fight for everything? He had made it to where he was by fighting harder than everyone else. He wasn't going to let some stupid graduate student and her husband ruin his career by telling people he was "supplementing his salary." *Jesus, how did they expect anyone to live on a professor's salary? Did being a scientist mean he'd taken a vow of poverty? Hell, no.* Why should people who sold toilet paper and toothpaste make millions while people who were furthering human knowledge make practically nothing?

Above him, like the struts of a giant Erector Set, the Golden Gate Bridge emerged out of the fog. He could see only a small section of its enormous span, its two ends disappearing into the fog like a ghost bridge connecting one world with another.

Beyond the bridge, the swells were even bigger than usual. It was going to be a rough crossing and take longer than he had anticipated. Elizabeth started to move again down in the open galley. He checked the radar and saw no targets in front of him, then went down to check on her. She seemed to have passed out again. When he came up, he saw on the radar that a large boat was moving toward him—on an interception course. *Oh, shit. Who could it be? Who's found out? How the hell did they find out?*

Skilling knew what he needed to do. He would tie something to Elizabeth quickly and dump her over the side. He found his anchor and rope, but there was no time. The boat was moving fast, impossibly fast. When he saw the boat, he realized it was worse than he'd thought.

The diagonal stripe down the front of the forty-seven-foot motor lifeboat was drained of its red color in the night. But in the moonlight, he could read the words next to it: U.S. COAST GUARD. *What the hell am I going to do now? Are they going to search for drugs?* Skilling quickly covered Elizabeth with a blanket, but he knew if anyone boarded his boat, they would see her in the open galley below. The boat was slowing, but its large hull was still spraying water and leaving an enormous wake in the rolling swell.

Skilling zipped up his black jacket and breathed deeply. The suspenders of his yellow foul-weather waders dug into his shoulders. He felt trapped. The muscles of his abdomen were tight as a knot, but Skilling smiled as the Coast Guard pulled alongside. The petty officer was dressed in a jumpsuit, covered by a parka, and crowned with a helmet. Everything had reflectors, and the helmet had a cross painted on top to ensure that anyone overboard had the greatest chance of being found and being found quickly. An hour in this fifty-four-degree water, and most people were as good as dead.

The voice came through a bullhorn: "Turn on—mari—rad—"
The words were clipped in the hissing wind.

Skilling glanced down at Elizabeth and picked up the white plastic mouthpiece of his marine radio as he switched it on. "Go ahead."

The words were punctuated by static. "There is a small-craft advisory in effect—sea conditions forty-knot winds—fifteen-foot swell—and growing—return to the nearest safe harbor."

Skilling's stomach and shoulders relaxed. Wind and waves he could handle. He had faced worse, and his boat was solid. In his most commanding voice, Skilling replied, "I'm a marine biologist. I have time-sensitive research out at the Farallon Islands. I will return to shore immediately after my research is complete."

Just then Elizabeth moaned from below. Skilling's heart stopped. Elizabeth moaned again.

"Roger. Proceed at your own risk."

After the Coast Guard retreated, Skilling kicked the throttle forward to get some speed. He wanted to go as fast as he could with the rolling swell, but the left engine was not giving its normal thrust. Had he bent the blades of the prop when he hit the rock? He needed to redline the engine to get it even with the other. Skilling knew he had to get there and get out quick. Maintop Bay was not somewhere you wanted to be when a storm struck. Heading into the waves, he had his engines trimmed down so the boat could hit the waves and cut through them like a knife.

Yet in this water, the boat was still pitching fore and aft. He switched his GPS chart plotter to the "roadway" view. It was as easy as driving down the highway—granted, a highway rolling in eight-foot swells. He knew the Coast Guard hated to make this crossing, even in their aluminum-hull boats that could roll completely over and stay afloat. If they had to go, they preferred to fly out by helicopter.

On fair days, which were few, you could see several of the largest Farallon Islands from the Golden Gate Bridge. But even fair weather could turn foul quickly out here, and the dozens, perhaps hundreds, of shipwrecks lying on the sea floor around the islands were silent testament to those who had misjudged the seas. The whole marine sanctuary was littered with the corroding hulls of boats, leaking oil. But the greatest dangers in the sanctuary were, as always, man-made.

Between 1946 and 1970, the military, in their postwar invincibility and shortsightedness, had dumped almost 50,000 drums of hazardous and radioactive waste near the Farallones. In another stroke of genius, a 10,000-ton aircraft carrier once used for nuclear target practice had also been dumped in these waters. It was amazing to Skilling that his sharks were not glowing. To him, it was all proof that humans would destroy themselves before long. The world was dying, so he might as well profit while it lasted. During a war, some people always made a killing.

Skilling checked his watch. Forty-five minutes to high tide, which was always the most active time for shark attacks at the Farallones. No one knew for sure why. He always assumed that it was when the most seals were flushed out of the coves by the rising water and left helpless, like floating sausages. Whatever the reason, the timing would be perfect. He'd arrive with Elizabeth just at feeding time.

EIGHTY-ONE

Midnight
Liberty Slough

LIEUTENANT JAMES still did not understand why there was such a rush to kill the whale, but he understood why they wanted to do it before sunrise, when it was too dark for the television cameras to get decent footage. Something did not smell right. But he had no evidence, and he could not disobey a direct order. He looked at the fax he had received, commanding him to harpoon the whale by 0600.

He had spent many happy hours hunting quail, duck, and deer. But harpooning Apollo felt like shooting fish in a barrel and offended his instincts as a hunter.

Scientists had recommended every reasonable possibility to rescue the whale, and many well-meaning people from around the world had suggested far less reasonable ones. His daughter Kayla had suggested trying to lure the whale back to sea by dripping salt water down the Sacramento River. He looked up at his daughter's drawing, with teardrop-shaped circles leading the whale back to the ocean and two girls riding on its back.

CONNIE'S CELL PHONE began to vibrate as the ring tone "Power to the People," by John Lennon, began to play. She looked at the caller ID. It was the vet calling her back.

"Hello?"

"Is this Mary Jane Williams?"

"Ah, yes, it is," Connie said, deepening her voice, trying to pretend that she was the assistant to the regional stranding coordinator for the National Marine Fisheries Service.

"This is Bob Townshend again. I got your message, but I'm just watching the live coverage on CNN, and it looks like they're planning to euthanize the whale. Are you sure they don't need me?"

"I assure you, Dr. Townshend, that the lieutenant governor has decided to pursue other means for the time being, but we will let you know if that changes."

"Well, no one likes to put a whale down, but call me if you need me."

"We certainly will."

THERE WAS A HEAVY KNOCK. The flimsy door rattled, and Lieutenant James opened it reluctantly.

"Lieutenant, some men are here to see you."

Lieutenant James adjusted his blue cap and stepped down the metal stairs. A spotlight above the door of the portable cast a circle of light.

"Halvard Nilsen," the man said in a Scandinavian accent, without holding out his hand. "I've got your gun."

"You got a form for me to sign?" Lieutenant James asked.

"No."

"No paperwork?"

"This is a gift." The man smiled, gesturing to the large gray polymer case. "I'll show you how to assemble and fire it."

"You a veterinarian?"

"I'm a whaler," Nilsen said.

Instead of sending over a vet, they send over a whaler? The more James heard, the less he liked what he was hearing. He wanted to know what was going on. "You guys connected with the consortium that owns this land?"

"No."

"Who called you in?"

"Dr. Skilling. He thought we might be able to supply you with the harpoon gun. They are not so easy to come by these days."

"Is that so?"

"This is a Norwegian model," Nilsen said. "It's smaller and lighter and more suitable for your boat."

Lieutenant James looked up at the sky and saw more clouds covering the moon quickly. The air was thick and smelled like rain. The barometer had been plummeting all day. A storm was definitely coming.

Nilsen pointed at the gray metal gun within the case. It looked like a miniature cannon. "The harpoon fits in the bore of the gun and attaches to the rope. This is the explosive head." The harpoon flared out into four large, hinged barbs and then narrowed into a torpedolike point. "When the tip strikes, a time-fused charge will explode in three seconds, driving the harpoon into the whale's side. As the whale wrestles with the line, the barbs will snap open, anchoring the whale and detonating the grenade." Like any professional, Nilsen obviously enjoyed the details of his craft. Lieutenant James listened, thankful that the veterinarian would be firing this thing and not him. "The explosion will cut into the lungs and other organs, if you're lucky, so it'll die quick. Sometimes they go fast, but it can take ten, even thirty, minutes or more. This is a big whale you got here. It helps if you aim between the shoulder blades."

Where the hell are the shoulder blades on a whale? Lieutenant James wondered. He asked the next question, not sure he wanted to know the answer. "What happens to the whale after it's struck?"

"The whale's rib muscles weaken, and when the air valves collapse, the water will rush in, suffocating the whale. She'll roll over when she's dead."

"*He.* The whale's a he."

Nilsen stared at him, then pointed to a crude metal rod on top. "This is the sight, and over here is the trigger." It was a little lever that one squeezed against the handle.

"If the vet doesn't show, are you going to fire this thing?"

"Oh, no, I'm afraid I can't," said Nilsen. "It must be the U.S. government that compassionately puts the whale out of its misery."

Lieutenant James prayed that the vet would get there by sunrise. Otherwise, he'd have to shoot the whale himself.

EIGHTY-TWO

1:00 A.M.
Farallon Islands

Aᴌᴌ Sᴋɪʟʟɪɴɢ ᴄᴏᴜʟᴅ sᴇᴇ in the moonlight was gray fog, so thick it eclipsed any possible line of sight. He slowed the engine, knowing he was close. Moments later the islands appeared out of the mist, granite icebergs jutting from the water, sharp and menacing. As he threw the throttle into reverse, the engines snarled and backed away. The landscape looked prehistoric, unfinished and barren. To Skilling, the shape of the islands had always resembled sharks' teeth, although superstitious sailors had long called them the Devil's Teeth for the many ships they had devoured. The Coast Miwok knew them as the Islands of the Dead, the place where bad Indians were condemned to live forever, like some spectral Alcatraz.

Skilling shook away a shiver and told himself that death was an inevitable part of life. He did feel a pang of guilt when he remembered that Elizabeth was pregnant. But the planet was already overrun with people. It wouldn't miss yet another child. Humans were like locusts. The only hope was that increasing infertility might someday end the plague they had become on the planet.

Skilling steered the boat skillfully around the gray-brown outcroppings, spattered white by the hundreds of thousands of birds that lived and defecated here. The sharp smell that blew off the island and filled his nostrils was a mixture of ammonia, rotting anchovies, decomposing salt water, and decades of accumulated fecal matter. The odor was so strong it was almost mind-numbing, and it often made first-timers wince or gag reflexively. Even Skilling had to get used to it each time he came out. Fortunately, the wind also helped to keep down the kelp flies that often covered one's skin and were particularly drawn to mucous membranes—mouths, noses, and in the case of seals, anuses.

Despite the Farallones' infernal number of torments, he found a strange charm in the place, and spending time with the white sharks made up for any discomfort. He looked at the shark-tagging pole resting in the metal hooks on the side of the boat. If he was lucky, he would accomplish two goals: getting rid of Elizabeth and tagging the largest shark ever recorded.

Although still on the lee side of the island, he could feel the gathering storm coming from the west. The swells made the boat buck like a horse as he motored past the Gap, and raindrops, heavy and swollen, started to pelt the boat. The moon freed itself from a smothering cloud, and he could see the black cormorants, black-and-white murres, and brown pelicans huddling together, preparing for the worst. The sea lions with their dexterous flippers had climbed high above the surf zone and were ominously silent, not barking as usual. The seals, who could not climb like the sea lions, were being pelted by waves in the coves. Some had already been dragged into the surf.

This "zone of death," just around the perimeter of the island, was where white sharks picked off many seals. Several looked up at him questioningly. Their black doll eyes always had the fearful stare of prey, but now they rocked their heads nervously, perhaps concerned about the squall that was quickly approaching. One rode a wave onto the black rocks and squirmed desperately up the shore.

Skilling could read the animals and the conditions and didn't like what he was seeing. But he had no choice—he had to steer around Sugarloaf and into Maintop Bay. This was never a completely safe proposition even in the best of weather, as the swells on the wind-ward side of the island were always unpredictable, and conditions changed quickly. But that was where the shark was.

He reconsidered simply tying the anchor to Elizabeth's feet and letting it drag her to the bottom. The sharks would eventually find her—but what if someone else found her first? No, it was safer if he knew for sure that the evidence of her demise had been digested in the stomach of the shark.

As he passed the Gap, he heard the islands whistling, as they often did in a storm. This time the sound was shrill, like a woman shrieking.

ELIZABETH BLINKED her blurry eyes as she came around. She saw something black scurrying across her face and felt the legs of a kelp fly as it brushed up against the hairs inside her nose. With her hands im-mobilized, she could not wave it away, and repeatedly tried to twitch her nose. It flew away at last but then landed on her lip and crawled back up the other nostril. She tried desperately to puff it out.

No luck. This kelp fly was used to stronger gusts than she could manage.

Elizabeth's eyes began to adjust to the dim light, and she realized she was in the galley of a boat. *Skilling.* Above her, she could see him steering, the side of his chiseled face like stone in the silvery light. He was standing, trying to balance as the waves battered the boat. Her body rocked precariously on the thin vinyl bench cushions. She tried to remember what had happened to her, and then the memories started to flood back: the stun gun, the injection, the struggle.

A wave of pain and nausea traveled from the side of her head down to her stomach. *He's going to drown me.* Then, with an even stronger wave of nausea, she realized, *No, he's going to feed me to his sharks.* She had heard the stories circulating in the department about the camera-shy monster shark that he had almost tagged underwater and had named Mother. She felt like she might vomit.

The boat slapped against a wave. She started to feel her arm against the cushion—her body was regaining sensation. Stretching her legs slowly, she made sure not to attract Skilling's attention. The boat lurched, and she swallowed the sharp bile in her throat, willing her stomach not to give her away.

Elizabeth looked at her hands. They were bound several times with hemp rope, which was part of a longer stretch of line that snaked up the stairs to the deck.

Skilling seemed to be preoccupied topside driving through the storm, so she was free to work on her hands. She began pulling them apart as the rope dug into her wrists. Breathing through the pain, she was able to bring her wrists a few inches apart but still couldn't pull them out of the rope handcuffs. In the galley light, she saw the skin of her wrists, chafed raw.

THE BOAT STAGGERED against the wind as Skilling entered Maintop Bay. The storm was arriving fast. *Perhaps this is not such a good plan,* he thought. But it was too late to stop now. He couldn't exactly call it off and decide to kill her on another day.

His legs absorbed the roll of the boat, buffeted by the ever-growing whitecaps. From a cooler, he pulled out the lower half of a newborn elephant seal. It had been crushed—no doubt by the bulls fighting for dominance—and he had kept it for a special occasion. The blood and entrails were seeping out. These dissections were always the perfect chum for baiting sharks. The deep, almost ferrous odor made him wince. He put the bloody mess in a burlap bag and threw it overboard after tying it off so that it hung at the surface and dunked like a tea bag with each swell. An oily chum slick began to spread out behind the boat.

Steering toward the blip on his RAPS display, he switched on his fish finder sonar. As the color screen flashed to life, it revealed a large red elliptical shape almost directly below him. Scar Eye.

Skilling descended the steps to the cabin. Elizabeth was still lying where he'd left her. Using her tied wrists for leverage, he hauled her over his shoulder, managed to carry her up the few stairs from the galley, and laid her down against the far gunwale. The waves were pounding the port side squarely, pushing the boat toward the island. He jumped back to the steering wheel.

"Jesus," he said as he gunned the engines. They were drifting fast toward the rocky shore, the fog hiding most of its brutal coastline. There were hidden rocks all around the island, too, and only his intimate knowledge of the dark gray waters kept him from running aground.

He looked down at the doubloon, trying to avoid looking at Elizabeth. *Unless you are a certifiable psycho,* he thought, *it isn't so easy to kill someone.*

He revved the engines, but his thrust was only half of what it should have been. His fist clenched around the throttle, as he knew that he had not just bent the propeller—he had sheared off the pin. He now had only one engine. Elizabeth's eyes flickered open. She was coming around. Now he would have to kill her in cold blood, with her staring back at him. *Damn, she isn't making this easy for me.*

When Elizabeth fell against the gunwale, she tried not to utter a sound. She opened her eyes quickly to see what was happening, but he saw her. She pretended her body was still paralyzed.

"Why are you doing this?" she said, noticing that the hemp rope was tied to one of the cleats on the starboard gunwale.

"Because you gave me no choice." Skilling looked at her and back at the rocks.

"Because I found out that you were working for the ESC?"

"I'm not working for anybody. I work for myself. They are just one of my . . . funders."

"Are they *funding* you to kill me?" Elizabeth was stalling, looking for a plan, as her eyes scanned the deck for potential weapons.

"No, I'm killing you because you could ruin everything that I've accomplished—my work, my reputation . . ."

Elizabeth's eyes found the wooden pole with the satellite tag attached to the end. "I'm not the only one who knows."

"I know your husband has seen the file. But don't worry, a bleary-eyed doctor driving home late at night, grieving the loss of his wife, can be very accident-prone."

Elizabeth started to panic. Frank's life was also at stake. Then she noticed the small red marine fire extinguisher.

SKILLING STEADIED HIMSELF with the gunwale and looked down at the binnacle, where the compass was lurching in all directions like a drunken sailor. The pain was excruciating. His eyes felt like they had been knocked out of their sockets, and he staggered on the pitching boat, falling to his knees. Over his shoulder, he saw Elizabeth holding a fire extinguisher. Dizzy, skull pounding, he tried to get to his feet, then gasped as his Adam's apple was forced against his throat. His windpipe was being crushed. He grabbed for his neck, trying to pry off the rope.

ELIZABETH PULLED the makeshift garrote with all her strength, bracing herself against his large back. She pressed her feet into the deck as if balancing on a seesaw, the boat rocking wildly beneath them. Hatred coursed through her veins like molten metal, making her strong. She could kill him right there, right then. Panting for breath, Skilling started to collapse forward, his hands futilely trying to grab the rope she had pulled tight around his neck.

Elizabeth felt a sharp pain as Skilling's elbow landed in her solar plexus, and she gasped as her breath and strength left her. She released her chokehold, and Skilling grabbed her by the throat. She realized the true inequality of their strength: He was six inches taller and at least fifty pounds heavier. She saw the killing fury in his eyes.

EIGHTY-THREE

SKILLING THREW ELIZABETH off the stern and made sure the rope was tied fast to the cleat. He pushed the throttle ahead and saw her bobbing up behind the boat in the glistening wake. Dark clouds were drowning out the moon, and he cursed the gathering storm. Now he wanted to see her eaten. How could she have thought that she could overpower him? His muscles were made for violence, for battle. But her futile struggle would make her death all the more gratifying.

He looked at the screen of the fish finder to see where the shark was. The large red spot was deep in the water column, no doubt seeing her outline on the surface, stalking, readying a surprise attack from below, as whites so often did. They could be methodical hunters or opportunistic, moving quickly when prey presented itself.

Skilling heard the fish finder beep. He had set its programmable parameters, and now, as he glanced down at the blinking shape on the screen, he saw another shark almost twice as large. It could only be Mother.

ELIZABETH COULD HARDLY BREATHE. The icy water was like a fist that gripped her body and froze her limbs. *Keep moving,* she commanded herself. *Keep moving.* She kicked furiously, trying to hold her head above water as the boat slowed down.

Whitecaps crashed around her as the boat appeared and disappeared beyond the swells. Her wrists, tied together, made it difficult to tread water. The boat was trolling her slowly. And then the full horror of her situation struck her: He was using her as human chum.

She kept kicking and struggling to breathe, trying desperately to free her hands. She knew her kicking would attract the shark, but she had no choice—the only alternative was to drown. Even if she kept her legs perfectly still, the shark could sense the beating of her heart, and there was no way to quiet its wild pumping in her chest.

Blood was fleeing from her limbs, and needles of cold dug into her skin. A voice in her head shouted, *Pull the handcuffs off. Pull them off.* It was her only chance of survival. The rope was loosening now that it was wet, and she dug the fingertips of one hand under the rope bracelet around the other, pulling desperately. The pain was intense, rubbing off skin, but the rope was moving. She felt a burst of hope.

Skilling sped up, dragging her head underwater and practically pulling her arms out of their sockets. Elizabeth gasped for air in the roiling wake and kept kicking, trying to stay afloat, stealing breaths and inhaling water with the air. The salt stung her throat and lungs as she coughed and sputtered.

She kept struggling against her cuffs but couldn't free her hands. She was freezing to death and could feel her body shutting down. At least it was better than being eaten alive. *Either way,* she thought, *I am going to die.* The thought was like a knife, severing her will. She stopped resisting, her body going limp as it bobbed through the waves.

The boat stopped. The line went slack. She began to sink into the dark, her hands still bound above her.

A few bright rays of moonlight penetrated the water. Elizabeth blinked but could see only a few inches in front of her. And then she saw something strange: a child's face with two black button eyes staring back at her.

My baby, Elizabeth thought. *I must save my baby.*

Her child deserved a chance to live. Elizabeth couldn't die. Not now. She fought to the surface for another breath, then saw the boat backing toward her.

Skilling had thrown the throttle astern. He was going to run her over and leave her bloody carcass for the sharks. No, this would not be her fate—or her child's.

She dove beneath the surface as the boat backed over her. The water was white, turned to chop by the propeller.

She was yanked back as the slack line fouled the propeller, grinding it to a halt. She heard the engine rev, but the boat was not moving.

THE SHARK SWAM *twenty feet from the rocky bottom and forty feet from the glittering surface—*

She saw the outline of her prey above—

Felt the wash of its frantic movements—

Smelled the blood of its wounds—

Sensed its heartbeat and breath—

It was necessary to be cautious—to surprise—

She had the knowledge of an experienced hunter and knew the moment had come—

She shifted direction with a twitch of her torso and a slight change in the angle of her pectoral fins—

She thrust her six-foot crescent tail—catapulting her toward the surface at full bore—

Water flowed over rows of two-inch teeth—her jaws ready to gape open—preparing for the killing blow—

Her dark pupils rolled tailward in their sockets to protect her precious sight from this creature's claws—

• • •

ELIZABETH FELT the pressure wave from below. She struggled, trying futilely to free her hands, as if somehow she could use them to defend herself and her baby. But the rope would not release her.

THE SHARK'S JAWS sank into the wriggling body—
  Her head wrenching from side to side—
  Through fat and muscle her rows of triangular teeth tore—
  Some snapping off as others held fast—
  A warm swell of blood covered her gums and spilled down into her throat—
  The smell and taste soothed her nervous system as her tail stopped whipping—
  The struggle was over—
  She would live to spawn more young—
  She began to descend—
  The flesh already entering the cartilaginous cavern of her stomach—

ELIZABETH'S BODY was thrown to the side. The turbulent sound in her ears was like a waterfall pumped backward.

First she smelled the blood in the water, like wet rusty metal, then she felt its oily slick, and when she finally opened her eyes, she saw the dark water spreading out around her.

How long do I have to live?

Her numb body mercifully could not feel any pain. She could hear the shrieking of the gulls as they flapped their wings around her, and she knew they would not wait until she was dead to start pecking at her flesh. She waved her arms, even though she knew she would go into shock at any moment. But as long as she lived, she would do anything to defend the child growing inside her. In that moment she felt no hatred toward the shark—there was no evil, no malice, in it. She understood, as she never had before, the hunger for life that drives all animals.

Elizabeth didn't want to feel her missing limbs, but the biologist in her needed to collect data. Her tethered hands began to probe downward.

Her chest and stomach were still intact and her pelvis, too. Her heart leaped with hope. She stopped her inventory to fight off the tornado of gulls that had gathered above her. Perhaps she had just lost a leg. But then she realized she would still probably die from blood loss. Her fingers descended her legs inch by inch.

They were whole.

Her mind raced, trying to understand what had happened. Just then she saw something floating in the water next to her.

It was the backside of a baby elephant seal. Its beheaded torso was still pumping out thick, oily blood into the water as the gulls pecked at the blondish-brown hair of the carcass, cutting off chunks with their flinty beaks. It must have been the seal's eyes she had seen in the water. Only then did she realize the truth. *Oh, my God, I'm going to live. I'm going to live.*

As she came to this realization, she also remembered that after the killing blow, sharks often returned to finish off their prey. She had to get out of the water as fast as possible, not only because of the shark but because the frozen water was becoming a coffin, shutting down her body. She looked ahead at the boat. Skilling was no longer chumming her, and now she saw why. Through the rising and falling swell, she could see him bent over in the stern, trying to cut the propeller free of the rope.

The bloody carcass floated next to her, giving her an idea. She hesitated and then plunged her hands into the warm, bloody entrails of the seal, halfway up her forearms. The heat felt good as she rubbed her wrists around the oily blubber. Now she pulled with all her strength, crushing her hands together like a bird claw so that they were as narrow as her wrists. She yanked and pulled and then tried digging her fingers under the rope, but the oil prevented her from getting a good grip. She would have to use her brute strength, what was left of it, and trust the oil to make her skin slick. She groaned hard, clenching her teeth and pulling her arms apart. One hand popped out, and once it had, the other cuff loosened. She was free.

Suddenly, the enormous head of the shark jutted out of the water beside her and bit into the beheaded seal. Every muscle in Elizabeth's body seized up. She choked for breath—the howling wind and cold were gone. Now there was only the shark.

One piercing eye stared back at her over bloodied two-inch teeth. She recognized intelligence in that eye. The shark had known how to identify its prey.

Slowly, she backed away and threw her numb arms one over the other. She swam quickly toward the boat, where Skilling was fighting a submerged rock with his bamboo gaff. Elizabeth had to get back in the boat without being seen. The flapping gulls shielded her as she clenched her unfeeling hands and tightened her jaw. Now she was the predator, stalking Skilling.

THE STERN OF THE BOAT was five feet in front of Elizabeth, listing to the starboard side, pelted by waves. Without its engines, it was foundering on the jagged coastline. Skilling was no longer thinking about her, only about saving himself and his boat.

Elizabeth heaved herself up onto the duckboard and pulled her body over the walk-through transom. She looked up. Skilling had not seen her, and the crashing waves silenced her awkward movements. On her elbows, she crawled across the deck rolling under her, and with her clawed hands, she grabbed the wooden tagging pole from its hooks.

She swung the pole at Skilling's head with all her strength, but he saw her and blocked her with the thick bamboo gaff. The rattle of the blow shook her arms.

He grabbed the tagging pole with his free hand and threw down the long gaff, which was useless in a fight. They grappled with the pole between them, the titanium tip of the satellite tag glinting in the moonlight. She knew the small harpoon head was sharp enough to pierce a shark's armored skin. As they shook the pole, the satellite tag broke free from the rubber bands that held it fast and rolled toward the gunwale.

Even with her newfound will to live, her frozen and exhausted body was no match for him. Skilling spun her around and pinned her against the railing. He took one hand off the pole and seized her throat. His cruel eyes told her that he cared only about killing her, regardless of the danger to him or his boat.

Elizabeth tried to gasp for air as he crushed her trachea in his grip. Her hand moved desperately over the rough deck of the boat, looking for the satellite tag beneath her.

She shot her eyes to the water just beyond the boat's stern and managed to yelp, *"Mother . . ."*

Skilling looked where her eyes were riveted.

Elizabeth seized the satellite tag, inching her fingers along the monofilament to the tip. She gripped its tiny scalpel-sharp point and dug it into Skilling's temple. She ripped it along his face, cutting him from his forehead to his chin. Skilling released the tagging pole and grabbed his bleeding face with both hands.

Elizabeth spied the rope, which was pulled taut between the cleat and where it was still tangled in the prop. She grabbed it to brace herself as the boat pivoted around the rock.

Screaming with pain and fury, he lunged at her, his hands like claws, his teeth bared. Another wave slammed into the boat.

Skilling staggered. Bracing herself with the rope, Elizabeth lifted her leg and kicked Skilling hard in the stomach. He lurched backward, tumbling through the transom and into the water.

His arms flailed for a moment in the water, and then he went under in the bubbling surf. He came up, fighting for air and struggling before going under again. Elizabeth tried to steady herself on the spinning boat but lost sight of him in the surf. Then she saw in the moonlight—

HER GRAY SNOUT *and gaping white mouth erupted out of the water like the swell of a violent wave—*

Mother's open maw—two times the width of her prey—swallowed the torso whole—

Rows of triangular white fangs—jutting from her distended pink gums—crushed him at the waist—

His yellow legs dangled from her massive jaws—

Mother's supreme bulk did not stop at the surface but lunged completely out of the water—

She rose ten feet in the air—propelled by her roaring tail—which was still lashing back and forth in midair its tips embowed by the force—

Around her mouth was a vast mane of silvery spray—

Water gushed out of her mouth over the limp legs—

Her four-foot pectoral fins hovered in the air—sluicing sheets of water—

The violent momentum of her attack forced her body into a complete roll—fins rotating—gray dorsal and back now facing the sea—

Her white underbelly hung suspended for a brief moment as the forces of the universe realigned—

Mother's upside-down pectoral fins were helpless against gravity—

White froth cascaded off her body as her enormous mass of solid muscle and cartilage began to fall almost perpendicular to the water—

*First her head sank into the dark water—followed by her vast under-
body and at last the black scythe of her tail that cut seamlessly through
the surface and disappeared into the deep—*

ELIZABETH'S EYES were released from witnessing Mother devour
Skilling, but her mouth remained agape. Her body swayed as the
boat lurched to the side—it was about to be swept onto the rocks by
a huge swell. She had to abandon ship before she, too, was broken
against the rocks.

Without a moment to consider, Elizabeth jumped into Sea Lion
Cove. Her breath stopped momentarily as if she had dunked her
body into a bucket of ice. Metal and fiberglass groaned and shattered
as the boat was thrown onto the black granite rocks. She heard much
shuffling and barking from the inhabitants of the cove as the boat
crashed onto the shore.

Elizabeth was surging up and down with the surf. She knew that
she could be knocked unconscious by the ceaseless waves, so she
pushed off from the rocks with her feet and hands, waiting for the
water to ebb before a large wave. Knowing the risk she was taking,
she scrambled out of the cove onto the sharp mussel-covered rocks,
shredding her clothing and the skin of her arms and knees as the
wave crashed over her. The pain was intense, but she breathed
through it and grasped the slippery rocks to keep herself from falling
backward. The wave receded and she crawled onto higher ground.
Deep nausea welled up inside her as she retched out all the seawater
and the terror she had swallowed with it.

We're alive. We're alive.

She collapsed against the rock and inhaled a great breath of
gratitude.

• • •

ELIZABETH LOOKED DOWN at her watch. The glowing numbers told her what she had feared. She was saved, but Apollo was still in danger. Dragging herself to her feet, she began to limp forward on the uneven rock. The wind howled against her as she climbed over the jagged and slippery granite shards piled on the hills of Cormorant Blind and East Seal. Half of each agonizing step was lost to an inevitable, backward slide. Only her determination to help Apollo kept her numb and exhausted body going. The rhythmic beam from the lighthouse was like a heartbeat of hope, and the moon fought its way through the clouds, revealing the flatter ground of the marine terrace. She could see the researchers' house.

She dragged her feet up the steps. The four small square windows on either side were dark. She was so cold her bones ached. It took every ounce of remaining strength to raise her hand high enough to bang on the door and awaken the resident scientists. The light switched on, and one of the biologists opened the door. The man had graying black hair, disheveled by sleep, and a two-day beard. Wide-eyed and openmouthed, he stared at her as if she were a ghost. But she knew she was not a ghost. Her body hurt too much to be dead.

EIGHTY-FOUR

5:00 A.M.

"**I** NEED TO CALL the Coast Guard."

Burt Thompson, one of the resident bird scientists, finally managed to speak. "Come in, come in. How did you get here?"

Elizabeth shuffled into the living room while her host hurried around the room, turning on lights. Her eyes blinked as she adjusted to the brightness. White skulls, stuffed birds, and three other researchers all stared at her. A marine radio whispered in the background, interrupting a stream of static with a weather warning. Thompson led her over to an armchair draped with a colorful Mexican blanket. Her body collapsed into the chair, and she could feel her muscles shaking uncontrollably. She saw a television in the corner. "Does the TV work?"

Her host crouched in front of her, pulling the blanket around her, trying to warm her.

"Thank you," Elizabeth said.

"You're in shock. Now try to rest."

"I'm afraid there's no time to rest. Please."

One of the other researchers flipped on the satellite television and handed Elizabeth the remote. She'd hoped the story would be on one of the local news stations, but to her surprise, CNN was showing live coverage of the "mercy killing." Apollo's plight had made worldwide news. The reporter was aglow with camera lights; behind her, the slough was dark in the predawn gloom. "It seems that time is about up for Apollo, who is supposed to be euthanized before sunrise today. Apparently, the decision has come as a surprise to many. We have just arrived with other television stations after an anonymous leak. There are also a few hard-core Apollo fans who have camped out overnight." The camera revealed several people holding up signs that said DON'T KILL APOLLO and ELIZABETH, WHERE ARE YOU?

"I need a Coast Guard evacuation immediately," Elizabeth said.

"I'm afraid that's not possible," Thompson said with the pragmatism and detachment of a field scientist. "There is no way they are going to bring a boat out in a storm like this unless it's a matter of life and death."

"It *is* a matter of life and death, and I don't have time for a boat. I need a helicopter."

The TV reporter continued, "Everyone here is asking what happened to Elizabeth McKay, the graduate student who was trying to communicate with the whale and has been called a modern Dr. Dolittle. Elizabeth has not been seen at the slough since yesterday afternoon. It seems there has been some controversy about the legitimacy of her research." A picture of Elizabeth flashed on the screen. It was the not particularly flattering picture from her graduate application. "With no sign of Elizabeth and no other options, Coast Guard Lieutenant Isaac James says he has no alternative but to harpoon the whale."

Thompson looked at Elizabeth, having recognized her. He picked up the plastic mouthpiece of the marine VHF radio and tried to hail a call on Channel 16. "Coast Guard, Coast Guard, this is Farallon Islands, over."

"Farallones, this is Coast Guard. Go ahead."

THIRTY MINUTES LATER, Elizabeth was on the cement helipad in front of the research station, wearing dry, borrowed clothing. *Air Station San Francisco,* an HH-65 Dolphin helicopter, was hovering overhead. Its red shell was glowing, and its four rotor blades whirled above, creating a downdraft of hurricane force. Its snout and domed front did resemble a dolphin. Thompson was shouting into a hand-held, talking with the pilot as Elizabeth climbed into the steel cage and was hoisted up.

While waiting for the helicopter rescue, she had used the research station's satellite phone to call Lieutenant James on his cell phone. But neither she nor Coast Guard Island in Alameda was able to raise him. She had reached Frank, who was beside himself with worry. She told him she would explain everything and asked him to meet her at the slough with the CD that she had dropped in the house.

"Welcome aboard, ma'am," the rescue swimmer said with the military formality that exudes confidence and safety. Elizabeth looked around at the crew of four men and then pointed to her ear, signaling for a headset.

"Where are the other survivors?" the copilot asked. His voice was hollow, as if in a canyon, and in the background she could hear the muffled noise of the rotors.

"Liberty Slough," she said slowly and forcefully to make sure she was understood.

"Liberty Slough? There are no survivors out here?"

"No," Elizabeth said as she looked down at the dark water and thought of Skilling in Mother's jaws. "No survivors."

"I don't understand," the copilot said as the pilot started to fly back toward the Golden Gate Bridge. "We were told this was an emergency rescue."

"It is. I'm the researcher who's been trying to rescue the whale at Liberty Slough," Elizabeth said. "I need to stop the Coast Guard from killing the whale."

"You're Elizabeth McKay?" the copilot said. "I saw you on top of Apollo!"

The rescue swimmer and mechanic were equally impressed.

"Wait until the guys back at base hear about our cargo!" said the mechanic.

"Lieutenant Isaac James and I were classmates at the academy," the pilot said, speaking for the first time. "He was number one in our class."

Elizabeth checked her watch. There was less than a half hour left. "I need you to take me directly to Liberty Slough."

The pilot shook his head, knowing the impossibility of her request. "Sorry, ma'am, our orders are to recover any survivors and return to base. Period."

Elizabeth's heart sank as she heard the pilot's radio check with base: "Sector San Francisco, this is Helo 6554."

"Helo 6554, this is Sector San Francisco. Send your traffic over."

"OPS, normal. Current position just west of Golden Gate Bridge. Five souls on board. Returning to base."

"Roger, out."

"You said you were friends with Lieutenant James, right?" Elizabeth said as they flew south toward the San Francisco airport. "Well, what do you think is going to happen if he kills Apollo? Do you want to be responsible for letting your friend ruin his career—and for the death of this whale?"

EIGHTY-FIVE

5:55 A.M.
Liberty Slough

LIEUTENANT JAMES was out of time. The veterinarian had not shown up, and it was up to him to finish it. He stood in the bow of the rigid-hull inflatable. The bright orange buoyancy tubes looked gray-brown in the gathering light. He had turned off his radio and cell phone to stop the barrage of calls from headquarters pushing him to kill the whale immediately. But as the sun peeked over the wetlands to the east, he knew that he was out of options. There was no way to get this whale out alive.

Apparently, no one had told the small crowd of gathered protesters that there was no hope. They were chanting, "Don't kill Apollo. Don't kill Apollo."

The cold gray harpoon cannon hung down on the gun mount, the weight of the harpoon tilting it forward. The machine gun usually mounted there had been removed to accommodate the new weapon.

As Apollo surfaced, Lieutenant James looked down the long metal sight and pointed in front of the dorsal fin, wondering where the whale's shoulder blades might be. He aimed the crude weapon with his right hand, two fingers on the trigger lever.

CONNIE'S CELL PHONE rang. It was Frank. Maybe he'd know where Elizabeth was.

"I have Elizabeth's CD," Frank said.

"Her CD?" Connie heard a loud noise like wood splintering and then sirens. "What was that?"

"A security barricade," Frank said. "Got to go. Just stop them from killing the whale." Connie saw in the distance Frank's car racing down the dirt road, with dust and a group of black security cars behind him. Connie looked at Lieutenant James. He was aiming the harpoon gun at Apollo.

"Teo! He's going to fire!"

TEO LOOKED DOWN at the orange boat floating near the bridge. He knew he had to do something dramatic to stop them from killing Elizabeth's whale. Teo climbed over the cement railing and jumped into the water. He swam quickly around to the bow of the boat and placed his body in the path of the harpoon.

LIEUTENANT JAMES HEARD a splash and then saw a man swimming from the bridge, distracting him from sighting on the whale. He knew it was one of the protesters. His heart was with them, but he had his orders. The boat sped to where the man was treading water, the bow wave covering him. The Coast Guard seamen pulled the protester in, despite his resistance, and quickly handcuffed him in the stern.

James looked back at his crew and the protester, all watching him silently. He hated to kill the whale, but he sure as hell was not going to make any of his men do it. He looked at the whale's back, still floating calmly, seemingly undisturbed. *Now, where are those damn shoulder blades?* He sighted on the whale again as it exhaled its last breath. Lieutenant James winced as he started to squeeze the trigger lever.

EIGHTY-SIX

6:00 A.M.

AIR STATION SAN FRANCISCO dropped out of the clouds with a roaring downdraft. Concentric circles of small waves spread out in every direction toward the shore. The helicopter hovered over Apollo, who dove beneath the water.

"Hold your fire," the Coast Guard pilot's voice shouted through the helicopter loudspeakers.

The helicopter lowered Elizabeth onto the bank in a cage. She climbed out and ran to the bridge, pushing aside the security guards who stood staring at her.

Frank drove right onto the bridge as the security cars chasing him stopped. His mouth hung open. She must have looked like hell, but there was no time to explain what had happened. He gave Elizabeth the CD.

"Play this!" Elizabeth shouted down to Lieutenant James, whose boat was still floating near the bridge.

She threw down the CD, which Lieutenant James caught in both hands, like a starving man receiving a morsel of bread.

Lieutenant James checked his watch. Elizabeth glanced at hers. It was already past six o'clock. Would Lieutenant James go against his orders? Elizabeth's heart stopped as she waited.

Lieutenant James tapped the CD case against his fingers.

"Please, just one more time," she said.

He looked up at her and slowly raised his right arm. He was holding up his pointer finger. He would give it one more try.

The crewmen lowered the speaker and tied it off to the side of the boat. After a few moments of silence, over the loudspeakers came the haunting sound of the whale song, which was also being broadcast through the water. Elizabeth heard creaks and moans and then the social sounds:

w-OP w-OP
EEh-EEh-EEh
w-OP w-OP
EEh-EEh-EEh

Would the song, recorded from Echo in Bequia, communicate to Apollo that his song had been heard and he could leave?

The song ended.

Silence.

Nothing.

The song echoed again through the slough.

On the banks, people stood silently. Even the wind had died down.

There was a slight swirl in the water.

What did she expect to see? A tail? A flipper? Apollo was not going to wave goodbye.

APOLLO HID *at the bottom of the slough—*
He heard the sounds from above—
His eyes bulged in the dark water as he listened—
He sloped his tail upward and hung like a floating dark cloud in the posture of the singer—

• • •

ELIZABETH'S HANDS RESTED on the railing of the bridge. Her shoulders fell as she witnessed her plan—the whale's last hope—failing. Her hands were trembling. Her eyes were tearing up. She exhaled in defeat.

It wasn't her *hands* that were trembling. It was the *bridge*. She looked for cars, but no one was moving.

She turned to Frank. "He's singing! Apollo's singing!" After a few moments, Apollo's song stopped.

APOLLO SHIFTED *his great weight—thrusting his tail—twisting his body—*

Ahead was the narrow passage—

IN THE GATHERING LIGHT, Elizabeth saw Apollo's dorsal fin above the water. He was swimming toward the bridge. "He's going!" she shouted as a wave of excitement flooded her body, quickly followed by dread. The tide was much lower than when Apollo swam under the bridge into the slough. Below, Elizabeth could see wooden pilings, the remains of a former bridge, jutting out of the water.

APOLLO DOVE DOWN—
Propelled forward by his powerful tail—
His skin scraping against the old wood—
He thrashed his tail—
But he could not move—
His flippers pinned to his sides—

• • •

"Oh my God, he's stuck!" Elizabeth shouted.

"He's a whale," Frank said, trying to comfort her.

"If he can't surface, he'll drown."

"We've got to move those wooden pilings," Frank said, pointing at where they stuck out above the water. "We need a rope."

Elizabeth echoed the request to Lieutenant James, who saw what was happening. Frank pulled off his shoes and jacket, climbed over the railing, and jumped into the water.

"Let me go," Teo was saying, holding up his handcuffed wrists and pointing to the water.

"He's a whaler," Elizabeth shouted.

"A whaler?" Lieutenant James said. He shook his head with disbelief but decided to follow Elizabeth's directions, which were working so far. "Okay. Let him go." Teo went overboard, dragging a thick line of rope attached to the boat.

Frank and Teo dove below the water, trying to tie the rope as low as possible on the piling. When they surfaced, Lieutenant James gave the order.

"Pull!"

Elizabeth heard the ferocious roar of the two Honda 225s as they raced away from Apollo. The rope's slack was quickly taken up. She heard the revving and straining of the engine tethered to the old piling.

After an endless minute, the piling started to move, first inches and then several feet. Apollo was able to surface with a great exhalation that rose twenty feet or more. Everyone cheered, even the security guards.

But Apollo still had to push his massive body over the piling and to the other side.

"He still can't get through," Frank shouted from where he was treading water below the bridge. He and Teo swam into the open water. They did not want to be near the whale when he breached.

• • •

APOLLO WHIPPED HIS TAIL in a downward power stroke and convulsed every muscle—

He propelled the front half of his body up and forward—

His skin scraped against the barriers—

He twisted his body and raised one winglike flipper out of the water—seeing the creature above him—

ELIZABETH HUNG OVER the railing and saw Apollo's eye looking up at her, glimmering in the morning light. She recognized once again that great and unknown intelligence.

Apollo's fin fell away as his giant body returned to the water, and a huge splash erupted in all directions. He had made it over the piling and was free of the bridge. The crowd cheered all around her.

Apollo "spy-hopped," raising his head vertically out of the water, and then began swimming back down the river with the Coast Guard boat trailing behind as an escort.

The black storm clouds hanging over the slough at last released their heavy load. The rain poured down on Elizabeth, a purifying stream. She shivered as she watched the water begin running into the holes in the bridge and down into the slough and back to the sea.

EIGHTY-SEVEN

Six months later
September 5
Russell Senate Office Building
Washington, D.C.

ELIZABETH LOOKED at her very pregnant belly. Through everything she had endured at the hands of Skilling and in the freezing ocean with the shark, her baby had been well protected in its own watery world. Now, at thirty-six weeks, the only place that Elizabeth wanted to be was in a warm bath where her body was buoyed up from the unrelenting weight of gravity.

How did I let Connie talk me into this? she wondered as she glanced up at the dark wood–paneled walls of the congressional hearing room. Frank was being surprisingly supportive and had even agreed to accompany her. He'd said he could deliver the baby on the plane if necessary. Elizabeth rocked from side to side in the hard wooden chair, trying to get comfortable, knowing that the ligaments of her pelvis were opening and the bones were softening for the approaching birth.

Although they were in the largest hearing room in the Russell Building, it was already full, and a crowd of people spilled out the door into the hall. The wooden table reserved for press was full, and a bank of television cameras was arrayed in the back. Connie had told her that many would be there for her, insisting that she brought some supposed celebrity status, but Elizabeth knew that environmental issues were generating their own interest.

Professor Ginsburg must have seen the nervousness on her face, because she patted Elizabeth on the arm and smiled warmly. Elizabeth wondered whether she should really say it the way she had planned. It was provocative, but it would get the senators' attention. Half a dozen gray-haired men were taking their seats around the long U-shaped wooden table. In the middle was the sole female senator. As the chair of the committee, she exuded confidence and professionalism. She looked over her reading glasses at Elizabeth and smiled. The senator was from California and had invited her to testify after the whale rescue. She was also a mother of two and was perhaps empathizing with Elizabeth's near-term discomfort.

To Elizabeth's side was a large screen on which she would show graphs of the rise in birth defects and childhood cancer, as well as the precipitous decline in fertility among men and women. The chairwoman called the meeting to order and invited Elizabeth to address the committee.

Elizabeth spoke into the microphone to make sure everyone could hear her as she began her testimony. "Every man in this room is half the man his grandfather was." There was a murmur of surprise and shock. "As you can see on this chart, sperm counts of men in the United States and twenty other countries have fallen over the last half century—by as much as 50 percent." Elizabeth turned to the chairwoman. "Senator, as women, we are equally if not more affected by environmental pollution. As just one example, no matter what we eat or where we live, our breast milk will pass on to our children a frightening array of toxins." Elizabeth presented a number of the facts that she had discovered, but celebrity status or not, she was eager to turn the microphone over to Dr. Ginsburg. "I'd like—"

"Isn't some level of environmental pollution," one of the senators asked, "an inevitable part of progress? It could take generations to know if there are lasting effects."

"We don't have generations to wait, Senator. Humans run the

risk of becoming the newest species on the endangered animals list."

"Are you saying this is about extinction?"

"Like the dinosaur . . . and the dodo bird," Elizabeth said as a chuckle fluttered around the room. "In truth, Senator, this is about more than extinction. This is about species extermination, including our own. To explain these threats more fully, I'd like to introduce Dr. Gladys Ginsburg." Elizabeth began to get up.

"One more thing, Dr. McKay, before we let you go." It was the female senator from California again. "I'd like to know if you really think that you were able to communicate with the whale—with Apollo?"

Elizabeth took a deep breath. The room was very quiet as everyone eagerly awaited her answer. "I wish I knew, Senator. As a scientist, I must say that any hypothesis about the cause of the whale's entrapment and its decision to swim back out to sea would be purely speculative."

"Do you believe that the whale was truly telling us that our children are in danger?"

"Whether we hear the warning from Apollo or from Dr. Ginsburg, Senator, the dangers we face are the same."

"Thank you, Dr. McKay."

Elizabeth decided not to mention that she was still not yet a Ph.D. She got up, using both arms of the chair to assist her.

Professor Ginsburg began by saying, "I would like to publicly thank Elizabeth McKay. We might never have gotten this hearing if it hadn't been for her and that charismatic whale."

"Dr. Ginsburg, what is it that you most want the committee to know?" asked the chairwoman.

"I want to begin with the good news, Senator. So many of the diseases that plague our world and that we thought were inevitable are actually environmental illnesses that are in fact preventable.

Today's epidemics include hormone-related cancers such as breast and prostate cancer, autoimmune disorders, learning disabilities, autism, degenerative diseases, preterm birth, obesity and diabetes, asthma, and infertility. As we stop putting these endocrine disruptors and other toxins into our environment, we will be able to save millions of men, women, and children from untold amounts of suffering."

As Professor Ginsburg continued her testimony, Elizabeth saw Professor Maddings by the door. He had come to be there for her and was beaming like a proud parent. She made her way toward him through the crowd, and together they slipped out of the hearing room.

"Brilliant, my dear," he said. "You were absolutely brilliant. And look at you." He gestured toward her full belly.

Elizabeth smiled. "I'm so glad you came."

"I wouldn't have missed it for all the blue whales in the world. I'm just glad to see you in one piece after what you've been through. Now, tell me, what I don't understand is why the whalers and that environmental consortium were working together."

"They weren't. Their interests just aligned, and both were willing to pay Skilling for his help. He had friends in all the wrong places."

"Well, that Skilling got his just deserts," Maddings said with satisfaction.

Skilling was not the only one who had. Elizabeth knew that the Japanese government was launching a formal investigation into the toxicity of whale meat and those who might have attempted to cover it up. The Environmental Stewardship Consortium had been disbanded, but Bruce Wood's article had helped launch a class-action lawsuit against the companies responsible for setting it up, and their collective stock value had been cut in half by negative press. One of Frank's patients, a former chemical company executive, was the star witness for the prosecution.

"And that white shark," Maddings continued, "must have been quite a monster."

Mother's breach attack flashed to mind—the power, the violence, and the grace. "No, not a monster," she corrected. "Really, just another hungry mother."

Frank opened the hearing room door, having managed to elbow his way through the thick crowd. He hugged Elizabeth over her big waist and kissed her on the lips. Frank shook Maddings's hand warmly.

"I want to tell you both the good news," Maddings said.

"Good news?" Elizabeth asked. Frank put his arm around Elizabeth, and she rested her head on his shoulder.

Maddings visibly struggled to contain his excitement as he clasped his hands together in triumph, grinning from ear to ear. "I got a call from the president of our university, who saw you on the telly and then called me. I was telling him about you, and he has some donors who will fund a state-of-the-art cetacean language research vessel for you."

"A boat?"

"A hundred-foot one, I should think. You could travel all over the world," Maddings said enthusiastically, clearly not noticing Elizabeth's downcast eyes. "And study the whales and the dolphins . . ."

She considered this offer of a lifetime, which would mean never being home, and then put her hand on her belly. "Maybe the donor would buy a fifteen-foot wooden boat for my research assistant in the Caribbean, and you could just give me back my old office at Woods Hole."

Maddings gazed at her in confusion, then must have noticed her head on her husband's shoulder. He finally understood Elizabeth's hesitation. "Maybe I can talk him into giving the money for a research lab for you at Woods Hole."

"You are forgetting that I don't yet have a Ph.D."

"I think I can talk the university into accepting the dissertation you've written. Perhaps we can consider that you've been on suspended leave. They do these things for pregnant mothers."

Elizabeth's face lit up. "I need to change some of my conclusions and can send it off to you before the baby is born."

"We'll accept it if I have to sign as all three members of your committee!"

Elizabeth embraced him. As they separated, her hands came to rest, as they often now did, on her belly, which stuck out like a comfortable armrest. The smile evaporated from her face as she had what she was sure was a Braxton Hicks contraction. There were still four weeks to go.

EIGHTY-EIGHT

Four weeks later
Sacramento

THE HOSPITAL had obviously tried to make the birthing room look less sterile, but had only partly succeeded. There was a cushioned green slide rocker and a maroon sleeping chair. Even the bed was wide and had a headboard, like in a hotel. The problem was that everything *did* need to be sterile. Birth was messy and potentially dangerous, and only so many of the risks could be controlled.

Elizabeth sat up on the white sheets, which were spotted with red drops where the blood of her baby's birth had seeped through the gauze pads. On the counter was the pink basin where the baby had been washed. Elizabeth was propped up on several pillows, and to her side was a rolling tray table with a plate of cold scrambled eggs and potatoes. She poked the yellow mound unenthusiastically with a fork.

Frank was lying next to her on the bed, and in his arms he cradled their tiny baby girl, Hope. He was gazing down at her rose lips, tiny nose, and red, puffy cheeks that peeked out from under a yellow infant hat.

The newborn looked up at him with blinking blue eyes that were just beginning to adjust to the shocking brightness of life. Frank was enraptured with his daughter as he smiled at her and gently stroked each of her ten wrinkled, inch-long fingers and ten even tinier toes.

Hope let out a thin, reedy cry, and Frank lifted the baby into

Elizabeth's arms and toward her mother's swollen pink nipple. Hope latched on with a power so intense that Elizabeth gasped. Her breast felt warm, and a primal feeling of contentment flooded through her body.

Frank fell asleep, his head resting on a pillow. Elizabeth's familiar longing for her mother to be there began to ache in her chest, but this time she realized that in some irreducible and immeasurable way, her mother *was* there, in a long cellular line of motherhood. It was at that moment, with her child at her breast, that she felt the bond of sacrifice and surrender linking a thousand generations before her. If humans were lucky and wise, it would continue for thousands of generations more. It was not just a cell line from human mother to human mother; it was countless threads of mothers in countless species, a tapestry of intricately woven and shimmering life.

Hope's eyelids began to close, leaving a tiny slit of sight. Her rhythmic sucking became softer, and her tremulous lower lip twitched. As she dozed off, she startled herself awake and began to suck all the more for fear of losing the nipple.

Elizabeth closed her own eyes and imagined the branching mammary glands like tributaries to a stream, gathering sustenance from her body. She felt like she was pouring love into her child. Every drop of this life-sustaining serum was distilled from her cells and everything that had made its way into her body through the air she breathed, the water she drank, and the food she ate. A new terror and protectiveness filled her, squeezing out the contentment. How could she protect her child? Why did she have to wonder what toxins would accompany her love and nourishment?

Hope wormed her arm out of the swaddling blanket and rested her palm on her mother's chest. Elizabeth thought about how much had been lost to her daughter and how much more there still was to lose. It was all so terribly fragile, like the infant in her arms, and she realized for the first time that what might be lost was not just a species, or hundreds of species, or even human life, but the very possibility of motherhood.

And fatherhood.

And family.

Her mother and father, despite death, despite distance, despite everything, had given her the greatest gift possible—life—in its endless cycle of destruction and restoration, and with all its embracing kindnesses and inevitable cruelties. And she wanted it for her daughter and her daughter's daughter and for every child and every creature that longs for a chance to live. Elizabeth felt like the door of a cage that had surrounded her heart was being pried open by Hope's delicate, nursing lips.

Tears streamed down her cheeks. Her desire to protect her daughter and the world that would feed her, hold her, and sustain her came not from guilt or fear but from love. She now understood that life did not need saving—it needed loving—and this, to her amazement, she knew how to do.

Elizabeth looked down through her tear-kissed eyes at the precious world of life and longing she held in her arms: Hope.

THERE WAS A KNOCK at the door. It was Connie, dressed in black boots, miniskirt, and red sweater. She smiled at Elizabeth but seemed nervous, since she knew nothing about hospitals, or birthing wards, or motherhood. When she saw Hope in Elizabeth's arms, she smiled and bit her lip. Embarrassed, she held out a gift that she hadn't had a chance to wrap. It was a sing-along children's cassette player with a built-in microphone.

"She can start making sound recordings as soon as she's able to press the buttons," Connie said. Elizabeth laughed gently, not wanting to wake Hope. Frank was still sleeping soundly, exhausted from the all-night birth.

"Dr. Lombardi." Dorothy, in her purple scrubs, was at the door. Frank quickly blinked himself awake. How many times, Elizabeth thought, had Frank been wrenched from sleep to help someone's child? "I'm sorry to interrupt the holy family, but there's a preemie on a vent in the NICU who's in distress."

"Can't the man have a little time with his own baby?" Connie demanded. "Is he the only doctor in the entire hospital?"

Dorothy glared back at Connie as she said to Frank, "I paged Dr. Lavorsky and Dr. Ramanujan, but no one's answering."

Frank looked at Elizabeth, not wanting to abandon her or their baby, but he knew what he needed to do. Elizabeth sensed his hesitation and said, "It could have been ours."

"You're right," Frank said as he got up from the bed. Elizabeth thought of the whales' song and wondered if Frank was thinking about it, too. At the door, Frank said, "I won't be long."

Elizabeth smiled, at peace.

Connie put a lullaby tape into the children's cassette player. The sounds that filled the room were of violins and cellos accompanied by the ancient and mysterious calls of whale song.

OUTSIDE THE GOLDEN GATE BRIDGE, *Apollo began slapping his tail rhythmically against the surface—*
He was heading south again—back to the breeding grounds—
The tide spilled out of the bay as he rode its current—
Then he dove down deep and turned upward in a graceful arc—
His mighty flukes thrust back and forth—
At last he burst through the surface in an enormous breach—
Apollo hung in the sky—his back arched in abandon—white foam falling—his tail stalk an axis on which he rotated—
And then his head fell back into the water—waves rippling for miles—

A giant cloud of white bubbles stirred by his bulk started to scatter—

Moments later, his thrusting tail launched him again skyward—

Leaving the life-giving waters—a silvery spray falling from his outstretched and eloquent body—

EPILOGUE:
REALITIES

ON SUNDAY, JUNE 18, 2006, the International Whaling Commission overturned a twenty-year-old ban on commercial whaling. Many believe that it is just a matter of time before commercial whaling will begin again.

FROM 1973 TO 1999, childhood cancers increased by 26 percent, making cancer the greatest health threat to children. Acute childhood lymphocytic leukemia is up 61 percent; brain cancer, 50 percent; and bone cancer, 39 percent.

THE BELUGA WHALES in Hudson Bay are so full of chemical pollutants that when their dead bodies wash up onshore, they must be handled like toxic waste.

AUTHOR'S NOTE

Each of my novels arises from a question to which I desperately want to know the answer. My first novel, *The Lost Diary of Don Juan,* resulted from exploring the question of whether it is possible to marry desire and love—passion and compassion—together for a lifetime. *Eye of the Whale* came from a very different question, one that is global as well as deeply personal. It is a question that many of us are increasingly asking: Can we survive as a species? And if we can, what might be stronger than ignorance, greed, and despair? Through writing this story, I found an answer to this question and a measure of hope. But as I learned from my research, there is shockingly little time to make changes that will preserve the health of our children, our grandchildren, and all intelligent life on our planet. I hope that for you this will not be the end of the story, but the beginning.

You can learn more about the research and the discoveries on which this novel is based at www.DouglasCarltonAbrams.com. You will also find a list of some of the organizations that are working effectively to protect us, marine mammals, and the world we share. Together, our actions will determine the ending of the unfolding story of life.

ACKNOWLEDGMENTS

To write a fact-based novel is to be constantly reminded of one's own limitations, the vastness of what there is to know, and the importance of relying on the kindness of experts. Any accuracy is due to their generosity; any inaccuracy is wholly my own fault.

The writing of this book has been an incredible journey, taking me to Tonga, where I was able to swim with and record the humpback whales; to Bequia, where I met local whalers; and to the Farallon Islands, where I went cage diving with white sharks. All along the way, I had extraordinary guides, whom I would like to acknowledge in the order in which I met them.

First, I must thank Libby Eyre, of the Biological Sciences Museum of Macquarie University in Australia, a marine biologist who took me into the wondrous underwater world of humpback whales and allowed me to videotape them and record their song. Libby was the first to believe in this project and to give me early guidance when I was literally just getting wet. Libby's colleague Bryant Austin not only arranged my trip through his nonprofit organization, Marine Mammal Conservation through the Arts, but also documented the whales we saw together for his extraordinary project of mounting life-sized whale photos in public places, especially in whaling countries. His work inspired the scene I set in Japan, and he also was an invaluable adviser on the technicalities of BASE-jumping.

Another early adviser for the whale science in the book was Roger Payne, Ph.D., the legendary co-discoverer of whale song and one of the leading whale scientists in the world. He is also the founder and president of Ocean Alliance, which, along with doing other important work, has been testing the health of the oceans around the world. Roger is in my mind the ideal model of a scientist-humanist. His love of the wild and the potential for humans to return to their rightful place within the natural world inspired my writing of the novel throughout. I highly recommend his book *Among Whales,* which through its poetic evocation and scientific exploration brings us as close as we can get to experiencing the grandeur of whales while on dry land. Roger is also a ruthlessly talented copyeditor.

Thanks also go to Iain Kerr, CEO of Ocean Alliance, for an eye-opening late-night meal and heartbreaking tales of our oceans from his five-year voyage aboard the *Odyssey,* gathering the first-ever baseline data on synthetic contaminants throughout the world's oceans. The fact about chromium in the Gilbert Islands comes from his and Roger's expedition. Roger introduced me to Bernie Krause, who explained the acoustics of hydrophones and shared his extraordinary humpback whale and killer whale sound files with me.

An equally invaluable guide in the area of endocrine disruption and ecotoxicology has been John Peterson Myers, Ph.D. Pete is CEO and chief scientist of Environmental Health Sciences and former senior vice president for science at the National Audubon Society. He is the co-author of the now classic *Our Stolen Future* and one of the world's leading experts on endocrine disruption. The lecture that my fictional Gladys Ginsburg gives is almost entirely based on his lecture and slide show, which I had the opportunity to see at the American Holistic Medical Association. The standing ovation he received there was just a small expression of the gratitude that he and his colleagues deserve for their incredible work educating us about the dangers that toxins pose in the environment. Devra Davis, Ph.D., is the author of the anguishing and fascinating *When Smoke Ran Like Water: Tales of Environmental Deception and the Battle Against Pollution*. Pete and Devra not only taught me about the issues, but were kind enough to read my manuscript to make sure that the novel accurately presented the facts. I would also like to thank Ken Cook and his pioneering nonprofit, the Environmental Working Group, for all of their dedicated work on behalf of the environment and his support of the novel. Sandra Steingraber, Ph.D., and her two poetic books *Living Downstream* and *Having Faith* were also a great inspiration.

Many legislators are trying to address the environmental crises we face. I would like to thank Senator Barbara Boxer, Senator Frank Lautenberg, and their colleagues in Congress who are working to help protect our environment and our children. Witnessing Senator Boxer chair the Committee on Environment and Public Works inspired the congressional hearing chapter in the novel. The testimony that was received that day on the human impact of global warming from then–CDC director Julie Gerberding, M.D., was heavily "edited" (many said censored). My daughter Kayla sat through the hearing at the tender age of eight and melted down only once or twice.

Brenda McCowan, Ph.D., who has been studying whale social sounds at the University of California, Davis, was extremely helpful in answering questions about whale communication and whale intelligence as well as about UC Davis, where much of the novel takes place.

In discussing the novel, my advisers and I were hypothesizing a mother-baby contact call. It was to our delight that Rebecca Dunlop, Ph.D., at the University of Queensland, discovered this exact social sound being used between mothers and their calves. Rebecca also confirmed the existence of social sounds in whale songs, although she believes their function may be different from their function in social communication. She was extremely helpful in explaining what can and can't be said about whale communication given our current state of knowledge. Pierre Béland confirmed my portrayal of an autopsy of a beluga whale, and his own lyrical writing about these "white whales" in *A Farewell to Whales* was very moving.

Marine biologist and whaling expert Nathalie Ward, Ph.D., was my host and guide on the wonderful island of Bequia and helped me to understand the culture and the role of the whalers. She has been studying humpback whales for more than twenty years as the director of the Eastern Caribbean Cetacean Network, and is the author of the definitive book on Bequia whaling, *Blows, Mon, Blows.* She has become a dear friend and helped to advise me throughout the writing of the book. Any authenticity in the rendering of Bequia is largely from her deep fund of knowledge and years on the island.

I am also indebted to the linguists who helped me with the subtleties of Bequian English. I would especially like to thank James Walker, Ph.D., of York University, who reviewed every line of dialogue spoken by a Bequian character. James helped me to appreciate the rich and unique qualities of Bequian English, which, he explained, can vary from speaker to speaker and from situation to situation. Once again, any errors here are my own.

I would like to thank the whalers of Bequia whom I had the opportunity to meet. One of the heroes of the book is a fictionalized whaler, and I tried to portray the whalers' love of the ocean, their cultural history, and their own deep knowledge and respect for the whales they hunt. The people of Bequia deserve my appreciation for their hospitality. I hope I have done justice to the beauty of their island and the warmth of their culture.

I was inspired to write the book by a whale named Humphrey, who swam up the Sacramento River in 1985. In amazing serendipity, while I was working on the novel, two more humpback whales—a mother-and-calf pair named Delta and Dawn—swam up the Sacramento. I watched the whale rescue firsthand and met two incredible individuals who were significantly involved in conducting this successful rescue. Frances Gulland, director of veterinary science at the Marine Mammal Center, one of the truly great organizations working on behalf of marine mammals, answered innumerable questions and read several drafts. Frances's devotion to the whales and to marine mammals in general informed and inspired Elizabeth's quest to save Apollo.

I also got to work with Coast Guard Lieutenant Robert Bixler. He helped me to understand the Coast Guard's role in the rescue and helped me to portray the numerous technical details about boats and helicopters in the book. Rob has that extraordinary mix of professionalism and kindness that inspires trust and admiration. If I ever need to be rescued at sea, I would hope Rob was captaining the vessel.

I also want to thank Rachel Thompson, a veterinarian at Discovery World, for her help figuring out how one might inject a humpback whale calf in the open ocean and what their veins would feel like.

Scott Davis was my guide into the extraordinary world of white sharks, where I could learn firsthand that so many fears about sharks are undeserved. Instead, I found a vulnerable apex predator that only on rare occasions attacks humans and that needs our greatest protection. Scott has a lot of experience tagging white sharks and was involved in the research that demonstrated that they migrate thousands of miles each year back to the same feeding grounds. Scott is currently the resident naturalist for eco-tour operator Great White Adventures, and it was thrilling to cage-dive with the sharks out in the frigid waters off the Farallones. Scott is a superb photographer, and I've included several of his images of sharks on my website.

Elizabeth's unusual half-Jewish and half–Native American heritage was inspired by my friend, the gifted novelist Greg Sarris, who has this dual tribal heritage. Greg is the tribal chairman of the Federated Indians of Graton Rancheria, a federally recognized tribe of Coast Miwok and Southern Pomo. I thank Greg for helping me with the development of Elizabeth's heritage and character. I also thank two Miwok language experts, Richard Applegate and Catherine Callaghan, although unfortunately the Miwok terms they helped me with were cut, along with a scene of Elizabeth visiting her father.

There is a great deal of medical science in the novel, and it certainly helps to be married to a physician. I also relied on the expertise of others, notably Loren Rauch, M.D., who is not only a good friend but also a superb ER doctor, and who among other things helped to confirm that Skillings's injection of ketamine would not have hurt Elizabeth's baby. For information on the increasing number of cases of hypospadias, I turned to Howard Snyder III, M.D., professor of urology in surgery at the University of Pennsylvania School of Medicine, who sent me many disturbing pictures of this growing phenomenon. I thank Betty Mekdeci of the National Birth Defects Registry for her advice and incredibly devoted work in protecting children and recording their suffering. She argued for a less hopeful ending to Elizabeth's story.

I especially want to thank Gordon Wheeler, Nancy Lunney-Wheeler, and the Esalen Institute, for offering me refuge to write much of this book. Esalen has been a hothouse of personal and cultural transformation for almost half a century, and I was incredibly fortunate to have the opportunity to draft much of the story in a room clinging to the Big Sur coast as whales migrated within sight.

I would like to thank my legion of family and friends who have read countless drafts and offered valuable guidance and support, including Karen Abrams, Mark Nicolson, Charlie Bloom, Lynn Franklin, Todd Siegal, Ana Munsell, Joshua Leavitt, John Robbins, Myra Goodman, and once again, Gordon.

One friend deserves particular acknowledgment. Heather Kuiper, DrPH, introduced me to the dangers of endocrine disruption and was there on a rainy day when the idea of the novel first arose and countless times thereafter. Old friends are invaluable. They are treasure chests of shared memories, but Heather is also that rarest of old friends: one whose friendship is not based on the past but on the future and the world we want to help create together.

A writer is always a student of the craft, and I want to thank my teachers Frank McCourt (for helping me to believe in myself as a writer), Jim Frey (for teaching me as we sailed in the Bay), Robert McKee (for flaying open the world of story), and Pilar Alessandra (for lending her story genius to this book and always knowing whether a character should go left instead of right). Thanks also to Janet Leimeister and the Capitola Book Café, and to all the brilliant booksellers whose devotion to books makes our business possible, and whose irreplaceable stores are the crossroads of our culture. I thank my film agent, Rich Green of Creative Artists Agency, for his belief in the cinematic potential of my novels.

Heide Lange is the ideal agent that every author dreams of having: a brilliant reader and adviser, a cherished friend and member of the family, and an infallible guide through the bewildering world of authorship. May every writer be blessed with such an agent. Heide's colleagues, Alex Cannon and Jennifer Linnan, and her daughter, Jessie Chaffee, also gave excellent readings.

Emily Bestler is the kind of editor that many people believe no longer exists in the publishing world. I now know why she has published so many bestselling novels: her devotion to the perfection of a manuscript through numerous drafts, her incomparable instincts for story, character, and style, and her unwavering support at every step of the publishing process. I also want to thank Emily's gifted colleagues, Judith Curr, Deb Darrock, Carolyn Reidy, Michael Selleck, Kathleen Schmidt, David Brown, Christine Duplessis, Laura Stern, Jeanne Lee, Stephen Breslin, and E. Beth Thomas. Laura, thank you for your own superb reading; Carolyn, for your confidence in me; and Judith, for your belief that "now was the time to write about our oceans."

I would like to thank my agents and publishers around the world who have worked so hard to bring this novel to a worldwide readership. The issues that the book addresses are obviously ones that affect all of us and can only be solved by all of us.

I thank my colleagues at Idea Architects, Michelle Defields-Gambrel and Zoe Elkaim, for their outstanding work on this book, their editorial gifts, and their tireless commitment to making sure it is read as far and as wide as possible. It is a joy to collaborate with such skillful and vision-aligned colleagues in creating a wiser, healthier, and more just world. My researcher, Jay Dautcher, Ph.D., is not only a great anthropologist and researcher. He truly knows everything about everything, and those few things that he doesn't already know, he can find out in a matter of minutes. Jay worked closely with me on this book and was an intellectual companion at every stage of the book's development.

I thank my father, Richard Abrams, for his early and continual faith in the significance of this project and his lifelong belief in me. A father's blessing is an invaluable gift. Speaking of blessings, I want to thank my children, Jesse, Kayla, and Eliana, who were constantly in my mind and heart as I wrote. It was really for them and all the other children who will inherit our small and precious planet that I stole so many hours from family life. As Kayla once wrote on a note that hangs above my desk, "His name is not Doug Abrams. His name is Dad." And it will always be.

More than anything, this novel is about the preciousness of life and in particular about the everyday miracle of motherhood. There are two mothers that I most want to thank.

Patricia Abrams, my own mother, not only endured nine months of pregnancy with me but also has continued to help gestate all of my books through their many developmental stages. She even helped me to hear whether there was life in each and every word. Now, that is maternal devotion. I am fortunate that my mother is also a brilliant editor and publishing professional. Thank you, Mom, for reading endless drafts, for offering your wise counsel, and for being the kind of guiding presence that made the entire process richer and more meaningful.

And at last there is, and thank the good universe, always is, my wife, Rachel. What an undeserved gift it is to bring life into the world with you. You are such an extraordinary mother and companion on the path of trying to raise a healthy and thriving family. Thank you for your endless emotional and literary support, your cherished honesty and insight into character, and all the innumerable joys of our pair-bonded life.